12/29/07

The Lion
of St. Mark

The Lion of St. Mark

Book One of
THE VENETIANS

Thomas Quinn

Thomas Dunne Books
St. Martin's Press ☙ New York

THOMAS DUNNE BOOKS.
An imprint of St. Martin's Press.

www.stmartins.com

Maps by Carolyn Chu

Book design by Phil Mazzone

ISBN 0-312-31908-8
EAN 978-0-312-31908-3

First Edition: July 2005

10 9 8 7 6 5 4 3 2 1

For my father

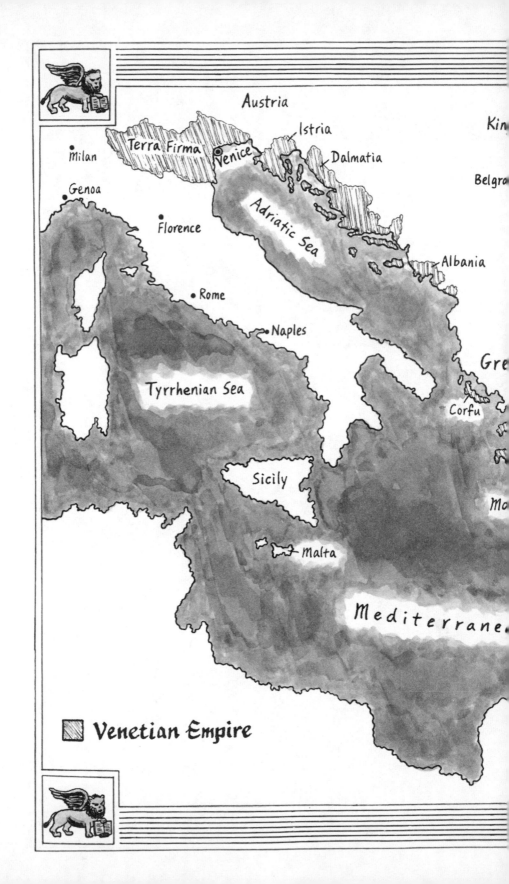

Austria

Kin

Milan

Terra Firma

Venice

Istria

Dalmatia

Belgra

Genoa

Florence

Adriatic Sea

Albania

Rome

Naples

Gre

Tyrrhenian Sea

Corfu

Sicily

Ma

Malta

Mediterrane

Venetian Empire

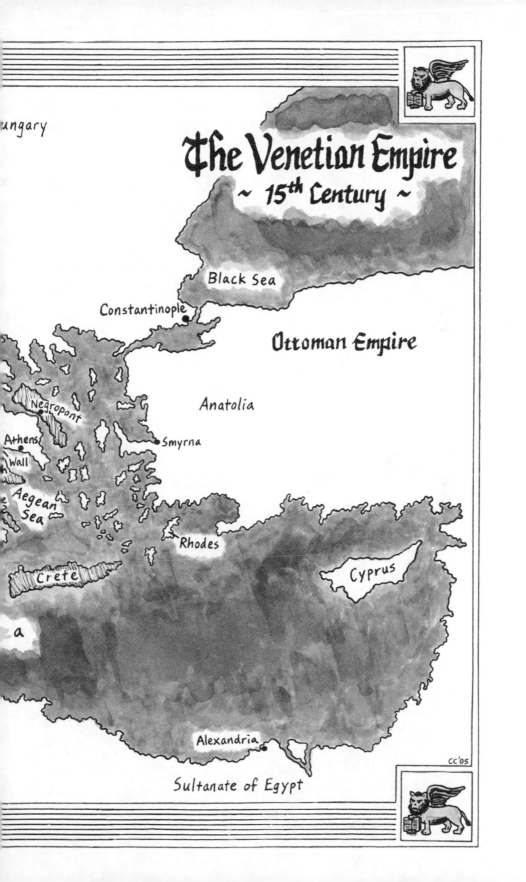

The Venetian Empire
~ 15th Century ~

Hungary

Black Sea

Constantinople

Ottoman Empire

Anatolia

Negropont

Smyrna

Athens

Wall

Aegean
Sea

Rhodes

Crete

Cyprus

a

Alexandria

Sultanate of Egypt

CC'05

The Lion
of St. Mark

1

The Relief Fleet

1452

The sudden plunge into the cold gray sea had filled the youth with such terror he thought his heart would burst from his heaving chest. Now, minutes later, he furiously worked his arms and legs as he struggled to ride up and over another mountainous wave. As he crested, needles of spray ripped from the sea by the howling wind stung his beardless face. Bone-penetrating cold was already sapping his strength—he had been in the frigid water for too long. As he struggled to ponder his fate, the cruel specter of death seeped into his thoughts, pushing any remaining hope of rescue from his mind.

Could it be? he thought. Have they really left me behind? Surely, someone must have seen me; heard my cries for help. He yearned for his two older brothers, Giovanni and Pietro, out there somewhere in the dark, beyond his reach. But too much time had passed since the lone flickering yellow lantern on the stern of the last ship had faded into the misty blackness. As the ships had passed him, one after another, no one on board could hear his pitiful cries for help as he desperately splashed his arms in the water, shouting vainly against the raging storm. Young Marco Soranzo was alone.

How wild the sea is, he thought, as another relentless wave crashed into his face, burning his nose and throat with its briny taste. Back in Venice, where the shimmering waters of the Grand Canal gently kissed the very stones of his family's stately palazzo, he had never imagined the sea could be so violent. Again, he strained his burning eyes to see a ship's lantern through the mist. He tried with all his might to will one to appear but none did. Marco no longer suffered from the seasickness that had driven him to disobey orders and sneak up onto the slippery deck, where the monstrous wave had surprised him as he was vomiting over the rail. Now, as he fought to stay afloat, his stomach was filled with the nausea of fear.

He had become no more than a piece of debris, gripped by the sea in all her power. He struggled to slowly turn in place as he surveyed his watery domain. Towering waves rolled by in the darkness, silhouetted against the misty sky, like grim executioners searching for their next victim. He thought about what it would be like to drown. He shuddered as he thought about being engulfed in a cold, black, silent coffin of water, with his heart still beating, while his mind struggled to deny the inevitability of his fate.

But where will I go when I am dead? Is the church right about salvation? Is there really life beyond death? Or is it a cruel fairy tale? What if there is nothing?

Suddenly, another wall of water crashed over him, this time driving him under with its terrible force. He instinctively fought his way back to the frothy surface as he coughed salt water from his lungs, gasping for a life-sustaining breath of air. He had reached the limit of his human endurance. He could not take any more pounding.

"I will choose my own time!" he vainly screamed at the relentless sea.

Finally, with his eyes and lungs burning and his heart broken, too cold to go on treading water, his exhausted body surrendered to the irresistible force of nature, dooming his still defiant mind, imprisoned within. As he recalled a few words of a simple prayer his mother had taught him, he slowly filled his lungs with one last deep draught of moist air. Then, with the roaring storm as his only requiem, in the final conscious act of his short life, young Marco Soranzo kicked his feet high above the waves and dove down into the dark, peaceful, eternal deep

Twice, they had searched the ship but they could find no trace of him. Coarse sailors and hardened marines vainly shouted Marco's name as though they were calling a lost dog. They stared into the familiar face of each shipmate they encountered, eerily illuminated by the dim lamplight. Some prayed aloud for Marco to appear while they silently cursed the bad luck that would surely befall the ship if he did not. Everyone knew it was a bad omen to lose a man overboard.

Thirty-one-year-old Antonio Ziani, captain of the ship's company of marines, was more concerned than anyone about the missing man. Marco Soranzo was one of *his* men—and just fifteen years old, with his whole life ahead of him. He had warned the seasick lad, several times, to remain below deck, sheltered from seas that were so heavy, even the surefooted sailors were forced to tether themselves to the rigging and railings whenever they were topside. One marine said he had seen the boy vomiting again, facedown in the bilge. Deathly ill, he had probably staggered up on deck for some fresh air to ease his misery and had lost his balance. The cause did not matter—he was lost at sea and nothing could bring him back now.

"We cannot take time to go back and search for young Soranzo," shouted Vice-Captain of the Gulf Gabriele Trevisan, above the roar of the storm. "Even if we could, we would never find him in this accursed weather. He is surely drowned by now."

As commander of the five Venetian ships, plowing their way through the Aegean Sea to the Venetian port city and naval base at Negropont, Trevisan was under strict orders to make all haste. That is why they were running with full sails—a dangerous maneuver in such a storm.

The light from the three-foot-tall iron sea lamp, swinging on the mast, made the saltwater droplets in Antonio's beard sparkle like stars in the night sky.

"I know, Gabriele," he replied, stoically, through the roaring wind and sheets of stinging spray that swept the deck.

At times like this he regretted the lonely responsibility of command. He had never liked visiting the families of men lost in battle or drowned at sea. This time, however, the task would be even more distasteful. Sailing in the ship astern of his were Captain Giovanni Soranzo and Lieutenant Pietro Soranzo. Antonio could only imagine their bitter reaction when they learned that Marco had perished. Worse, how would they react when they realized that they had sailed past the very spot where Marco had probably been swimming for his life, leaving him to drown? He wondered how he would react if he were told his own younger brother, Giorgio, had been lost at sea right under *his* nose?

The big merchant ship lazily strained at her anchor chain; barely rolling in the shimmering gray water. It feels good to be dry for the first time in days, thought Antonio, as he ran his fingers through his beard. Like many Venetians, his light brown hair and fair skin contrasted markedly with that of southern Italians from Rome and Naples.

He was a patrician, a *nobile*—a member of the ruling class of the Serene Republic of Venice—*La Serenissima*. Like his father, and all *his* fathers before him, Antonio's pride in his family's heritage was matched only by his devotion to the Republic. Every thought and action was driven by values purposefully and carefully instilled in him by his forebears. He was bound by honor, law, and custom to serve in any capacity the Republic deemed fit. If he refused, he could be fined, have his property confiscated, or even suffer imprisonment.

More than any other country in the world, Venice had fused rank and privilege with responsibility. The day he had first heard about the mission to go to Constantinople's defense he had volunteered for the dangerous undertaking. Only a coward, he reasoned, would wait to be ordered to go. Of the seven hundred Venetians on board the five ships, more than one hundred were *nobili*.

The voyage from Venice had been miserable in the rough, raw November weather. As he gazed across the tranquil harbor in the dim twilight, he fixed his steel-gray eyes upon Negropont's massive crenellated city walls. He welcomed the steady deck under his feet, afforded by the sheltered anchorage and the passing of the storm, as he studied the battlements. He wondered how Constantinople's compared to them.

Nagging thoughts of young Soranzo haunted him. He had not caused his loss, but the sense of responsibility he felt, as the boy's commanding officer, weighed heavily on him. Marco had not died a glorious death in battle—the ideal of every Venetian who went to war. Instead, his life had been wasted. Soon Antonio would have to face Marco's older brothers and tell them the tragic news. Most men would accept the boy's fate as the fortunes of war, but his gut told him that they would not. Captain Giovanni Soranzo was proud, uncompromising, and vindictive—the very qualities that, in war, made him such a formidable foe. Pietro, his other brother, he imagined would also be made of the same tough stock.

The House of Ziani and the House of Soranzo had been enemies ever since their grandfathers' joint business venture had collapsed into mutual recriminations more than forty years before. Then they had chosen not to resolve their differences in the courts. That only would have resulted in unacceptable compromise. Instead, they each sought to prevail in their rivalry by investing, trading, and manipulating as each battled to dominate and ultimately ruin the other. The fathers passed this legacy on to their sons.

The fleet had reached Negropont, on the island of Euboea, in under three weeks—faster than expected. Located between Athens and Constantinople, it would be their only stop on the voyage. Tomorrow, after reprovisioning with food and fresh water, they would quickly depart on the final leg of their journey with the morning tide. Vice Captain Trevisan was not even going to take time to repair the damage caused by the storm.

As daylight faded, Antonio gazed across the harbor at the four other ships riding on their anchor chains with their crimson and gold flags hanging limply from the masts, like shrouds in the still evening air. He looked down at his feet and thought about the series of events that had placed him, at that moment, on the little square of wooden deck so far away from the comforts of the Ca' Ziani, his family's palazzo back in Venice.

Two years earlier the Byzantine emperor, John VIII, had died before he could convince his people that Constantinople, virtually all that remained of his Byzantine Empire, could not survive without support from the West. The West's resolve to honor an agreement it had solemnly made to help defend the city, in return for accepting Roman Church doctrine, died with him. His son, Emperor Constantine XI, was unable to improve the situation. Constantinople was now more vulnerable than she had been at any time since 1204. Then, crusaders on the way to the Holy Land, led by the blind doge of Venice, wily, old Enrico Dandolo, had sacked the city in a shameless display of greed that would forever stain the Republic's honor. But now, thought Antonio, Venice would redeem her honor and atone for her past sins by helping to defend the city.

As damaging as John's death had been to the Byzantine cause, a second death was far worse. The Ottoman Turkish sultan, Murad II, had died just after John VIII. With him died any hope of peace between the Byzantines and the Turks. His son, Muhammed II, had sworn to take the city. Just twenty-one, he was known to his subjects as *Hunkar*—"Drinker of Blood." On his accession, he immediately built a massive fortress, called "Cut-Throat Castle," on the western shore of the Bosphorus, just north of Constantinople.

Its powerful guns allowed him to stop and tax all shipping into and from the Black Sea—a major source of commercial traffic for the West. Venetian merchants with considerable trading interests there were outraged at his piracy.

Antonio had been present in the Sala del Maggior Consiglio, the Great Council Chamber, when news exploded into the room that the sultan had seized a Venetian ship that had tried to run his gauntlet without paying the tax. The sultan had beheaded the crew and impaled the brash captain alive on a wooden stake as a warning to others not to evade the toll. Antonio knew and admired the late Captain Rizzo and was sickened and enraged, as many Venetians were, at the sultan's wanton barbarity.

A motion to abandon the Byzantine capital to her fate was quickly defeated in the Pregadi, Venice's senate, by a vote of seventy-four to seven. Instead, Venice would send help. Wise men said Venice had more to lose by walking away from her responsibilities than by defending her trading interests. They reasoned that if the sultan perceived any weakness in the hearts of the Venetians, it would only be a matter of time until the Republic's own Greek possessions would fall to the Turks and their valuable monopoly on trade to the spice-rich East would be irreparably damaged. Now the time had come to pay for the privilege of being born a Venetian noble. Antonio would fight for his country *and* his fortune.

Vice-Captain Trevisan's orders were to help the city's defenders, without antagonizing the sultan further. It seemed to Antonio that these instructions conflicted. There were about seven hundred sailors and marines on board the five vessels, carrying a precious cargo of arms, armor, and money to fund bravery or bribery as the situation called for. Including those already in the city, there would be about a thousand Venetian defenders altogether, once their small fleet arrived. The sultan would quickly understand the Republic's intentions. How could one thousand armed Venetians not antagonize the sultan? He had just impaled one Venetian alive just for evading his damned toll!

Trevisan emerged from the doorway under the fighting castle at the stern.

"I have sent word to all the officers to come aboard for a council of war. Before they arrive there is something I want to discuss with you."

He looked hard into Antonio's eyes. "It was my fault, not yours, that young Soranzo was drowned. I made the decision to not turn back and search for him. Leave it to me to break the news to the boy's brothers."

"I appreciate your intentions, Gabriele, but I still feel partly responsible. I failed to ensure that he remained safely below deck where he belonged."

"Why let this unfortunate event cause trouble between you and Captain Soranzo? Marco was the only one who disregarded your orders and went up on deck." Trevisan smiled ironically. "Many of us will die before this is all over. In the end, the loss of one marine, though it seems important now, will not matter. And if the Soranzos both survive, time will lessen their grief as it does for all those who experience such a loss."

"Time does repair one's grief, but they will be at the peak of their anguish at the very time that we all must think of nothing but accomplishing our mission. The tragic news may divert their attention from what is most important."

"I know there has been bad blood between your families in the past, but now we must think of nothing but saving Constantinople. To this end, I have no doubt that they will do their duty as you will do yours."

Trevisan placed his hand firmly on Antonio's shoulder.

"I am fortunate to have such an honorable man to command my marines."

"To deserve that honor you speak of, I must do my duty and be the one to inform them, as distasteful as it will be."

"Very well, then. As you wish, I will leave it to you."

He had served with Vice-Captain Trevisan two years before, when they were sent to destroy a nest of Albanian pirates, near Corfu, but it was his position as a fellow patrician that enabled him to speak frankly to his superior, now, about their mission.

"Gabriele, I have never visited Constantinople and seen its defenses, but you have. Do you think we can successfully defend the city?"

Trevisan squinted as though in pain, momentarily revealing his stony teeth through his thick beard, and then slowly shook his head.

"I fear it will be most difficult. If the city had not fallen once before, I would say her defenses were virtually impregnable. Except for Venice itself, they are the strongest on earth. The city is completely surrounded by thirteen miles of thick masonry walls. Imagine a great triangle. On the north face along the Golden Horn, a branch of the Bosphorus by which name the city's main harbor is known, a wall stretches for three and a half miles. The horn itself is protected by a massive iron-chain boom that, when raised to the surface of the water, blocks entry by enemy vessels.

"The second face, to the southeast along the Sea of Marmara, stretches for five and a half miles. Unmarked shoals and rocks make it nearly impossible to land there. The point of land that juts out between these two faces has currents so strong that, in my opinion, no ship can remain there long enough to even launch a small boat.

"The third face runs southwest on the landward side. The dry moat and triple walls that protect it are the largest in all of Christendom and stretch almost four miles from the Golden Horn all the way to the Sea of Marmara. The moat is sixty feet across and no less than fifteen feet in depth. Behind it is a stone breastwork ten feet high. Behind the breastwork is the outer wall, twenty-five feet high and ten feet thick with too many towers to count. The inner wall is forty feet in height and fifteen feet thick, with over a hundred towers, most exceeding sixty feet in height."

Antonio listened intently, encouraged, as he imagined the massive defenses. Trevisan knew the city well as a port of call in times of peace and from information provided to him by the government.

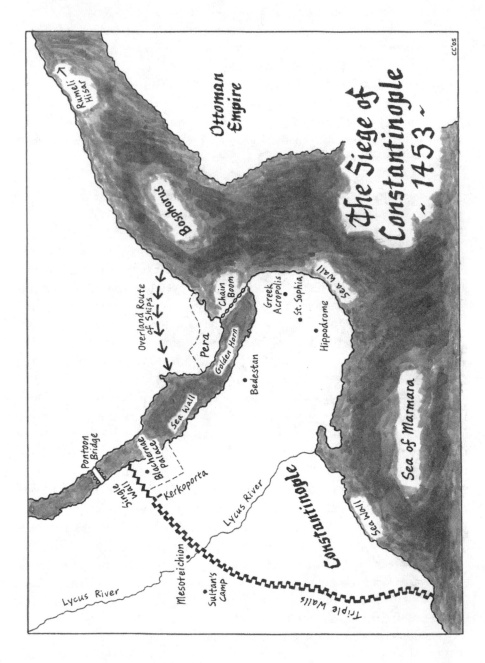

The Siege of Constantinople ~ 1453 ~

Ottoman Empire

Rumeli Hisar

Bosphorus

Overland Route of Ships

Chain Boom

Sea Wall

Greek Acropolis

St. Sophia

Hippodrome

Pera

Golden Horn

Bedestan

Sea of Marmara

Sea Wall

Pontoon Bridge

Sea Wall

Blachernae Palace

Single Wall

Kerkoporta

Lycus River

Constantinople

Sea Wall

Lycus River

Mesoteichion

Sultan's Camp

Triple Walls

CC'05

"Where will you post the marines? Will we fight on land or on our ships?"

"Our orders are to fight on our ships, unless the danger on the walls exceeds the danger posed to us in the Golden Horn. Then I am to place you and the marines under the emperor's command to defend the walls."

Antonio had no more questions. He looked into Trevisan's face. His expression was firm, quietly confident. Antonio knew his company of four hundred marines could defend little more than a few hundred yards of the walls. How many Greeks from the city, he wondered, would fight beside them to defend their homes and families—and how many Turks would be outside the walls trying to smash their way in?

The Soranzos climbed aboard, brazen and loud, talking like proud men who had faced death and lived to tell about it. They were trading tales with some of the other officers who had arrived before them about stormy voyages past. They both looked imposing, strong, and determined. Captain Giovanni Soranzo was renowned in Venice as an expert swordsman. His large forehead made his dominating icy-blue eyes seem smaller, but their menacing gaze disarmed nearly everyone who felt their power.

Though Soranzo's family was the principal shareholder of one of the Republic's oldest banks, the captain left the oversight of his business to his uncles and cousins. He preferred the navy. Antonio briefly studied Pietro, who had chosen to emulate his brother, choosing martial exploits over mere business transactions. That is the difference between us, he thought. I count my winnings in ducats and they count theirs in blood.

Antonio purposefully crossed the deck to where the officers mingled. The conversation abruptly stopped. Captain Soranzo turned to acknowledge him with a faint smile just visible through the beard that covered his brown weather-beaten, face.

"Ah, Captain Ziani, did my brother, Marco, perform well on his first voyage?"

"Captain Soranzo, Lieutenant Soranzo, I must speak to both of you privately."

Their smiles disappeared as the two brothers glanced at each other, unable to hide their concern at Antonio's serious tone. As they strode together across the deck to the other side of the ship, Antonio felt as if he was walking between two powder kegs with a flaming torch in his hand. This is going to be hard, he thought, best to tell them directly. As they stopped along the rail, he turned around to face them. A mild breeze rustled their beards and disheveled their hair. He felt a strange vibration in his head as he began.

"I regret to tell you that Marco was lost at sea."

He paused to give them a chance to absorb the hard news.

Captain Soranzo's face was transformed into an agonized mask of pain. He squarely faced Antonio, stepping in front of Pietro, preempting his brother's response, and grasped Antonio roughly by the shoulders. "Tell me what happened."

Antonio related the few stark details and explained that because of their orders they had not turned back to search for Marco or signaled the other ships.

"I do not fault Vice-Captain Trevisan for pressing on, refusing to go back and search for Marco. I would have done the same," Soranzo hissed through his clenched teeth, his angry face flushed scarlet. "But I demand to know the reason why a boy of fifteen was allowed to go up on deck *alone* in such a dangerous storm? All alone!"

As Pietro appeared from behind his older brother and stepped toward Antonio, the captain's arm shot out to restrain him, palm outstretched.

"*You* were his commanding officer. *You* were responsible for him. I hold *you* accountable for Marco's death! When this business in Constantinople is finished, by God, I will deal with you!"

Soranzo's eyes burned into Antonio's like hot coals, glowing with hatred, with greater intensity than he had ever seen before—even in the eyes of an enemy, an instant before he had mercilessly cut short his life.

"We all mourn his death, Captain. Though he was young, he had earned the respect of his comrades. But I gave strict orders for no one to go up on deck, for any reason. He disobeyed them."

"Captain Ziani, before a battle, as a Venetian officer, I presume you order your men to fight with courage. If one man turns coward and tries to run, do you simply let him go? Or do you take charge of his actions and prevent his flight, forcing him to obey your orders, as any *competent* officer would?"

The words bit deeply into Antonio's pride. He was becoming angrier as he held his ground, defiantly returning Soranzo's piercing stare.

"Captain Soranzo, if one of your sailors, while he is ashore in a foreign port, takes another man's woman and sleeps with her and her man comes home and discovers them, killing your man for the insult—are you at fault? Did that sailor not make his own decision to tempt fate and accept a dangerous situation for himself? Are you at fault for not following him to that house and pulling him from that bed to save his life?"

As Antonio waited for Soranzo to answer his questions, the captain wrapped his powerful arm around Pietro's broad shoulders, and together they turned and slowly walked away, supporting each other in their shock and grief. Antonio stood against the rail, alone. The captain's bitter words had turned Antonio's remorse into anger. The encounter had been far worse than he had anticipated.

Vice-Captain Trevisan motioned for the officers to assemble. He had sent the entire ship's crew ashore on their last night in Negropont. This would ensure that nothing said in the council of war would be heard by them—giving rise to dangerous rumors. As Antonio looked at his comrades, he could see that most of them were younger men. Old men would not undertake such a venture, he thought cynically. They have too much to lose. Most of the men in this group had volunteered to go to Constantinople to cover themselves in glory by saving the city from the infidel Turks. He smiled as he thought: old men invented the concept of glory to entice young men to sacrifice their lives to finish the wars they started.

Vice-Captain Trevisan took his time. Not until he had looked into each man's face did he begin to speak, slowly and deliberately.

"This is the first chance we have had to meet together since we sailed from Venice. It is time for me to tell you more about our mission and to give you your orders.

"Tomorrow morning we will sail with the tide and make straight for Constantinople. I do not know whether hostilities have yet begun. If they have not, there should be nothing to oppose our entry into the harbor, but be on guard for Turkish warships, just the same. We will fight only if they attack us first but I do not expect that will happen. Once we arrive, we will unload our cargo and then join the emperor's fleet anchored in the harbor. Our mission will be to prevent any Turkish ships from entering the Golden Horn and attacking the seawalls. If there is no attack we will send as many men as we can to fight on the land walls but we will not risk our ships under any circumstances." He paused to search the many anxious faces. "Now, you must all look to your men. We will be forced to spend many days on board our ships and we must maintain our fighting spirit and readiness. I hold you each responsible for the fitness of the men under your command."

The words stung Antonio, though he knew they were not directed at him. Surely, upon hearing them, he thought, the Soranzos will have their accusing eyes riveted on me. A quick glance told him he was right.

Captain Soranzo now spoke. "Who will command the marines we send ashore to fight on the land walls?"

"Captain Ziani. He is the most senior marine captain and, I might add, the most experienced. We have fought together before. I have complete faith in his leadership."

"And if the sailors fight on the walls?"

"I will lead them personally and you, Captain Soranzo, as the senior ship's captain, will take command of our ships in my absence."

Some of the officers began to talk among themselves, envious of the posts assigned to Ziani and Soranzo, but most were relieved to hear they would most likely remain on board their ships with their crews, avoiding an unfamiliar land battle. A Venetian preferred fighting with his feet on a wooden deck rather than on a stone wall.

"Who will be in overall command of the city's defenses?" asked another.

"I do not know," replied Trevisan. "There are men from all over Christendom on the walls. Companies of Papal, Genoese, Cretan, and even a few disaffected Turks have joined the Greeks. However, I expect that the emperor will claim that honor for himself."

At the mere mention of the hated Genoese, the men grumbled discontentedly. Trevisan angrily raised his voice to quell the disturbance.

"In the coming battle, there will be no Greek, no Roman, no Genoese . . . and no Venetian. There will only be Christians—and Turks. There will be no more talk of factions. We will only defeat the infidels if we fight as one. What can we accomplish if we fight as Contarini, Morosini, Soranzo, Ziani, and Trevisan, with no faith in each other?" The point was forcefully made. They would have to put their prejudices and jealousies aside, no matter how strongly felt, to survive.

"Any more questions?" spit Trevisan, in a tone intended to discourage them.

"Yes," said Pietro Soranzo as every head turned in his direction. "Why must I serve with Captain Ziani and not with my brother? I want to fight under his command."

The deck was awash in shocked silence. Pietro's place was with the rest of the marines under Antonio's command and everyone knew it—including him. Trevisan, attempting to repair the breach of discipline, cast an angry glance at Pietro's older brother who, upon seeing it, was forced to speak.

"Pietro, your place is with the marines. If they fight on the land walls, you will serve under Captain Ziani," said the elder Soranzo, his voice dripping with disdain.

Pietro dropped his head. He realized his rashness. He had embarrassed himself and his brother, though he cared little that he had insulted Ziani.

Antonio could forgive the youth's indiscretion. He could forgive him because of the profound grief he knew he must be suffering over the loss of his brother. But he regarded Pietro's public display of contempt for him as a warning sign—he would have to keep his eye on this young man.

Hearing no more questions, Vice-Captain Trevisan dismissed the officers who somberly returned to their ships. Later, just before retiring to his cabin, Antonio saw Trevisan, alone, pacing on the deck near the stern and joined him.

"Gabriele, why not let Lieutenant Soranzo fight under the command of his older brother as he has requested? He is young and must learn how to act like a patrician."

"I will not! I will not tolerate or reward his impertinence," he said, holding up his hand to prevent any objection.

"Very well, Gabriele," he replied.

"Why do you defend the boy's foolish behavior?"

"I do not know. Perhaps it is because I cannot stop thinking about how I would have felt if it had been my brother who had drowned."

"How is Giorgio now? He must have been gravely ill to miss this."

"Yes. The fever came on so suddenly we thought we were going to lose him at first. And then, his poor health was hardly helped by his disappointment at being left behind. But by the time we return to Venice, I expect he will be fully recovered."

Antonio and Giorgio had always been closer than any brothers they knew. When they were young, Antonio used to defend his little brother when they played soldier with the other boys and things got rough. When they reached adolescence, Giorgio grew to surpass him in size and strength. Then, he was Antonio's protector—some would have said enforcer. He recalled when Giorgio bravely fought off three boys while he nursed a bloody head that one of the boys had split open with his wooden sword.

Not as clever as Antonio, Giorgio made up for it with his robust sense of humor and worldly ways. He was a natural leader. Men followed him because they liked and trusted him. He would always courageously place himself in front, at the point of greatest danger. Three times he had served the Republic in war with distinction. With his neatly trimmed black beard, dark mysterious eyes, and aquiline nose, he had a magnetic effect on everyone who met him—he was imposing to men and irresistible to women.

Over the next two days, the five Venetian ships crossed the Aegean and sailed up the Dardanelles into the Sea of Marmara. They proceeded north, through the night. By daybreak the crews could see the massive golden dome of the Hagia Sophia—the Church of Holy Wisdom—rising out of the morning mists. Soon the vast expanse of the city sprawled for miles along the western coast. As the small fleet drew even with the city, near the headland, they could clearly make out the massive seawalls. All along the battlements, brilliantly colored flags of a dozen nations seemed to salute the Venetians, as they fluttered out of the soft haze that was slowly burning away in the warm December sun.

With sails unfurled and their huge battle flags, each with its golden Lion of St. Mark, gazing defiantly across the Bosphorus, the fleet sailed around the headland and made for the Golden Horn. Soon they could hear thousands of people cheering them on from the city walls. Loud reports boomed and puffs of white smoke rose above the walls as the city fired a three-gun salute in their honor. For the first time in days, the Venetians could smell humankind above the salty sea air. The city's tiled rooftops seemed to rise up to greet them, uplifted by her citizens' restored spirits. They could hear bells ringing from a hundred churches celebrating their arrival. They were proud to be Venetians.

Every man was on deck enjoying a brief respite before the work of docking and unloading the ship would begin. As they stood at attention, broad grins painting their faces, bright eyes gleaming with anticipation, they knew they had brought the only means of survival to the city's defenders.

After an hour, they approached the great rusted iron-chain boom, draped with seaweed, which stretched almost a thousand yards across the entrance to the harbor. One end was anchored deep in the wall of nearby Pera, a Genoese trading town just across the Golden Horn. The other end was connected to a winch device within Constantinople's walls to enable the defenders to raise and lower it. A cannon barked the signal to lower the chain. Within minutes, it was submerged. The ships safely crossed over it and entered the refuge of the Golden Horn. A dozen piers of all sizes dotted the southern shoreline. The Venetians made for the longest and in another half hour they were docked. It was just before noon when they began unloading their precious cargo of food and arms.

As Antonio debarked from his ship, confidently striding down the gangway onto the broad stone pier, he was mobbed by jubilant dockworkers, soldiers, and assorted well-wishers who pounded him on the back, hugged, and kissed him. Young girls sobbed tears of joy as they strewed crimson and white rose petals at his feet. Despite the press of the crowd, he assembled his men to be sure they were all present and accounted for. Marines from the other four ships soon joined his company, forming ranks, nearly four hundred strong. The crowd's wild cheers fed their hungry pride.

Presently, a well-dressed, officious-looking man of fifty pushed his way through the mob and held out his hand to Antonio. Despite the cool air, he was sweating like a galley slave; his red face seemed to be bursting through his chestnut beard.

"I am *Bailo* Girolamo Minotto. How many are you?" he asked with great urgency, barely controlling his excitement. Minotto was the Venetian official who headed the Republic's colony of traders in the city and had come to greet his countrymen.

"I am Captain Antonio Ziani. We are seven hundred, counting the sailors."

"That will help, that will help . . . ," he muttered as his voice dissolved.

"We have brought with us six thousand bladed weapons, twenty thousand crossbow bolts, four hundred suits of armor, and a hundred barrels of black powder," he added proudly. "We have also brought you much grain and salted fish."

"It is brave men that we need most, Captain. What good are all these weapons if there is no one to wield them? When do the rest of the ships arrive?"

Antonio looked at him incredulously.

"There are no other ships—but there is talk that another fleet will be dispatched in the weeks to come. Has there been any sign of the Turks?"

"No, not yet, but the prices of luxuries are falling and staples are rising. That means the Turks will be here soon and will blockade the city, laying siege to it." Seeming to have lost interest, Minotto suddenly turned to his left, ignoring him completely.

He followed Minotto's gaze to see a tall handsome man cloaked in a long purple robe walking in the midst of a large richly dressed retinue. It was the emperor, accompanied by the patriarch and the rest of his court. Spotting Minotto, he walked directly to where he and Antonio were standing and looked impatiently at the *bailo,* waiting for him to make introductions.

"Your Majesty, allow me to introduce, eh, I am sorry, Captain . . ."

"I am Captain Antonio Ziani, commander of Venetian marines, Your Majesty," he said as he bowed respectfully.

"Thank you for your faithfulness to our cause, Captain Ziani."

"Your Majesty, your presence here honors us all. We offer our service to you in the name of St. Mark and Venice."

"This is a great day for Christendom! May God bless your arms and may you slay many a Turkish infidel," said the emperor. Then, as quickly as he had appeared, he politely took his leave and continued along the pier, greeting every new arrival he could—even common sailors and soldiers.

He watched the emperor move with ease among the crowd, graciously welcoming the Venetians while all the time honoring his own citizens, never once betraying that he was carrying the weight of the world on his shoulders. He was the picture of grace, majestic in his motions, every inch an emperor. An extraordinary man, thought Antonio. But could he provide the military leadership to save the city and his throne?

2

Constantinople

In January, shortly after the defenders ushered in the new year of 1453, Giovanni Giustiniani Longo, a Genoese soldier of fortune and an acknowledged expert at defending fortresses, arrived with seven hundred handpicked men, two ships, and a German artillerist named Johann Grant. Soon after, the pope's legate, Cardinal Isadore, arrived with two hundred more soldiers. A few others trickled into the city after that but there were no more large reinforcements. The defenders barely numbered a disappointing eight thousand. This included about five thousand Greeks from the city—a poor response to the emperor's call to arms to the more than twenty-five thousand men old enough to fight. In addition to the men defending the walls, the fleet was comprised of ten imperial ships and eight each from Venice and Genoa. All eight Venetian ships and seven imperial ships were placed under the command of Vice-Captain of the Gulf Trevisan.

Though the Turks were expected to commence their siege any day, there was nothing more the Venetians could do to ready themselves. Fresh food and water were delivered each day from the city to the crews of the ships anchored in the Golden Horn. As March arrived, bringing its unpredictable assortment of weather, boredom had become their greatest enemy.

For several long months the Venetians remained on board their ships in case of a sudden attack by the Turkish fleet, but the attack did not come.

Each day the crews, virtual prisoners on board their ships, peered over the rails at the magnificent city that seemed so close they could reach out and touch it. They talked endlessly about home or the impending battle. Battle-hardened veterans tried to outdo each other with tales of their exploits, each lie bigger than the last, as the wide-eyed younger men soaked up every word. But as each day crawled by, morale began to wane.

Ever since the Venetians had arrived in early December, Trevisan had permitted no one to go ashore, except for a few officers to arrange for provisions. Recognizing that the crews' confinement could lead to a breakdown of their discipline and a reduction of his command's fighting effectiveness, he now wisely decided to allow the officers to take fifty men ashore each day, to sample the delights of the city. No one knew how long the Turks' inactivity would allow this arrangement to last but, to the men, it was a godsend.

It would be Antonio's first day in Constantinople in more than a month. He had patiently watched, with his impatient men, as Trevisan had ensured that each of the other seven Venetian ships under his command had taken their turn to go ashore. At times it had seemed as though their day would never come. Now, as he climbed from the boat onto the expanse of the stone pier, he looked over his shoulder, back toward his ship. He was euphoric as he contemplated his escape from her crowded, reeking confines. He smiled as he watched his pleasure-starved marines eagerly disembark from the boats, joking and good-naturedly taunting each other. Suddenly, he felt a hard tug on his sleeve.

"You are Venetians, no?"

He quickly spun around. At first he did not see the intruder, but standing before him was a strange little man, so short that at first glance he thought he might be a dwarf—like those he had seen perform on the quay in Venice.

"Yes," said Antonio, annoyed, as he quickly returned his attention to his men.

But the persistent man pulled on his arm again. He was dressed in tattered clothes and reeked of cheap wine, burnt garlic, and mutton. He had a head like a knot in an old oak tree. His swarthy complexion and wild black hair flowed in unkempt ringlets to his shoulders. His Italian was excellent, unlike most Greeks who, Antonio thought, were inept at the language. His high-pitched voice assaulted Antonio's ears as he spoke loudly, as though he was an actor on a stage.

"Your Honor, you are looking for something, no? I can help you find anything you desire," he boasted as he flashed a grin, his bushy eyebrows dancing like smoke billowing from a campfire.

What an irritating little man, he thought. In Venice, most patricians would have been indignant that such a person would have the impertinence to speak to them without first being spoken to, let alone grab hold of their sleeve . . . twice!

"If you will point out where the taverns are located, that will do," said Antonio with finality, wanting nothing more to do with him.

"Of course, you and your men would like to drink some wine, no? Follow me then, Your Honor. I will take you to a place where a sailor can find good wine, fair food, and bad women." He winked and then quickly turned and waddled across the pier, disappearing through a large open gate in the wall that towered twenty feet above them.

Ignoring the invitation, Antonio formed up his fifty marines into two lines. Then, with fine military bearing, he and his second in command, Lieutenant Sagredo, led them through the gate, two abreast. As they marched into the cold stone passageway, made vile with age, he could tell that, being so near the taverns, for centuries the gate had doubled as a privy. On the other side of the wall was the debauched and noisy world of the parasites who preyed on sailors and merchants in every port in the Mediterranean. A wide gray and black stone street, paved with refuse of every sort, ran along the inside of the seawall far in both directions.

To Antonio's front was a sprawling marketplace that extended into the city. Acres of dwellings, taverns, and inns were crammed together amid a maze of narrow streets, many little more than alleyways. Their uneven rooftops etched a ragged outline against the swirling purple and gray winter sky, dappled with racing fluffs of cloud. The looming walls blocked out most of the morning sunlight, making the air seem colder. Scents from a myriad of spices blended with woody smoke, assaulting his nostrils and masking the underlying odors emanating from the filthy streets.

He looked back at his men. They were ready to cut loose and enjoy themselves for the first time in months. They had all seen thriving marketplaces before but only a handful had seen anything rivaling this.

"A carouser's paradise, a debaucher's dream!" said Sagredo with a wry grin.

"It is as though Satan, himself, has let every sinner in hell out for the day, to all gather in this place just to greet us," observed Antonio, shaking his head.

At the sight of fifty finely clad Venetian marines, with their distinctive sea caps, the motley inhabitants of the precinct burst into a frenzy of activity, as if on cue, to better hawk their wares, pour their wine, and sell their bodies, each shouting a more outrageous advertisement than the next to outsell the competition. As the marines began to break ranks, each with his mind set on gratifying his favorite vice, Antonio shouted to them.

"Remember, we must meet back on the pier as soon as the church bells ring eight. Any man who is late will be severely punished. Do not move about in groups of less than four and stay out of fights! If there is any trouble these pleasure trips will cease."

His words trailed off, lost on the most aggressive veterans who were already crossing the street and melting into the crowd. He had lost control. It was easier to maintain discipline, he thought, when men faced death than when they sought pleasure. He began to wonder if this trip was really such a good idea. How many would be missing at eight bells? But the men desperately needed relief from their monotonous routine on board ship. This day might afford some of them the last pleasures they would ever know in their short lives. He watched them drag Sagredo into the nearest tavern where they would expect him to buy the first round of drinks. Soon drunk, most of the marines would end up in the arms of the ubiquitous whores, who would trade their flesh for the marines' silver *torneselli*. What Venetian could resist the lure of such a trade?

Left alone by his men, out of respect for his rank, Antonio blinked and looked around, adjusting his eyes to the dim light and shadows. It was then that he noticed his nemesis. He was fifty feet away, sitting by himself on a stone bench across the street, eyeing Antonio intently with a broad grin on his face as he swung his legs, back and forth, like a child. Antonio moved obliquely past him in order to cross the street, unmolested, and join the others. But as soon as he took his first step, the man slid off his perch and made straight for him, his stubby legs pumping fast.

He wanted him to go away and yet, strangely, he felt drawn to him in the same way one's curiosity overcomes one's revulsion to a corpse. He continued walking toward the tavern, looking straight ahead, but the man, suddenly, was there, directly in front of him, underfoot, blocking his way. Antonio abruptly stopped to avoid running over him.

"Now that you have seen to your men's needs what do *you* require, Your Honor?" said the man, anticipation scrawled across his upturned face.

He looked down at the gnome and sighed. "Why do you plague me so?"

"A thousand apologies if I am bothering you, Your Honor. I am simply grateful that you have come to defend my city. I only want to show my appreciation in some small way. As you can see, I could hardly be expected to take up the sword or the axe to defend my home. But by helping its defenders I am helping the defense too. No?"

His intense pride was evident as he inclined his prominent chin in Antonio's direction. Though he made a ridiculous picture, his dramatic tone told Antonio that he was quite serious. He was trying to oppose the Turks in his own modest way—the only way he could. That was more than most of these cowardly Greeks who lived in the city were doing, he thought.

Suddenly, he struggled to remove something from a small leather sack. Then, with a broad smile, he proudly held aloft a large golden medallion attached to a long golden chain.

"It was given to me by the emperor John VIII for service to the Empire."

"For killing Turks?" asked Antonio with a wide grin, warming to him.

"For figuring out how to remove shit from the city!" he replied, unperturbed. "Not Turks, though. I am talking about the kind of shit people make. I hear you Venetians do not have that problem since you have your canals to remove the city's waste."

Antonio was being drawn into a conversation with a man who, minutes before, he was embarrassed to be seen talking to.

"Have you lived in Constantinople all of your life?"

"Oh yes, Your Honor, all twenty-seven years. My mother was a royal prostitute in the service of the emperor himself, one of his favorites I am told. My father was a captain of the imperial guard—though one can never be sure. They say that when my parents first laid eyes on me, fresh from the womb, my mother swore and my father cried. I was an utter disappointment. So they orphaned me to the Monastery of St. George. It was those monks there who raised me and provided me with my education. They taught me mathematics, philosophy, and history and many useful languages."

Antonio had never met anyone like him before.

"What do they call you?" he asked as he bent slightly, maintaining eye contact.

"I am called Seraglio—named for the place where I was conceived and born. Do you know the term, Your Honor? Well, a *seraglio* is the high-class brothel where the emperor keeps his favorite women, closely guarded night and day by his eunuchs."

"Seraglio, will you show me Constantinople?" he said abruptly. "I want to see the palaces and churches, to walk along the walls and feel the wind in my face. I want to know this place I am going to fight for."

"I would be delighted, Your Honor, if you would only tell me *your* name," said Seraglio as he held out his fleshy hand.

As he grasped it firmly he could feel the dislocated bones ripple in his hand.

"I am Captain Antonio Ziani of the Venetian marines."

"I am honored to make your acquaintance, Captain," he bowed. "Follow me."

Antonio watched as his new companion scampered across the cobblestones and into a tavern across the street from the one where his men were now fully engaged in their revelry. As he entered the half-full place, he could see Seraglio sitting at a table in a corner, alone, pouring wine into a single wooden cup. He sat down across from him.

"Where do you live, Seraglio?"

"Here, in the cellar. I bring the owner business in return for meals and a warm place to sleep. For him, it is a bargain. It does not take much food to fill my stomach," he laughed. "It is hardly a prestigious job but it provides me with life's essentials.

"A tour of the city must begin with a cup of wine. You drink. I will talk!"

Though he was not four feet tall, there was more life in him than in any normal-sized man, thought Antonio. As he studied him, he noticed that his fingers were gnarled like the roots of an old swamp tree. Earlier he had seen that his arms extended below his knees, and his legs were so bowed they seemed to almost form a circle.

"Seraglio, what happened to your hands? Were you born like that?"

"Yes, but life in the monastery made them worse."

"How?"

"As the years passed, I did not grow taller like the others. I tried my best to get along with them," he sighed, dropping his eyes. After a pause, he continued.

"When you are only three and a half feet tall you learn to be quick with your mind, because when you encounter trouble you cannot run away from it. I was born small and unattractive, but I became truly ugly from the beatings I received from the other boys.

"One kindly brother who felt sorry for me taught me to box, so I could defend myself from their bullying, but it was hard on my knuckles and fingers. The younger boys, cajoled by the older ones, all wanted to fight me, to prove they were not so young."

"Did they beat you for your impertinence?"

Seraglio confidently met Antonio's gaze, ignoring their difference in station.

"Look, Your Honor. Look at these scars on my face. Look at my hands."

He laid them on the table between them. His stubby fingers were splayed crookedly apart.

"Not the hands of a scribe or a copyist, are they? Now you see why I excelled at languages. The monks gave up trying to teach me calligraphy.

"No, Your Honor, impertinence does not drive humans to do that. They all wanted to fight me—but not because of my actions. It was because I was different than them. You should have seen them line up—like they were going to receive communion."

"But, Seraglio, why would they all want to beat you? Surely you must have done something to provoke them."

He looked intently at Antonio. "Do not states do the same thing to each other? Have we provoked the Turks? Why do they want to beat us? I will tell you why. It is because we are different—but in this case, it is our religion. Turks want to defeat us so they can make us like them." He sighed. "Perhaps it would be better for us if they did."

Suddenly, he shook his head violently, as though fighting off sleep.

"No, I must not say that! God, forgive me. In our case, we Greeks are not just different than the Turks—we are better. That is why Byzantium must survive." For the first time, Seraglio was silent, somber, not his usual ebullient self.

"How old were you when you left the monastery?"

"Sixteen."

"What did you do?" asked Antonio.

"I was first employed as a tutor in a school here in Constantinople where I achieved notoriety for my command of languages. Eventually I was chosen to be translator for the emperor's chief architect, a man named Alexius, whom I would come to love as the father I never knew. You see, craftsmen and workers came from all over the empire to work here. Fortunately, for me, Alexius spoke only Greek and Latin. I speak Greek and Latin too, but I am also fluent in Turkish, French, and Italian and I can manage all right with some of the Slavic languages. Alexius would communicate with these foreign workers through me. I have worked on nearly every major building in the city, including the emperor's palaces," he said with pride.

"An impressive and important post," observed Antonio. "What happened? Why do you live in this ramshackle tavern, hawking wine and women to drunken sailors in return for little more than the means to stay alive?"

Seraglio looked down at the floor. "Alexius died unexpectedly and there was no money left for the emperor to build. When Constantine took the throne, two years ago, he poured his remaining treasure into mercenaries and bribes in his desperate attempts to keep the Turks at bay. He had no need for an architect's translator then. One day they just told me to leave my quarters in the palace. After wandering the streets of the city for days, I finally found this place. The owner thought I was entertaining and clever. Finding no better arrangement, I accepted his offer. That was almost two years ago. You might say that ever since then, I have been underemployed," he grinned ironically.

Antonio swallowed the rest of the cheap bitter wine and changed the subject.

"Tell me about your city."

Seraglio shifted in his seat as his head inclined to the side. Finally he spoke.

"Well, Your Honor, that is a lengthy subject. Eleven hundred years ago, the Roman emperor Constantine marked out the limits of the original city on a barren point of land below the Bosphorus. Just four years later, Constantinople was ready to be dedicated. They say many thousands of workmen died building her and many more died expanding her over the years. For ten centuries she has been the greatest and richest city in the world. Nine hundred years ago almost one million souls lived within these walls, though but a tenth of that number live here today.

"I have seen the official census from the year 450. It lists five imperial palaces, over four thousand mansions, three hundred twenty-two streets, and fifty-two gates in the city walls. Our roads led to every corner of the Roman Empire. Great squares and baths abounded. Our Hagia Sophia is still the largest church in the world. The Hippodrome presented circuses and races, holding seventy thousand spectators—it still stands, though there is not much sport to watch there these days—a few muggings perhaps."

Antonio clasped Seraglio's arm. "Take me to see the Hagia Sophia."

"I will, but first, you must see the rest of the city. We will save the best for last."

On their six-hour walk, Seraglio pointed out the city's sights, filling Antonio with facts and figures about each building's construction. When they were finished, Antonio had two overwhelming impressions. First, the city was massive, three or four times larger in area than Venice. Second, it was much older and in a terrible state of disrepair, owing to the horrific sack in 1204 from which the city had never fully recovered and to the declining fortunes of the Byzantine Empire over the two hundred and fifty years since.

As the satin red sun began to sink in the cold gray sky, they finally stood in front of the great church. It was the largest church Antonio had ever seen, even larger than Venice's own Basilica of San Marco. Dominated by its giant dome, the structure and surrounding complex was virtually a small city within a city.

"This is the Hagia Sophia, the Church of Holy Wisdom, Your Honor," whispered Seraglio. "Prepare to meet God." He smiled at Antonio, his homely face softening with pride. As they entered, removing their hats and bowing their heads, Seraglio began to speak in hushed tones draped with reverence. The sweet musty scent of exotic incense filled Antonio's head—making his first impression more surreal.

"It required ten thousand workmen and cost the emperor Justinian three hundred and twenty thousand pounds of gold to pay for it," whispered Seraglio. "It took five long years to finally complete the work in the year 537."

Antonio visualized the vast gleaming golden pile. He was amazed. It had taken almost a century to rebuild the smaller Basilica of San Marco after a disastrous fire destroyed the original church on its spot.

"When the emperor Justinian cast his eyes on the finished work, he cried, 'Glory be to God who has thought me worthy to accomplish so great a work! Solomon! I have vanquished you!' "

Seraglio pointed to the golden altar, then to the distant transepts.

"It is built in the shape of a Greek cross—two hundred fifty feet by two hundred feet. Look to heaven, Your Honor."

Antonio slowly raised his eyes until he fixed them on the vast dome.

"The dome is supported on a square of marble walls measuring one hundred by one hundred feet. Its apex is one hundred eighty feet above the floor. Only the dome of the Pantheon in Rome is larger. Now, behold the beauty of God's realm."

Antonio's eyes drank in the grandeur of its interior while he tried to burn a vivid image in his mind so he could recall it later. It was a panorama of color. Marble of every hue decorated the floor and walls—pink, gold, blue, green, white, red, purple, and yellow, more colors than one could see at carnival time back in Venice. Fantastic carvings adorned almost every foot of stone fascia. Mosaics rivaling the artistry of San Marco's were everywhere and more numerous. Forty massive silver chandeliers augmented the many large windows, bathing the cavernous place in soft yellow light. The interior, devoid of pillars, gave the impression of a scale, even larger than its reality. Silver, gold, pearl, ivory, and silk decorated the body of the church as wondrously as jewelry and fine clothing decorate the human body. Antonio had the same sensation as those who had entered before him—this place was not built by hands of man, but by God!

The church was not very crowded. As Seraglio talked quietly, explaining each architectural detail, Antonio could see a few people in small groups, the morning service was long ended and the evening service had not yet begun. An ancient woman worked meticulously, armed with her clutch of rags, laboriously cleaning the soot deposited by candles on the cracked marble slabs in the floor and on the forest of wooden chairs.

The church looked like it had seen the passage of almost a thousand years. As Antonio knelt to examine a prominent jagged break in one slab, Seraglio spoke.

"A massive earthquake once struck near the church. Every building around it was destroyed but the church survived. The people said it was the hand of God that saved it, but I say it was the skill of the architect and the men who built it."

Seraglio laughed at his own observation, but Antonio seemed lost in his thoughts.

"You have said little since we entered the church, Your Honor," whispered Seraglio. "Do you have anything like this in Venice?"

"I am awestruck, Seraglio. I thought our own Basilica of San Marco was the greatest church in Christendom, but this . . ." Words failed him.

"And to think, Your Honor, that just a few hundred years ago, you Venetians were ransacking this place, stealing her most valuable jewels and relics just minutes before your filthy French crusader friends could lay their hands on them. I just do not understand my fellow man." He fell silent.

"Seraglio, I am a Venetian. I have come now to atone for that great crime."

"I know, but where is the *rest* of the Christian world? Do they not know what danger we are in? Do they not know that after taking this city the sultan will be filled with an insatiable lust to possess their great cities too?"

Antonio could only slowly shake his head. There was power in this man. His body was of no account but his mind was keen and perceptive, his words true and forceful.

They walked back to the tavern in silence. Seven bells had rung already. It was nearly time for Antonio and his men to return to their ship.

"One day, you must come to Venice and I will show you my city—though she is not nearly as old and venerable as Constantinople, she is no less impressive, and in some ways more so. And she bears no scars from the depredations of her enemies." He embraced Seraglio, and then smiled as he took leave of him.

"I should like that very much, Your Honor. Surely it must be a place to make angels blush with envy," he said with a sadness he could not hide.

"After all, it is to Venice that we Greeks are looking for our salvation in our time of distress, no? So Venice, you see, must be the greater of the two cities."

Antonio turned to leave, but then quickly spun around and faced his new friend. "You are a noble man, Seraglio. If the Turks defeat us, make your way, without fail, to the harbor. I fear that if you do not leave this place, you will perish in the sack. Our ships will afford the only means of escape if the Turks breach the walls."

Seraglio nodded his understanding. "Do not worry about me, Your Honor. *You* are the one who must take care. Go with God!"

3

The Siege

On Good Friday evening, Antonio and the other senior officers from every contingent of troops in the city were summoned to a council of war to be held at the emperor's Blachernae Palace. Rumors had circulated all day that Emperor Constantine would name the Genoan Giovanni Giustiniani commander-in-chief of the city's defenses. As Antonio entered with Trevisan through the massive bronze doors, he was filled with excitement. Surely, they would finally be told the details of the plan to defend the city.

There were more than a hundred men gathered in the great hall. He surmised that every leading soldier, cleric, and government official in Constantinople was present. They spotted Catarin Contarini and the rest of the Venetians seated at the back and found two empty chairs next to them. Antonio noticed that the room glowed dimly in the eerie yellow light—only half of the precious candles and lamps were lit.

The emperor was in front, dressed in his familiar purple robes and seated in a simple wooden chair—deliberately shunning his jewel-encrusted throne directly behind him. Next to him was a hard-looking man wearing a soldier's clothes. The crowd was whispering Giustiniani's name. It must be him, thought Antonio.

"So that is our famous commander," sighed Trevisan, leaning close. "The emperor has made a good decision. I hear he knows his work."

Constantine suddenly rose, quieting the murmurs. He waited for complete silence as the flickering lamps made every piece of metal in the room sparkle like gold.

"Today, I have appointed Giovanni Giustiniani as commander-in-chief of the city. I grant him any power he desires. I command all of you to obey his orders as though they were my own."

An enthusiastic cheer rose up from the Genoese officers clustered on Antonio's right, nearer to the front. Everyone was pleased with his appointment to the vital post, even the Venetians. His reputation was beyond question. As the emperor nodded to him to begin, Giustiniani stood and smiled at the audience.

"We have many advantages and we shall use them wisely."

His words immediately began to inspire confidence among the defenders as he began to reveal his strategy, sparing no detail.

"Our plan is simple enough. We will prevent the Turks from entering the Golden Horn with the great chain and our ships. That will force the sultan to attack from the landward side. There we will defend the outer wall, leaving only armed monks and other irregulars to defend the seawalls along the Bosphorus that we judge to be impregnable. As long as our fleet can prevent him from placing his ships up against our seawall in the Golden Horn we will have just enough men to adequately defend the landward walls."

Giustiniani held his listeners in rapt attention. Everyone knew that in 1204, the Venetians and their crusader allies *had* placed their ships up against the seawall along the Golden Horn to successfully storm and sack the city. But back then the Byzantine fleet was of no account. Now, Venetians would defend the harbor.

"The Turks will, no doubt, attack our weak points at the Mesoteichion and the Blachernae Palace sections of the land wall. That is where the emperor and I and *Bailo* Minotto and Catarin Contarini will lead the defense, personally. The sailors and marines will fight on the extreme northern section of the wall, when not threatened by the Turks in the Golden Horn. Since there is only one wall there, we can surely use the extra men."

Giustiniani then meticulously detailed each defending company's post and orders. The defenders were heavily armed and ready to fight. Food and water were plentiful, the city having had a year to prepare for the inevitable siege. The Venetians all approved of the plan. As the council of war ended, Antonio thought about his own orders. As long as his marines fought on the

ships they would be fine, but he knew defending the walls would be an unfamiliar post for them.

Most of the Venetian officers attended an Easter Mass in the Hagia
Sophia on April 1. After the service, they returned somberly to their posts.
The next morning, the first scouts from the sultan's army, followed by large
bodies of cavalry, appeared outside the walls in front of the city. The emperor ordered all of the bridges across the moat burned. Over the next two
days, the sultan assembled his army of eighty thousand men. In compliance
with Islamic law, he offered to spare the city and its defenders if they would
surrender—otherwise, death, rape, pillage, and slavery would be the only reward for their bravery. The emperor refused his offer. The great siege had
begun.

S ultan Muhammed II was a terrifying man. Two years before, hearing the
news that his father, Murad II, had died, he had rushed back to Adri-
anople, his capital, to claim the sultanate as his own. He feared that his own
legitimacy would be challenged because many in the court believed his
mother was a beautiful Christian slave girl whom his father had taken as
his favorite wife. Muhammed's first act as the new sultan had been to have
his half brother drowned to avoid any possibility, later, of sharing or losing
power to him. Next he had the assassin executed. Then he had married the
boy's mother to a slave.

He would show no mercy to the defenders of Constantinople, or to his
own troops, from whom he demanded blind obedience. To cement his own
authority in the dangerous world of Turkish political intrigue, he had to
take Constantinople. If he failed, he knew he would probably be deposed
and killed. The Turks loved their sultans when they were conquering—
leading them to glory for Allah. Weakness in their leader was intolerable,
unthinkable. The sultan had decided to risk everything, even his life, on
capturing the greatest prize imaginable—Constantinople, the city that had
eluded Islam's designs for nearly eight hundred years.

The sultan was a study in contradictions. He spoke six languages perfectly, yet he would grunt like a beast as he watched a friend he had embraced, just the day before, impaled alive on a wooden stake for some small
affront. He was wiry and yet he possessed immense strength for his size. He
thought nothing of cruelly taking any man's wife for a night of pleasure, yet
he would spend hours stroking one of his five thousand hunting falcons,
as he delicately rearranged its feathers. He had no time for diplomacy,
though he devoted unlimited time to learning the ways of war, especially the

use of the newest weapon of terror—artillery. He was precocious and all-knowing, sometimes ranting at his generals for hours, yet he would patiently listen in silence to Urban, his artillerist, explain his craft in the minutest details. His narrow hooked nose and pinprick eyes gave him, rather, a hawklike intensity as he stared out from under his immense turban. Pashas, beys, *vezirs, emins,* and *mollas* alike agreed that a momentary glance from the sultan could freeze a man's spine. His bushy coal-black beard could not hide the thin lips beneath that decreed pain or death to those who would displease him. His philosophy as a leader of men was simple: the leader who never forgives is rarely disobeyed—and never more than once.

He kept his court loyal to him by the adroit use of rewards and punishments and employed both, liberally and publicly. His spies were everywhere, preventing conspiracies against him. He was even known to disguise himself and move among his soldiers, listening to their whining in camp. More than once he had ordered a soldier beheaded on the spot for uttering a careless or defeatist remark.

He ruled his sultanate by two maxims. First, *divide and conquer*—mete out favors to your internal court parsimoniously, dividing men against each other, discouraging those prone to disloyalty from joining to rebel against you. Second, *conquer and divide*—achieve great conquests, dividing the spoils generously, uniting men in a common cause, encouraging those prone to support you from flagging in their loyalty.

The Turkish camp was quiet. The outnumbered defenders wondered when the Turks would begin their attack. As soon as the sultan's emissary had returned with the defenders' refusal to accept his surrender terms, he began his bombardment of the massive city walls. His plan called for maintaining pressure against the seawalls, to tie up the defenders that would be desperately needed at the point of attack. Then he would blast the land walls into rubble with his guns—the finest in the world. They were terrifying new weapons that could wreak mass destruction on buildings and populations with merciless mechanical efficiency. Finally, he would storm the breaches created by his artillery, using his vast superiority in numbers to overwhelm the exhausted defenders.

One night, soon after the siege began, a supply boat came alongside Antonio's ship with provisions, fresh water, and news.

"Each day, they level sections of the walls with their guns," said the Greek. "They use the resulting rubble, dirt, and branches from trees to fill in the moat. Last night we killed almost a hundred as they labored under the walls, with our guns and archers. They rush up to the moat with their load of rocks or tree trunks and scurry back like rabbits to the safety of their lines. Then, when night falls, we clear the moat and build the walls back up using the same rubble, adding wood and cotton bales—anything to create an obstacle to the Turkish assaults that will surely come. You should see the courage of the women and children who lend a hand!"

Vivid images filled Antonio's mind as the man cast off in his small boat to return to the city. He could envision hundreds of people, working like ants, as they desperately struggled to rebuild the walls, knowing a half-hearted effort could mean defeat and the brutal sack of their city.

In the first days of the siege, Muhammed probed Constantinople's defenses with two attacks. The first was by his admiral, Suleiman Baltoghlu, a blustery Bulgarian soldier of fortune and governor of Gallipoli, who swore to break the chain boom across the Golden Horn but his attack ended in failure, unable to defeat the Christian ships on guard outside the chain. The second was a token attack on two small outlying forts.

Their fall gave the Venetians their first taste of what it would be like to fight the Turks. The day after, they heard that the sultan had impaled the prisoners he captured, alive on wooden stakes in front of the city walls, just out of range of the defenders' mercy arrows. The thought of these poor victims, writhing in excruciating pain, until death finally ended their misery, instilled fear and anger in the Venetians. They knew then that there could be no surrender. A glorious death in battle was preferable to such torture.

As the sultan's artillery continued to reduce a section of the outer wall of the Mesoteichion to ruin, Baltoghlu now launched a new, massive attack against the chain boom, this time with most of his fleet. The Venetians would now have their first engagement with the Turks.

Antonio and Trevisan peered over the bow, straining to see the smaller Turkish ships approaching from the east, barely able to make them out in the late afternoon light, inexorably rowing toward them. The Turkish vessels sat low in the water; they were designed to accommodate their rowers, who were all slaves. The Venetian and imperial ships, having only sails, were designed to sit much higher.

"Their decks must be six feet lower than ours."

"Yes, they are too low in the water to bring their guns to bear on the decks of our ships," observed Trevisan, "nor can they easily board us."

They could already hear the Turks' cheers faintly rolling across the murky waters of the Golden Horn. In another ten minutes the Turks would be on them.

"Do you think we can handle them? There must be more than a hundred of them out there and we have but fifteen ships."

Trevisan grinned like a cat in a warm basket.

"Antonio, have you ever seen Greek fire used in battle?"

"I have heard many tales of it, but, no, I have never seen it used before."

Trevisan turned and barked, "Prepare to repel boarders with Greek fire."

A young lieutenant raised a lantern high above his head on a stout pole, giving the prearranged signal to the two adjacent ships that, in turn, repeated the action, quickly passing the order down the battle line in both directions.

The four handpicked Greek sailors, like the others who had been placed on each Christian ship, responded to the order, slowly rolling two large iron barrels along the deck toward the bow. Antonio noticed they wore the grim expression of executioners.

Greek fire was a viscous incendiary mixture of naphtha, quicklime, sulfur, petroleum, and a secret ingredient, known only to the Byzantines, that stuck to surfaces and when ignited was almost impossible to extinguish. It even continued to burn in the water. The Byzantines guarded its secret formula under penalty of death. In more than six hundred years, it had been poorly copied by others, but never duplicated.

They watched as two of the Greeks carefully positioned the barrels along the ship's rails, one on each side. Then the other two each appeared with two large bronze tubes, attaching one end to the barrels and projecting the other over the side. They would be used to channel the gelatinous mixture away from the deck and hull out over the water. Then they quickly returned with two bellowslike machines they would use to pump the contents of the barrels through the bronze tubes.

No sooner had they completed their work when cannon fire burst from the bows of the nearest Turkish ships. Small iron balls bounced off the stout hull timbers of the larger Christian ships and splashed harmlessly into the water.

"Their guns cannot be elevated to rake our decks. Our ships *are* too high for them," observed Trevisan, then he shouted, "Now we have them!"

"I will ready my archers," replied Antonio as he turned and walked briskly to where Lieutenant Sagredo had assembled his twenty marines armed with their crossbows.

Antonio wondered if any of the rowing slaves were Venetians, captured in some faraway place only to die by the arrows and flames of their countrymen.

"Two minutes!" shouted Trevisan.

Both sides engaged first with spirited cheers as Venetian sailors and marines drowned out the more numerous but distant Turks. The enemy continued to fire their guns but with no effect. Each time they scored a hit on the ship's hull, the crew would loudly jeer as the shot bounced off.

"Steady, men," cautioned Antonio. "On my order, pour it into them."

Time seemed to stand still. In the twilight, Antonio could see the ragged line of Turkish vessels fast approaching. He could make out individual Turks in the nearest boats—their white headgear and garments contrasted with the darker naked skin of the sweating slaves rowing furiously at their feet.

Suddenly, the stench of burning sulfur filled Antonio's nose and stung his eyes. The Greeks had ignited the contents of the barrels. Acrid smoke wafted from the bow as the Greek firemen donned masks to cover their faces and thick leather aprons and gloves to protect their bodies and hands. The bolts in his marines' deadly crossbows seemed to him like child's toys compared to the Greek fire that would soon rain down on the hapless Turks.

He was shocked by what he saw next. The bow of the nearest Venetian ship off their port beam abruptly seemed to burst into flames. Just as Antonio was about to shout a warning, the flames leaped down the side of the ship like a dragon's blast in search of its prey and spread out on the water just under the prow. In the inferno he could see a Turkish vessel burst into a fiery ball, lighting the area around it as though it was daylight. Flaming figures, with robes blazing, dove over the sides. Their horrible shrieks pierced the twilight. Just a hundred feet away, he could plainly see Turks frantically ripping their burning garments from their bodies. The Greek fire stuck to them like suits of fiery armor—burning them horribly. Soon, a score of dead bodies were floating between the Venetian ships like flaming, crackling islands burning themselves out in the darkened sea.

He turned his attention back to his crossbowmen. The nearest Turkish vessel was now just twenty yards off. He decided to wait until the Greek fire had been poured on the Turks before ordering his men to fire—no point wasting bolts. The Venetians' hearts pounded as every eye was riveted on the four Byzantine firemen. As the first Turkish boat bumped against their starboard hull, he heard one of the Greeks shout a command. Immediately, another man began furiously working the hand bellows, pumping the contents of the barrel over the side. The man-made volcano spewed instant death, immolating the front half of the Turkish vessel. He could clearly hear the victims' wild screams above the din of battle raging all around.

No one cheered on board the Venetian ship. This was an efficient kind of murder the Venetians had not seen before. The stench of burning flesh and putrid sulfur combined to assault their nostrils. It sickened them. The Turks, tightly packed into the bow for their abortive assault, were all burned to death. The few slaves who had not been caught in the flames abandoned their benches and, chained together, leapt over the side, hanging on to their oars for flotation. The empty Turkish vessel slowly drifted away from Antonio's ship, out of control, a flaming wreck.

Bravely, the nearest Turk on the port side attempted the same tactic, even though he had just witnessed the fate of the other attackers. In less than a minute this new threat had been mercilessly eliminated in another sheet of flames. The marines had broken ranks to run to the side of the ship to get a better view of the carnage. Antonio now quickly formed them up again just in time. Now the Turks, seeing the effects of the Christians' terrifying defense, had wisely chosen to attack the sterns of the Venetian ships away from the Greek fire deployed at the bows. It was then that Antonio finally gave the order to fire. The Venetian crossbowmen, knowing that the Turkish cannon posed no danger, repelled them with carefully aimed, murderous volleys at close range.

Within twenty minutes, the engagement was over. Almost a quarter of the Turkish ships were burned as Baltoghlu retreated in disgrace. The Turks had killed only one sailor on board Antonio's ship. Just two had been wounded. No Turks had set foot on the deck of a single Venetian or imperial ship.

The next day, spies revealed to the defenders that the ever-resourceful sultan had ordered his ships' gun mounts modified to achieve higher elevation. They also saw him move some of his land guns into positions where they could bombard the Christian ships outside the great chain from the north shore of the harbor. Soon one imperial ship was sunk by a direct hit, the massive iron ball smashing through the hull near the waterline. The emperor ordered the rest of the fleet to retreat inside the protection of the chain and out of range. The defenders did not want to lose another ship to the land-based guns.

For the next two weeks, all of the Turks' probing attacks were on land. Finally, on April 18, their first major assault fell on the Mesoteichion. Giustiniani personally led the defense there, killing more than two hundred Turks without losing a single Genoese. Their armor proved impenetrable. The sultan began to feel the sting of failure.

Two days later, Turkish sentries spied ships approaching the city from the

Sea of Marmara. They were three Genoese war galleys, filled with troops, escorting a large imperial transport, laden with much-needed corn. Inside the city, the walls were soon alive with citizens, deliriously cheering their allies on to the safety of the harbor.

In the Turkish camp, the sultan received the news with anger. As he turned to his commanders, his slim face was contorted with rage.

"Admiral Baltoghlu has left the approaches to the city unguarded as he has concentrated his fleet before the Golden Horn," said Muhammed coldly. "Go and find him. Tell him I require his presence here at once."

The young Janissary did not have to be told to ride like the wind, as if his life depended on it. The sultan was known to have men flayed alive for failing to deliver his orders promptly. The rider quickly disappeared over the ridge behind the sultan's ornate scarlet and gold tent. Its sheets of dyed canvas billowed like fiery clouds in the fresh sea breeze blowing in from the Bosphorus.

The angry sultan turned around to face his assembled court. Though some thought him too young to command such a formidable host, the absolute power he wielded combined with his uncompromising will held powerful men, some of them three times his age, in a perpetual state of fear. He ruled without a trace of mercy.

As the sultan and his court watched, in the distance, the four Christian ships slowly beating their way up the Bosphorus, Admiral Baltoghlu rode up with his retinue, breathless and red-faced. He was annoyed at the unexpected summons to appear before the sultan, yet too afraid to show it. As he dismounted the sultan spoke.

"Why did you leave the Bosphorus unguarded?"

He had expected his master to ask that very question. He had rehearsed his answer a hundred times in his mind as he rode to the sultan's camp. But now, his dry throat betrayed him. He coughed nervously before answering.

"I received news of their approach hours ago, master. I knew if I was too quick to oppose their passage they might have turned back. With the northerly wind in their faces my rowers could not have kept up with them and the Christians would have easily escaped to the south. Now, as Allah is my witness, I have them!"

Baltoghlu confidently smashed his fleshy fist into his open hand and grinned at the sultan, convinced by his own words.

"From what I can see, Admiral, those big ships will push your *fustae* aside like kindling wood. Are you certain they have not laid a trap for you?" The sultan stared straight ahead at the much larger man, without a trace of humor in his eyes. The admiral's confidence began to crack.

"Master, I tell you they will not reach the harbor. I will see to it personally!"

"Very well, but heed this. Capture or sink those ships or do not come back alive!"

Baltoghlu swallowed with difficulty and bowed. Then he turned and mounted his barely rested horse and hastily galloped off, his staff behind him trying to keep up.

All who had witnessed the exchange watched as the unfortunate admiral departed. No one, down to the lowliest slave, expected that he would successfully carry out the sultan's orders if his past performance were any guide to what would happen this day.

Baltoghlu's entire fleet of one hundred and forty-five craft was soon rowing out to intercept the four brave intruders. Triremes, biremes, and galleys joined assorted smaller craft filling the narrow Bosphorus from shore to shore, blocking the Christians' way.

Both the city and the besiegers' camps cheered their ships on in the fight, like gladiators in the arena. It was a windy day, which favored the Christian ships with their large sails and made rowing difficult for the Turks in the choppy water, but the swift Bosphorus currents were against the Christians, slowing their progress. The Turks tried to board the loftier enemy ships but were repelled with arrows and javelins. As the four big ships crashed through the hulls and oars of their assailants, they sailed on toward the safety of the Golden Horn, relatively unscathed.

Just as they rounded the headland, within sight of the chain boom, the wind died. They were becalmed. The fighting was savage as the Turks moved in for the kill. The four ships defended themselves with hot brands, arrows, javelins, rocks, and small guns. Finally, they lashed themselves together in a sort of floating fortress, shifting marines from one deck to another as needed to repel the Turks who surrounded them. After more than two hours of hellish combat, as the late afternoon sun began to set, the wind suddenly began to blow again, and the four ships, bludgeoned, but not broken, again crashed through the smaller Turkish craft toward the safety of the protective chain across the entrance to the Golden Horn. They had chosen to run rather than fight to a certain death. The Turks, most of their rowers exhausted, were able to pursue them with no more than a third of their fleet—the rest of their crews were fought out.

Venetians, Genoese, and Byzantines on board their ships had been helplessly watching the savage battle since the combatants had come into sight, unable to go to their comrades' aid. Just as the flaming orange sun disappeared behind the western hills, the beleaguered ships made their final desperate run toward the harbor. The three Genoese war galleys surrounded the transport, using their oar power to propel the slower food-ladened Byzantine ship, her once-proud sails now in tatters. One galley was leading, with one on each side of her. Only the outside banks of oarsmen could row on the two galleys alongside the transport, causing them to crawl slowly across the waves.

"Those brave fellows are rowing for their lives!" shouted Lieutenant Sagredo.

"Like a pregnant doe protected by her fawns, pursued by a pack of famished wolves," observed Antonio icily.

Soon the surface of the water was painted black by the moonless night. The only colors visible were the dark gray of the sky, dimly lit by the last rays of the sun and the flaming orange torches and fires that dotted the decks of the oncoming ships. Turkish *fustae* darted like phantoms in and out of the firelight as they tried to find a weakness in the Genoese defenses. The groans and cries of men locked in mortal combat drifted across the water.

"The winds are dying down again, Antonio. I fear they cannot hold out for too much longer," observed Trevisan.

"Gabriele, let me go to their rescue. All I need is three ships!"

"My orders are to avoid any risk to our ships, you know that," replied Trevisan.

"We must not let them perish out there, like those poor devils from the forts that the sultan impaled alive in full view of thousands on the walls."

"What would you do, Antonio? If I agreed to your request, you would be playing into the Turkish admiral's hands. He would like nothing better than to engage a small portion our fleet outside the boom and destroy it."

Antonio was desperate. He had seen enough. It was time to act.

"The night is so dark, the Turks will not know how strong we are—only that we are coming. If we gather the trumpeters from all of our ships on three of our galleys—in the blackness the Turks will think our whole fleet is coming out to meet them."

The two friends stood face-to-face in the lamplight, like two rocks, neither budging an inch. Finally Trevisan broke into a broad smile.

"Very well, Captain Ziani. Assemble your trumpeters."

The order for every ship's trumpeter to assemble on three Venetian galleys was quickly communicated to the closely packed Christian fleet. In fifteen minutes they were ready to execute their ruse. As the blaring notes cut through the evening darkness like screaming demons, the rowers pulled like their lives depended on it. The Turks, worn out and fearful of the might of the combined Christian fleet, lost heart. They turned their ships around and headed for the safety of the Bosphorus.

M uhammed was so enraged he ordered his bodyguards to bring Baltoghlu to him at once. Every attempt his admiral had made to defeat the Christians had failed. This could not be allowed. Soon the fifty mounted Janissaries the sultan had dispatched returned. In their midst, on foot, was the unfortunate admiral, stumbling for his life as he tried to keep pace with their spirited Arabian mounts. Seeing their arrival, a fearsome eunuch ducked unnoticed into the sultan's tent.

A minute later the sultan suddenly emerged, a bunch of purple grapes dangling from one hand. As he delicately placed one in his mouth, every man present waited in total silence. Only the flapping of the tent and the fluttering crescent-adorned banners flying above it broke the quiet in the flickering torchlight.

"You have failed me for the last time," said the sultan, without emotion. "Since you have aided the accursed Christians time and again, you will die like one."

The sultan turned and nodded once to the captain of his bodyguards. As he had a hundred times before, the captain clapped his hands twice, unleashing a flurry of activity, and then he disappeared into the sultan's tent. Baltoghlu looked around frantically, his feet rooted to the ground. Sweat dripped from his ruddy face, already bruised and bloodied from the rough handling he received from the Janissaries, as it formed tiny droplets in the dirt at his feet.

Suddenly, four men took hold of Baltoghlu, two grasping each of his massive arms. He did not resist, but instead began to groan like a defenseless cow seized by a pride of starving lions. The sultan began to pace as he waited for the captain who had disappeared into the red and gold tent. As Baltoghlu wildly searched the faces in the crowd, he saw a score of men that only yesterday had bowed to him, paying him great respect. Now they were like a group of children looking at a dog crushed in the street under the wheels of a runaway cart. Their cold dead stares told Baltoghlu that it was the end. His knees buckled but the powerful Janissaries held his slumping body erect.

The captain emerged from the tent, followed by a Janissary carrying a long, rough wooden stake about six inches in diameter and eight feet long. Each end was sharpened into menacing points. In the dim light, it was difficult for some to see what they were carrying, but every man there knew the sultan's intention. Baltoghlu was to be crucified but not upon the hated symbol of the infidels. Instead, he would be impaled alive.

As those with weaker stomachs turned away uncontrollably from the horror of the scene and the *mollas* shielded their holy eyes, Baltoghlu's whimpers defeated his attempts to beg for mercy. Even facing death, he was incompetent.

"Master!"

An old man stepped forward. The sultan's court was hushed.

"Speak," said the sultan, his grim face twisted into a look of surprise.

"The admiral has, without doubt, failed you—he has failed all of us. But he has never been a man of the sea. He is a ruler of the land—the governor of Gallipoli. Surely, placing him in command of the fleet put him beyond the bounds of his abilities."

"Have I erred then?" asked the sultan, devoid of the slightest emotion.

"No, Master, we erred when we did not beg you to consider the all too predictable results of your decision. It is we who knew Baltoghlu best and we failed you."

The sultan narrowed the sweep of his eyes to the small group of men behind the speaker, who, he knew, were all loyal to the doomed admiral.

"Who, among you, agrees with this man?"

Baltoghlu surely would have been one, except that he could not see—his face was an inch from the ground as he prayed fervently to Allah for his deliverance and he could not hear—his loud prayers prevented him from hearing his friend's plea on his behalf.

Another man stepped forward, then two more. Soon, all seven men who had come to Constantinople with Baltoghlu were standing before the sultan. As he measured their resolve, he could feel their collective will pushing against his like a block of stone. These fools would die for this miserable admiral, thought the sultan.

With the privilege that is afforded absolute power, the sultan decreed two immediate and seemingly incompatible orders.

"Very well, perhaps a death sentence is too severe for a man who devoted his life to my father's service."

Baltoghlu, who by now had been allowed to rise to his knees by the dumbfounded guards, began to cry as he sensed a ray of hope. Then the sultan turned to his captain and said casually, "Remove his garments and give him as much gold as he deserves, a hundred pieces should be sufficient. Then cast him out naked into the world—banished forever. Never let me lay my eyes on him again."

His new sentence pronounced, the sultan slowly turned and disappeared into his tent. His guards closed the opened flaps behind him signaling that he was retiring for the night. Baltoghlu's brave supporters looked at each other in disbelief. They had been certain they would meet the same fate as their leader for daring to question the sultan's right to do as he pleased—but this? Allah be praised! They began to congratulate each other like guests at a wedding.

As the Janissaries released Baltoghlu's arms he fell to the ground. The Janissaries began to tear off Baltoghlu's silken robes and ornate jewelry; four huge slaves appeared, each carrying a long rod of gold. He offered no resistance and in a minute he was naked—his sweaty, hairy bulk shivering in the cool April night air.

"Take hold of him," commanded the captain. The slaves dropped the golden rods and roughly pushed Baltoghlu down onto his stomach in the dirt. He began to whimper. This time, he knew there would be no reprieve. His supporters could only look on. There was no one to appeal to now. The sultan had gone to bed. Only his fiercely loyal guards remained to do his will.

A strange-looking man appeared at the side of the sultan's tent. He picked up the four shimmering golden rods, each about five feet long. Baltoghlu's gift of gold from the sultan would do him no good. As the strange man stood over his prostrate victim, the slaves each placed stout cords around an ankle or a wrist and stretched Baltoghlu out, painfully pinning him to the ground. He looked at Baltoghlu and then, expectantly, at the captain, awaiting the order to begin.

"The sultan has commanded that we give the former admiral as much gold as he can carry. Do be generous, Samir. After all, these men have vouched for him with their lives. Since he can carry none in his hands, see how much you can lay on his back."

The man nodded as he dropped three of the four rods next to Baltoghlu. As he flexed the remaining instrument, he turned to the captain and sneered, "I'll plate him with gold—like a door fit for the sultan's palace." Then with a lightning-fast swing of his arm, the golden rod bit the air. It made a sweet zinging sound like some heavenly musical instrument, so pleasing to the ear, as it cut a thin, foot-long stripe in the dirt next to his victim. As he turned toward Baltoghlu, he pulled a handful of powder from his robe and knelt beside him.

"Now, now, Admiral, I have done this more times than you," he laughed. "The rod will bite and sting terribly as it does its work but this salt here will save you from the red swelling and pus that often kills a man after he's had his plating."

As he stood, he slowly drew his right arm all the way back and then, faster than an eye could see, the golden rod screamed as it tore into Baltoghlu's exposed pink flesh.

"Give him a hundred," said the captain, in a grim monotone.

The lasher nodded and began to whip Baltoghlu relentlessly with savage strokes. In a minute, the admiral was unconscious. Fifteen minutes later, he was cast out of the camp, his back and buttocks split down to the bone, dressed only in his disgrace without even a cloth to gird his loins. No one, not even his loyal retinue, lifted a finger to help him or shed a tear of pity, for fear that if they did, they too might share his golden reward.

The April morning broke sunny, clear, and crisp. The siege had lasted eighteen days. Antonio and Vice-Captain of the Gulf Trevisan talked on the deck as the fresh sea breeze rustled their matted hair and unkempt beards. Squawking gulls flew lazily overhead, oblivious to walls and battle lines, immune to the death and destruction below.

"What do you think the Turks will do next?" asked Trevisan.

He valued his subordinate's judgment—even so more since Antonio had distinguished himself in the engagement to save the four relief ships with his ruse that had sent the terrified Turks packing, as they heard the trumpeters announce the attack of what they thought was the entire Christian fleet.

"It appears, Gabriele, that though we are greatly outnumbered, Giustiniani knows his business. I hear that he and his men have butchered the Turks each time they have attempted to storm the walls. As long as, when they tire, his men are reinforced by defenders from the seawalls, the city can hold out until help comes."

"Do you think help *will* come?" asked Trevisan, his expression severe.

"It must," Antonio shot back quickly. "How can all of Christendom simply turn its back on Constantinople, abandoning her to the savagery of these infidels?"

"I wish I were as hopeful as you, Antonio. I am afraid that Constantinople has stood for so long, Western Christians think the city is impregnable. And after eight crusades against the Muslims, I think the West may have lost interest in fighting them."

"I hope you are wrong," sighed Antonio ruefully. "Otherwise, we are doomed here. Eventually, our food will be exhausted."

"I believe our one hope for deliverance lies with the Turks themselves," said Trevisan. "They cannot maintain such a large concentration of men for long. Like locusts, they have eaten the nearby country bare already. They are also prone to palace intrigues and have a vast empire to defend. Surely, the sultan cannot maintain his presence here much longer. We must hold out until the Turks lose heart and withdraw. That is why our action against their fleet the day before yesterday was so important."

"What you say makes sense, Gabriele."

Each man stood silently along the rail as he recalled the vivid images of the brave Christian crews fighting their way into the Golden Horn and their narrow rescue.

"Tell me." Trevisan paused slightly. "Have you spoken to the Soranzos?"

"No," replied Antonio quietly, as memories of that sad night flooded back into his consciousness. "The one time I saw Pietro he did not speak a word to me, except to acknowledge my orders or to extend a military courtesy. I have not seen the captain at all since that day in Negropont."

"I have tried to speak with Soranzo about the incident myself, when I have been on board his ship. It is not good to have such dissensions in time of war, but he refuses to talk about it." Trevisan turned now and placed his strong hands on Antonio's shoulders and spoke in an uncustomary lowered voice, "Be careful. I do not know to what lengths they will go to gain satisfaction for their younger brother's death. One thing I do know is that they hold you solely responsible for it," he said gravely.

Antonio looked Trevisan squarely in the face, saying nothing.

"I have not changed my opinion on the matter. The boy disobeyed orders, went on deck, and was swept overboard. That is all there is to say about it. I will tell that to the Great Council and the doge when I make my full report, when all this is over."

Trevisan signaled that he was finished discussing the subject as he turned to look out across the Golden Horn. As they gazed, in silence, beyond the harbor at the old Genoese trading settlement of Pera, situated on a headland jutting into the harbor, they could see the great iron chain rising out of the water into its moorings in the town wall. Antonio turned from the side of the ship and began to walk back along the deck. Suddenly, he heard Trevisan swear. As Antonio looked back in his direction, he froze. Was such a thing possible? In the distance, he could see a ship's mast moving behind the town of Pera—but how? There was no water there—just dry land!

"Fourteen years ago, in our war with the Milanese, we moved our ships almost six miles on a causeway, built of logs, between the Adige River and Lake Garda," said Trevisan, awestruck. "It took two weeks and two thousand oxen to complete the task."

He turned and looked at Antonio, his mouth agape. Trevisan could no longer speak; his composure was so shaken by the shock of what he saw across the water.

The sail they saw belonged to the first of the Turkish ships to be pulled from the Bosphorus and laboriously transported a mile overland to the Golden Horn. Soon, every Christian ship's deck was filled with sailors and marines, standing transfixed, as they witnessed the unimaginable turn into stark reality. Even the city walls behind them were soon filled with spectators to this military engineering marvel, as their higher vantage point gave them a perfect view of one of the greatest feats in the annals of warfare.

The sultan, realizing that his time was running out, needed a miracle. He decided to create one on the backs of his soldiers, sailors, and slaves. On that day, he transported seventy ships, some of them large triremes and galleys, each weighing more than one hundred tons, over a roadway made from logs and planks and greased with animal fats and oil. In some places the vertical climb was more than three hundred feet. It required thousands of oxen and men to pull the ships. Their sails provided momentum as they literally sailed across the one-mile neck of land to be launched into the Golden Horn, under the protection of the Turks' powerful land-based artillery.

By nightfall, the work had been completed in full view of the city's defenders, who were powerless to stop it. The Turks had bested the Venetians' earlier feat, moving almost three times as many ships, many larger in size, in a single day!

The sultan had defeated the chain boom and placed his ships in the Golden Horn. Now it was only a matter of time before he would attack the Christian fleet. Once it was defeated, both the land walls and seawalls could be threatened simultaneously. The long seawall along the Golden Horn would then have to be defended in earnest, night and day, robbing the deteriorating landward walls of almost a thousand irreplaceable defenders.

By the beginning of May, the city started to ration food—Pera, under pressure from the Turks, was refusing to supply any more provisions to the city. Some people were going hungry. Morale was dropping.

When some suggested that the emperor leave the city to save himself, he replied, "I thank you all for the advice which you have given me but how could I leave the churches of our Lord, and His servants the clergy, and the throne, and my people in such a plight? What would the world say about me? I pray you, my friends, in future do not say to me anything else but, 'Nay, sire, do not leave us!' Never, never will I leave you! I am resolved to die here with you!"

His entire court wept with him as his display of resolute courage gave heart to the defenders. But the city could not survive without relief. More than a few hoped the emperor would finally decide to yield to the sultan but he remained steadfast. Two days later, the defenders sent a Venetian brig, disguised as a Turkish ship, out of the harbor to find the Christian fleet that must surely have been dispatched to save the city.

Continuous bombardment on the land walls and constant vigil on the wall along the Golden Horn were wearing down the defenders. They were continually deprived of sleep. The first weeks in May, the Turks attacked the land walls twice. First they threw thirty thousand men against them, then fifty thousand. Still, the valiant defenders, proving the power of defense over offense and armor over flesh, resisted successfully.

At one point, the Turks built huge wooden siege towers with gangways extending over the moat and the top of the outer wall, but the defenders burned them with Greek fire. Then the Turks built a wooden causeway over the moat, to speed the attack on the outer wall, but some brave volunteer defenders blew it up under cover of darkness. The sultan was reaching the limits of his patience. So were his commanders.

But, behind their massive walls, the Christians were running out of arrows, powder, food, and hope. While few had been killed, the seven thousand defenders still answering the call to arms were mostly all wounded in some way, many weak from hunger and loss of blood. The first signs of sickness had finally appeared. The Venetians aboard the ships, under constant threat of attack, were unable to assist in the defense of the land walls as the Genoese and Greeks bore the brunt of the Turkish attacks.

Antonio spotted the marines near the bow, as far away from Vice-Captain of the Gulf Trevisan's cabin as possible. They were angry. Antonio pushed his way into the center of the crowd—there were at least a dozen of them. He was surprised, this time, to see a few reasonable men shoulder to shoulder with the usual complainers. No one said a word. Brunetti, the self-appointed ship's lawyer, spoke first.

"Captain Ziani, we have been in this godforsaken harbor for nearly six months and in all that time we have hardly seen the enemy."

"Have you forgotten the pig roast we had in their honor, so soon, Brunetti?" taunted an older man, nicknamed Saggio, who was admired by the crew for his wisdom.

"There was nothing glorious about incinerating a few miserable Turks and their unfortunate slaves," hissed Brunetti, as he pushed the older man, almost knocking him down. "I came here to fight like a man!"

"It is the endless waiting that we all despise most, Captain," added one of the quiet marines. "We endured a perilous and miserable journey to get here. We came to fight the Turks and, instead, we sit here every day listening to the sounds of battle, but we can see nothing and do nothing. The Greeks who deliver our rotten food say that the defenders are near the end of their rope! Are we to be of no account?"

Antonio shared their frustration. The Turk's plan was working well. The marines aboard the Venetian fleet in the harbor were useless while the land battle raged every day and night just a mile away, beyond the Blachernae Palace, but they had to be vigilant in case the Turks attacked in the Golden Horn. Normally, the Venetians would have attacked the portion of the Turkish fleet in the harbor, but they were safely under the protection of the sultan's land-based artillery. It would be suicide, he thought.

"Be patient a little longer. I will speak with Vice-Captain of the Gulf Trevisan. If things are as bad as you say, we will surely be thrown into the fight soon enough."

On May 23, the little Venetian brig appeared just over the southern horizon. The entire civilian population of the city soon filled the walls along the Bosphorus as the ship ran for the harbor in broad daylight. It miraculously evaded the Turkish picket ships and made its way into the harbor protected by the guns of the Christian fleet. But it brought crushing news. After searching for three weeks, they could find no sign of any fleet coming to the city's rescue. Some of the sailors on board had argued that they should run for Venice, but the captain had dutifully turned his ship around and returned to Constantinople.

The tension was reaching the breaking point. The sultan was plagued with bad news too. He received word that the Hungarians had renounced their peace treaty with him. Many of his commanders believed an attack by them was now imminent. Worse, his army had foraged the countryside around the city bare. There was little food remaining to feed his hungry men and animals. Finally, to appease his subordinates, he sent another envoy to the emperor offering to spare the city if it surrendered. Constantine asked for terms, but the sultan demanded too much tribute, many times more than the city could afford to pay. Finally negotiations broke down. This sealed the city's fate. The sultan's commanders now agreed it would be a fight to the finish. The Christians, knowing their foe's resolve, grimly prepared for the final battle—and victory or death.

· · ·

When Antonio asked him for permission to take his marines ashore to fight, Vice-Captain Trevisan, also spoiling to get into the epic battle, gave it immediately. He ordered Antonio to depart with all of the nearly four hundred marines from the five ships the next morning, saying he would arrange for them to be posted alongside the Blachernae Palace, just north of where the emperor and Giustiniani were leading the defense. Trevisan had heard that the threat there was so great, he was willing to risk leaving only the sailors on the ships to defend them, should the Turks attack in the Golden Horn. The sailors would not be able to put up much of a fight though, without the marines. They would have to rely on their sails to escape. In that event, the brave Venetian marines would be left behind to suffer the same fate as the other three hundred Venetian soldiers already on the city walls, led by Catarin Contarini.

The next day, May 27, dawned crisp and clean. They awkwardly climbed down into the waiting boat with difficulty, stiff in their body armor, weighted down with the heavy weapons and supplies each man carried. Their eyes looked nervously at one another in anticipation of what lay ahead, as they joined the craft transporting the marines from the other four Venetian ships and rowed for the nearest pier.

Antonio gazed up at the dark, ominous walls that engulfed them in the shadows they cast across the gray water as they approached. They amplified the sound of the oars slapping the water and made the men whisper their nervous conversations.

Suddenly, an unfamiliar stench insulted Antonio's nose and made the skin underneath his armor crawl. His eyes watered and his throat burned, though he had just drunk some tepid water before he had embarked only minutes before. He had never smelled anything like it before. It was the reek of death on a massive scale—thousands of bloated abandoned bodies rotting in the hot Grecian sun. The sultan would not permit his troops to recover their dead who had fallen near the walls, decreeing that it was too dangerous. He knew this abomination would further incite his men to hate the Christians.

They disembarked onto the nearly empty pier, struggling to keep their balance as they climbed out of the bouncing boats. There was no one in sight but a few old men who made the lines fast, mooring the boats, and a soldier who had been detailed to guide them to their post. The regular dockworkers had long ago been armed and sent to the walls. There had been no cargo for them to handle for weeks.

After assembling his men and ensuring that all were present, Antonio marched his marines through a large gate in the wall and across one of the sprawling courtyards of the Blachernae Palace, the emperor's majestic home in happier times. The once magnificently manicured plants and trees were now hopelessly overgrown. Lush green weeds obscured the lavishly paved courtyard, reminding him of how quickly man's tenuous battle with nature is lost once his attention is diverted to other things.

A feisty little black dog, too quick to be someone's dinner, barked his objection to their intrusion, running before the advancing marines, turning occasionally to bravely snap at them. For a fleeting moment he thought about Seraglio for the first time in weeks.

As they approached the highest wall of the courtyard on the western side, an impressively uniformed imperial guard pointed to the southwest corner, his crimson plume fluttering in the breeze. There, behind a garden of overgrown ornamental trees, ragged from neglect, was a large iron-trimmed wooden door at the foot of a tall tower. An imposing captain of the guard, accompanied by a four-man escort, was waiting for them. He unlocked it with a large rusty key. The door was obviously seldom used. It took all four guards to push it open on its rusted, shrieking hinges. None of the Greeks spoke Italian and only a few of Antonio's men spoke any Greek. They could only communicate with grateful looks of approval to one another—the Venetians' expressions admiring the stoic courage of the Greeks, the Greeks thankful for the Venetians' steadfast presence beside them. No words in any language could have said more.

Inside, through the tower's open door, they could see the dark image of a man descending the circular stairs, shouting orders to unseen subordinates. As he boldly stepped through the door into the light, the sun's rays instantly painted his gray form in glorious colors. On his head was a shiny steel bascinet with wings of gold and a tall white ostrich plume. An elongated nose jutted defiantly from the helmet, creating the illusion of a fierce bird of prey. A flowing dark-red cape covered his steel body armor obscuring everything but his dented breastplate and the gorget that protected his throat. As a breeze blew his cape aside, it revealed a terrifying battle-axe, bloodstained with use, hanging at his side. He stopped a few feet from the Venetians and faced them, measuring them with eyes that had judged the courage of men, like them, a thousand times before. He slipped his right hand out of his gauntlet and raised his klappvisor.

"Are you in command of these fine-looking soldiers?" he said as his eyes stabbed impatiently at Antonio. He was obviously a very busy man who was under tremendous pressure. More than one hundred thousand people's lives depended upon his decisions. Antonio nodded that he was. The man forcefully grasped Antonio's hand and smiled suddenly.

"I am Giovanni Giustiniani. Welcome to hell!"

Antonio shook his outstretched bare hand. "I am Captain Antonio Ziani, commander of the Venetian marines."

"Thank you for joining us, Captain." He turned to the Venetians and, removing his bascinet, said in a loud voice that betrayed his Genoese accent, "I never thought I would see the day I would be pleased to be fighting with Venetian marines at my side."

The men laughed heartily at his unexpected joke but quickly grew silent. Antonio noticed traces of dried blood on the steel greaves covering Giustiniani's legs. He wondered if it was Turkish blood or his own.

"There is little time, so please, Captain, allow me to direct your men to their fighting posts on the wall and in the towers." Antonio nodded respectfully.

"I have assigned you to a place of honor. You will be responsible for defending the southernmost section of the Blachernae Palace wall. Here, the two land walls and parapet to the south converge into the single wall that runs north, along the palace, the rest of the way to the Golden Horn. The Turks will surely attack here. You will take up your positions in this tower and extend along the wall, toward the Golden Horn, through the next two towers, making altogether three towers and two sections of wall in between. The Turks have concentrated their artillery fire at a point about a half mile south of here. You are fortunate. Down there, we have to rebuild the wall every night."

The Venetian marines listened in awe as Giustiniani spoke. He was a famous *condottiere*, a commander who sold his services to the highest bidder. Known throughout Europe, the respect he was according them buoyed the marines' confidence.

"Now listen to me carefully. This tower is called the Kerkoporta, which means Circus Gate. Do not be fooled by its name or because it is shorter than the other towers. It is the most important tower along the entire four miles of our land walls. While every tower on the inner wall has a door between it and the city, only eight have outer gates in the side facing the Turks—the six to the south are protected by the outer wall. But from here, northward, there is only *one* wall. We have completely blocked the gate further north with masonry. We did not have time to block up this one so the outside door *must remain locked*. You are to defend this outer door with your very lives!"

"Now . . . I need volunteers—one brave officer and twelve stout-hearted marines."

A score of men along with one officer stepped forward. Antonio strained to remain still as Giustiniani quickly formed twelve of the marines into a company, sending the rest back to their ranks. Giustiniani looked sternly at the officer.

"What is your name?"

"Lieutenant Pietro Soranzo, at your service," he replied smartly.

"Do you give me your sacred word, Lieutenant Soranzo, that you will defend this tower, even to the death, opening the gate for no one?" His fierce eyes narrowed.

"On my honor, Signor Giustiniani. No Turk will pass."

Giustiniani turned again to face the rest of the marines.

"I see most of you are wearing armor. You others, remember to keep low. Push any ladder the Turks raise up on the walls to the ground immediately. We have no more oil or Greek fire, so it will be by the sword, axe, and crossbow that you will repel them. If the Turks take this wall, there will be nothing left to stop them." Pausing, he looked upward to the heavens, the end of his thick beard springing loose from the gorget that protected his throat. He knelt on one knee and began to pray.

"May God look with favor upon our arms and graciously give us the strength we will need to repel the infidel." Slowly rising back to his feet, he finished, "Have courage and for God's sake, do not lose heart. We must hold out until relief comes."

Many of the veteran marines cast glances at one another upon hearing this last exhortation. Old Saggio rolled his eyes in disgust. They would fight bravely, but at this point, even the newest recruit knew the city would not be reinforced.

Giustiniani saluted the Venetians and then, replacing his headgear, departed as quickly as he had come, entering the tower and hurrying back up the stairs, his armor clanking with each step. Antonio watched until he disappeared. As he turned back to his men, Pietro Soranzo was standing before him with the other lieutenants.

"I would hardly call this miserable little tower a place of honor!"

"You have your orders, Lieutenant Soranzo. Take another twenty-five men to assist you. I will place fifty more in each of the other two towers. The rest will be posted along the two sections of wall between the towers. The men concentrated in the towers will be our reserves to repel the Turks wherever they attempt to scale the walls."

Pietro glowered at Antonio as he turned to obey his command. In fifteen minutes, every man was at his post. The rest of the day was quiet as the Turks made final preparations for their great assault.

Farther to the south, at the Mesoteichion, Giustiniani concentrated two thousand of his best men. There, the Turks' guns had leveled an entire section of the outer wall and destroyed two adjacent towers. The whole expanse was now no more than a pile of rubble and junk with rows of earth-filled barrels to protect the defenders from arrows. To discourage cowardice, Giustiniani and Constantine locked the single gate through the inner wall near there. There would be no retreat.

4

The Assault

May 28 dawned quiet and still. The sultan, all his preparations made, had given his army a day of rest. He instructed his new admiral, Hamoud, to spread his ships all along the coastline of the city from the Golden Horn to the Sea of Marmara to tie down as many defenders as possible. Any opening was to be exploited, no matter what the cost. On the landward side, the entire Turkish army, still seventy-five thousand strong, was to attack everywhere and overwhelm the exhausted defenders. Officers were instructed to kill any man not advancing. The sultan planned to pour in fresh troops in successive waves, employing over two thousand scaling ladders, until the defenders could resist no more. By evening, all was ready for the grand assault.

Within the great city, the inhabitants sensed the end was coming. The emperor celebrated mass in the Hagia Sophia as the leaders of the city gathered for a final service. Rivalries and internal strife were forgiven and forgotten. This service was to be the last rites of a great empire and was presided over by her emperor and her patriarch. All day, the church bells tolled as if to complete their lifetime of allotted rings before being torn from their belfries by the victorious Turks. Evening found each participant in the great event, with sharpened senses, reflecting on a myriad of his deepest thoughts.

On board his ship, Vice-Captain of the Gulf Trevisan prepared to resist the inevitable attack by the Turkish fleet without his marines. He wondered what would become of his friend, Antonio Ziani, and his brave men. Swords and axes were distributed to the sailors who would fight alone if the Turks tried to board their ships.

Captain Soranzo gazed across the Golden Horn. He still marveled at the sultan's feat of moving all those ships over a mile of undulating land. How could we have thought we could resist such a force? he thought. As he looked to his left, over the top of the Blachernae Palace to the land walls far in the distance, he thought of Pietro. He wondered if he would ever see his brother again. This had been a costly venture, in personal terms, for the House of Soranzo—far more costly than he could have ever imagined. His mouth drew tight at the thought of Antonio Ziani, somewhere out there, alive.

Pietro Soranzo leaned over the massive wall and looked down at the ground forty feet below, then up at the taller towers on either side of him. He was more angry than afraid. His patrician pride had been wounded. He was disappointed by the assignment Giustiniani had given him—regardless of the commander's assertions.

This miserable little tower, dwarfed by all the others, would make a pitiful coffin, he thought. He resolved that he would *not* die there— no matter what. As he looked up to his right he could see the red plume on Captain Ziani's bascinet just visible over a crenellated tower wall, a hundred yards away.

"Look at that bastard," he muttered out loud. "How grand he looks. He will have an opportunity to cover himself in glory on these walls, but he threw away my brother's life before he had the same chance. Marco should be here beside me. If I ever get out of this alive, so help me God . . ."

Antonio looked out at the Turkish lines. Dusk was falling as hundreds of tiny fires began to dot the horizon from north to south. He had never seen such a host. He decided to walk the length of his position to encourage his nervous marines wherever he could. They were rested, well armed, and ready for a fight, but they were scared. If I can only calm the men's fears, he thought, they would fight like lions.

Shortly after Antonio returned to his position, near the center tower, he could see his men there were reacting to the panorama unfolding to the south. The Turks, after a day of quiet, were finally springing to action. Out of the dusky twilight, he could see thousands of the enemy running with baskets of earth and rocks, others carrying tree trunks, headed straight for the dry moat. The defenders, their arrows, balls, and powder in short supply, could only watch helplessly as the Turks filled in strategic places, making causeways for their final assault. The defenders had to save their firepower for targets so close—they could not miss. After a while, their work done, the Turks grew quiet again.

An hour after darkness, the thousand twinkling campfires began to blink out. Soon, all were extinguished. Loud creaking betrayed the sound of turning wheels. As he squinted in the soft moonlight, Antonio could see the Turks moving their artillery, on his left, up to almost point-blank range— right where Giustiniani and the emperor were making their stand. Soon all was blackness, save for the faint moonlight, obscured by thick clouds. He passed the word to his officers to tell the men to try to get some sleep, though he knew few would be able to. He thought about their ships, beyond the ornate rooftops of the Blachernac Palace, in the relative safety of the Golden Horn. What were the chances that he and any of his men would reach them if the Turks breached the wall? He decided he would make straight for the harbor, if the battle were lost, no matter what.

An hour after midnight, a single Turkish trumpet pierced the damp night air with its shrill off-key notes, offending the defenders' ears. Two or three more now added their unique blasts. Drums began to beat wildly. Suddenly, the entire length of the Turkish line came to life, like a great fire raging out of control. At first there were a few distinct cheers, then a cacophony of screams and shouts, and finally, a mighty rolling roar that reverberated up and over the city walls, piercing the ears of the weary defenders. *"Yagma, yagma!"*—"To the sack, to the sack!" the Turks screamed.

"Here they come!" Antonio shouted, as he turned to the men on his left and right.

He pushed down his klappvisor and drew his sword, as his eyes searched through the slits for the enemy below. Church bells began to peal, beckoning the women and children into the illusory sanctuary of their churches. He wondered how many cowardly, able-bodied Greeks would seek their protection this night. He could not understand why a man would prefer a death cowering in some dank basement to dying honorably—on the walls, defending his home and loved ones. A Venetian could never understand that.

The sultan sat on his majestic white Arabian stallion and prepared to observe his army win him his great victory. Not a moment too soon, he thought, as he turned to an aide and dispatched him with an order.

"I have promised the *bashi-bazouks* they would have the honor of leading the attack today. Go and tell Karem Pasha he is to advance at once!"

These were the regular troops of his army that came from every corner of the Ottoman Empire and beyond. Their only pay was the booty they could take in war. As they ran to the attack, chain mail hanging down to their knees and their distinctive white caps armored with strips of iron or mail, they screamed bloodcurdling cries.

As the sultan's retinue quietly waited on their master, he turned and spoke.

"Their morale is fragile, like a dog who beholds a strange cat. If the cat runs, the dog is fearsome in his pursuit, throwing all caution to the wind. But if the cat raises his back and bares his claws, the dog thinks better and doubts his own ferocity—he loses heart and cowers. So it is with my wonderful *bashi-bazouks*. They are fearsome if winning a battle, but quick to retreat if resistance is spirited."

He called for the commander of his military police.

"Have you armed your men with clubs and whips as I have commanded?"

"Yes, Master," replied the man. "They will beat any stragglers back into the ranks, showing no mercy, even to the walking wounded, just as you have ordered."

The sultan nodded his approval and turned back toward the city. In the moonlight he could see thousands of his white-helmeted soldiers struggling across the dry moat, many carrying their heavy scaling ladders. In some places they were laying the ladders across the ditch and expertly scampering over the moat along their wooden uprights. When they finished, they picked up the ladders and carried them to the walls.

Despite his troops' valor, the sultan could soon see that his initial attack would fail. Karem Pasha rode up to the sultan just as his men rushed toward the breaches blown in the twenty-five-foot-high outer wall by the sultan's cannon. Wave after wave of his men were struck down by bolts shot from the Christians' deadly crossbows. The crossbowmen's body armor made them impervious to the arrows fired at maximum range by his archers from the Turks' side of the moat, almost two hundred yards away from the wall. Firing blindly in the direction of their enemy at that distance, they could not see their targets in the predawn light. Since the *bashi-bazouks* supplied their own weapons, many bows were ancient, having been passed down from father to son.

"You will have to replace those old-fashioned bows with the crossbows we capture in this siege," the sultan remarked casually to his subordinate. The commander bowed politely as he thought of his men who were being slaughtered by the hundreds right before his eyes, for lack of effective weapons. The gold spent to purchase those precious jewels that dangled from the nipples of the sultan's harem whores could have purchased several thousand fine new Saxon crossbows, he thought with disgust.

As the defenders toppled one ladder after another, sending five or six screaming Turks to their deaths or to a life as a crippled beggar, the rear ranks began to realize the futility of their mission.

"See how the Christians are using those long poles to push our ladders away from the walls," lamented the *bashi-bazouk* commander. "Their armor protects them too well."

"Not a man has reached the top. Not one! Why are those fools trying to scale twenty-five-foot walls to their front, when we have knocked them down over there!" the sultan screamed as he pointed to the place where his artillery had turned the once-formidable walls into a pile of rubble not ten feet in height.

"No more than one tenth of my men can occupy that space. The rest, hungry for booty, have decided to scale the walls to try to get a share of the city's riches. They know the Christians' most savage defense will be where they are most vulnerable—at the breaches," analyzed the pasha, correctly. The sultan lost his patience.

"Vulnerable! How could they be more vulnerable than when they are teetering twenty feet from the ground on those wobbling ladders, built by treacherous slaves, while a hundred Christian crossbowmen try to murder them faster than others can push the ladders over, sending them to their deaths? Send in the Anatolians," he commanded.

These were the sultan's regular Turkish troops, all mounted for rapid movement. As the order to attack was passed down the lines a cry rose up behind the sultan. Thick dust enveloped and choked his army as waves of dashing horsemen emerged from the clouds and thundered toward the walls, less than two hundred yards away. They galloped up to the moat, dismounted, and launched their attack as the sultan's guns unleashed a preplanned volley. As soon as they had delivered their deadly blasts the Anatolians sprang to the walls climbing over the moat on the ladders left by the retreating *bashi-bazouks*. The attack was so rapid, the defenders had no time to repair the damage.

A quarter mile away to the north, Antonio felt the same frustration he and his men had experienced as they had sat idle for weeks, on board their ships, listening to the sounds of battle raging on the walls. They were repeating their frustration all over again as they stood at the ready on their section of the wall—unengaged. They could clearly hear the sounds of the battle raging at the Mesoteichion although they could not yet see it.

He knew the time for decisive action had arrived and decided to go to Giustiniani's aid. He quickly picked one hundred men who were wearing armor, about a quarter of his force, and ordered them to follow him, leaving

Lieutenant Sagredo with the rest to hold the Venetians' position on the wall. As they clattered along the wall toward the sound of battle, encased in their life-protecting armor, they could soon hear the screams of thousands of Turks, as they climbed their scaling ladders leaning against the twenty-five-foot outer wall where the defenders had chosen to make their last stand.

Every attacker was hoping to claim a rich prize of booty or else entrance into paradise—a warrior's reward for dying in the cause of Allah. Driven on by these thoughts and in dread of their sultan's wrath, the Turks were contemptuous of death.

The marines soon reached the scene of the carnage and charged into the fight with a fury only fresh troops can muster. They viciously repelled the Turks, pushing over their ladders as they neared the top of the wall. It was impossible to see the arrows and stones whizzing through the air; a few lucky shots wounded several Venetians as they penetrated the seams in their steel plating. Each man could only pray that God and his armor would protect him. The Venetians fought savagely. Four times, some Turks reached the top of the wall. Each time, they killed them all, throwing their corpses down, like rocks, on the attackers below. After an hour, this attack, too, began to falter. As the first rays of the morning sun began to appear in the east behind the defenders, the weary warriors had won a brief respite as the Anatolians retreated. They caught their breath, bound up their wounds, and foraged for arrows among the dead.

In the meantime, all along the land walls and at many points along the seawalls, the Turks probed for openings. Everywhere they were repelled. But too many defenders were tied up too far from the point of decision where Giustiniani's bloodied band of men defended the shattered walls of the Mesoteichion.

Just after sunrise a lone Turkish cannon fired a huge stone that tore out a complete section of wooden palisade that the defenders had hastily built to fill in a hole in the outer wall. Seeing their good fortune, hundreds of Turks rushed the moat in front of the breach. Luckily, Constantine himself happened to be at the point where the attack was aimed. The Christians, fighting for their very survival with Constantine in the lead, overpowered the Turks and drove them back and down into the moat, mercilessly killing them all.

The irresistible weight of my numbers is finally beginning to tell, thought the sultan. Seeing the great carnage, he knew it was time to press home his final attack. He kicked his heels into the flanks of his horse. The beast reared on his hind legs and vaulted forward. As he rode out in front of his Janissaries, twelve thousand handpicked killers, said to be the best troops in the world, he wheeled his mount around in circles, looking first at his men, and then pointing at the walls.

"There, over those walls, lies Constantinople. Only those walls and their mortal defenders stand between you and the richest city on earth! Those defenders are infidels, who have desecrated our most sacred sites and butchered and enslaved our women and children. They are an abomination in the eyes of God! Allah has promised indescribable delights to any man who would die for him in a holy *gaza*."

The stoic Janissaries stood silently at attention, displaying no emotion.

"Today, I take your orders from the Holy Koran."

He raised his arms, his fingers stretched out toward heaven, and shouted.

"Let those fight in the Cause of God who sell the life of this world for the next life. To the one who fights in the Cause of God, whether he is killed or achieves victory, we shall soon give him a great reward. And why should you not fight in the Cause of God and of those who, being weak, are mistreated; the men, women, and children whose only cry is, 'Our Lord! Save us from this land whose people are oppressors and bring to us from You someone who will protect us.'"

He lowered his voice slightly, to compel all within earshot to listen more intently.

"Those who believe, fight in the Cause of God, and those who reject faith fight in the cause of evil. So fight against the friends of *Shaytan*."

The sultan led the twelve thousand, in serried ranks, up to the moat. The Christians watched silently, conserving their energy and their remaining arrows.

"God will reward those who will perish in this final battle according to his promise." Reaching into his robes, the sultan produced a paper and held it aloft.

"Here is my promise for the first man who reaches the top of the inner wall. To him I will give an entire province of my sultanate and riches beyond compare."

The Janissaries finally released their pent-up emotions with a thunderous roar that struck fear into the hearts of the defenders.

"Fatih! Fatih! Muhammed Fatih!" they screamed. "Conqueror! Conqueror!"

The sultan slowly waved his hand forward. The Janissaries began to move but not in a wild rush like the previous attackers. Their disciplined attack was unlike any seen by the defenders previously. They successively placed ladders against the heavily damaged wall, as thousands of them began to climb. Their bowmen kept up a steady withering fire on the defenders from close range, forcing them to keep their heads down, unable to rise long enough to topple all the ladders. The Janissaries pressed home their advantage.

Antonio ordered his men to hold their portion of the wall just to the north of the Mesoteichion. They kept up a withering fire on the flank of the attackers until they ran out of arrows. Soon, the sheer numbers of Janissaries, clearly visible now in the full morning light, began to lap along the wall inclining beyond them to the north to within two hundred yards of the Kerkoporta.

Seeing his original post would soon come under attack and with his supply of arrows exhausted, Antonio ordered half of his tired band of men to fall back to their original position on the double, leaving the rest to try to cover Giustiniani's flank. As they ran along the top of the outer wall, each man struggling with the weight of his armor, they could see Turks below, carrying scaling ladders, moving along the base of the wall just below them. It would be a race. As the wall bent slightly left and then right, Antonio frantically looked to the north for the crimson and gold Venetian battle flag proudly fluttering above the marines he had left behind to defend the Kerkoporta.

Pietro Soranzo was furious with Antonio Ziani for leaving him and the others behind while he went to fight the Turks with Giustiniani. Now, to his front, the early light had revealed a battery of four large guns preparing to bombard the section of the wall held by him and his men. He peered from the top of the Kerkoporta tower, down the wall toward the Mesoteichion. He could faintly make out the waves of Janissaries crawling over the moat and scaling the walls. After looking once again, at the menacing Turkish artillery, he went off to search for Sagredo—the officer Ziani had left in command.

"Sagredo, those guns over there are preparing to blast us to pieces!"

The lieutenant angrily shook his head. "No, Soranzo. Our orders are to defend this wall, not to risk our command in such a reckless venture."

"You fool! When we were ordered to stay put, those guns were not aimed at our heads. Everything has changed. Did Captain Ziani have orders to go to the aid of the Genoese? Shall we show less initiative than our commander?"

"But your orders were to open that gate for no one."

Pietro persisted. "There is nothing to our front but those guns. They have no infantry support. We cannot just sit here and do nothing. Look, the guns are less than a hundred yards from the gate. If we attack now, we can destroy them and return to our post here on the wall before they have time to fire their first shot. If we just sit here they will slaughter us all. Besides, Sagredo, the Turks will never expect us to attack them."

Sagredo looked nervously at Soranzo, then at the guns. Saggio grinned and reached for his battle-axe. Now the others, who had witnessed the exchange, began to crowd around, brandishing their weapons too. It is no use, thought Sagredo. Their blood is up and Pietro is probably right. It *would* be suicide to do nothing. Tired of sitting on the ships, now they were on land and still they had not yet tasted Turkish blood. Besides, he thought, it would be a glorious thing to put four of the enemy's guns out of action.

"Go! Kill the crew and carry off the wooden staves they use to swab the sparks from the barrels in between discharges. Without them, the guns will be useless. But for God's sake and ours, Pietro, be quick about it!"

Barely waiting for Sagredo to finish, Pietro dashed along the wall back toward his men, closely followed by Saggio who led another twenty-five marines, sent by Sagredo to support him. The Kerkoporta gate was actually a large wooden door, about six feet wide and eight feet high, secured by three heavy rusted iron bars that extended six inches into iron brackets bolted deep into the stone wall. Pietro tried to move the rusted bars with his hands, but they would not budge. Grabbing one man's mace, he began to batter one of the bars; several others joined in, hammering the other two bars back. In less than a minute, they had smashed all three bars out of their brackets. The door was free.

Pietro turned toward his men—now sixty strong. "No noise, no shouts. To the left of the gate, the Turks have piled enough debris in the moat to enable us to easily cross it. Saggio, take twenty of your men and guard this side of that causeway across the moat. Lie down so the Turks will not see you. The rest of you, follow me." Finally, selecting six men, he said, "You stay behind by this door. If we do not make it back, close it and lock it. Do not let anyone in. Ready, men?"

With a mighty heave, Pietro pulled the door open and dashed out. Crouching to make themselves less visible, he and his men ran to the edge of the moat and jumped in. It was filled with dirt, rocks, and large branches to within four feet of the top. While they clumsily stumbled across the bridge of debris, bending low, they were hidden from the unsuspecting Turkish artillerists just seventy-five yards away in the cover of a small grove of trees. Reaching the far side of the moat, they formed up for their charge.

"Rush them fast. Kill everyone, even the oxen. Remember to grab the staves."

He cast one final look at the scared but excited faces of his crouching marines.

"Now!"

In half a minute they were all out of the moat, running as fast as their legs could carry them toward the stunned Turks who, by now, had spotted them and were desperately scrambling for their weapons to resist the surprise assault.

Up on the wall, Antonio could not believe his eyes! He slowed to a fast walk to steady his vision as he squinted through his bascinet at the scene below. About a hundred yards to his front, he could see the unmistakable tunics and salades of Venetian marines running out from under the wall and into the moat. He looked down quickly to his left at the company of several hundred Janissaries moving along the wall toward them. From their actions, he could tell that neither group on the ground had seen the other. Then a thought hit him like a hammer blow. Who was left guarding the Kerkoporta gate?

He broke into a run shouting, "Follow me, men, quickly!"

The marines obeyed, doubling their pace. There were just twenty of them now. The rest were wounded or too tired to keep up. As he neared the tower, passing a few thinly posted Greek defenders, below Antonio could see Venetians climb from the moat and rush the clump of trees. His eyes moved from them to where the Turkish battery was already preparing to repel the attackers. Antonio's band was now closer to the gate than the Janissaries below, and moving faster. The Turks' progress was obstructed by the litter of war strewn in their path. He could tell they could not see the marines outside the walls attacking the guns. Their attention was focused completely on the wall, searching for a weak point to scale with their ladders and attack.

As Pietro jumped to his feet, he was suddenly struck by doubt that they could overpower the Turks. They were not as well armed as the Venetians, but there were twice as many of them. As he ran, he hoped most of them would not be soldiers but slaves instead, who might run away.

"Turks!"

The marine on his left suddenly grabbed Pietro's arm and pointed back toward the wall. Pietro turned to his left and froze. He could see that a large body of Turks behind them, moving along the strip of ground between the moat and the wall, would soon block their retreat route back across the moat. He fell behind the rest of his men as they sprinted toward the Turkish guns, unaware of the new danger to their rear. Pietro made an instant decision to save the gate, leaving all the men ahead of him, attacking the guns, to their fate. Turning quickly, his stomach churned with fear—not of death—but from his terrible mistake in judgment. He ran back toward the gate and leapt into the moat. When he reached the other side, the closest Turk was just fifty yards away.

The Janissaries, seeing their guns were under attack, also began to stream across the moat, but their veteran commander spied Pietro running back toward the wall up ahead and wisely surmised there must be an open gate there. He shouted to his men to follow him but, in the noise of battle, only about fifty heard him and obeyed his order.

Antonio and his band of twenty marines quickly covered the remaining distance to the Kerkoporta tower. He cursed Pietro Soranzo, wishing it had been he who had been washed overboard on that fateful night instead of his brother Marco.

The three groups of soldiers converged on the tower, almost simultaneously. Below, Pietro shouted to Saggio and his doomed marines as he ran past, "You must hold them off at all costs!" Saggio had seen the Turks coming and knew he was outnumbered more than two to one. The six men Pietro had left to guard the gate saw everything through the partially opened door. As they jerked their breathless lieutenant inside, Pietro ordered them to slam the door shut behind him. As Saggio stole one last peek over his shoulder, he saw the heavy door close. Venetian marines deserved better, he thought.

"No retreat for us now, lads," he shouted. "Stand and sell your lives dearly!"

Pietro fought to catch his breath as he collapsed on the hard stone floor. Things had moved too fast. As he sat there, chest heaving, three marines began to smash the iron bars with their maces, furiously trying to hammer them back into the brackets in the wall—though it would doom every man stranded outside to certain death.

From high up on the wall above, Antonio heard the door slam shut and not a second too soon as the Janissaries piteously cut down Saggio and his brave men. In a few seconds they would be at the door. The Kerkoporta was under attack and the man in charge of its defense had almost left it unguarded! He quickly posted his men atop the tower and spotting Sagredo, ran toward him to find out what had happened.

Pietro was mortified. The mace blows that had freed the rusty door, only a few minutes before, had bent the iron bars. As the frantic marines tried to beat them back in place, locking the door, they suddenly felt the first wild banging. Using all their strength, Pietro and his six men desperately tried to hold back the fierce Janissaries who were seven times their number. The door quickly began to give way as their feet slipped on the smooth stone floor. The Venetians hacked at the first arms to protrude through the widening crack between the door and the wall. Severed hands and bloody fingers splattered on the floor. Finally, with one great heave, the big door flew open, tumbling the seven Venetians onto the floor. In a few seconds it was over. They were massacred. Pietro Soranzo fell with his throat cut, ear to ear, one arm outstretched, still tightly holding his axe in his lifeless fingers. His corpse lay sprawled across the doorway, as though barring the way into the city, obeying Giustiniani's order in death, if not in life. The victorious Janissaries trampled over his lifeless body as they spilled into the Blachernae Palace courtyard; they were the first Turks to break into the city.

5

The Fall

Farther south, just as they beat back the first rush of the Janissaries, Constantine, with Giustiniani at his side, shouted to his valiant men, "Bear yourselves bravely, for God's sake! I see the enemy retires in disorder! If God wills, ours shall be the victory!"

No sooner had the words passed from his lips when Giustiniani was hit with a bolt from a crossbow, so powerful, it penetrated his armor. In excruciating pain and bleeding badly, in his utterly exhausted state, he begged his companions to remove him into the city so he could bind up his wound. Constantine pleaded with him to remain on the walls, but it was no use, he was delirious. Pitying him, Constantine gave the Genoese his key to the gate in the inner wall, which Giustiniani himself had locked the night before. They opened it and carried him as gently as they could through it. When the Genoese saw their leader retiring, not knowing he was wounded, it was too much for them. In a mad rush, they converged on the single open gate to save themselves, preventing its closure. Now the emperor, with his loyal Greek troops, remained alone to fight the dreaded Janissaries.

Across the moat, the sultan could see the confusion in the Christian ranks. He immediately ordered fresh troops to the attack as the Christians, with their backs to the Turks, poured through the gate into the city.

Now crestfallen, Constantine could see commotion to his right at the

Kerkoporta. A red Turkish flag with its white crescent waved from one of the towers alongside the Blachernae Palace. Somehow, he thought, the Turks must have overwhelmed the Venetians and gained entry into the city there.

From their perch on top of the Kerkoporta tower, Antonio and his few remaining men could see Janissaries pouring into the palace courtyard through the door below. Running down the circular stairs, they found three stragglers at the bottom and killed them. Antonio saw the seven dead marines. One was Pietro Soranzo, splayed like a broken toy, eyes wide open in shocked disbelief, betraying his final thought.

As they tried to shut the wide open door, through the opening they saw more Turks coming toward them. Surely they had seen the Janissaries enter. Like a magnet, they would rush to the portal and enter the city. It was then that they discovered the door's bolts could not be closed. Antonio resolved to hold the tower and prevent the Turks from climbing it and gaining the top of the wall. Lining two men across the tower stairs halfway up from the bottom, with the rest behind them, he shouted, "Let no one pass, not even Satan, himself! Hold and I will go to find more men to reinforce you!"

He bounded up the stairs, his heart pounding as he fought the rigid armor that encased his legs. Looking to his right, along the wall toward the Golden Horn, he could see the thin line of marines still at their posts—there were at least a few men left on the wall. Why were they all looking back toward the city? Where was Sagredo? It was then that he saw it. On top of the tallest tower of the Blachernae Palace, a short way inside the wall, he could see the red and white Turkish banner proudly flying, whipped by the fresh sea breeze. Below it, on the battlements, he could see a few Janissaries waving their swords in defiance as imperial palace guards poured into the tower through a door below.

Suddenly, he could hear the clash of steel ringing from the stairway in the tower behind him. He quickly spun around. Thirty feet away a fierce-looking Turk emerged victorious, wiping the blood from his sword. He raised the weapon over his head and rushed headlong at Antonio. Reaching for his axe, he threw it at his assailant with all his might, striking him in the chest. The Turk slumped to the stones, dying in a pool of blood that quickly spread around him.

There were Turks already inside the Blachernae Palace and now more were trying to gain access to the wall. The men he had left to guard the tower steps only a minute before were now surely dead. Alive, they would never have allowed the Turk to pass. The city's defenses had been breached. Now there will be hell to pay, thought Antonio.

To the south, the Turks were scaling the inner wall by the thousands.

Most of Giustiniani's Genoese soldiers had disappeared through the inner gate. The rest, unable to escape, were slaughtered. The battle was over. It was time to save as many men as he could, thought Antonio. Their only hope was to make it out to the ships in the Golden Horn before they sailed from the harbor to make good their escape.

Antonio ran north along the wall and quickly found Lieutenant Sagredo, still at his post. After gathering up the remnants of his command, about fifty marines in all, they began to make their way along the wall, as fast as they could, toward the harbor. As they neared the place where the land wall connected at a right angle with the seawall along the Golden Horn, they could see hundreds of Turks streaming over the top, unopposed. The defenders there, seeing the battle was lost, had run away. Their way was blocked. To avoid them, Antonio quickly turned around and led his men back to the tower they had just passed through and descended its stairs to the Blachernae Palace grounds below.

"Stay close together, men!" he shouted.

He suspected the Turks' attention would quickly turn from fighting to sacking. A force of fifty heavily armed marines would be more than any small band of pillagers would dare to take on. If they could only get through to a pier and find a few boats to row out to one of their ships, they could escape—but which way to go?

Antonio tried to find the route they had taken on their march from the pier to their post on the walls, but it was no use. Everything looked unfamiliar, different. Desperate, he sent out a few small parties of men in several directions with orders to find a way to the pier and return for the main body. Several times, while they waited, small groups of shouting Turks ran into the courtyard, but quickly discovering the Venetians' strength they darted back into the shadows, preferring to pillage instead of fight.

Finally some marines emerged from a doorway across the courtyard, shouting for the rest to follow them. As they all ran down a narrow street, the seawall loomed up ahead above the rooftops. On they went, down a short hill and across the wide street that ran along the inside of the seawall. On their left, they spied an open door that revealed a glimpse of the royal blue water of the Golden Horn. As they streamed through it out onto the pier, the harbor was a panoramic mass of confusion. Smoke and fire billowed from a dozen ships. Christian ships were firing at Turks in scores of small boats, who, afraid the army would get all the plunder, were ignoring the Christians and rowing straight for the city. There were no defenders on the walls. The city lay wide open for the sack.

"There are no boats!" cried one marine. "We are lost!" shouted another.

Every eye was on Antonio. They had endured all, survived all. I will not give up, he thought, but the pier was empty. He thought of the thousands of boats he had seen in his life, the hundreds of gondolas that plied the Grand Canal back in Venice. What he would give for just a few of them now.

"Your Honor!" a voice barked from the wall above. Antonio looked up to see its unmistakable owner hanging over the side, a familiar smile on his face.

"There is no time to waste, follow me!" His head began to move along the wall to the left. Antonio quickly led his men back through the open door and along the inside of the wall in the direction Seraglio was moving. To his right, two hundred yards away, a company of Turks spied the Venetians and erupted into bloodthirsty screams as they fiercely brandished their weapons and broke into a run. The race was on.

After a two-minute run, Antonio and his men reached another door in the wall. As they rushed through it Antonio could see three small boats at the far end of the pier, abandoned by Turks who had gone in search of plunder. They quickly turned them over and heaved them into the water with loud splashes. After his men climbed down into the two largest boats as fast as they could, careful to avoid capsizing them, Antonio stepped into the smallest of the three craft with the six remaining marines, who were already running the oars into the oarlocks. Suddenly, Seraglio appeared in the doorway. He stood motionless, staring intently at Antonio.

"What are you waiting for!" shouted Antonio as he waved for him to come. Relieved, Seraglio scampered across the pier and jumped into the water alongside the boat, already pushing away from the pier. Two men leaned over the side and quickly fished him out of the water and with one motion heaved him into the craft, soaking the others. As they strained at their oars, the exhausted men smiled at their unlikely savior. Straight ahead they could see a big Venetian ship, easily identified by her large crimson and gold Lion of St. Mark standard, still snapping proudly in the breeze, like a beacon amid the smoke and confusion of battle. Antonio hoped the crew could tell they were Venetians, so they would not fire on the occupants of the Turkish boats thinking they were filled with the enemy. They had lost their flag back on the wall.

As his men put their strong backs to the oars, Antonio turned around to look back at the dying city. It was an unforgettable sight. The company of Turks stood on the pier, but Antonio and his men were out of range of all but their insults and a few arrows. Their prey having escaped, the Turks soon turned back to the sack. Above them, beyond the wall, far off in the distance, Antonio could make out the majestic dome of the Hagia Sophia, transcending the carnage in its midst, oblivious to the fate that would soon befall her. There were only a few telltale wisps of smoke snaking skyward above the city. The sultan knew it would be more valuable if left intact. He had given orders that Constantinople should not be burned.

Intermittently, Antonio could hear women shrieking above the roar of almost two hundred thousand souls raucously celebrating or bemoaning the sack of the city. He shuddered as he imagined the horrible price the raging Turks would be exacting after besieging the city for fifty-eight days. The smell of death filled his nostrils but another familiar scent, the odor of garlic and burnt mutton, soon overwhelmed even that. He quickly looked around the tiny craft. There, wedged tightly into the prow, was Seraglio.

As he painfully unfolded himself and stood up, Seraglio said, "I first saw you and your men running down the hill to the harbor. After avoiding some very nasty Turks, I climbed to the top of the wall. From there, I could see you on that empty pier. I prayed that the Turks had not let their boats drift away. God has provided—no? Will you take me back to Venice with you, Your Honor, or throw me overboard?"

Listening, a few of the marines were laughing for the first time in days.

"If you do, I will surely drown for I never learned how to swim."

"As you once said to me, my friend, you do not take up much space and eat little. Your courage has saved us."

Antonio's men nodded in agreement.

"Captain Ziani, look!"

Antonio's eyes followed the man's pointing finger out toward the Venetian ship. The two other boats, with more rowers, had already reached it. They were climbing up ropes onto the deck as the crew hung over the side, like a giant caterpillar, helping the many wounded on board with their arms. Antonio watched as his men strained to row faster. His chest was taut, as he breathed heavily. Suddenly, he sensed something. His eyes scanned the ship. Then he saw it. Up in the rigging, sailors were unfurling the sails.

They could see the dripping anchor slowly rise out of the water below the prow. They were preparing to get underway. Too far distant for their shouts to be heard above the fray, they waved their tired arms at their comrades, in vain.

"They are going to leave us!" screamed a frightened young marine.

"No, they are preparing to sail to the safety of the open seas away from this accursed place," replied a seasoned veteran. "It has nothing to do with us."

"Look! They are heading straight for us!" pointed another.

Everyone turned in the direction of the man's outstretched arm. There, about the same distance from them as their boat was from the Venetian ship, were six boatloads of shouting Turks. The Turkish commander was pointing in the marines' direction, ordering his men to divert their course from the city to intercept them.

"Row for your lives, men," Antonio exhorted.

He turned toward the Venetian ship. The distance between them was opening. She seemed to be ignoring them as she slipped away. There would be no escape now.

After maintaining their discipline all day, his men panicked. How could they have come so close to deliverance, only to be left alone to face the fearsome Turks and certain death? It was incomprehensible. Antonio squinted as he tried to make out the ship's officers amid the crew and refugees in the chaos on deck. He scanned the big ship from bow to stern but it was already too far away to identify them.

Captain Soranzo stood on the deck, peering out toward the city. The little boat in the distance seemed to be motionless as they began to move away under the billowing sails. As it disappeared and reappeared, amid the choppy waves in the harbor, he made his decision. He must save the ship and the hundreds who had sought refuge on board.

"Captain Soranzo! We cannot leave them," snarled a marine lieutenant, as he bared his teeth in anger. Despite his thick beard a deep gash was visible on his face where the whiskers had been cut away by a Turkish blade. Two rough-looking sailors restrained him at a respectful distance from their captain.

"Captain Ziani is in that boat."

"My orders are to bring this ship back to Venice. We have already taken on many survivors. I will not risk the lives of more than three hundred men to save a handful more. Besides, those Turks will take them before they can reach us. They will be a regrettable but unavoidable sacrifice on this day when so much has already been lost."

All eyes turned in the direction of the little boat. Six larger craft filled with Turks had surrounded it. Captain Soranzo was right.

"But there is still time to save them. They are Venetians. We cannot leave them. I beg you, Captain, to turn about. Perhaps we can drive the Turks off."

"It is too late," replied Soranzo, calmly. "The wind and tide prevent it. It would take far too long for us to turn back for them. You have fought well today. Be content that you have escaped with your life and your honor intact." He looked at his men and said, "Take this brave fellow below and sew him up."

Alone on the fighting castle, the elevated wooden platform at the stern of the ship, once again Soranzo gazed intently at the little boat far off in the distance, now surrounded by Turks. He thought of his dead brother, Marco, and of Pietro, who by now had also surely perished. As he turned away from the forlorn scene and returned to his work, his thick beard concealed the slight upward curving of the corners of his mouth. Justice.

A s the stern of the ship grew smaller in the distance, the pessimists hung their heads and sobbed while the optimists prepared to repel the Turks, who were now closing fast and clamoring to board them. Each man, in his own way, prepared to face death.

Antonio looked at their faces—not a trace of fear on his own.

"Well, men, shall we give them a fight or swim for it?"

"It is half a mile to the shore, they will spear us in the water like fish, killing us one by one," replied one man.

"If we fight, at least we can kill a few of the bastards."

Antonio gave them their orders. "Prepare to fight like Venetians and die with honor." The marines prepared to obey him in grim silence.

"Be sure we get their commander—the one with the big turban," ordered Antonio.

The Turks were within arrow range, but none flew. They would use cold steel. One boat crossed the Venetians' stern as another crossed their bow. Two Venetians faced half a dozen Turks on each end, as they prepared to board. They offered no quarter. The Venetians expected none.

Suddenly a loud cheer rose from the Turks as they jumped fearlessly across the narrow gaps between the boats. A few fell into the water, but the rest quickly assailed the marines. In a few seconds all the marines were down. A Turk crashed his sword onto Antonio's bascinet, knocking him senseless onto the bottom of the boat. As another Turk slit the throat of one marine, Seraglio shielded Antonio with his little body as best he could and shouted loudly, "Ransom!" in perfect Turkish. The attackers were stunned.

"Stop!" shouted their commander from his boat, alongside. "Spare him and the one he is protecting. Kill the rest and bring the little one to me."

Two Turks picked up Seraglio and threw him into the water near the commander's boat with a splash. One pulled him up quickly into the boat and lifted him to his feet. As he wiped the saltwater from his eyes, the Turkish commander spoke.

"You are not Turkish. Who are you?" He began to laugh as he contemplated his grotesque little prisoner, "What are you?" The entire company of Turks burst into laughter at the sight of their fierce leader questioning the gnomelike man.

"I am called Seraglio. My master is a very rich man." He turned and pointed to Antonio who was still unconscious. "His name is Captain Antonio Ziani. He is a Venetian patrician. I am certain his family would pay handsomely to secure his return. I am also certain so great a master as your sultan would reward you handsomely for capturing him, and me, of course." He smiled bravely.

Visions of great wealth danced in the minds of the Turks. He was right; the sultan *would* reward them for capturing such a man.

"Your quick wits have saved your master, but who would pay one *akce* for you?"

"My master's family will gladly pay my ransom," he lied.

"Who would pay a ransom for a slave?" laughed the commander.

He was right, thought Seraglio. Why would Antonio Ziani's family, who knows nothing of me, purchase my release? What if Antonio does not recover from his wound? Seraglio's quick mind found the answer.

"What I say matters not. Ask my master when he revives. If he confirms my words, spare me, if not . . ."

"If not, I will impale you on this oar for troubling me with your babbling."

Seraglio shifted uncomfortably on the wooden bench.

The discussion finished, the Turks rowed for the city, pleased with their commander's decision to chase after the Venetians instead of joining in the sack of the city, like the other sailors. Their share of the sultan's reward for capturing a Venetian patrician to ransom would be far more than their share of booty.

The sack of Constantinople lasted only a day. The sultan, intending to make the great city his new capital, had given orders to his military police to limit the physical damage to private homes and businesses. No public buildings were to be looted or damaged in any way. Any who disobeyed were to be summarily executed. Even rapine was discouraged, though hardly prevented, since the sultan planned to sell one half of the population—fifty thousand souls—into slavery.

That afternoon, Sultan Muhammed II entered Constantinople, for the first time, to claim as his prize—the greatest city in eastern Christendom.

. . .

Antonio's eyelids fluttered open as he slowly regained consciousness. Their captors were rowing them back to the same pier they had left a short time before, when they had tried to make it to the last Venetian ship to leave the harbor.

"What happened?" he whispered groggily, rubbing his head where the dried blood matted his hair. It throbbed painfully as he tried to focus his tired eyes.

"They killed everyone else in the boat, but I was able to convince them to spare us for ransom instead," whispered back Seraglio.

"No talking!" shouted a Turk, his black mustache jumping as he spit each word.

In a few minutes they arrived at the pier. Seraglio cared for his wounded friend, while four guards stood watch over them to protect them from marauding bands of Turks who were prowling all over the fallen city. Before long, the Turkish commander returned with another officer who wore a Janissary's uniform.

"Here they are," the commander proudly proclaimed to the sultan's officer.

"You speak Turkish," the officer said rapidly, as if to test Seraglio.

"As well as you," he shot back with calculated defiance.

"Who are you?"

"I am this man's companion. He is a patrician whose family will surely pay a large ransom to the sultan for our safe return."

Not content to trust Seraglio, the Janissary pulled his dagger from his sash and held it to Seraglio's throat. Turning to Antonio, he raised his eyebrows and then held his other hand out, palm up, and began to lift it up and down. Antonio understood.

"My family will pay for him too," he nodded as he firmly patted Seraglio.

The officer sheathed his dagger and smiled back at Antonio. With a quick motion, he signaled the two prisoners to follow him. They made their way through winding city streets, toward the Blachernae Palace, passing scores of dead, lying in grotesque bloody heaps—but saw no women or children. Their bodies would be lying inside the buildings, where the Turks would have sated their sexual pleasures in private, as was their custom. Groups of Turkish soldiers and sailors scurried to and fro, their arms laden with booty. Others carried large sacks on their backs bulging with their newfound loot.

As they entered a large courtyard of one of the many mansions that dotted that part of the city, the officer abruptly raised his hand and stopped. He pointed to a door. The guards opened it and roughly pushed their captives inside. The dank storage cellar was to be their prison. The Turks slammed the door shut, leaving Antonio and Seraglio in near darkness. Alone, they began to speak in hushed voices as the oppressive smell of the ancient walls and earthen floor filled their noses.

"It feels good to still be alive at the end of this day," sighed Seraglio.

"How did you convince them not to kill us?" grimaced Antonio as he rubbed his still-aching head.

"To be honest, I was thinking of myself first. I concluded they were going to kill us both unless I could give them a good reason not to. I decided to spend some of your money. I told them you were rich and that your family would pay a ransom."

Seraglio chuckled as he placed his gnarled hand on Antonio's leg and continued. "I fear that now, Your Honor, if your family does not pay my ransom too, the Turks will be so angry that they will kill us both."

"We will worry about that when the time comes, Seraglio. And from now on, please call me Antonio."

The two men talked about their experiences earlier that terrible day, recounting the death and destruction they had both witnessed. When they considered what had happened in the harbor, they agreed the Venetians on board the ship must have seen their boat as the Turks pursued them. But why did they not come to their rescue? Antonio suspected the reason why but did not share it with Seraglio.

The waning sun cleansed the city with its golden rays, filling every place it could reach with its soft light. The loose-fitting door to their prison allowed slits of light through on all four sides, eerily framing Antonio as he sat against the far wall.

"I suppose tomorrow they will take us and the other Venetian and Genoese *nobili* who are still alive and confine us all in a prison for safekeeping until they can determine whether or not Venice and Genoa will pay our ransoms."

"You mean Venice may decide *not* to pay?" Seraglio could not believe his ears. "What could possibly prevent your families from paying, no matter what the cost?"

"For one thing, as a show of defiance, the government could decide it is not in the interest of the Republic to honor the sultan's request."

"You really think your countrymen would sacrifice you and the other nobles as part of a political game they are playing with the sultan?"

"No game, Seraglio. It is deadly serious. If the sultan believes he can extort vast sums in ransoms every time he captures Venetian nobles, it would encourage him to pursue other attacks against our possessions. Another consideration is that the sultan may simply ask for far more than we are all worth."

Are my ears actually hearing these words? thought Seraglio, too respectful to speak out loud to his friend. Antonio, sensing Seraglio's confusion, continued.

"You see, Seraglio, to Venetians everything is centered on our Republic. We *nobili* exist to further Venice's honor and prestige because it is we who benefit most from her prosperity. If it costs too much to obtain our freedom from the sultan, we must die. When we went to Constantinople, we knew that we might suffer that fate, as many Venetians have in wars past. Would it not be better for Venice to lose her men alone, than her treasure too? You see, it is by means of our wealth that we will obtain our revenge on the Turks for what has happened here. If we die, others will take our place but how would they fight without ships, and arms?" Antonio bowed his head. "All that costs money."

He grew quiet but fatigue prevented Seraglio from completely understanding. As night approached the two men fell asleep again, still drained by their ordeal.

They could hear footsteps approaching. Suddenly the door swung open. The full force of the morning sun's light stabbed at their eyes, temporarily blinding them.

"Out, you two! You have an audience with the sultan," laughed the guard as he motioned for them to follow him.

Seraglio rose to his feet and dragged himself up the four steps, followed by Antonio. Outside were two more guards, who marched them through a maze of narrow streets until they finally could see the Blachernae Palace up ahead, near the very same wall Antonio and his marines had so valiantly defended the day before. The city was deathly quiet. Only a high-pitched sort of wailing split the silence, far off toward the Bosphorus on the eastern side of the city. Soon the unfamiliar chanting grew into a chorus that rang out from every quarter of Constantinople. Antonio had never heard such sounds. He was intrigued, yet annoyed, since he could not understand the language they were singing. Seraglio labored to catch up to Antonio, who was walking four paces ahead of him. Drawing even, he placed his hand on Antonio's arm and whispered, "The *muezzins*. They are calling the faithful to prayer."

Antonio turned and looked into his friend's face and thought he saw a tear glisten in the corner of his eye. There would be no more church bells rung in Constantinople.

As they turned a corner and stepped through the huge decorated iron doors into the imperial courtyard, they saw a scene unlike any they had ever witnessed before. Along the far wall, about sixty yards away, lay the human refuse of war. About two hundred men of all descriptions stood, sat, leaned, or lay along the base of the massive edifice. Far above, on the walls, were Janissaries in green and white garb, spaced twenty feet apart, each with a newly acquired Christian crossbow at the ready in his hands.

Between them and the forlorn-looking prisoners were hundreds of Turks milling about, many speaking loudly—some arguing. They were dressed as soldiers and civilians but all wore the expensive clothes of the important and the attitude of the mighty. Antonio had seen a circus once as a young boy. The scene before him reminded him of the panoply of colors that had always lived in his memory from that memorable day.

The vast courtyard was filled with a cacophony of loud voices—so alien to ears accustomed to the sounds of the Piazza San Marco. The Turks sounded as though they were all arguing with each other. Few were conversing. It was as though whoever could talk louder would prevail—not like at home where the stronger the point, the more subtly it could be made. A Venetian persuaded with ideas, conveyed by strong words. These Turks persuaded with words conveyed by strong voices. Perhaps it was because the most powerful Venetians, the doge and his advisors, were usually older men and sometimes physically enfeebled. In contrast, these men seemed to be trying to wear down their opponents by giving them headaches. Despite his grave circumstances, Antonio allowed himself a smile, safely secreted behind his unkempt itching beard.

Their guards led them along a perpendicular wall until they reached the higher outer wall and turned right, depositing them among the other prisoners. Antonio searched for a familiar face as he began to move among them. After a minute, his eyes found the Venetian *bailo* Girolamo Minotto. He was sitting with his back against the wall, his legs outstretched, a picture of complete physical and mental exhaustion. His eyes were closed and his head thrown back, revealing a deep slash across his lower neck, just above where his armor breastplate would have protected him. His son, whose concerned expression made him look much older than his twenty-two years, was by his side.

As Antonio, followed by Seraglio, continued to pick his way among the defeated men he recognized more Venetians. His eyes carefully examined the other prisoners. Almost all were wounded, some grievously. Many were afraid. All were dejected.

Recognizing Minotto, he knelt and grasped the man's hand.

"*Bailo,* it is Captain Ziani. We first met on the pier when I arrived last November and again at the last Easter service—" Minotto interrupted him.

"Captain Ziani, you, too, have survived. What news do you have of the others?"

"I was just going to ask you the same thing," said Antonio quickly as he looked at Minotto's son, searching for some indication of the *bailo*'s condition. The young man was oblivious to Antonio's unasked question as his adoring eyes never moved from his beloved father. Antonio could see the black-encrusted streaks on the young man's face where his tears had mingled with the blood and dirt of battle.

"Ziani!" called a nearby voice.

Antonio spun to his right just in time to see Catarin Contarini kneel down beside him. He was genuinely pleased to see the older man.

"We thought you were dead," he said as he looked at Antonio almost admiringly.

Antonio noticed his arm was in a sling—his bandaged hand was too small—he had lost some fingers. Only his thumb protruded from the filthy cloth wrapped around it.

Contarini began to recount events.

"The Turks massacred most of my men, the Genoese fared no better."

"What news is there of Giustiniani?" asked Antonio.

"He was badly wounded and left the walls shortly before the Turks entered the city. They say he escaped. He is the one man the sultan wanted most to take alive—excepting the emperor, of course. Such a famous *condottiere,* Giustiniani would have brought a fine ransom."

Antonio had a fleeting vision of the day he had met Constantine on the pier.

"What do you know of the emperor's fate?"

"He perished defending his city with his last breath. They say his body has not been found. His bodyguards stripped him of any sign of rank so that the Turks could not hang his mutilated body like a butchered piece of meat in the marketplace. The Turks have been looking everywhere for him. They have tortured many Genoese and Greeks who were captured near where he was fighting. They say he and the sultan actually laid eyes on each other—

at least the sultan saw *him*. Imagine that," said Contarini. "Anyway, he is surely dead."

"Prince Orhan and a few other Turks opposed to the sultan fought in a tower until they were all killed or captured. The prince almost escaped disguised as a Greek but he was betrayed by one of his own men and executed on the spot."

"What of your men?" asked Antonio.

"Most were killed, but I am certain a few fleet of foot made it out to the ships. Do you know how many of our ships escaped, Antonio?"

"I am not certain. Three or four, I think. Vice-Captain Trevisan must have escaped with at least that many," he replied optimistically.

"I am afraid not," said Contarini with a sigh. "Like you, he led some men ashore. What is left of our vice-captain of the gulf is huddled over there, against the wall."

Antonio's eyes followed his pointing finger to a group of men near the far corner. He could see Trevisan sitting silently, by himself, in a sort of trance.

"Captain Soranzo was left in command of the fleet."

Was that ship in the harbor under his command? Antonio wondered.

"Who are those men?" Antonio pointed to a group of strange-looking men, whom the Turks had separated from the rest of the prisoners.

"Cretans," said *Bailo* Minotto, who had opened his eyes and now joined in the conversation. "They held out until just a few hours before sundown. The Turks were so impressed by their courage it is rumored that they are to be set free."

Suddenly a wave of commotion swept across the courtyard. Chaos erupted as scores of Turkish soldiers roughly herded the dazed prisoners into one corner of the courtyard. Those who did not immediately comply were kicked and beaten into place. More than a few felt the flat of a sword's blade, but none were killed.

As the Turks backed away from their prisoners a troop of *sipahis,* the sultan's elite cavalry, rode into the courtyard through the large main gate followed by still more mounted men—this time, Janissaries. Then, every Turk in the vast courtyard turned and bowed in unison in the direction of the gate.

As they arose, they began to cheer wildly. The large crowd that had gathered near the gate soon parted, revealing a man riding a horse and wearing a huge white turban and sporting a long black beard. As he approached the corner, packed with the prisoners, hundreds of nervous guards tightened their grips on their weapons. He reigned in his spirited mount just twenty feet from the nearest captive and wheeled around to salute his men. A thunderous cheer echoed off the high walls that surrounded the courtyard.

"*Fatih! Fatih!* Muhammed *Fatih!*" screamed the Turks.

As the sultan turned again and faced the prisoners, the courtyard fell silent as though commanded by a signal—but there was none.

"Infidels! Behold the power of Allah, Scourge of Christendom and his servant on earth. I am Sultan Muhammed II, named for Allah's Holy Prophet and like him, I, too, will conquer all before me."

The sultan repeated his words in Greek and then in Italian. Then he continued.

"Yesterday, your Church dedicated to the whore St. Sophia, was whitewashed, its blasphemous images destroyed forever. It will now be the first mosque in my city—the new capital of the invincible Ottoman Empire. The only vestiges of your religion left there are the pathetic priests whose lives I spared—their loyalty to their god so weak, they agreed to whitewash the insides of all the other churches of my city."

The prisoners, who were now grouped with their countrymen, could only stare at one another in silence, knowing their fate was entirely in the sultan's hands.

"If you listen, soon you will hear the midday prayer sung from a hundred towers. In a few months these will be replaced by proper minarets." He spun his horse around to the delight of his subjects who successfully fought back their urge to cheer and remained silent out of respect to their sultan.

"Now we shall get down to business. You Venetians and Genoese surely understand these words, do you not? After all, like a swarm of leeches on the back of an old cow, you have been sucking the wealth of Byzantium for hundreds of years."

He turned his back to the prisoners and shouted, "First, we will divide the spoils!" His delirious soldiers, unable to control themselves, broke into deafening pandemonium.

For the next two hours, the sultan divided the spoils of war, pausing only to observe the midday prayer. Each of his commanders was awarded his share. Special care was given to those who commanded the troops who had little or no opportunity to pillage—military police, much of the navy, and the support troops in the camps. Included as booty were vast numbers of slaves. He ordered four hundred young boys and girls packed off as slaves to each of the rulers of Tunis, Granada, and Egypt. Then he allowed his most important commanders and officials to name women and men they wanted as personal slaves. Many had already been sampled for their talents. Then large groups of the city's population were designated to be slaves. When he had finished, he had accounted for almost fifty thousand people to be transported from Constantinople and sent to the far-flung corners of his vast empire, never to see their homes again. Many families were divided from one another. Only a few lucky ones were allowed to buy their freedom.

As the day dragged on, the prisoners' thirst was terrible as the hot afternoon sun beat down directly upon them. The Turks who were mostly free to move about sought the cooling shelter of the shade created by the walls. Many of the sultan's commanders had left to distribute their shares to their men and to collect their human booty.

"There will be many tears in the city this night," whispered Antonio. Most around him were thinking the same thing.

Now, finally, the sultan turned his attention back to his prisoners.

"I have decided to spare the lives of most of you—those who are worth more alive than dead. But I fear that I have been too generous to my beloved soldiers and sailors this day. Now I must replenish my treasury with your ransoms."

Most of the captives heaved sighs of relief as they listened to his words, especially the rich and powerful since their ransoms could surely be paid.

"Who will speak for you, so I may negotiate the ransom amounts?" he asked.

Quietly, at first, each group of countrymen began to discuss who would represent them in dealing with the sultan. While the Genoese, Greeks, and other survivors debated at length before finally making their selections, the Venetians quickly chose their leaders. *Bailo* Minotto was the first. Catarin Contarini was next. Eventually, seven others were elected. Some of Venice's most powerful families were represented among them; all had previously served the Republic in elected and appointed offices.

Once all the representatives were finally chosen, they began to move away from their countrymen and cautiously approach the sultan. In all, more than thirty venerable men stood between the other two hundred prisoners and the long ranks of Janissaries.

"Each of you will write down the amount your family will pay for your release. All sums are to be in Venetian gold ducats. Value yourselves highly— your lives will depend upon it. I count thirty-four among you; the seventeen who write the lesser sums will be immediately beheaded. But be careful, any man who writes a sum that proves too large for his family to pay I will have impaled alive on a wooden stake."

Thirty-four rich and powerful men instantly regretted their wealth, their social status, and—most of all—their vanity as they received chits and wrote down their prices. The two hundred other prisoners slumped against the wall and heaved sighs of relief.

In ten minutes it was finished. A Janissary captain collected the chits and wrote each man's name and ransom on a board. The sultan sat astride his horse like a statue, suppressing his excitement. He had just taken the greatest city on earth, but now he would take something as satisfying. Now he would strip these infidel mercenaries of their money or their lives.

When he had finished, the captain respectfully approached the sultan and handed the board to him. He read silently, occasionally nodding his head, but he showed no emotion. He handed the board back to the captain, speaking too softly for anyone to hear.

"Those whose names I read will sit down!" shouted the captain with authority.

He began to read. "Minotto, Doria, Contarini . . ."

He continued until he had read seventeen names. As each man was named, he quickly sat down on the stone pavement, relieved. When the captain was finished, most of the seventeen still standing were trembling.

"You men are not only pathetic infidels, worthless to Allah, but you also have no value in your own minds," sneered the sultan as he dismounted.

Then he turned to his captain and commanded. "Remove them from my sight."

Some wept bitterly, one man fainted, others valiantly resisted, in vain. Soon the courtyard was cleared of the unfortunate low bidders.

"Now," said the sultan loudly, his eyes ablaze, "down to business."

He motioned with his arm for the remaining seventeen prisoners to come forward. As they rose to their feet, several whispered among themselves, hastily planning their negotiating strategies. The sultan motioned with his hand for them to follow. Led by Minotto, they walked through a funnel of Janissaries, who forced them to stay far enough behind the sultan to ensure his personal safety. As he neared the open gate the sultan stopped and turned again to face the seventeen. A smile slithered from his beard as he motioned for *Bailo* Minotto to come forward alone.

The others watched as Minotto walked resolutely toward the sultan. Then, without a warning, a great shout went up from the crowd of Janissaries. It was over in a heartbeat. All seventeen of the greatest and most powerful were mercilessly beheaded. As their bodies dropped, their heads made sickening popping sounds as they bounced on the hard stone pavement and rolled in all directions. One man's feet continued two steps after his head was lopped off, like a chicken with its neck snapped. Blood gushed from the decapitated bodies, forming crimson pools on the large gray stones. The rest of the prisoners instinctively surged forward, but the well-armed Janissaries forced them back to their places to reflect on the horror of the barbarous act they had just witnessed.

Unnoticed by the crowd, the sultan had remounted. He slowly rode forward toward the prisoners, now closely guarded by more than three hundred Janissaries. His expression was like a man who had just won a bet—not one who had just murdered seventeen men in cold blood.

"A sultan is not required to know everything, but he *is* required to know *how* to know everything. What I did not know is how much to ransom all of you for. Now your countrymen have told me and I am no poorer for my troubles."

He smiled at the prisoners in an odd, almost kindly, understanding way.

"I have good news! I have spared the first seventeen men who were led away. Their families will pay a ransom equal to the amount given by the seventeen I executed. As for the rest of you, your families will pay dearly. If your letters fail to convince your families back in Venice, Genoa, or Rome to pay your ransoms, I will execute you. Until then, you will be imprisoned in Rumeli Hisar under the watchful eyes of Governor Abdullah Ali."

Then the sultan, his final decrees delivered, wheeled around his magnificent white Arabian charger and retired slowly through the open gate. An oppressive pall descended upon the courtyard as each prisoner contemplated, in his own way, what he had just seen and heard. Only the most steadfast were not broken in spirit.

Shortly after the sultan departed, the dispirited prisoners were herded down to the wreck-strewn harbor. Few spoke—there was little to say. They had been through the hell of a protracted siege, deprived of sleep, food, and, in the end, for many, blood. Most were weak and many were suffering from fever. Fortunately, to the disappointment of the guards, the sultan had given strict orders not to mistreat them. Woe to the Turk who was responsible for the death of a prisoner the sultan intended to ransom!

As the ragged parade of survivors limped and staggered through the sea gate onto the pier, the smiths were waiting for them. The pier reverberated with the clanking sounds of iron on iron as the Turks shackled the prisoners in threes. As soon as the rough metal bands had been hammered around their ankles, rubbing them raw, the men were prodded up a gangway aboard a big galley that was to transport them to the castle.

Antonio and Seraglio had been careful to stay together on the march to the harbor. Seraglio, relatively healthy compared to the others, was able to keep up with his quick, short strides. As they climbed aboard and down the wooden stairs into the hold, the reeking stench of excrement overpowered the prisoners, many of whom vomited, contributing to the smell. As they felt their way through the dark, lit only by a small lantern at each end of the ship, the two hundred prisoners cursed and complained as they tripped over the benches and oars. Sometimes stepping on another, sometimes stepped upon, tempers were short. Chained together, Antonio, Seraglio, and young Minotto filed slowly along an empty bench and sat down, picking up the heavy oar and resting it on their laps. Antonio and Minotto barely had enough legroom to row. The Turks, peering through the air vents in the hatches, loudly mocked their once-proud enemies, adding to their misery.

"The Turks are fools," said Minotto. "There is not enough room for a man to straighten his legs properly to row with his full force."

"They want to make our rowing difficult and futile," replied Seraglio.

"He is right," said Antonio. "This is a prison ship, not a warship! Would a war galley's hold be covered in this stinking filth? See how they have crammed in extra benches so they can accommodate us all? They want the journey to be slow and hard; the castle is only five miles away but it will take us hours of backbreaking work to get there."

At first, every man tried to keep his feet still since the slightest movement would soon cause the rough shackles to tear his skin and his two chained comrades to suffer similarly. But once they began to row, they soon forgot the pain.

The journey to the Rumeli Hisar took four interminable hours as the men fought against the strong current that runs swiftly through the straits between Europe and Asia. From Constantinople to the promontory on the western bank, where Rumeli Hisar stood, the Bosphorus narrowed in places to less than five hundred yards wide.

The Turks did not need to force the men to row hard, given the deplorable conditions down in the hold. By the time the ship berthed, the rowers were a sweating, heaving mass of sore muscles and bleeding hands and feet. As they pulled in their oars, the men gasped for air in the oppressive heat, beards and backs dripping with foul perspiration. Tired of raining insults down on their captives, the Turks had closed the hatches, hours before, to prevent the stench below from wafting up onto the deck, adding to the prisoners' misery.

Antonio and the others sat hunched over, panting, their parched throats burning with thirst. Suddenly, the door to the hold flew open, revealing a huge bare-chested Turk, with a flowing, thick black beard, silhouetted in the bright sunlight. With a grunt, he signaled to the men to come up the stairs. Satan himself, with all the demons of hell could have been waiting up there and they still would have come up out of that seagoing latrine. Antonio and the others suffered in silence as they waited for their turn.

"What do you think will happen now?" asked young Minotto, his youthful energy contrasting with the grim resolve of his older comrades.

"What do you care?" shot back a stocky man. "I hope they just let me die! I cannot take much more of this."

"Easy, signore," said Antonio. "We cannot let the Turks think they have broken our will. We must behave like Venetians."

The others looked at Antonio with a mixture of admiration and disbelief.

"Nobili," the man uttered under his breath as he shook his head in disgust.

After an insufferable wait, Antonio and the others finally ascended the stairs. As they sucked in deep draughts of sweet, fresh air, it intoxicated their senses. Though the temperature was still hot, it felt like a cool spring breeze compared to what they had just experienced.

They slowly filed up the gangway, made slippery with bodily filth, tripping and stumbling as the short lengths of chain binding them together restricted their natural leg movements. At the top, they joined the crowd of prisoners milling about on the pier. Most were gaping at the massive stone battlements of Rumeli Hisar. The imposing structure towered ominously above them on a foundation of solid rock, overlooking the Bosphorus.

"The sultan chose this sight well," observed Seraglio. "Those guns control the straits. No ship can pass unless the Turks permit it."

"Look, over there!" cried one man.

Across the water they could see the broken timbers of a once-mighty ship that had been blasted to bits by the sultan's cannon.

Antonio counted sixteen black muzzles along the castle wall facing the water. Each cannon was larger than any he had ever seen on a Venetian ship. He wondered if the wooden skeleton was the remains of poor Captain Rizzo's ship that had tried to run the gauntlet without paying the sultan's toll—what balls the man had, thought Antonio.

One of the men put his hand on Antonio's arm and pointed with the other, high above them. There, flying from the tallest towers, were four giant Turkish battle flags, each with its white crescent proclaiming the dominance of Islam over the castle, its inhabitants, and the vanquished prisoners far below. A few men close to Antonio cursed in their feeble attempt to hide their humiliation and shame.

Through the crowd of heads and shoulders, Antonio thought he caught a glimpse of Vice-Captain of the Gulf Trevisan.

"Come with me," ordered Antonio as he and the two men chained together with him began to carefully push their way through the others. Finally reaching Trevisan, he gently placed a hand on his shoulder.

"I thank God that you are alive, Gabriele."

Getting no response, he gently pulled on Trevisan's arm, slowly turning him around. It was then that Antonio noticed, for the first time, a weeping red gash that ran from his ear to his chin. He seemed oblivious to the black flies buzzing and crawling around the ugly wound.

"What happened to you?" asked Antonio. Nothing.

"Vice-Captain of the Gulf Trevisan," he said loudly into his friend's face.

Suddenly a trace of understanding showed on his countenance. A glimmer of life danced in his eyes. His cracked lips trembled, as he seemed to comprehend slightly.

"Captain Ziani," he said in an empty monotone voice, "it is good to see you. Where are your men?"

"Most were killed on the walls. About forty made it to one of our ships."

"The ships. Captain Soranzo . . ." Silence.

"What about Captain Soranzo?" Antonio grasped Trevisan's hand, but the faint spark in his eyes was extinguished as quickly as it had appeared.

"Captain Ziani, it is good to see you."

"It is no use trying to talk to him," a coarse voice interrupted.

Antonio turned to see a small man he recognized as an officer from one of the Venetian ships that had come to Constantinople with Catarin Contarini's men.

"He has lost his mind. You are lucky that he even recognized you."

Antonio sadly accepted the man's pronouncement and released his gentle grip. He knew that, in this condition, Trevisan would probably not survive their imprisonment.

Suddenly his thoughts were interrupted by rhythmic footfalls crunching on the stone path leading from the pier to the castle. A troop of Turks, led by an officer in a resplendent uniform, had marched down from Rumeli Hisar to take charge of the prisoners. The transaction concluded, the prisoners were formed up to begin their trek up a winding path to the castle.

As they crossed over the moat and marched through the outer gate into the sprawling yard, a chaotic scene, typical of castle life, greeted them. Along almost the entire length of each wall were scores of small wooden buildings with red tile roofs. At first, the hundreds of people there stopped and stared at the Christian prisoners but, knowing they would not be spending any money, the people soon turned back to their business.

The prisoners were led across the yard and into the large stone castle keep. Rumeli Hisar reminded Antonio of the massive castles he had seen in his travels though France and Germany. In a few minutes he and five of his fellow prisoners were shown to their new home—a stone cell deep in the bowels of the castle, measuring nine by ten feet. As the tired men took their places on the hard cobblestone floor, the Turks closed the heavy wooden door with a dull thud. They were alone and welcomed the chance to finally rest.

A small barred window three times the height of a man above the floor and too small for a man's shoulders to fit through provided the only light and ventilation. In one corner was a small pile of straw. In another were two large wooden buckets, one filled with water, the other empty. They all quickly found a way to recline, each man occupying his three feet of space from side to side, as they lay three on one end and three on the other, their backs against the walls, chained together like galley slaves.

"So this is to be our new home," said one man ruefully.

"It is not so bad," retorted the ever-optimistic Seraglio. "If we were not to be ransomed, we would have been consigned to a galley or else sent to some godforsaken place with much backbreaking work and little hope."

The men reflected on his words. Minotto suddenly cracked a smile, the first since his father had been murdered by the sultan, and said ironically, "This cell is the best thing that has happened to us in days. Imagine that. What has our world come to?"

"Man is a most adaptable and tolerant creature," philosophized Seraglio. "First he fights, then he resists. Then he merely complains about his new and deplorable condition. In time he acquiesces and then soon, he accepts and finally makes himself comfortable in his new circumstances, no matter how spartan. In the end, he finds enjoyment in his condition—even humor. We Greeks call it the humor of the condemned."

Benedetto, who up until now had said nothing, hissed, "You may think this is funny, but I say that if it were not for you and your cowardly Greek brethren, we would not be here in this dung hole at all. We would have beaten the Turks and held the city." Antonio knew Benedetto. He was tough, ill-tempered, and prone to violence.

This unpleasant exchange was interrupted by the sounds of heavy footsteps and slamming doors, growing ever closer. Soon the door to their cell opened. Five powerful-looking Turks dressed in crimson and black robes stood in the doorway. Their leader spoke to them in Turkish while his men set down wooden plates of food for the hungry prisoners. Seraglio translated for his comrades.

"He says that each afternoon we will be fed, our water bucket will be refilled and the waste bucket will be emptied. If anyone becomes sick, he will be unchained and taken to a special cell for the sick to prevent the rest of us from also becoming ill."

Seraglio spoke quickly to the man, who laughed and departed.

"I told him that we would like lamb and fresh bread tomorrow."

"The humor of the condemned," said Lando with a wry grin. "I hope you did not make him angry. I would not want to have him withhold any of this fine food from us."

Lando tipped his wooden bowl toward his comrades revealing some soup made from cornmeal and a few pieces of sinewy mutton in a cold watery broth. Minotto, in turn, held up a plate of moldy, unleavened bread. No one laughed—not even Seraglio.

So began the confinement of the six prisoners in their own little world within the walls of Rumeli Hisar. They talked of home and the siege. The men were thankful when the Turkish jailers came for a few minutes each day to remove their waste bucket and give them their single meal—it was their only relief from the endless monotony.

As the weeks passed, the prisoners' beards grew more ragged—except for young Minotto, whose fuzzy face contrasted with the others. It was impossible for him to hide his expressions from them. But the lice that frolicked in the whiskers on his fellow prisoners' faces more than compensated him for that disadvantage.

By this time, Minotto and Benedetto both were shirtless. They had finally torn theirs into pieces and used the rags to wipe themselves after using the waste bucket—when each suffered from dysentery. Antonio, relatively well, had decided to keep his shirt to roll up for a pillow so he could sleep on the rounded stones more comfortably.

Only those who have known long confinement could imagine the despair that settled like a dense cloud in their cell. The hard uneven floor made sleep difficult. Worse, Benedetto snored thunderously whenever he lay on his back. His mean disposition prevented any one man from attempting to stop him, alone. Only when all the others had been awakened would they dare to wake him and incur his wrath.

At first, they tried to exercise together to maintain their fitness, but the lack of space and the ever-present shackles made it too difficult. Soon, after some were weakened by illness, any further attempts to exercise were abandoned.

The summer days were stifling and the cell was always filled with the foul smells of bodily functions. Hardly a day passed when at least one of the men was not sick from the rotten food—his intestines violently protesting their treatment despite the man's valiant attempt to spare the others from the resulting stench. They all looked forward to when the bucket filled with the vile contents from the last twenty-four hours would be removed and a few minutes or, occasionally, hours would pass before the odors would again build up in the cell. Even this, they slowly became accustomed to—just as Seraglio had predicted.

It was not all heartbreaking deprivation and hopelessness. After all, they were Venetians. To keep their sanity, Antonio encouraged the prisoners to wile away the long hours in conversation. Soon, each knew much about the others' lives and experiences.

Seraglio taught some basic Turkish words and phrases to his comrades. Minotto used his long thin fingers to remove their lice. Benedetto was the champion pebble tosser. Everyone marveled at how he almost always was able to place his pebble closest to the step that led up to the door. Antonio calculated that he had already won enough ducats to buy half of Venice. Lando had only one talent, but it amused the other prisoners every time he employed it. He was the bucket passer. Each day when the guards came with new food and fresh water and removed their waste bucket of recycled food, he would imperceptibly splash the robe of the guard who took it from him with a small amount of its contents to the delight of his snickering comrades.

The last was the enigmatic Dona. Unlike the others, he seldom spoke but when prodded, he would sometimes astound them with his prodigious feats of memory. They would recite lists of articles, places, or people and he would enumerate them in the same order, sometimes up to one hundred items at a time. Seraglio had calculated that Benedetto's winnings from pebble-tossing athletics paled beside the millions of ducats Dona had won from the others using his brain.

As so often happens when a group of strangers are thrown together by circumstances, each settles into his role and plays it with relish, securing his special place in his new society. So it was with the six prisoners in the dank cell at the end of the corridor in the deepest dungeon in Rumeli Hisar.

6

The Report

Of all the western European states, only Venice had sent a large fleet to reinforce the city. What had become of it? After much argument and debate, it finally was permitted to set sail on May 9, far too late to save the city. When it encountered several ships bearing the survivors of the great siege, the Venetians sadly turned around and made the long voyage back to Venice.

The first word of the fall of Constantinople reached Venice exactly one month to the day on June 29. About four thousand men, women, and children were killed outright in the sack of the city in addition to the thousands of soldiers and sailors who had lost their lives defending it. About twenty-five hundred Christians escaped on ships. Many were Venetian and Genoese soldiers and sailors along with some wealthy civilians who could pay for their passage. The brave Genoese commander, Giustiniani, was among those who made it to the ships, but he died of his wound five days later.

The real damage done by the fall was not to the city itself, or even to the Byzantine Empire, which had virtually ceased to exist by the time of the siege. The worst damage was the threat Venice now faced of losing her eastern Mediterranean possessions to the vengeful Muhammed II. Now the Republic's fight to the death with her larger, more warlike enemy would begin.

. . .

The Senate had summoned him to answer questions about the siege and fall of Constantinople. As the highest-ranking survivor, it was Soranzo's duty to account for Venetian ships, lives, and property as he related his eyewitness account. He had submitted a written report two weeks after returning. The members of the Senate, having read the report, had sent for him this day so they could question him at their pleasure.

He walked across the brick-paved Piazza San Marco and entered the Doges' Palace through the Porta della Carta and stopped briefly to scan the decrees and other documents that were routinely posted on the outer wall on each side of the famous door. Two caught his eye. One urged every citizen of the Republic to do his part to help construct fifty new war galleys by year-end. Nearly everyone expected full-scale war with the Turks. He smiled as he read a notice just below it. It warned the city's more than six thousand prostitutes to be sure to register with the government and to pay their taxes dutifully under penalty of imprisonment. The Arsenal, Venice's massive shipyard, and the brothels, he thought, would be the two busiest places in Venice that summer.

He crossed the courtyard, climbed the broad staircase, and went inside, eventually reaching the fourth floor, where he walked the familiar route to the Senate chamber. As he entered the ornate room, unannounced, heads turned to examine the intruder. The loud voices he heard surprised him. Normally this was a dignified and impressive group whose members would awe their visitors. However, this day, sheer pandemonium reigned in the stately chamber.

Soranzo found an empty seat along the far side of the room under two large windows. Seated with his back to the wall, he slowly scanned the room. Every member of the Pregadi, the "invited men," was present. They were the sixty select members of the larger 480-man Senate who were empowered by the larger body to make foreign policy decisions. To them were added a sixty-man Zonta, also drawn from the Senate in times of crisis to expand the Pregadi. Dressed in their simple black robes, they were all seated on fourteen long rows of wooden benches, perpendicular to the doge.

Doge Francesco Foscari sat at one end, wearing his official robes of gold-embroidered white satin with a white ermine collar and golden *corno,* a horned cap that replaced his jewel-encrusted tiara that was too heavy to wear except for short ceremonial occasions. Seated beside the doge was his inner circle of six advisors, one from each of the six *sestieri,* the districts of the city, dressed in long blood-red robes, and the three other members of his

Signoria, his closest advisors. To the doge's left, also dressed in black, were members of the secret Consiglio dei Dieci, the "Ten." Their identities, normally concealed from the population, were known to anyone important enough to attend a meeting such as this. The Ten were the power behind the power in the Republic. They were chosen by the Great Council as a committee of public safety—a watchdog on the doge, the Signoria, and the Pregadi. Three members of the Ten would be locked in the Doges' Palace each month, unable to leave under penalty of treason. These Inquisitori di Stato were commissioned to root out corruption or treason within the government. They trusted no one and questioned everything. Thirty more government officials, mostly military and administrative leaders, completed the assemblage.

The Republic's paranoia was so extreme that the doge could not open mail, leave the Doges' Palace, or be in a room alone with his family members, except of course his wife, without a member of the Ten present. The patriciate policed itself with even greater fervor than it policed its citizens, fearing treachery and rebellion from within its own ranks far more than from the population it ruled.

As he waited respectfully for the assembly to conclude its current business, Soranzo thought of how the Republic went to almost ridiculous lengths to ensure a fair election of the doge. In nine successive steps, representative groups of senators would elect and in turn, be elected until forty-one were finally vested with the voting power to choose a new doge on a tenth round of voting. This unwieldy process guaranteed that only those who had built broad, powerful support could be elected.

Soranzo returned his attention to the powerful men, as the business in progress since he had entered the room was nearly completed. There would be nothing more important in the day's session than to discuss his report on the fall of Constantinople. They were rapidly disposing of less important matters.

He examined the old doge closely. Francesco Foscari had held power for more than thirty years, longer than anyone in the last seven hundred years. He looked tired and worn. His early reign had seen the death of true democracy in the Republic as power had shifted from the larger Senate to the smaller Pregadi. Soranzo remembered the uproar, years before, when Foscari had ended the Arengo, the general assembly of all adult citizens in the city. Since 1423 the *nobili* had ruled alone, unfettered by the populace at large. His dogeship had been marked by almost constant warfare with Milan that had consumed many millions of ducats. At this stage in his reign, he was not popular. Soranzo and many others no longer held him in such high esteem. Perhaps it was this lack of popular strength that had led to his inde-cision regarding the dispatch of a large relief fleet to Constantinople that had been sent too late to try to save the city.

Soranzo felt contempt for these overfed bureaucrats who had debated *ad nauseum* while they had delayed the help Constantinople needed to survive. Now there would be hell to pay with the Turks. Better to not have sent any help at all than to have helped halfheartedly, as they had. The rest of the Christian world had done less, he thought, except, of course, Genoa, which also had important financial interests there, possibly even greater than Venice's. He blocked the considerable financial losses his family had suf-fered, not to mention the loss of his two brothers, out of his mind. They were too painful to think about at a time like this.

Finally, the preliminary business at hand was finished. Soranzo's thoughts were interrupted as the doge stood and spoke loudly.

"Captain Soranzo, thank you for your informative report regarding the events at Constantinople. Has your wound healed satisfactorily?" Giovanni looked down at his shoulder and then nodded his assent. Not much of a wound really, he thought.

"We have noted the losses that, sadly, include over six hundred men, many from families represented in this room. Of course, we are hopeful that some now counted as lost will eventually return. In the confusion of the evacuation, many were dispersed and will require time to make their way back to Venice. We all pray to God for their safe return. We are hopeful the Turks will ransom all of the surviving *nobili* back to us." There was com-plete quiet, as many nodded their agreement. The room was too cavernous to hear most speakers without observing total silence. The doge continued.

"The Turkish ambassador to Egypt has told our ambassador there that the sultan has already made his ransom list and it is, this very moment, on its way to Venice.

"We calculate our financial losses in Constantinople to exceed three hundred thousand ducats, equaling five months of state revenue. We also sent eight ships to Constantinople, two galleys, one brig, and the five mer-chantmen of Vice-Captain of the Gulf Trevisan's squadron. In your report, Captain Soranzo, you state that three of the merchant ships were lost. Do you know what happened to them?"

"Yes, Doge Foscari. Two merchant ships were lost in the Golden Horn, unable to make good their escape because they were too far away from the Bosphorus at the time of the final attack. We saw the Turkish flags raised on their masts after the Turks boarded them. Their gallant crews set them afire. We rounded the headland before we could confirm they had been destroyed.

There has been no word of the third ship. The reports of her fate are conflicting. Some say she, too, was set afire in the harbor. Others say the Turks took her. One thing is certain. She did not leave the harbor with us."

"What of Vice-Captain of the Gulf Trevisan?" asked the Captain-General of the Seas, the Republic's highest-ranking naval commander. "Your report states he went ashore to fight on the walls the day the city fell and did not return."

"That is correct. He told me before he went ashore that he could not resist the call to honor. He wanted to fight with his countrymen. Contarini's men and our marines were all on the walls defending the city."

"Captain Ziani was also lost, along with most of his marines?"

"Yes, Captain-General," replied Soranzo. "Two days before the fall, Vice-Captain Trevisan and *Bailo* Minotto agreed to the emperor's request for fresh troops. Captain Ziani led almost four hundred marines to the walls, but only two score survived. All the other marines are presumed dead, including Captain Ziani." Soranzo seethed at the thought that Pietro was also among them. He wondered again, for the hundredth time, how it had happened. He hoped Pietro had died a hero's death—and a quick one.

"Now, what are we going to do about the Turks?" sighed the doge as he turned to the assembled leaders of the Republic.

The captain-general of the seas spoke first. "We have ordered the construction of fifty new war galleys by year-end. Plans are in place to levy the usual war taxes. We are now planning for the defense of our Greek possessions, but it will be difficult. Where the sultan will strike next is anyone's guess, but surely he will seek retribution for the assistance we provided to the emperor."

Most of those present nodded their agreement. "We believe Athens, the Isthmus of Corinth, and the whole of the Peloponnese will be his next target. We have ordered the Corinthian wall across the Isthmus repaired and have ordered additional troops sent there," said the captain-general.

"Very well," said the doge with a deep sigh. "Let us send a peace proposal to the sultan to find out his price. In the meantime, let us make full preparations for war."

The doge looked at Soranzo and nodded. Understanding, he rose and strode from the room. As a guard closed the door behind him, Soranzo was surprised when the man ordered him to remain there, waiting outside the chamber.

"Why?" he asked the tall young man.

"The doge wishes to talk to you in private."

He had spoken to Pasquale Malipiero, his mentor and one of the most powerful men in the government, about Antonio Ziani's conduct and the deaths of his two brothers. He surmised that Malipiero must have spoken to the doge about it.

Soon the doors opened and the meeting participants began to file out. Soranzo was struck by how they seemed to ignore him as they walked by after listening in rapt attention to his every word just moments before.

The last to emerge was the captain-general of the seas.

"Come with me, Captain," he said in an impatient voice.

Soranzo returned and this time sat near to Doge Foscari. The only men present were the doge, the captain-general, the doge's counselors, and the Ten, one of whom was Malipiero, who spoke first.

"Captain Soranzo, your report states that the marine commander, Captain Antonio Ziani, was incompetent. As proof, you say he lost one of his men overboard on the voyage to Negropont. This, of course, is a serious charge since you claim his loss was completely preventable. Since the marine did not die in battle, Ziani could be charged with a violation of the law."

"Are you quite certain he could have prevented it?" asked another.

"Yes."

"Are there any other witnesses who can attest to this? You have brought a serious charge against Captain Ziani. Though he is dead, it will be a stain on his family's honor."

"And a stain it should be. You could ask Vice-Captain Trevisan, but unfortunately, he has not returned. You could have asked any member of his ship's crew, but that ship was one of the two burned and lost in the harbor. You could have asked my other brother, Pietro. He was a marine officer who fought with Captain Ziani on the walls, but by now it is clear that he was killed also. I can only imagine how Captain Ziani may have caused his and the others' demise. No, signore, I am afraid that I am the only one left alive who knows what happened."

"Are you sure you are not making these charges because the marine lost overboard was your younger brother?" interjected another one of the Ten. "What is the accidental drowning of one marine compared to the enormity of our loss in the siege?"

"Signore," he patiently replied, "war has taught me that a commander who shirks his responsibility for one man will soon shirk it for his entire company."

"What about the marines who survived and made it to your ship?" asked another.

"None were witnesses to young Soranzo's demise," responded Malipiero.

Charges like this were seldom made and were regarded with the utmost seriousness by the government, especially at a time of national emergency when unity among the patriciate was vital. The doge decided to end the discussion.

"I am directing you, Captain-General, to make a full investigation into these charges against Captain Ziani. Perhaps later, if we can ransom back some prisoners you can find some other witnesses. Take the necessary time to find the truth."

Every man in the room knew that bad blood had existed between the Soranzos and the Zianis many years ago, but it had been a long time since anything this serious had come between them.

Soranzo emerged from the Doges' Palace into the bright summer sunlight. He knew he had portrayed his enemy in the worst possible light, to ensure he would pay for the deaths of Marco and Pietro. Even though Ziani was surely dead, at least his family could be made to bear the shame of his actions. He smiled visibly. A dead man cannot refute a charge leveled against him. Perhaps, he thought, the Republic, which normally required two witnesses to corroborate a charge of treason, cowardice, or dereliction of one's duty during war, would make an exception and rely on his testimony alone. The only man who could tell a different version of what had happened that stormy night was Trevisan—and surely he was killed on the walls of Constantinople.

As Soranzo walked home, he thought about his family. Shortly after he had returned to Venice, he had made the decision to take responsibility for his brother Pietro's young wife, Maria, and her eight-year-old son. Enrico was already a strong-willed boy and reminded him of Pietro when his brother was the same age. Maria would not have to rely on him for much—she came from a wealthy patrician family, but it would be a great burden to assume the unfamiliar role of surrogate father to Enrico. To fully play the part, he had decided that he would adopt the boy and raise him as his own son.

Soranzo wondered what kind of a father he would be—never having had a son of his own. His thoughts turned to his late rival, who had perished childless. Now, the leadership of the House of Ziani would pass to his brother, Giorgio, whose impetuousness, such an asset in battle, would make him foolish and vulnerable in business. Soranzo smiled as he thought about the golden opportunity that lay before him. He intended to put them in their place, once and for all—just as he would move in for the kill against a grievously wounded opponent. He would make his grandfather proud.

The House of Ziani had fared better than his own with the fall of Constantinople. They were a powerful trading family. Their wealth was in their close trading relationships and in their ships and crews that transported their wares. They owned half a dozen seagoing vessels and many smaller ships that sailed around the lagoon and up the northern Italian rivers, collecting and distributing goods for the lengthier ocean voyages. None of the merchant ships lost in the siege had belonged to them.

In contrast, Soranzo's family, always investors in trading ventures, had sustained significant losses in the debacle. They had been part of the consortium that had financed the supplies on board the relief fleet. There would be no payment now. He estimated losses from this at more than three thousand ducats—half a year's profit!

Added to that loss were other supplies that Venetian merchants, backed by the House of Soranzo, had been selling to the Byzantines at inflated prices in the months leading up to the siege. They had finally been paid with bartered goods—but the emperor had conveniently waited until it was too late for his partners to remove them before the Turks began their siege. Their only option had been to arrange for them to be stored in a warehouse until he could find a way to ship them back to Venice after the siege had been successfully resisted. He had known at the time that it was a risky plan, but it was the only way he could hope to recoup his family's investment.

The ship he had commanded had caused his family still more losses. Though it did not belong to his family—they owned no ships—another trading family, the Morosinis, had furnished it to the government. To be made its captain, he had agreed to pay the owners for any damage it sustained. Storm and battle damage had exceeded two hundred ducats. This had proven to be a useless expense since he had not been able to use it to bring the stored goods back to Venice.

Now, with Antonio dead, he would undermine the House of Ziani's trading relationships and claim them for himself and his partners, who would be only too happy to recoup the sizable losses they suffered in the fall of Constantinople at the Zianis' expense. But first, he would wait until his rivals were weakened by the damaging findings of the captain-general of the seas' investigation. Then he would concoct a scheme to embarrass Giorgio in the eyes of his business partners.

As he rounded the corner to the street where his family's palazzo stood, he smiled as he considered all of the possibilities. While a disaster for the Republic and a devastating financial and personal loss for him, Constantinople could at least provide the Soranzos with the opportunity to bury the House of Ziani forever.

7

The Prison

The six prisoners were bored to death in their tiny cell as each day slowly crept by. Nothing broke the sameness but the daily visit by the guards. Even activities that had diverted their attention from their mean circumstances weeks before now only reminded them of how miserable their lives had become. Their only hope was that their ransoms would be paid, buying their freedom at last.

One day, in their sixth week of captivity, as the footsteps on the stone floor approached their cell door, they sounded different. There were more than usual. When the door opened they saw an officer and two heavily armed soldiers with their jailers.

"Him," pointed a jailer, as the five prisoners turned toward Seraglio.

"Come with us," the officer said in Turkish. The two guards stepped into the cell and broke the chains that connected Seraglio to Antonio and Minotto and led him away.

As the jailers delivered their daily ration of food and removed their waste bucket, Antonio wondered what the Turks were going to do with him. Seraglio was a Greek—not a Venetian. Did the Turks doubt his ransom would be paid? Would they kill him, like so many others who had no value? His physical deformities would prevent them from making him a slave. Antonio suddenly realized that he might never see his friend again.

The soldiers stripped and scrubbed Seraglio with soap and stiff brushes until his skin was red. His nostrils flared as they splashed him all over with strong perfume. Then they dressed him in a simple white robe, tied with a thin royal blue cord. Satisfied, the soldiers then escorted him up from the bowels of the castle to the governor's quarters.

A big eunuch pushed open the door. Inside, he could see a large Turk with a long brown beard and a white bejeweled turban seated at a large table, busily reading an official-looking document. Seraglio examined the impressively decorated room. The walls and parquet floor were covered with rich tapestries and an exotic Persian rug. A large carved marble tracery window provided a magnificent view of the choppy blue Bosphorus and the Black Sea, far beyond. In one corner stood a suit of highly polished armor—the kind the Venetians wore. In another was a detailed model of the castle. Ignoring the intruders, the man continued his work as Seraglio and the officer stood quietly at attention until, finally finished, he laid down his quill and raised his eyes.

"Are we treating you well?" he asked in perfect Greek, sounding as though he was bored with his own question, though his eyes betrayed his interest.

"The food is excellent," Seraglio shot back, in Turkish.

"I will have that remedied. And the accommodations?"

"They are surely fit for a sultan but perhaps you could help me with one thing. We are having difficulty determining if the guards are removing the food or our excrement each day when they visit us to see to our well-being. Would it be too much to ask you order them to mark each bucket so that we may distinguish between them? We have tried using our eyes and our noses but without success. Confusing them could be most unpleasant." His insult delivered, Seraglio bravely awaited the Turk's wrath.

The man slowly rose to his feet and gazed down at him, as a schoolmaster would regard a child—not with contempt but as one who pitied his ignorance.

"Your sense of humor is as good as your Turkish. Be thankful you are in the presence of Abdullah Ali, the sultan's humble servant, and not in the presence of the sultan himself. If you were, he would have your tongue ripped out for your insolence. Why would we waste good food on men who have tried to kill us?"

"Why would we worry about having our tongues torn from our mouths, when without them, perhaps we would not have to taste the dung you feed us?"

"What is your name?" asked the governor of Rumeli Hisar.

"I am called Seraglio."

"How many languages can you speak fluently?"

"Five, Your Honor. Greek, Turkish, Italian, Latin, and French."

"I have need of a translator so that I can talk to a Venetian patrician. The guards tell me you are the servant of one who is in your cell."

"That would be Captain Antonio Ziani. But I am no servant. I have been his companion since we were drawn together by fate and the fortunes of war."

"Which language do you speak best?"

"The language every man values most, Your Honor—truth."

"You are fluent in that rarely spoken language as well? I thought truth, like Latin, was a dead language in the Christian world, used only in your precious Bible and on old Roman ruins and ritualistically spoken in church—without feeling or understanding. The only truth that is alive in the world today is the word of the Great Prophet."

"Perhaps, but Captain Ziani also speaks it—although with an Italian accent, just as, no doubt, you speak it, Governor, but with a Turkish accent."

"You are clever, Seraglio. You and Captain Ziani shall dine with me tonight. You will translate for us so that we may better understand each other. Do not let your fluency in speaking the truth fail you. I speak more than a little Italian. How much more you may ponder, but it will be enough to know if you are interpreting our words accurately."

The governor called out to the officer, "Take him back to his cell. Tonight, two hours after dark, bring him and Captain Ziani back to me. Have a dinner prepared for us."

When Seraglio returned, he reeked of the pungent perfume. The other prisoners recoiled from the strong scent as he recounted his meeting with the governor. They were amazed that he had invited Seraglio and Antonio to dine with him later that night.

The six prisoners debated about what the governor wanted with Antonio and Seraglio. One thing was certain: they would be required to pay for their meal, somehow. Turkish generosity toward Christians always had a price.

A few hours later, loud footsteps announced that their adventure was about to begin. The guards bathed them and dressed them in simple white garments, dousing both of them with perfume—Seraglio's skin and hair had already reabsorbed the ever-present stinking odor of their cell. After a few minutes' walk, they stood outside a room with a large ebony door, appointed with golden metalwork in a dazzling oriental pattern.

As the guards pushed open the doors, they revealed a small piece of heaven on earth. The room was not large but seemed vast compared to their tiny cell. A single woolen carpet, dyed a rich green hue and laced with deep chestnut tones and golden threads, almost completely covered the floor. Delicate golden sconces caressing oil lamps lit the mahogany-paneled walls. A single round table, prominently set in the middle, dominated the room. It was low to the floor, as though weighted down by the many heavy plates and dishes piled high with exotic fruits and breads. Along the far wall, on a high serving table, a whole roasted pheasant and a large trout sizzled and steamed, filling the air with the sweet smell of their aromatic spices and succulent juices. Seraglio's empty stomach smiled through its pangs of hunger at the thought of such a feast.

The guards motioned to them to sit. They flopped down onto plush red and green silk-embroidered pillows decorated with woodland scenes depicting brave hunters and ferocious animals. As the guards left them alone, Antonio decided not to eat anything until the governor joined them. Seraglio followed his example.

They stared intermittently at the food and then at each other. After they had endured what seemed like endless torture, the door finally opened. A large powerful-looking man drifted into the room like a cloud, all draped in white with wisps of blue and gold twisted into his silken sash. On his head was a large white turban trimmed with a royal blue ostrich feather. As he removed his red pointed slippers, he bowed deeply to his guests. A eunuch entered carrying a large bowl of water laced with lemon slices, three towels draped on his arms. The governor washed his hands and face and then sat motionless while Antonio and Seraglio respectfully repeated his ritual.

"Captain Ziani, welcome to my table," he said in labored Italian. Then he prayed, "May God, who has provided this meal, protect his servant Muhammed and these humble souls who partake of His bounty." Antonio was self-conscious as he crossed himself, peeking at the governor to gauge his reaction.

"You both must be hungry. I suggest that we eat first and then talk."

Before Seraglio could translate the governor's words they attacked the delicacy-filled plates with their hands and fingers, ignoring the golden forks and knives set on the table. They ate like common beggars, stuffing food into their mouths as if the governor might change his mind and order it removed at any moment.

Their hunger sated, they washed down their meal with a delicious mixture of white Greek wine laced with raw honey. The governor had obviously gone to great lengths to accommodate them, providing it in violation of Islamic law.

"Tell me, Captain, why did you come all this way to fight such a hopeless battle for such a forlorn cause? You must have known that the sultan had the power of God and a hundred thousand men on his side." He stared unabashedly at Antonio while Seraglio carefully translated his words.

Antonio took another drink and then answered.

"Because my honor demanded it and my country expected it. It seems, Governor, that we created a dilemma for God—each of us invoking His name in our cause."

"Surely you do not think that God was on your side instead of ours?"

"It seems to me God showed no preference since rivers of Turkish and Christian blood mingled together as both sides suffered," interjected Seraglio carefully.

The governor's eyes narrowed.

"True, much blood *was* shed, but there can be no doubt that God favored the sword of Islam and granted us the victory. I offer as proof the fifty thousand Christian slaves we have taken to glorify our cause. In time, they will all become Muslim."

The governor leaned back, self-satisfied as Seraglio translated.

"God's kingdom is not of this world. Some events are the work of man alone—he has given all of us free will and the power to choose to do good or evil."

"The words of your great prophet, Jesus."

"What do you know of Jesus?" Antonio replied, caught off guard.

"Jesus Christ was a great prophet of his people but more important, he was a herald to the coming of The One Prophet—Muhammed."

"I am surprised you have such respect for Jesus."

"Yes, Captain, I do, but I have no respect for his followers. You Christians have perverted Jesus's teachings. Just look at all the misery you have created through the years with your petty kingdoms and your bloody wars. Look at how you desecrated the very birthplace of your Jesus in the Holy Land during your futile crusades."

Antonio could feel the anger in his words before he heard their meaning. He was thankful for Seraglio's meticulous translation. It gave him time to think.

"But, Governor, are you Turks any different as you seek to conquer the West? Why can you not be satisfied with your own righteousness and leave us, who do not choose to worship your God, alone?" Antonio riveted his eyes on their host. "It appears to us the sultan pursues his expansionist wars to gain land, wealth, and secular power rather than to ensure a place in heaven for the unhappy inhabitants of the territories he conquers. He wants all that we possess."

The governor shook his head. "You are mistaken, Captain. He *does* want to save those inhabitants you speak of. Throughout history, there has been but one true religion. In the beginning, it was Judaism. But Christianity replaced the less perfect doctrine of the Jews fifteen hundred years ago, when God saw that the rabbis had perverted His one true religion into a ridiculous set of impossible laws and rituals. Six hundred years later, the same thing happened again—for the last time. God saw that Christianity had fallen victim to the same sort of perversion, except your failing was greater than the Jews'. You turned away, becoming infidels, and you remain so today. How can you dispute the facts? Two times I have read your Bible from cover to cover, yet I can find no words forbidding priests to marry. Where does it say that a man may obtain forgiveness from a priest? And why would God admit a man into his precious heaven, filled with its indescribable delights, when he has only *said* that he believes, but he has not performed the good works that *prove* he believes? And what about your schisms? What do you say to that, infidel?"

Antonio fought back anger. After weeks of humiliation by these arrogant Turks, now the governor was trying to strip him of his faith in his religion.

"It is God's will that as the Jew begot the Christian, so the Christian, in turn, has begotten the Muslim, so that the one true faith, refined and perfected, is now ready to be spread throughout the world to every human being."

He made it all sound so simple, so logical, thought Antonio. His eyes unconsciously darted to Seraglio, who, sensing his plea, sprang to his friend's aid.

"Governor, it is true, we Christians have engaged in much internal strife."

The governor nodded in agreement, as Seraglio seemed to be proving his point.

"But answer me this," he continued. "You predict that, in the end, the God of Islam will be the one true God of all peoples. Why, then, eight hundred years after the death of Muhammed, does our God still reign in the hearts of so many people? Why are the Western kingdoms relentlessly growing in power? While you Turks have finally destroyed what was left of the sickly Byzantine Empire, hardly more than the city of Constantinople, the

Moors, who are Islamic, are inexorably being pushed out of Spain and now retain little more than their capital city of Granada. Is it not true that Islam's attempts to expand eastward have been successfully resisted by the Hindu people there? And if the followers of Islam are truly God's chosen people, his kingdom on earth—why did God not save you from the Mongol hordes that ravaged Islam just two hundred years ago, nearly destroying it? This proves that God does not favor Islam at all."

"It is true that no civilization has suffered more grievously in such a short time as our forebears, the Seljuqs, did at the hands of the great Genghis Khan. In forty years the Mongols almost wrecked seven hundred years of progress and slaughtered half of Islam." The governor's face shook with passion. "But Islam survived this test and now Allah has placed His servant, Sultan Muhammed II, on His earth to deal the infidels their final defeat and unite the world forever in worshipping only Him."

Antonio, inspired by Seraglio's forceful arguments, reentered the debate.

"Governor, God's will is like the wind. Though we cannot see it, we know the wind is there because we can see the motion it creates as it stirs and scatters the leaves. God makes His presence known by the way He moves men to accomplish great things. And the greatest of those is man's civilization—his sprawling cities, vibrant commerce, majestic places of worship, great universities, productive manufactories, his science and invention, and most of all, his laws and his morals. But all of these are dependent on his wise government, which determines if his civilization is saved or destroyed, and his religion, which determines whether his soul is saved or destroyed.

"The Mongols came and ravaged Islam because it was too weak to resist. In Islam your government is controlled by your religion, making your government—your sole protector in this world—weak. After they trampled Islam, the Mongols swept on to the gates of Vienna. There, they met the West, where our governments are separated from our religion. Our worldly power defeated the Mongols. So you see, Governor, the world is not as you say it is—no matter how much you want it to be so."

The two men fell silent as Seraglio attempted to translate Antonio's eloquent words, mindful of the governor's warning to translate accurately. When he had finished, time seemed to stand still. Finally, the governor's deep voice broke the silence.

"You would be right, if a strong civilization here on earth were God's aim, but He cares only for the obedience of his believers. As you said, he cares not for this world."

"Then, I ask you again, why does the sultan covet the world? Why can he not see that the victory he harvests today, will sow the seeds of his bitter defeat tomorrow?

"When the West sank into the abyss of the Dark Ages, Islam preserved and improved upon the knowledge of the ancients. But we have emerged from the darkness, reclaimed our heritage, and improved upon it greatly, leaving Islam behind. The outcome is inevitable. Our civilization will defeat yours because governments can wage wars more effectively than a religion. Islam has become the handmaiden of Christianity because you have failed to progress as we have. Earlier, you ridiculed the Jewish rabbis for perverting their religion with restrictive laws—leading to the rise of Christianity. But do you not see? Your *mollas* have perverted your religion with their own set of restrictive laws."

Antonio's firm gaze met the governor's. Neither man looked away.

"It does not have to be that way, you know," said Antonio solemnly.

Satisfied that he had won the debate, he watched Seraglio as his friend translated.

The governor, wearied by his guests' relentless arguments, leaned back on his pillow and looked skyward, as if asking Allah to intervene.

"You are wrong, Captain." He slowly rose to his feet and straightened his robes.

"You still do not understand. We seek only to obey the will of Allah, as it is written in the Koran. So, you see, it *does* have to be that way. The sultan is God's servant on earth, doing God's will, and that is that."

The governor then did something unexpected. He walked around the large table, cluttered with the remains of their well-eaten meal, and embraced Antonio.

"You fight well, Venetian—better with words than the sword." He smiled at Seraglio. "And you do indeed speak truth fluently, my Greek friend."

He walked toward the door and reaching it, turned to face his guests.

"I have arranged for you to have your own cell, good food, and clean water. May God grant that your ransom be paid or I will truly regret ordering your deaths."

As he pulled the door open he turned one more time. "Seraglio, you will be pleased to know your new cell has only one bucket in it. Do not eat from it."

With an ironic grin, he departed. Alone, Antonio and Seraglio looked at each other, still wondering what the governor's aim had been.

They were escorted to their new cell. Now there was plenty of room. The next day, when the guards brought their meal, it was warm and edible. But as they ate the savory cubes of meat and fresh vegetables they were haunted with guilt. They knew the governor was feeding their fellow prisoners barely enough to keep them alive.

Exactly one week later, the governor summoned Antonio and Seraglio for another sumptuous meal. Again, they ate first and then talked.

"When we last met, you claimed that your civilization was superior to ours." The governor's face was grave. "How is it superior?"

"From what I understand, in Islam's sultanates the power to rule is not shared but invested in one man only—it is absolute. It is possible for a bad king or prince to remain in power, unchallenged. In the West, monarchs also rule with great authority but they share power with nobles, who own a large portion of the land. These nobles often depose a bad king and replace him with someone more capable and acceptable to the people."

"In our civilization, bad sultans are usually assassinated," said the governor, casually, dismissing Antonio's response.

"Perhaps," said Antonio. "Here, your holy men are in league with your leaders and, together, they control the people. In the West, church and temporal leaders sometimes disagree. Often, the church courageously reins in monarchs who commit sins against their subjects. Once, the pope even made the Holy Roman Emperor do penance barefoot in the snow for a week."

"That could never happen here," shot back the governor. "It would only confuse our people and could lead to dangerous thinking."

Antonio smiled, "In our world a man can set his own course, following the example set by his monarch. In yours it would mean death. Our people's discontent leads to invention and discovery. In your world, nonconformity is discouraged—even fatal."

"But we must maintain order or else, with so many diverse peoples, we would quickly become divided and vulnerable again—as we were when the Mongols struck. Tell me, Captain, which state of all those in the West has the best government?"

"Venice," said Antonio proudly.

"I thought you would say that," said the governor. "Why Venice?"

"We are ruled by laws, jealously guarded and refined by men who are elected by the people they represent and who are, for the most part, incorruptible."

"I am told you have no king or prince."

"That is true. Our duke, or doge as we call him, derives his position for life after election by his peers in the Great Council. He is one of the nobility. In Venice, the dogeship cannot be passed on from father to son. In this way, we avoid the inevitable wars brought about by arguments over rights of succession—we have replaced the sword with the ballot. No other country has such a system for determining its ruler."

"When a sultan dies, his eldest son and rightful heir immediately has his brothers killed to avoid that problem." The governor continued, "Yours is not the first republic. There have been others before, in Athens and Rome, and they did not endure."

"Venice has been a republic for nearly eight hundred years. The Athenian and Roman republics lasted for only a few years until they were destroyed by ambitious men who became too powerful and ruled as despots—like your sultan."

"But how, then, has Venice managed to remain a republic for so long?"

"By recognizing that the greatest threat to our freedom comes from within—not from foreign enemies. No one is permitted to have too much power, not even the doge."

"So, Venice endures because no one Venetian is too powerful? What about the Church?" asked the governor. "It must have more power than any man in Venice since there is no strong monarch to resist the will of the holy men."

"Ah," said Antonio. "That is the beauty of Venice. Our first religion is business. We believe in God, but we do not allow our religious beliefs to force us to do things that make no sense. In this, we are different from many other Christian countries or yours. Other states despise us for our independence and pragmatism and question the depth of our religious faith, but it is the Venetian way and it has made us the envy of the Western world."

"Why are you worthy of envy?"

"For one thing, we welcome foreigners—they are good for business. And unlike you, we value our women. We treat the Jews as valuable members of our society; they may even become citizens with almost as many rights as Christians."

"I presume you have only one wife, Captain. How many children do you have?"

"I have one wife, yes, but no children . . . yet." Antonio sighed, thinking of Isabella.

"What! No children? I have four wives and twenty-seven children. What civilization can long survive without many children? I knew I would find your weakness sooner or later," he laughed.

They talked until it grew late. Finally, the governor grew tired and announced their time had ended. Before he left them, he told them they would be required on the same night each week, as long as they remained captives in his castle. Antonio asked if they could be reunited with their fellow prisoners but the governor refused to permit it.

Later that night, when they were alone in their cell, Antonio noticed that Seraglio was uncharacteristically quiet. They sat together, in silence, for a long time.

"What do you think the governor is up to, Antonio? Why has he singled us out for better treatment than the others? Why will he not allow us to see them?"

"I have been asking myself the same thing, Seraglio. He must want something."

"He will wait until we are properly prepared before he makes his request. A snake coats his victim in saliva before he attempts to consume it," replied Seraglio.

"There is something else bothering you, Seraglio. What is it?"

"I was just thinking about what it will be like to live in Venice. I know so little about the place that will become my home—the place where I will probably die."

"What would you like to know?"

He thought for a moment.

"First, why does the city of Venice not appear on any ancient Roman maps?"

Antonio closed his eyes as he slowly leaned back against the hard stone cell wall.

"In Roman times, Venice did not exist. Then, the Rialto Islands were uninhabited, but eventually hardy fishermen, who worked their abundant fishing grounds and used the salt pans there to preserve the fish, settled there. From the beginning they were dependent on their boats to trade their fish and salt for essentials from the mainland.

"As the Roman Empire declined over the centuries, eventually, it was too weak to resist the barbarian invasions that swept down the Italian peninsula from the Alps, beginning in the fifth century. The people who lived on land bordering on the lagoon that surrounded those islands began to flee there as a place of refuge. Soon the settlements prospered and grew, so that when Attila ravaged the mainland, some refugees elected to remain on the islands instead of returning to their ruined towns and farms.

"The island folk were always fearful of their more powerful barbarian mainland neighbors, so they helped the Byzantines when they reclaimed part of Italy. In exchange for military protection and trading privileges, the islanders became subjects of the Byzantine emperor and adherents to the Eastern Orthodox Church—rather than the pope in Rome. They called themselves Venetians. The word comes from the Latin *Veni etiam,* which means, 'Come back again.'"

"How do you know so many details about these events that took place so long ago?" asked Seraglio. "Do all Venetian patricians learn these things?"

"Every male child is well educated in the history of our Republic. We believe this is essential if we are to preserve our way of life." Antonio's tone became grave as he continued, "How can a republic long endure if its citizens forget the intentions, exertions, and most of all, the sacrifices of their forebears? How can we improve our institutions if we forget our mistakes and transgressions, our achievements and glorious victories?"

"Who taught these things to you?"

"Our family has always had a tradition that a grandfather passes this heritage on to his grandsons. My grandfather Lorenzo Ziani was my tutor. His words were a source of inspiration—a calling that I could not deny. Since then, I have lived each day as though the spirits of my forebears were watching me, expecting me to continue the work they could not finish before they died. It is a great responsibility."

Seraglio was struck by his friend's seriousness. Venice had found a way to instill her people with an unwavering sense of destiny. Seraglio surmised that this, above all else, was Venice's secret weapon—her "Greek fire." But it was infinitely more powerful because it strengthened her every endeavor in war *and* peace, yet, unlike Greek fire, this secret weapon could never be copied or stolen.

Antonio continued, "Venice was officially founded in 726 when the Byzantine emperor ordered all religious icons and images destroyed as idolatrous. Venetians were outraged. The pope, in Rome, also opposed this action. It was then that we cast off any remaining ties to Byzantium and the Eastern Orthodox Church. Now without a country, we formed our own government, created a dukedom, and elected our first *dux* or duke."

"I have heard that Venice is like Constantinople in many ways," said Seraglio.

"From its earliest times Venice modeled herself on Constantinople—not Rome, like all the other Italian cities. Our Basilica of San Marco was modeled after your Church of the Apostles. More important, we emulated Byzantium's commercial prowess built on trade backed up by sea power. We soon produced a fleet of privately owned ships to serve us in peacetime and war and a strong naval tradition to provide brave sailors and marines to man them. Throughout history, Venice has fought many battles on land, but it has been her navy that has protected her in times of her greatest danger.

"Our warships and the waters separating the Rialto Islands from the mainland, more than two miles apart at their closest point, have prevented attacks by the waves of invaders who have swept down the Italian peninsula. The Goths, Ostrogoths, Huns, and Lombards all wisely chose not to invade the islands of the Rialto.

"Even the great Charlemagne traded recognition as Holy Roman Emperor by the Byzantine emperor, legitimizing his rule over the rest of Italy, in return for his pledge to guarantee Venice's independence. For the next sixty years, the Franks occupied themselves with other conquests in Germany but finally Charlemagne's son, Pépin, made the first serious attempt to take Venice by force. Our small but intrepid navy and the disease that ravaged his army in the swampy lagoon defeated him.

"Its commander and one of our greatest doges, Agnello Participazio led the transformation of Venice from a town of mud houses to a city, built on land drained, buttressed from the sea, and set on wooden pilings driven deep into the mud."

"You mean to say that Venice is built upon pilings?"

"Yes, Seraglio—millions of them.

"Soon, our canals began to take shape, transforming the Rialto's irregularly shaped islands into a labyrinth of sedate waterways and over one hundred bulwarked islands, connected by small footbridges. A wide waterway, the serpentine Grand Canal, divided our city in two. Under Participazio's rule, the Doges' Palace and Church of San Marco were begun, as was the huge Piazza San Marco on the island of Rialto, which became the seat of the government and the doge's residence.

"Now, with our sovereignty assured, we sought to increase our status in the world. We replaced St. Theodore, our traditional patron saint, with the more venerable St. Mark. In 828, Venice became the defender of his remains when they were stolen from their resting place in Alexandria, Egypt, by two Venetian adventurers and smuggled back to Venice to rest in the church that bears his name. This gave rise to our battle cry 'For St. Mark and Venice!' but more important, it legitimized Venice as a first-rate city-state watched over by one of the greatest patron saints in Christendom."

"But why was it necessary for Venice to possess the saint's actual remains?"

"You see, Seraglio, Venice had always suffered from her more modern origins. She is not nearly as old as Rome or the other great Italian cities. For many years Venice sat astride East and West: a Byzantine fief presided over by a Roman pope. We needed to be independent of both East and West. We needed a unifying cause.

"Ever since those merchants brought St. Mark's remains to Venice, our doge has been charged with protecting them. To do this, he must bring together the political, military, *and* religious enthusiasm of the people in times of dire need. No one in all of Italy has such a relic to unite and inspire the hearts and minds of his people like that."

"I am beginning to understand. A republic intent on keeping its government and its religion separate requires a supremely noble cause, like preserving the sanctity of one of Christendom's most revered saints, to break down that wall you have built so carefully, in those rare times when the very existence of your Republic is endangered and every means must be employed to ignite the people's will to defend it."

"Exactly!

"By the end of the first millennium we had built on almost all of the remaining land on the Rialto Islands that had previously been used to grow food. Our fisherman had to range farther to the south to catch enough fish to supply the city's needs. But we could not rely solely on fish for food. A reliable supply of grain was essential to our survival. In peacetime, we could procure grain from our nearby mainland territory or by trade with more distant provinces. During war, however, our *terra firma* lands were vulnerable to invasion and could be closed to us by enemy blockade. Even in peacetime we could not depend on an adequate supply of food without tapping the rich breadbasket of Dalmatia, to the southeast, and the fishing grounds of the lower Adriatic. Similarly, we could not depend on the perpetually warring northern Italian city-states for wood, pitch, and other naval supplies. To protect the trade that was our lifeblood, we had to have unfettered access to the lower Adriatic. So began our expansion from a city to an empire."

Seraglio was uncomfortable as he sat silently in the dark, shifting his small body against the rounded stones on the floor and walls of the cell.

"It is still hard for me to envision an entire city built upon wooden pilings driven into the mud. After all, Constantinople was built upon solid rock."

"It was done, Seraglio. It required vision and courage, persistence and ingenuity. You might say that Venice was built twice. First, to claim her footprint from the sea, her wooden roots reached deep through the mud into the bedrock below. Then, to carve her silhouette from the sky, she rose up with her impressive palazzi, churches, and public buildings. It took centuries to do it but you should see her now. She is magnificent."

"I look forward to that day with great anticipation."

Each smiled, unseen by the other in the darkness. Antonio's story of Venice's founding would be the first of many he would tell during their long captivity.

.   .   .

The day had passed without much conversation. It was stifling in their cell even though it was sheltered from the sun's rays. It had only one small window, too far above them to provide even a wisp of fresh air. Many times Seraglio had weighed how he would ask his question. Finally, he could no longer suppress his curiosity.

"Antonio, tell me, why is there bad blood between you and Captain Soranzo?"

Antonio sighed and looked long at the ceiling, as he searched for how to begin.

"Forty years ago my grandfather, Lorenzo Ziani, was the head of our family. The Zianis were known throughout the world as preeminent merchants. Our ships plied the Mediterranean and farther, some voyaging as far as the Black Sea, the Baltic, and to that terrible destroyer of ships, the storm-plagued North Sea, in search of trade.

"The House of Ziani controlled large shares of the fine-glass market to the north and salt to the east and west. After selling our cargoes at handsome profits in a hundred ports in Britain, France, Spain, Germany, the Levant, and even Muscovy, our vessels would return to Venice laden with steel tools, weapons, and textiles of all descriptions. Our ships roved from Rostock to Flanders and Lisbon and Damascus. We also controlled part of the spice trade from India and China through its termini in Egypt and Syria.

"You see, Seraglio, to succeed, a trader must be able to do two things well. First, he must possess that rare instinct—to know how to buy cheap and sell dear. But that is just the half of it. Nothing has greater influence on the price people will dare to ask or be willing to pay than the amount of a good that is readily available in relation to the people's demand for it. Second, you must have the means to influence that availability—and that is what my grandfather, like his forebears, excelled at. My family has always invested in the best ships, captains, and crews to enable us to move goods faster and more reliably than our competitors. Whenever demand suddenly rose in a port . . . we were among the first to be there to sell. When it plummeted . . . you can bet we were also there, buying up as much as we could find.

"But no one has unlimited resources, except perhaps a king or the pope. Because it required many chests of gold ducats to purchase the goods to fill our ships, my grandfather always sought out partners to share the costs, the risks, and, in return, the profits of our ventures. For every great Venetian family engaged in trade there is another engaged in assembling the ducats to make the trading venture possible—the banker. One cannot survive without the other. You might say that, together, they make their daily bread. By law, a Venetian citizen is permitted to invest in a *com pane*—a 'bread sharer' enterprise. Returns on high-risk voyages can be up to a thousand percent while investors can make twenty-percent interest on their loans to the trading partners."

"But," asked Seraglio, "why would your grandfather not employ his own funds?"

"In time, you will understand, my friend," replied Antonio. "Let me explain.

"To succeed, each merchant must master naval architecture, know the tides, geography, foreign tongues, and how to spot shoddy or counterfeit goods. He must know how to load and unload ships and how to pick good and trustworthy men to crew them. Most of all, he must be able to attract clever, honest men to captain his ships. Each of these captains must be a trader in his own right—an extension of the merchant, himself. Finally, he must have instinct—whether prices are likely to rise or fall. With this, the merchant can divine the future, knowing when and where to buy and sell.

"The investor, on the other hand, must know how to raise money quickly, at the lowest interest rates, how to provide marine insurance and how to structure each contract so that he and his merchant partner assume a minimum of risk while reaping the greatest share of the profits possible. I have never met a man with the capacity to excel equally in both. If my grandfather could not—no one could!

"One day, Alvise Soranzo, the captain's grandfather, approached my grandfather with a problem. He had secured a coveted contract to supply the Republic with that most precious of all naval stores—the tall pine trees that grow straight as an arrow, that are required for a war galley's masts. The government had been sourcing them from the lower Adriatic, but constant warfare in Dalmatia with the Hungarians had prevented their harvest and export. The war had also made the goods normally traded for the tree trunks almost worthless to the beleaguered populace there, who wanted only food, wine, and military stores. The Republic was forced to desperately secure them elsewhere.

"Soranzo had a source—and what a source! The Hanseatic League, through the port of Danzig, would not only supply the masts, but they would pay handsomely for the fine goods that a ship sent to retrieve them would bring. Soranzo's problem was that the masts were for the Republic's newest galleys. They were so long only a few ships could carry them—one belonged to the House of Ziani. The *Lion* was large enough to carry all forty logs, lashed to her deck, in one trip. Even then, she would be unstable in the rolling swells with the logs stowed on deck, so he had arranged for casks of wine to fill the hold for extra ballast. Soranzo had thought of everything. He even sent his son, Francesco, the captain's father, to accompany the *Lion*. That was the fatal flaw in his plan.

"You see, my grandfather's eldest child, Caterina, was almost eleven when the first of her four brothers, my father, was born. For a long time, Lorenzo had resigned himself to his wife's inability to produce a son. At first he nurtured and taught her to be a merchant—just like a son. This sort of thing was unheard of then as it is now, but a powerful merchant like Lorenzo Ziani would not be told what to do. Once my father was born, he, of course, became first in line to head the House of Ziani. Caterina became my grandfather's prized possession—to be married off to a rich patrician.

"At the time, Caterina was thirty-one and had a face like the Madonna and the charms of Venus. They say there was not a man in Venice, young or old, who would not have fallen for her. But alas, the men she loved were not rich enough for my grandfather's taste, and the ones he favored, she rejected. Exasperated, he sent her to Bruges to learn the lace business.

"Apparently, Caterina and Francesco Soranzo had been eyeing each other for some time. When the *Lion* called on Antwerp en route to Danzig, my father, who was aboard, was not surprised to see that she was on the quay to greet them. He told me that Caterina and Francesco were inseparable for the entire week they were in Antwerp. When the *Lion* and Francesco sailed for Danzig, Caterina cried bitter tears. It was the first time my father had ever seen her cry. It was then that he knew she was in love with Francesco Soranzo.

"The voyage to Danzig was easy enough. The great hulking tree trunks were waiting on the pier when the *Lion* docked. The efficient crew off loaded their cargo—about twenty tons of salt, fine Murano glass, Bruges lace, and some military supplies purchased by the Teutonic Knights. My father and Francesco had become friends on the long voyage from Venice. It was while they were in Danzig that Francesco confessed his love for Caterina. My father was delighted with the prospect of not losing his sister to a stranger but instead, gaining such a fine brother-in-law.

"Years later my father confided in me that Francesco was so possessed by Caterina's charms that his mind was barely on his work. He was off buying gifts for her when he should have been on board helping to ensure the cargo was properly accounted for, since his family had contracted with the Germans for the logs.

"After casks of wine and heavy ingots of lead and iron were placed in the hold to provide ballast, it was time to load the eighty-foot-long logs. My father always said that he had argued that the ropes used to secure them were not thick enough, but the German foreman insisted they were, saying he had used ropes like that a hundred times before. Francesco agreed with him. A few days later, they sailed for home.

"Caterina had made my father promise to stop for one day at Antwerp to take on water and stores for the long and unpredictable trip that would carry them far out into the Atlantic until they reached the coast of Spain on their way back to Venice.

"From the time they arrived, Caterina was irritable and cried inconsolably when they all had dinner that night. It was as though he no longer knew her. Perhaps it was her strange transformation that had caused Francesco to change too. He seemed to easily lose patience with Caterina and even with my father. It was as though he wanted to be rid of them both. His only desire, it seemed, was to sail for Venice on the morning tide. To end the unpleasantness, my father suggested that they all turn in early for the night, but he was certain that Caterina and Francesco had made a pact to meet again later, in secret.

"The next morning, Caterina shocked my father by informing him that she was returning with them to Venice on the *Lion* and that she would occupy his cabin, one of just three on board, the others belonging to the captain and Francesco. My father begged her not to come with them, fearing my grandfather would be furious, but she would not hear of it. Francesco supported her. My father was overwhelmed and finally relented.

"At first, the voyage was uneventful. Caterina remained in her cabin, a recluse, taking all of her meals there. The cabin boy who waited on her said she was seasick the whole way. My father thought that was odd since the seas were not rough and she had always been a good sailor. That was the clue that made my father realize there might be another reason why she suddenly wanted to return to Venice.

"On the third day, they had just passed the familiar sight of Cherbourg harbor when a storm began to rage. Within an hour, they were in the clutches of a full gale. Men prayed for their lives as the ship was driven toward the rocky coast. With the *Lion* in danger of foundering, the captain tried to save the ship by beaching her.

"The fierce seas tossed the *Lion* about like a toy boat in a child's bath. Just a hundred yards from shore, as she heeled over hard to port, a huge wave crashed over her side. Suddenly, the ropes lashing the massive logs on the starboard deck, high up in the air, gave way, releasing them in an avalanche. In an instant, the ship was doomed. As the *Lion* rolled over and began to sink, everyone on deck was thrown into the sea. The strong swimmers and those who could grab hold of something to keep them afloat made it to shore. My father and Francesco swam near the wreck, but there was no sign of Caterina. She had gone down with the ship, apparently without ever leaving her cabin. It was a disaster—for my father, my grandfather, and for Alvise Soranzo. If things had ended there it would have been bad enough, but soon after, the recriminations began.

"It started with the marine insurance Soranzo had arranged for the venture. Usually my grandfather had always used his own insurer, but Alvise Soranzo had insisted on using his as a condition of the partnership. Now they refused to cover no more than half of the loss because, they said, based upon accounts by witnesses to the wreck, the cargo had been improperly secured. Soon the two partners began to argue about who had caused the shipwreck. Of course, it was the storm, but men always prefer to blame each other rather than nature for their misfortunes.

"The friendship between my father and Francesco was broken. Each was forced by his domineering father to accuse the other of incompetence—they both played their roles brilliantly. Poor Caterina was almost forgotten. At first the former partners sought redress in the courts with the insurers. Later, they brought suit against each other. Seeing that the courts, as usual, would likely force them to compromise, my grandfather and Alvise Soranzo each dropped their suits. They decided, instead, to seek vengeance on the field of battle, which was for them the world of business. From that point onward, our families have fought each other as viciously as Christians fight Turks—scraping and conniving for every advantage—to gain at the other's expense, each seeking to dominate the other and relegate his enemy to irrelevance in the world of Venetian business.

"To be honest, Seraglio, as long as I can remember, I have never had much to do with the Soranzos. When I learned that Marco Soranzo was to serve under me, I saw it as an opportunity to end this long-standing hatred and the open conflict it has sometimes caused. Our grandfathers hated each other. My father, Vincenzo, and his erstwhile friend, Francesco Soranzo, continued the mutual acrimony. I thought I could be different. I thought I could be better than them—stronger than them. But I did not realize how the cruel hand of fate could remorselessly push me back on the path taken by my father and his father before him. I think, perhaps, it is man's destiny to hate and be hated. Without hatred in this world, how else could a man become so desperate that he would turn to God for his last hope of salvation?"

8

The Mission

That morning when he had received an urgent summons to meet with the doge and his Signoria, Captain Soranzo told his wife that he would be home in time for their evening meal. Now, as Doge Foscari looked at his counselor charged with the financial affairs of the government, Signor Guardi, and nodded, he was not so sure.

"Captain Soranzo, last week we received a list from the sultan of the Ottoman Turks with the names of the *nobili* he is holding as hostages and his price for their release. Since he insists that every man's ransom be paid or else he will execute them all, the Senate has authorized you to pay their ransoms with funds from the state treasury. We shall settle accounts with the individual families later."

"It is unthinkable that a family would not pay for the release of a father or son or brother," interjected the doge, as he looked at the others in the room.

Those who disagreed with the decision sat in silence. They had not wanted to pay, fearing it would encourage the sultan to attack again to take more hostages to ransom, but they had been overruled by the majority, who all had relatives in the sultan's prison. Once the decision had been made, every man was required to publicly support it.

Guardi continued. "A fast merchant ship is waiting in the Bacino di San Marco for you to assume command and sail with the tide.

"The ship has no rowers—only sails. We wanted to be sure you would have adequate space below deck to transport all the ransomed men."

Guardi produced a tan leather-covered folio and handed it carefully to Soranzo.

"Inside are all of the ransom notes written by the hostages in their own hands," said the doge, his voice burdened with sadness. "By the omissions we have concluded that more than sixty patricians perished at Constantinople, including six Contarini, five Trevisan, three Balbi, two Mocenigo, and two Morosini."

"Sixty," Soranzo repeated loudly, as he opened the book to examine its contents, but Guardi quickly cleared his throat, demanding attention. Soranzo closed it and looked up, careful to conceal his annoyance at being interrupted.

"I have taken the time to examine each ransom note," said Guardi. "There are a total of fifty-eight. The sultan has demanded a combined ransom of almost twenty-six thousand ducats for their release." His ashen face showed the strain. His treasury would be severely reduced until repayments from the families could replenish it.

"You have no more than an hour and a half to catch the tide," interjected the captain-general of the seas abruptly. "You had better leave at once."

"Do I have any other instructions?" Soranzo asked respectfully, uncomfortable with the lack of details about what he was to do once he arrived in Constantinople. A score of questions echoed in his head, but he knew that they expected him to faithfully carry out his orders and to think for himself if they failed to provide specific guidance. His question was answered only with silent stares. The meeting was finished.

As Soranzo left the chamber he heard footsteps following closely behind him.

"Captain Soranzo, I do not have to tell you that this mission is crucial to the Republic—and to your career. Do not fail to bring back every man whose name is contained in that book. Do not let the Turks retain a single one. If any has died, you must return with his body, but in that case, you must endeavor to pay no ransom. At the very least, try to pay less than the original amount demanded by the sultan."

That is easy for you to say, thought Soranzo, as he saluted his superior.

"We will be lucky to get them out, alive or dead, Captain-General."

"I suppose you are right, Captain, but you must make them work for it. Show them that we will not bow easily to their rapacious demands."

Soranzo nodded his agreement.

"One more thing, Captain. Give me back the folio. I will ensure it gets safely to your cabin on board the ship, along with chests containing the gold."

Soranzo would have to wait to inspect the folio's contents. He had not had time to see if it contained a ransom note from Antonio Ziani. Their conversation finished, he turned and walked speedily to the stairs leading down and out of the Doges' Palace.

There would be just enough time for him to give instructions to his cousin, Cosimo, who would manage the family business while he was away and to say good-bye to his wife, Beatrice, and his adopted son, Enrico. He hurried the short way home, his mind racing. As he walked into the garden he could smell the savory aroma of the evening meal. He was hungry but there was no time to eat if he was to sail with the tide.

He slipped through the side door that led to the main room on the ground floor. There, several offices ran across the back wall. Normally, the main floor of a Venetian's palazzo would be filled with goods of all descriptions, but the Ca' Soranzo belonged to investors. Their commodity was gold. They did not need space to store barrels, crates, and sacks—just ducats on their way to and from the bank. He went directly to where his cousin Cosimo, his uncle's eldest son, would, as usual, be poring over the accounts. He was better with numbers than people. As Giovanni's second, he was a perfect business partner. There was not a percentage he could not shave or pad or a payment he could not delay. Most of all, he was loyal and possessed the one attribute Giovanni admired most in men engaged in business—he was greedy in his business dealings on behalf of the family but never for his own personal gain. Giovanni trusted him with the family's money.

"Giovanni! How was your meeting with the doge?"

"I have been ordered to go to Constantinople to ransom back the prisoners."

"I tell you, Giovanni, your star is rising."

Having little time, Giovanni abruptly changed the subject.

"Cosimo, I must go and pack my things. While I am away, I want you to make quiet inquiries with all of your associates. Find out who the Zianis' investors are on their principal trade routes. Also, find out how much they are paying for marine insurance and who provides it. Finally, have Vettor follow Giorgio Ziani. Tell him to be discreet. I want to know what his vice is."

"That last request for my brother will be most difficult," protested Cosimo.

"Why?" shot back Giovanni.

"Not every man has a vice," he said with finality.

"Is that so? Would you be shocked, then, to learn that I know even *you* have one?"

The blood drained from Cosimo's face; perspiration formed on his brow.

"You think I do not know about that little mare who is not much more than half your age that you take for a ride twice a week? What would your wife say about that? I will not even ask where the money comes from to pay for that cozy apartment near the Fondaco dei Turchi you have her stabled in."

Cosimo knew he was innocent of misappropriating the family's money for the apartment—he had scrupulously used only his own funds. But he had been caught red-handed keeping a mistress—and she was younger than a respectable age—just fifteen. He tried to change the subject, as though he could erase it from his cousin's memory.

"Do you want me to do anything else, cousin?"

"Yes. Here is what I want Vettor to do. . . ."

When he had finished, Giovanni patted Cosimo on the cheek, eliciting a weak grin. He had been hard on Cosimo, but he had no time for anything but blind obedience. Cosimo could be dangerous when he thought too much. His capacity for loyalty and selective greed was only exceeded by his lack of courage.

"I must be off," he said as he turned to leave.

"Giovanni."

He turned back toward Cosimo.

"How did you know?—About the girl?"

"How do you think I knew Vettor was the right man to spy on Giorgio Ziani?"

Soranzo turned to go upstairs. He was the head of the family and Cosimo would obey him. They both knew that Giovanni would never make good on his threat to tell Cosimo's wife about his infidelity, but the point was made. Giovanni used sensitive information like this to hold him tightly in his iron grip, always making sure Cosimo's first aim was to please him. He commanded his family like his ship.

After ordering his servant to bring his sea trunk down to the street, Soranzo climbed the back stairs, unnoticed, and went straight to his room to gather his remaining personal belongings and say good-bye to his wife and adopted son. When Giovanni had finished, he rushed back downstairs and out to the street, where two servants were struggling to lift his heavy sea trunk onto a cart.

Soranzo proceeded straight to his ship, boarding it with a half hour to spare. After inspecting the veteran crew and meeting the officers, he gave the order to make sails. As the crew sprang to action, Soranzo leaned against the rail and gazed out over the water. The city looked serene in the twilight. To the west he could see the waning copper sun just above the red-tiled rooftops and blazing golden domes of the churches. How different his mission to Constantinople would be this time, he thought, as he inhaled the fresh sea air. He could faintly smell the evening meals, cooking in a thousand homes, wafting across the glassy surface of the water. As he lowered his eyes to watch the reflection of the city's lamps beginning to sprinkle the water with bursts of orange light he suddenly remembered the folio. The ship began to slowly move away from the quay and into the lagoon. With nothing more to do on deck, he turned from the rail, and went to his cabin.

In the privacy of his seagoing sanctuary he placed the book on his table and opened it to the last page, knowing the efficient Guardi would have bound the letters in alphabetical order. There it was! The name he had hoped would be there— Zeno. Ziani was dead. But he had to be sure. For the next half hour, he poured through the book, carefully reading each page several times, running his fingers over the smooth surfaces—fifty-eight pages in all—each with a name at the bottom and Antonio Ziani's nowhere to be found. He allowed himself a sigh as the tenseness in his neck muscles relaxed.

Weeks later, one chilly morning, his ship passed what he supposed was the spot where his brother had drowned the previous November. As he watched the ship's wake cut a jagged white furrow in the choppy gray water, he dropped a single silver *lira piccola* into the sea and silently saluted Marco's memory.

It was a new year—seven months since the fall of Constantinople. Antonio and Seraglio had dined once each week with the governor. Despite their heated debates, the governor provided them with their own cell, good food, and clean water.

This night began like all the others, but soon they could tell that the governor was not himself. He seemed nervous. Seraglio waited until they finished eating to speak.

"Governor, you do not seem to be yourself tonight. Is something troubling you?"

Abdullah Ali stood, as he always did, before saying something important.

"A Venetian ship has arrived in Constantinople. It has come with the sultan's ransom and to carry the released prisoners back to Venice."

They looked at each other. Soon we will be free! they both thought. But why, then, was the governor so morose? Could it be that he will miss us? thought Seraglio.

"I have received the names of those whose ransoms have been paid," the governor stated plainly as he riveted his eyes on Antonio's.

"Captain Ziani, your name is not on the list. I am sorry."

The governor's words hit Antonio like a blow from a heavy mace. Seraglio sunk to his knees, devastated.

"But I wrote my ransom letter like all the others," Antonio protested. "Why was it not delivered? What will happen to us?"

The governor broke away from Antonio's piercing stare and looked at Seraglio. The tension in the room was unbearable. He was about to reveal if they would live or die.

"It matters not what happened to your letter now. But do not despair. I have decided to do something I never thought I would do," he said, wiping his brow with the sleeve of his white robe, staining it with his perspiration.

"I have decided to ask the sultan to spare your lives. If he does, he will exact a heavy price from me. He could even have me killed or enslaved for my insolence." He looked steadily at his two guests, shifting his penetrating gaze from one to the other.

Seraglio fervently thanked the governor for his intercession, but Antonio was not so quick to respond. He remembered what he had thought the first time they had been invited to dine with him. What is his price? Can I afford it? He decided to speak boldly.

"Abdullah Ali, I am deeply touched by your offer, but I am puzzled. Why would you assume such a risk?"

"Our empires are now at war but they will not always be. When we finally defeat you Venetians and there is peace, we shall need wise men like you to help us rule Venice. I think that you are the kind of man we could rely upon to help us."

The governor rose in his usual way and backed toward the door.

"Be patient, my friends. Trust me. Rely upon me for your salvation." His grave countenance melted into a broad smile. "You have no other choice."

He bowed to his two guests and departed.

Back in their cell, Antonio and Seraglio discussed the unexpected news and the governor's offer as they talked in hushed tones late into the night.

"Do you think he can convince the sultan to free us?"

"It is all we can hope for. If he cannot, Seraglio, I fear we are doomed."

Seraglio shook his head as he thought about the governor's precarious position. The sultan was not a man to be challenged—even by a governor. His rule was absolute.

. . .

Abdullah Ali, governor of Rumeli Hisar, rode toward the sultan's camp just beyond the castle walls, two times the distance of an arrow flight away—his Janissary bodyguards insisted on this precaution to prevent assassination attempts.

He rode through the sprawling complex of multicolored tents, each flying a white-crescented red banner, taking the familiar route. When he reached the sultan's tent he dismounted. Recognizing him, the sentries bowed respectfully. Though the sultan now possessed four former imperial palaces in Istanbul—he had recently renamed Constantinople—he had moved his court nearer to the castle in anticipation of the arrival of the Venetian, Genoese, and papal ships carrying gold to exchange for their hostages. Now that the first ship had arrived, he had summoned the governor to plan their negotiating strategy. The methodical and calculating sultan left nothing to chance. As the governor entered the sultan's tent, he saw a sight that never ceased to amaze him.

The tent appeared much larger from the inside than from outside. It was raised up on massive poles cut from tall Lebanese cedars and covered an area the size of a large courtyard. Hundreds of oil lamps lit the inside so brightly that it was indistinguishable from the daylight outside. Not a blade of grass was visible beneath the fine Persian carpets that covered the floor. It was cool, so the sultan did not need the large fans used to circulate air within the enclosure on warm summer days. Always careful, the sultan had holes cut in the tent for the ropes to pass through so the scores of slaves who operated them could be kept safely outside—posing no threat to his personal safety.

In the center sat the young sultan holding court. A score of eunuchs and beautiful young girls from his harem waited on him. His *harem agasi,* the chief black eunuch of the palace, stood guard behind him, arms folded, a menacing scowl on his face. A gaggle of nervous ambassadors and other envoys, garbed in exotic luxury, milled about waiting for their five minutes' audience with the conqueror of Constantinople. As the governor approached, the sultan waved his hand once. His guards immediately cleared the tent.

"Abdullah Ali! Welcome to *my* castle. It is not so grand as yours, but far less expensive, I can assure you." He grinned at his subject through his flowing beard. The governor did not fear him and the sultan knew it. That is why the sultan respected him.

"You sent for me, Master?" The governor bowed as deeply as his large frame would allow him to. His left knee always ached in cool weather since he had fallen from his horse in a victory over the Persians ten years before.

"The Venetian ship has arrived first. Her captain has come to pay the ransom and repatriate the hostages. He told Karadja Pasha that he was not empowered to ransom any man that has died." The sultan grew serious. "What shall we do about that?"

"Master, I would tell him plainly that if his aim is to save a few ducats, we can kill every one of his hostages and he can keep all of his precious gold. Unless, of course, he would like to bring back the prisoners' mutilated corpses, for which we shall only charge him nine-tenths of the ransom." They both laughed.

"I swear you could not possibly have had a mother, Abdullah Ali. You must have been born in a foundry instead of a tent. You are as hard as steel!"

"What shall we do, Master?"

"Tomorrow you shall meet with Captain Soranzo and accept the ransom gracefully—after having every ducat counted to be sure they have not shortchanged us. Then do what you wish about the dead. How many are there?"

"Five, Master. That leaves fifty-three alive, although three are gravely ill. I doubt they will all survive the long voyage back to Venice."

"I hear you have befriended a Venetian patrician."

"Yes, Master, his name is Antonio Ziani."

"Why have you shown such hospitality to infidels?"

"To study the Venetians. I have learned from you how to keep my enemies close."

"That is all well, Abdullah Ali, but to what end?"

"When I received the ransom notes to check against the list of prisoners, I removed one before you had them sent to Venice. It was Captain Ziani's. I decided to pay his ransom myself, placing the captain forever in my debt."

"Do you think that you can buy an infidel's loyalty so easily, Abdullah Ali?"

"If I did not think it so, I would have left him with the other starving prisoners. When I told him that his name was not on the list of hostages to be ransomed, I thought his heart would stop beating in his breast. His little servant prostrated himself and thanked me for putting my life in danger by asking you to allow me to pay their ransom."

The sultan stroked his beard, as he often did when he was deep in thought.

"I suppose he could be useful to us once we take Venice. We shall need cooperative Venetians to help us rule effectively, to tell us all we need to know."

"In the end, he owes his life to me—and ultimately to you, Master."

"Tell him that I made you pay triple his ransom to buy his freedom."

"As you wish, Master."

"Are you sure this Captain Ziani will pay his debt to you when it comes due?"

"Nothing is certain except the will of Allah and the superiority of our arms over the Christians, but I believe he will."

"It is my experience, Abdullah Ali, that time begets ingratitude. Trust me, once Ziani is safely back in Venice, he will forget your courage and your generosity."

"I have anticipated that since I, too, have experienced ingratitude from others.

"I have separated him from the others and fattened him up with sumptuous meals. This difference in his treatment compared to all the other prisoners will make Ziani vulnerable to charges of collaborating with us."

"So blackmail will prevent ingratitude," observed the sultan, nodding his head.

"So it would seem, Master."

"Well done, Abdullah Ali. You are a good student."

"And you, Master, are a good teacher."

The governor bowed deeply and then turned to leave. One never lingered after a successful audience with the sultan.

"Just one more thing."

"Yes, Master."

"It is a clever plan, but I still would not trust a Venetian. They hate us."

"True, but I think this one can be useful."

"Useful to you, perhaps, but I have no use for *any* Venetian—dead or alive."

As he rode back to the castle, Abdullah Ali was satisfied. He had deceived Antonio and Seraglio, and the sultan had complimented his bold plan to secure a reliable ally among the Venetian patriciate. However, as his horse cantered up the path to the castle gate, the sultan's words of caution still echoed in his head.

The day dawned ominously as a depressing rain fell in sheets, making the journey on horseback miserable. By the time Captain Soranzo neared the great castle of Rumeli Hisar he was soaked through to his skin and shivering uncontrollably—hardly a good way to prepare for the tough negotiation he knew awaited him. He turned around to be sure the heavy cart was still keeping up. It would be like these bastards to steal the gold and kill the hostages, he thought. Up ahead, the castle's darkened battlements and towers loomed in the distance, as they disappeared up into the gray mists.

An hour later they reached the castle and rode into the yard. They dismounted and entered the keep while some Janissaries unloaded the heavy chests and carried them inside. Soranzo was led into a large room with a long table pushed against one wall. A big Turk was seated there with his back to him, writing. Four small windows near the ceiling cut the dusty air with their shafts of light as they painted the gray stone floor. The only decorations on the walls were two large Turkish battle flags, like the ones Soranzo had seen waving over the walls of Constantinople after the Turks had taken the city. Finally, the man placed his quill on the table, stood, and turned to greet him.

"I am Abdullah Ali, governor of Rumeli Hisar."

"I am Captain Giovanni Soranzo. I have been sent by Doge Francesco Foscari to pay the ransom the sultan has demanded for the Venetian prisoners. According to my instructions, I am to claim fifty-eight men."

"Unfortunately, Captain, five have since died of wounds sustained in the siege."

"That is most regrettable since I am not authorized to pay a ransom for the dead." He defiantly held the governor's gaze to more forcefully make his point.

"But, Captain, those five men required more expense to care for than the living and we took great pains to embalm their bodies for the long voyage back to Venice. Certainly their grieving families will pay for that?"

Soranzo paused, pretending to consider the governor's question.

"I am authorized to pay only half of *their* ransom—and not a ducat more."

"Then you shall have to return empty-handed. The sultan has ordered me to kill every Venetian prisoner unless you pay the full ransom for each of them, living or dead." He smiled, "But I will risk my neck and accept ninetenths for each of the dead so that you can report to your doge that you skillfully negotiated a good deal from the Turks." Abdullah Ali reached out his fleshy hand toward Soranzo. "We are agreed, then?"

What a hopeless position I have been put in, thought Soranzo. Better to quit now and return with them all. I would rather be known as the man who paid too much than the man whose bad judgment led to the deaths of so many brave and important men. He slowly reached to grasp the governor's hand, but Abdullah Ali suddenly pulled back.

"Captain Soranzo, I have some unexpected good news for you. After we sent the prisoners' ransom notes to your doge, we were amazed to find another Venetian hiding in the city. The sultan will also set him free if you will pay his ransom too."

Soranzo slowly nodded as he saw the trap closing around him.

"And how much will this new prisoner cost me?"

"Exactly one-tenth of the dead prisoners' ransoms. A trifling sum, I am sure you will agree. Perhaps you know this man. His name is Captain Antonio Ziani."

Soranzo leaned hard on the table, trying to maintain his composure.

"Did you say Antonio Ziani is alive?" replied Soranzo, concealing his shock.

"Yes. Do you know him?" said the governor in a businesslike tone.

"Of course, but we heard he was killed."

"Well, now you can rejoice that he lives—unless you will not pay his ransom."

For a fleeting moment Soranzo thought about how sweet it would be to leave Ziani to his fate, but he knew he could not. Months before, when he had left Ziani to his fate in the Golden Horn—that was different. Then, he had to think of the safety of his ship and the passengers and crew. To leave Ziani to the Turks now would be nothing but cold-blooded murder. Even he could not do that. Instead he would crush the man in his own way, at a time of his own choosing.

"I want to see the prisoners before I pay."

"That is impossible. The sultan has forbidden it. Tomorrow fifty-nine Venetians, alive and dead, will be delivered into your care for their return to Venice."

"Very well, Governor, you have obtained every ducat I have brought with me."

"And you, Captain, have saved yourself much trouble, since you have obtained the release of every prisoner, even the dead ones and, of course, Captain Ziani, who you might say, has come back from the dead."

The two men shook hands.

"Now, I shall count the gold."

Giovanni looked at the corner of the room where the Turks had placed the chests.

"Break the seals and count every ducat," the governor ordered his men.

It took four men two hours to finish their tedious task.

"Twenty-five thousand six hundred exactly. The doge is an honest man."

"I will be sure to tell him," replied Soranzo sarcastically.

"Now I must leave you," said the governor as he bowed. "One day maybe we will meet again—perhaps in Venice?"

"Not unless you are there as my hostage."

The governor laughed.

"By the way, your Italian is excellent."

"Yes, but it was not always. My frequent conversations with Captain Ziani helped a good deal. Farewell, Captain Soranzo, may Allah grant you a safe voyage home."

Finished, the governor turned and disappeared through a doorway leaving Soranzo to ponder his parting words. On his long ride back to the ship, he turned them over and over in his mind. Why was Ziani having conversations with the governor?

The downpour had turned into a steady drizzle by the time the crew had finished helping the feeble passengers on board. Though shivering with cold in the January winds, they were warmed by their first taste of freedom in months. Now, with the passengers all safely below, the crew weighed anchor. As Soranzo leaned over the rail of the rolling ship he gazed out at the spot where he had last seen Antonio Ziani. Beyond it, over the roof of the Blachernae Palace, somewhere on the wall, Pietro had perished. He was not looking forward to returning to Venice with the man whose reputation he had so blatantly attacked, now alive. At least the law required that Ziani be quarantined for a week with the other former prisoners as a precaution against spreading the plague.

Two hours later, standing on the fighting castle as the ship slowly crossed the Sea of Marmara, Giovanni Soranzo addressed the former prisoners for the first time.

"Venetian heroes! We thank God for your safe return. You have fought with valor and covered yourselves in glory."

"For Venice and St. Mark!" arose a weak cry from the throats of the former prisoners—reinforced by the crew's loud shouts.

Antonio gazed up at the proud Venetian battle standard, whipped by the wind as it billowed above him. Its winged lion seemed to smile its approval as it welcomed its sons back home. He shifted his eyes to Soranzo, so strong and self-assured on his perch. He had not spent the last seven months languishing in a stinking Turkish prison.

"The doge has ordered the ship stocked with good food and drink. Can your stomachs handle it?" shouted Soranzo.

The former prisoners weakly laughed and soon cheered again as the crew began to break out wine and cheese and baccalà, salted fish, a Venetian specialty. The men quickly broke ranks and began stuffing themselves.

Crewmen brought food down to the three gravely ill men who had remained below deck.

For a brief moment, Antonio thought he saw Soranzo look at him. It was a look of disdain—hardly the admiring glance one would give to a hero. He wondered again what had happened that last day of the siege. Was it he who abandoned us to the Turks?

For the rest of the voyage, Antonio and the others were kept below to keep from interfering with the efficient crew who constantly worked the sails to squeeze every knot of speed from their ship. Two of the sick men were dying. One had already succumbed to dysentery. Time was of the essence. Soranzo stayed in his cabin whenever the passengers were on deck to get fresh air. Only once did he speak to the former prisoners when several of them had requested a meeting with him. It was then that Soranzo learned more about how the Turks had separated Ziani and Seraglio from the other four prisoners in their cell. When the two did not return, the rest thought the Turks had killed them both.

Afterward, alone in his cabin, Soranzo wondered. Why had Abdullah Ali met with Ziani? Why did he single him out from all the other prisoners? And why had the governor lied to him about Ziani being found in Constantinople after the ransom notes had been sent? The prisoners had told him that Ziani had been captured on the day of the fall, not afterward, and he had written his ransom note like all the rest. Was there a possibility he could cast doubt on Ziani's loyalty? He decided he would use the next four weeks of the voyage to devise a new plan to attack his enemy. He would strike first, while Ziani was quarantined on the ship after their arrival in Venice.

Below, in the hold of the big ship, exhausted almost beyond endurance, Antonio Ziani drifted off into a deep, peaceful sleep. He dreamed of Venice, his carefree childhood, and his Isabella. He could not have imagined that his ordeal had only begun.

9

The Homecoming

It was still cold, though the sun had risen an hour ago. Antonio stood at the ship's rail and squinted as he gazed to the north, through the morning mists, at the familiar skyline of his beloved Venice. He had been away more than a year. In the distance he could just make out the majestic red and white brick tower of the Campanile of San Marco, the tallest structure in the city. He smiled as the familiar *basso* voice of *il Marangone,* its massive bronze bell, summoned thousands of Venetian workers to the Arsenal, as it had each morning for as long as he could remember.

The long voyage had been frustrating beyond endurance. He and the other liberated prisoners had spent virtually the entire time in the dank hold of the ship as the crew took precautions to prevent a possible outbreak of the always-dangerous plague. The ship's company had gone ashore the day they had arrived, while Antonio and the other former prisoners had to wait seven more days before they, too, could be reunited with their loved ones. To be so tantalizingly close and yet be unable to leave the ship had been one more cruel torture for them to bear.

On the voyage Antonio had seen Soranzo only once—that first day on deck when he had addressed the ransomed men. It was just as well, thought Antonio, as he looked at the crimson and gold flag hanging limply from the mast. It reminded him, for a moment, of that terrible day in the Golden

Horn, when he had expected to die as the big Venetian ship had hoisted its anchor and slowly sailed off, sealing his fate. If not for Seraglio's quick thinking he would be dead. During the long voyage, two ever-present thoughts, like beacons in the night, had kept him sane. He would soon be reunited with his wife and he had saved a life that was truly worth saving— the irrepressible Seraglio.

Now, for the first time in months, he allowed his mind to caress Isabella. He thanked God that Venetian law required a two-year waiting period before a missing man could be legally declared dead. Otherwise, he was sure, a woman as beautiful as she would have been betrothed to another by now and all of his property redistributed among his relatives, since he had no children of his own. He missed her and longed for her.

Finally, near midday, the crew returned and maneuvered the ship the short distance to the main harbor. They anchored near the Doges' Palace on the Riva degli Schiavoni, the Quay of the Slavs. Soon the elated passengers were spilling out of the small boats used to ferry them to the shore and heading for home. Antonio walked into the Piazzetta between the government buildings on the left and the Doges' Palace on the right. It did not take Antonio long to find someone he knew. The old man was a friend of his father's. He said that Antonio had originally been listed as missing and presumed dead but that Captain Soranzo had reported, on his return, that Antonio was alive and aboard the ship with the others. Antonio also learned that it was rumored that the Turks had separated him from the other prisoners. Having no money, Antonio borrowed a handful of silver coins from the man, with a promise to promptly repay him.

"Seraglio, I must leave you now to go to Isabella and attend to my family's business, which requires my attention after so long an absence. I may be a few days."

Antonio pointed to his right.

"There is an inn, just down there, called the Acropolis. The owner, a man named Nikos, is a friend. Tell him you work for me and he will give you food and lodging. Take this, to provide for any other needs you may have," he said, handing Seraglio three silver *lire piccole,* each equal to one-twentieth of a gold ducat. "Wait for me there. Be patient. I will come for you and then I will show you Venice."

"I will do as you say. Do not concern yourself with me."

Seraglio smiled in response, his teeth peeking through his unkempt beard.

Antonio hurried the short distance to the expanse of the Piazza San Marco. He could see *cittadini* sitting idly talking or lazily walking about in the cool air. He admired the immense expanse of brickwork carpeting the piazza, which caught and reflected the warming rays of the winter sun. The people were oblivious to Antonio and the ordeal he had survived. Life went on in Venice, as it always did, shielded from the horrors of war by her impregnable wall of water. For most of her people, the only reminder that Venice had lost a great battle would have been the lists of names, posted on the Porta della Carta, of those who had died at Constantinople and would never return from that faraway place. By now, even they would be gone, replaced by some other news the government deemed important for the people to know.

He wondered how many of these people, strolling in the piazza, so preoccupied with their own lives, really cared about Constantinople's fate. His eyes roamed past the marble-clad portico of the Basilica of San Marco as he stopped and turned to his right. He fixed them on the imposing edifice of the Doges' Palace. There—they would have cared. He imagined the beehive of activity within its walls as the doge, his counselors, and the Senate had contemplated Venice's plight following Constantinople's fall. There would have been recriminations and disagreements, so typical, whenever powerful men debated the cause and effect of a debacle of that magnitude.

Suddenly, he felt as though a great weight had been lifted from him. Thoughts of politics and war faded. He wanted to see Isabella right now. He could think of nothing but her. He quickened his gait and soon reached the far end of the vast public square. As he wound his way through the familiar maze of narrow streets he had walked thousands of times before, he began to feel like he was really home.

His family's palazzo was known in the city as the Ca' Ziani, a Venetian adaptation of Casa Ziani. It was ostentatious, like the many palaces that adorned the Grand Canal. The home of a venerable patrician family that boasted two doges and three procurators of St. Mark's, it was grand beyond all comprehension by *popolano,* or commoner, standards. In less than five minutes, he could see the familiar façade at last.

He quietly opened the door and stepped into the wide hallway that led to the main room on the ground floor. To provide security, the palazzo provided only one other entrance, which was on the dock that ran along the Grand Canal on the opposite side. It was used to conveniently load or unload merchandise and to permit access to guests who arrived by boat.

Like all merchant patricians' homes, the Ca' Ziani was both his family's residence and their place of business. Merchandise was warehoused in a cavernous atrium that ran the entire length of the building, from the street to the Grand Canal, comprising most of the ground floor. As he picked his way through the dimly lit labyrinth of goods, in some places piled almost to the ceiling, his heart began to beat harder as he read the familiar markings that indicated their contents. He could smell the blend of spices and freshly sawn pinewood. Everywhere he could see boxes of fine metal goods, small casks, each containing an exotic spice imported from the east and large barrels filled with delicate Venetian glassware, embedded in sawdust to prevent breakage.

Business must be good. He smiled at the thought of his younger brother, Giorgio, who had guided the family's affairs while he was gone. He could hear voices emanating from the unseen rooms that lined the two sides of the warehouse. The time for the midday meal had not yet passed. The dozen warehousemen, usually employed by his family, had not yet resumed their unloading and loading. The others, immersed in their work, did not notice him as he ascended the main stairway to the second floor. As he crept up the broad staircase that led to the large reception room, a noise startled him. Months of straining his ears in the darkness for sounds of danger had made his hearing more acute. A strange sound was coming from the top floor where the bedrooms were located. Someone was singing. As Antonio neared the landing he could hear distinct voices. He smiled as he recognized Isabella's velvety strains as she sang soft and low. She was happy. He surmised that she surely must have known by now that he had survived.

He still wanted to surprise her, so he removed the cheap leather shoes he had been given when he boarded the ship in Constantinople and tiptoed silently down the long corridor. Suddenly, a young servant girl emerged from a bedroom just in front of him and entered the hallway, not seeing Antonio behind her. He quickly sprang two steps and embraced her, covering her mouth with his hand to stifle her surprised scream. Her wide-open eyes smiled up at him as he felt her body relax in his arms. Holding a finger to his lips, he slowly removed his hand. Understanding his intention, she grinned broadly as she turned and ran away, disappearing down the stairs, giggling like a child.

"Maria, is that you?" Isabella called from the bedroom. "I need you. Come now."

Antonio pushed the door open with his foot and stood there like an apparition, silhouetted in the golden afternoon light that filled the room. Isabella was seated in a chair with her back to him. Her mother was sitting on a stool facing her and Antonio. When her mother looked up, she swooned and slid from her stool onto the floor. With a sudden start, Isabella stood and turned to face Antonio. Her expression instantly changed from fright to elation as Antonio's image filled her beautiful dark eyes. Her white teeth shone brightly as she smiled. As their eyes met and he beheld her folded arms, tears welled in his eyes. Could it be? Is God so good to me that He saved me from the hell of Constantinople *and* He has given me a child? But how, he thought? Isabella was not pregnant when he had departed for Constantinople that November day, over a year ago.

"Antonio, I thought I had lost you!"

"Isabella!" He whispered and gently embraced her; careful not to crush the fragile infant she was gently suckling at her breast.

"Can this be? We have a child?"

"Yes, yes, Antonio, a son, praise God! I first learned I was with child after you sailed. If only I could have told you! He was born last May—on the twenty-ninth."

Antonio's head was reeling—powerful emotions filled his heart. Just the thought of it all was more than he could take in. He had a son, praise God! Born on the twenty-ninth of May, a day that would forever be chiseled into his memory—the same day that Constantinople had fallen. As he tenderly kissed her, he felt her naked breast, soft and warm, lightly touch the inside of his arm.

Her mother, recovered now, vainly tried to break their embrace to hand Isabella a shawl. They ignored her and kissed a long time. Finally, the old lady pried the restless baby from her daughter's arms and sat back on her stool, slowly rocking him to stop his crying. Isabella, now unencumbered by her tiny bundle, threw her arms around her husband's neck as Antonio lifted her from the floor and lovingly laid her on her back, on the bed. She lay there, arms above her head, smiling like the first time they had met. The shawl teased him as it revealed too much of her body.

"I need a bath," he said as he smiled at Isabella's mother. She rose and quickly left the room, with the baby on her shoulder, obedient to Antonio's implied command.

"I thank God you are home safe, Antonio. At first, when they said you were lost I refused to believe it—even when I saw your name among the dead posted on the Porta della Carta. But after a while, as the months passed with no news to the contrary, I confess that I resigned myself to your fate." A tear slid down her soft cheek. She looked up at him with love-filled eyes.

"Were you hurt?"

"No, Isabella, I am well, and I am happy, now that I am home."

"You can imagine my indescribable joy when I heard from my uncle that you were on that ship—alive."

He looked down at her, drinking in her beauty. Antonio's life had turned completely around since he had walked into the room. He forgot all of his anxieties and reveled instead in his love for his wife and in the intoxicating pride of fatherhood.

"What happened?" she said.

"I was captured and ransomed like the others, but then events took a strange turn. I was befriended by the Turkish governor of the prison where we were all held."

Her smile vanished. "Was it as bad as they say? Did the Turks kill everyone?"

"Many were killed but many more were sold off as slaves. I regret to say, most of my marines were killed and so were many of the other *nobili*."

Suddenly the door opened. Isabella's mother had returned. Antonio quickly rolled from the bed and planted his feet squarely on the floor, facing the woman.

"I had a servant prepare a warm bath for you," she said, handing him a large towel. "Antonio, my brother attended a session of the Senate earlier this week. You must speak to him about the terrible state of affairs. He said things are bad."

"Where is he now?"

"Where he always is at this time of the day—drinking with his friends in one of those taverns near the Rialto Bridge," she sighed. "He becomes so involved in his conversations, he often misses the evening meal."

Antonio turned back to Isabella. "I love you. Thank you for not losing heart."

"How could I lose heart when I could look into your son's little face and see your likeness? It has been as though you were here with me all along. Look at his eyes. They are just like yours."

She sat up on the edge of the bed and held out her hands. He grasped them firmly.

"I wanted to name him for you, but I was afraid. I thought it would be bad luck as long as your fate was unknown."

Her chin quivered as tears began to fill her eyes and redden her nose. "And then I heard them say you had been killed." She fell apart, the shock of his return and its life-altering impact finally sinking in.

"Though he is almost eight months old," she sobbed, "he still has no name."

He thought for a minute and then a broad smile cracked his unkempt beard.

"We shall name him Constantine—after the city—to honor all of the brave men who died there. His name will be a constant reminder to him, like a charm around his neck, of the importance of honor and loyalty. We could not give him a better name."

She smiled as her mouth silently formed the name over and over. She liked the sound of it, though it was strange. She had never heard of anyone with that name before.

Isabella's mother cleared her throat.

"Your bath is getting cold."

Antonio smiled at Isabella and quickly left the room, stripping his clothes off as he walked down the hall to his waiting bath. In a few short minutes, he had scrubbed his long matted beard and hair and bathed using strongly scented soap. In his haste to finish, still dripping wet, he splashed his body all over with expensive perfume and slipped into a long white silk nightshirt. As his still-wet bare feet slapped along the gray marble floor, leaving footprints behind, he felt exhilarated as he reentered the bedroom.

"Now, Signora Ruzzini, if you will excuse us, I will remind my wife of the best reason why she married me." She obediently closed the door behind her, shaking her head and muttering to herself, too old to recall her own youthful passions. Laughing out loud, he turned and fell onto the bed, slid under the silk sheet next to Isabella, and embraced her with a fiery passion fueled by a year's separation. He was dizzy with desire. They made love, familiar and divine, as though they had never parted.

Afterward, with their hearts pounding and chests heaving, they lay beside one another silently conversing, at first, just with their eyes, as only lovers can do. After a while Antonio rolled onto his back and looked up at the ceiling.

"He is handsome, you know."

"He looks just like his father," she smiled.

He soon began to doze lightly, wavering between consciousness and sleep, but his mind could not rest. After a few minutes, he revived. Something was incomplete, out of place. Then he remembered, as Signora Ruzzini's words came back to him. What news did her brother Domenico have? Soon, as so easily happens with a man, unfinished business replaced finished pleasure. He hated to leave Isabella's warm and tender embrace, but his sense of duty and gnawing curiosity got the better of him.

He kissed her lightly. "I must find out what Venice is going to do and what part I am to play. I am going to see your uncle but do not worry, I promise I will bring him home in time for supper."

He kissed her once again and then slowly rose from the bed but he controlled his urge to dress too quickly. He did not want her to feel used. When he had finished, he leaned down and gently stroked her long curls as he kissed her one last time, long and passionately. Then he stood and walked quickly from the room.

News of his return had already swept through the house. As he reached the ground floor, a small crowd of cousins and employees was there to greet him.

"Antonio!" shouted his brother, Giorgio.

They embraced, laughing heartily at the sight of each other, as all the others looked on, smiling their approval.

"I am off to find Domenico. He says he must see me right away. When I return, you can tell me all about the business."

Giorgio shouted as Antonio turned to leave, "War is always good for business. We are recouping our losses from Constantinople. All of our ships are accounted for."

Antonio was elated as he emerged into the afternoon light and walked quickly toward the Rialto Bridge. The temperature had dropped but the cool January air could not chill his renewed spirits.

As he weaved his way through the streets and over the short, steeply arched bridges spanning the dark, placid canals, he thought, How fortunate can one man be? He was home at last and the proud father of a healthy son!

Reaching the wooden Rialto Bridge, he soon spied Isabella's uncle, Domenico Ruzzini, sitting with his friends at a table in an inn by the Grand Canal. He was one of Venice's most powerful patricians. Isabella's father, Domenico's brother, had died when she was a child. Domenico had raised her as his own daughter. It was he who had given his permission for her to marry. He had also generously provided her with a large dowry. He was like a father to her and a trusted friend to Antonio.

Antonio approached the older man who, seeing him, broke into a lusty grin. He was not a tall man, but very heavy. His corpulent face burst out from under a shock of white, unfashionably long hair, giving him the look of a man standing on the windblown prow of a ship, even though he was sitting calmly, drinking a cup of wine, which he did frequently. His white beard was sparse and cut short. He was dressed, like Antonio, in a simple black robe, the garb of a patrician when in public, as mandated by law. Ostentatious dress, except on celebratory occasions and during carnival, was prohibited.

"Antonio, you *are* alive! Bless the Virgin Mother for our good fortune!" Like most Venetians, he was not a religious man, but he often invoked religious oaths.

"What happened? We thought you were lost until last week when we heard you were on the ship that arrived from Constantinople with the other ransomed prisoners."

Antonio threw his arm around the man's broad shoulders and kissed him on the cheek as he pulled up a chair.

"As the Turks poured into the doomed city, I led a small remnant of my marines back to the harbor. We tried to make it to our ships but we were attacked by some Turks as we rowed for our lives. They killed everyone except me and a quick-witted Greek who saved my life by convincing the Turkish commander that I was more valuable ransomed than dead. After I joined the other captured survivors, we were all made to write ransom notes—but mine never reached Venice. I cannot understand why."

"Neither can I. When you were not among the ransomed we thought you were dead for sure, but tell me, how did Captain Soranzo obtain your freedom, then? There was only enough gold sent to pay for those we knew were being held."

He changed the subject, not wanting to tell him of his experience with Abdullah Ali in such a public place where prying ears were always inclined to eavesdrop on a conversation between two black-robed *nobili*.

"You would not believe what it was like when the city fell, Domenico."

Isabella's uncle shook his head gravely. "Was it as bad as we heard?"

"Worse than you could ever imagine—such slaughter and suffering. How many men made it back to Venice besides us?"

"Antonio, there is trouble," he said, ignoring the question. "I am reviled by the thought of delivering such bad news to you on the same day when you have, no doubt, met your new son for the first time, but the Pregadi met this week."

Antonio pulled back slightly to better see Domenico's face. He was distraught.

"When the first survivors of the siege returned at the end of June, Captain Soranzo was the senior officer. It was his duty to report to the Senate what had happened." His eyes narrowed and his face flushed. "After he gave his report, he met privately with Doge, his counselors and the Ten. He accused you of incompetent leadership, claiming that your failings cost the lives of hundreds of our marines. Do you realize how many members of the Senate lost relatives who were under your command?"

Antonio began to speak, but Domenico held up his hand and continued.

"As proof, Soranzo said that you caused the drowning of his youngest brother, Marco, and based upon the horrific losses sustained by the marines on the last day of the siege, you may have caused the avoidable deaths of his other brother, Pietro, and many others as well. Until now, I was afraid that there would be no other witnesses to dispute the captain's story. But now both you and Vice-Captain of the Gulf Trevisan have returned safely. You can imagine how bad things looked."

The joy that had filled Antonio, following his reunion with Isabella and the unexpected news that he had fathered a son, suddenly turned to anger and frustration. His thoughts turned to poor Trevisan, who, though back in Venice, would be of no help.

"Vice-Captain of the Gulf Trevisan's head wound and battle shock have rendered him an imbecile. At first, though his words were understandable, his thoughts were not. But his condition worsened on the long voyage home. Now he rarely speaks at all. He appears doomed to spend the rest of his days unable to communicate."

"I see," said Domenico as he sadly shook his head.

"Domenico, it sickens me to think that I risked my life for the same men who now question my competence, my honor. What were *they* doing while I was fighting the Turks? I will tell you. They were sitting on their asses stuffing their faces with good food and wine!" He calmed slightly. "So it will be my word against Soranzo's then? What do you think the Senate will do?"

"When we have told our story, probably nothing. We know that about forty of your men made it back to Venice on Soranzo's ship. It is very strange that these men made it out to his ship, but you did not."

"There were almost fifty marines who made it back to the harbor with me. We found three boats. Two boats reached a Venetian ship, but the Turks intercepted mine. Surely some of those marines who made it back have refuted the charges against me."

"When they were questioned their recollections shed no light on what really happened. One man, a Lieutenant Sagredo, accused Soranzo of leaving you, but others swore he was simply trying to save the ship and all the survivors on her. None of the marines saw what happened to Marco or Pietro Soranzo."

"Soranzo's brothers were both at fault. Marco disobeyed my orders and was swept from the deck in a storm while he puked over the side. Pietro foolishly attacked the Turks, leaving a vital gate in the wall unguarded and breaking a solemn promise he made to Giustiniani to defend it with his life. The Turks first entered the city through that very gate. Though a Turkish victory was probably inevitable, his actions cost the lives of all of his men who were massacred outside the wall because of his recklessness. Other marines were also killed when they were cut off by the Turks once they captured the gate."

Antonio turned toward Domenico, his eyes blazing with anger.

"I will not let Soranzo dishonor me!"

"Listen to me," pleaded Domenico. "If you attack in the Senate, hurling charges at each other, you will only damage your reputations and future opportunities for important posts in the government. Of course, I will help you in any way I can. I have powerful friends, as you know. But you must not give in to anger and rekindle that old feud between your families."

"I appreciate your counsel, Domenico, but the man is a damned liar."

Domenico breathed a long sigh. "What you have told me about Pietro Soranzo is a serious charge—more damaging than the ones Giovanni Soranzo has leveled at you. And just like his, yours is made by a man who is alive, against one who is presumed dead and cannot defend his honor."

"What did they decide to do about Soranzo's charges against me?"

"The doge directed the captain-general of the seas to investigate and report back to the Senate after the hostages were returned, since they would be the only possible witnesses who could corroborate or refute Soranzo's version of what happened."

Antonio leaned close to Domenico and asked, "What should I do?"

"First thing tomorrow, we will see the captain-general of the seas. No doubt Soranzo has already made his case to *his* powerful allies in the government. Now we shall make ours."

Ruzzini leaned forward and slapped Antonio on the knee and said, "So what do you think of that little boy of yours?"

"He looks just like his great-uncle," Antonio lied with a broad smile.

"He would be lucky to resemble me!" He laughed heartily. "I have had so much pleasure in this long life, I hope he will be as fortunate." He tilted his head awkwardly and asked, "What will you call him? Have you discussed it with Isabella?"

"Yes. We shall call him Constantine."

Domenico leaned back in his chair, expelling his breath in a long sigh, as it creaked under his weight. As his eyes inclined skyward, he began to slowly nod his head.

"An inspired choice. He shall always wear it proudly. When people ask him how he came to be named Constantine, he can say, 'My father risked his life to save the magnificent city whose name I carry. While the rest of the Christian world wallowed in their comfort, greed, and indecision, he was one of the gallant few who answered the call to come to her defense.' He smiled approvingly at Antonio. "Surely your courageous service will not be stained by a conniver like Captain Soranzo. I will see to it."

"Thank you, Domenico. You are a true friend."

. . .

E arly the next morning, just after dawn, they went to see the captain-
general of the seas. Antonio related his story of what had happened.

"It seems your version of events varies so greatly from Captain Soranzo's—they both cannot possibly be true."

The captain-general wanted nothing to do with a controversy between
two powerful and well-connected patricians. He remembered that his father
had told him when he was a child that "When two large dogs fight over a
piece of meat, the man who would try to stop them is usually bitten."

Antonio clasped his hands tightly together beneath the large table and
looked quickly at Domenico, fighting to control his anger and frustration.

"True, true," Domenico nodded. "You are in an impossible position. Perhaps you should tell the doge that you must delay your report until Vice-
Captain of the Gulf Trevisan has recovered sufficiently to give his
testimony."

"Yes, that would make sense, Signor Ruzzini." The man leaned back in
his chair. "That is precisely what I shall do. I will inform the doge and his
counselors that the truth lies locked inside Trevisan's head. Only he can tell
us what really happened."

Domenico turned to Antonio, "Fair enough, Signor Ziani?"

"And if Trevisan never recovers his senses?"

The two older men stared at each other, mutually understanding.

"Then the matter will be unsolvable, and like all things that are, it will
fade in importance as it is forgotten, except, of course, by you and Captain
Soranzo."

The meeting was finished. They thanked the man for his time and departed. Back in the piazza, Antonio expressed his appreciation to Domenico
for interceding on his behalf. As he watched his mentor depart in the direction of his usual haunt near the Rialto Bridge, Antonio turned and headed
for home. Now he finally had time to catch up on business with Giorgio.

He was pleased with Giorgio's report on the accounts and the overall
state of their business. Under Giorgio's leadership, it had apparently carried
on all right, despite their losses in Constantinople and the ruin of their trade
routes to the Black Sea, now completely cut off by the state of war that existed between the Ottoman Empire and Venice. Now their discussion
turned to the family's most valuable asset.

"What is the condition of our fleet?" asked Antonio.

Giorgio shook his head. "The ships are in good shape, two are on voyages as we speak. The *Eagle* is due from Alexandria this week with a cargo

of grain and the *Tiger* left just two weeks ago with a cargo of fine goods, including two hundred barrels of Murano glass, bound for Marseilles. Our two other ships are in dry dock. The barnacles had built up, so I ordered them both to be scraped. When they have finished with the *Raven,* she will be requisitioned by the Senate for use as a troop transport."

Antonio noticed that Giorgio never looked up as he spoke.

"Why do you seem troubled, then, Giorgio?"

"Some things have happened since you were away that I must tell you about."

His eyes narrowed and his voice became quiet, guarded. He turned around to see if any of their employees were nearby out in the warehouse. They were alone. Giorgio leaned forward, sucked in a deep breath, and continued.

"First, though it pains me to do it, I must confess a transgression to you."

Antonio sat in patient silence while Giorgio worked up the nerve to tell him what was wrong. It is a girl, thought Antonio. He has fallen for a commoner.

"I have lost some money—a lot of money."

"But how, Giorgio?"

"I have taken up gambling . . . or, should I say, gambling has taken up me."

Antonio leaned back in his chair and expelled a long, painful sigh. If only it had been some girl. Antonio was almost afraid to ask his next question. Giorgio spared him the trouble.

"I lost more than six hundred ducats. It did not seem like it was that much money at the time I was losing it, but I have totaled my losses and that is the amount."

"Have you paid your debts? It would not do for you to get a reputation for not paying your debts promptly—even if they are from gambling."

"If only my stupidity was limited to foolish wagering I would not be so ashamed. I wished to avoid reproach . . . from you. So to hide my gambling, I borrowed my wagering money, intending to pay it back with my winnings. As my losses mounted, I had to choose between borrowing from the business, leaving a record that our employees would discover and question or else borrowing from another. I chose the latter."

"Who loaned you the money?"

"He was the only man in the room I knew who could help me."

"Who was this other man, Giorgio?"

"I had no choice; it was Vettor Soranzo."

Antonio jumped from his chair and raised his outstretched hands. It could not get worse, he thought.

"Why, Giorgio? Why him of all people?"

"I know, Antonio, I know."

"No, Giorgio, you do not know. His cousin, Giovanni, thinking I was dead, told the doge and the captain-general of the seas that I was incompetent and responsible for the deaths of his two younger brothers and most of my men. He has tried to ruin me."

Giorgio hung his head in shame.

"Have you any idea of the suffering this man has caused me? You have wounded me like never before."

Antonio fought to calm his emotions. Then he continued.

"What has been done has been done. Now, we must deal with the problem. Tell me how it happened."

Giorgio looked up at his older brother, grateful that, like a true Venetian, he never allowed his feelings to cloud his business judgment.

"I went to the gambling house for the first time about two months ago."

"Why did you go there? You have never gambled in your life. As far back as I can remember no one in our family has ever gambled."

"My friend, Nicolo Steno, convinced me to go. To be honest, I only went to try my luck with the ladies. I had no intention of gambling but he made it look so easy. I tell you, once I tried it, I did not have the willpower to stay away from the table."

Nicolo was the grandson of the former doge Michele Steno, whose family were merchants, like the Zianis. Antonio did not know him very well.

"I used my own money at first and I won. It was exciting and it seemed so easy. I could not resist increasing my bets. But before long, the dice ran against me. Soon I needed money. Steno was no help—he was broke too. It was then that Soranzo stepped forward and loaned me thirty ducats. Once a week, Steno and I returned to try to get even. Sometimes I won, but mostly I lost. The god of the dice seems to let you win just often enough to keep you always coming back."

Antonio struggled to remain quiet and allow him to continue.

"In the end, my losses became so severe that, three weeks ago, I borrowed five hundred ducats from Soranzo to cover them. I only stopped when I realized how badly I had risked our good name."

"What security did you pledge for the loan?"

"Vettor said I did not need to repay him."

"He must have wanted something?"

"Instead, he said he would forgive the debt if I would do him a personal favor."

Antonio could feel his anger returning. He could only imagine what

Vettor Soranzo had opportunistically proposed, to take advantage of Giorgio's weakness.

"He said he had a friend who wanted to provide marine insurance to the city's merchants but he had not been able to break into the market. You know how difficult that can be. He only wanted a chance to work with the House of Ziani—to get him started."

"So instead of making a standard insurance contract with the Candianos, you insured one of our ships with him instead? Which one?"

"The *Tiger.*"

Antonio's frustration boiled over. "Do you not see, Giorgio? This has all been a plot orchestrated by the Soranzos. They laid a trap for you and like a fool you fell right into it. Now you have risked the *Tiger,* her crew, and cargo and you have damaged, perhaps irreparably, our relations with the Candianos, who have been insuring our vessels for fifty years. Surely, Vitale Candiano must have confronted you about this?"

"Within a day of her sailing, he came here asking why I had not insured the *Tiger* with him. I was ashamed and could offer no excuse, except that I did it for personal reasons I could not reveal. Candiano said I had made a terrible mistake; he grew angry and finally swore he would never insure a Ziani ship again."

"You have weakened our family's reputation among the *nobili.* Where there was deference, there will now be mistrust. You have squandered years of careful work."

Giorgio's chin sunk to his chest as he accepted his guilt, but Antonio continued.

"Did you ask Vettor for references to ensure that this man could pay on a loss?"

"Vettor said that Steno would vouch for him—I asked him and he confirmed that the man had adequate resources to cover the *Tiger,* even if she was a total loss."

"How do you know Steno was not in on the plot too?"

Silence.

"Giorgio?"

"I do not."

"What is this insurer's name? Who is his family?"

Giorgio slowly ran his trembling fingers through his thick black hair. "He is not a Venetian—he is from Provence. His name is Pierre DeMars of Marseilles. My God, Antonio! What have I done? The *Tiger* is bound for Marseilles."

Antonio stood motionless, staring at his distraught brother—thinking.

"What shall we do?" pleaded Giorgio.

"I want to see Signor DeMars. Where is his place of business?"

"Near the Church of Santa Caterina."

A plan of action quickly formed in Antonio's mind.

"Let me see the insurance contract."

Giorgio slowly opened a drawer in his table and produced a rolled paper. Antonio read it silently, carefully examining each paragraph. It was a standard Venetian insurance agreement—there was nothing unusual about it.

"I am going to do some checking of my own on Signor DeMars. Meet me at Santa Caterina at three hours past midday and I will tell you what I have learned. Be sure to bring this contract with you." He added, "Have you told anyone else in our family about this?"

"No, no one else."

"Good, we shall keep this between us, for now."

Antonio reached out to help his defeated brother to his feet and embraced him.

"You are my brother, Giorgio. The Soranzos have taken advantage of my absence and your human weakness. Their malevolence must be met with strength. That is the only way to deal with aggressive actions by others who mean to do you harm."

"It would have been better if I had gone to Constantinople in your place."

"If you had gone to Constantinople instead of me, *you* might have perished in the siege. As bad as things are, at least we are both alive and able to fight them together."

Antonio smiled bitterly, turned, and walked from the room.

Immediately after leaving Giorgio, Antonio went to see three powerful merchants, all friends of the family. None of them had ever heard of a Monsieur DeMars. Antonio concluded that DeMars had never been in the marine insurance business. He was a fraud.

Now, he had to think. The image of his father's face and the sound of his voice surfaced amid his swirling, jumbled thoughts. "When you need to think . . . go for a walk. Divert your attention from the problem you need to solve. Fill your mind with other things—noble and beautiful things—and the solution will come to you."

It was an unseasonably warm winter morning as Antonio walked across the Piazzetta between the two ancient columns near the Doges' Palace. He had decided that he would make good on his promise to introduce Seraglio to Venice. This would provide the perfect diversion from his troubles. While he showed his friend the city, his subconscious mind could mull over the problems he faced, pondering questions, searching for answers. He was confident the solution would come, like it always did. When he reached the water, he turned left and walked along the Quay of the Slavs toward the Acropolis.

As Antonio strode briskly along the quayside, he calculated the losses his brother's mistake had cost. Worse, one of the merchants had told him that Candiano was carping about Giorgio's foolish mistake to anyone who would listen, in an effort to preserve his family's reputation. But before Antonio could grapple with the future, he knew he had to deal with the present. He decided that later, after he had met Giorgio, they would go together to confront DeMars with his treachery.

10

The Deception

The Acropolis was a three-story masonry building, wedged in among a half mile of warehouses, shops, inns, and manufactories that ran the length of the broad stone quay that formed Venice's main port along the Bacino di San Marco. More than a hundred ships, of all sizes and types, filled the harbor—one of the world's busiest. This morning it was alive with motion and commotion as dockhands and deckhands skillfully exchanged their precious cargoes. Antonio walked through the door of the inn, his fine black robes immediately arousing the interest of a few aged sailors lying about on the crude furniture inside. They rarely saw a patrician set foot in the Acropolis, but Antonio's demeanor indicated that he was familiar with the place. The clerk recognized him at once.

"Good morning, Signor Ziani. Your little Greek friend is upstairs, in the first room on the third floor. He is still asleep, I suspect." A toothless laugh wheezed through a thicket of black whiskers that obscured half of his face.

Antonio nodded and walked briskly up two flights of stairs and, reaching the room, slowly opened the door. It was pitch-dark except for where a triangle of white light from the hallway illuminated the floor and far wall. The bed was empty. As he opened the shutters to let in the morning light, there in the corner of the room, he saw Scraglio sitting upright in a large wooden chair. He was sound asleep. His short legs and little feet extended straight out, just beyond the seat. Antonio kicked one foot. Seraglio snorted loudly but still remained there sound asleep.

"Seraglio!" Antonio shouted loudly into the living corpse's ear.

One eye fluttered open. The large brown eyeball slowly rolled to the side and then, moving with a purpose, fixed on his tormentor. Then, as Antonio's image registered and his brain came to life, he quickly slid from his comfortable perch and stood at attention on the floor, fighting to keep his balance.

"Antonio, please tell me that this is not the day that I am to see Venice."

His tired ashen face, bloodshot eyes, and pungent breath that reeked of wine betrayed his damaged condition.

Seeing Antonio recoil slightly, he admitted, "I drank too much wine last night. Can we postpone the tour until tomorrow?" He yawned. "My stomach does not feel so good . . . and my head aches terribly. Perhaps a few hours of sleep will repair my body."

"No, Seraglio. The tour is today but do not worry. Here in Venice, we have a remedy for those who have drunk too much wine."

"A remedy? Impossible! Only time can cure the effects of fermented grapes." Suddenly Antonio seized him by the back of his shirt and in one easy motion lifted him from his feet, throwing him over his shoulder and onto his back.

"Sleep, I must have some more sleep," he pleaded, as Antonio quickly descended the stairs, carrying him like a large sack of grain. He continued through the foyer, out through the open door and into the bright morning light.

"A good bath will cure you!" said Antonio loudly.

"But I have already had one—last night!" Seraglio pleaded in vain.

"Not in the lagoon," said Antonio as he heaved him, kicking his legs like a toad, into the blue-gray water that lapped gently against the wooden bulwark four feet below.

Seraglio made a splash like a cannonball. Popping up for air, with clumps of his long hair stuck to his face, he looked like one of the buoys, trailing strings of seaweed, that marked the fishing pots and nets scattered throughout the lagoon. A few curious people stopped to watch.

Antonio, laughing, dropped a nearby rope into the water. As Seraglio clutched it, Antonio quickly pulled him up and dropped him onto the stone quay. As he rolled to a stop, a dark pool of water spread its stain on the dry stone pavement around him. Seraglio looked up and smiled with one eye open, a large piece of dark green seaweed covering the other. The excitement over, the curious onlookers went on with their business.

"I feel better already," said Seraglio as he looked up at his friend and wiped salt water from his pink eyes.

"Do you expect me to parade you around my city looking like that?"

"I only had three pieces of silver and the wine here was cheaper than the food."

Antonio took Seraglio into one of the many small shops that lined the Quay of the Slavs and purchased some new clothes for him. After drying and dressing he emerged looking like a new man. With his brown face and yellow cloth shirt bulging out of his loose-fitting green trousers, Seraglio resembled a sunflower.

"Now you look like a proper Venetian *cittadino*."

"I look like a perfect fool! These trousers are too long," he protested as he pulled them up for the third time, only to have them slide back down to his waist again.

"We will have them altered to fit you better later. Now let us sit and drink some wine and plan our day," suggested Antonio.

"You drink, I will sit," grimaced Seraglio, still not completely recovered.

They sat outside at one of the many large taverns that interrupted the long line of grain warehouses and bakeries that the efficient Venetians operated across from the wharfs where the grain was unloaded from the ships.

"So tell me, Seraglio, what is your impression of Venice so far?"

"I have only been here a day and a half but I am quickly acquiring knowledge of the place. My acute Greek senses have made many discoveries. Venice has made strong impressions on each one of them."

Antonio leaned back, intrigued.

"First, my nose," he said as he tapped his fleshy protuberance. "The lagoon smells of the sea, salty and fishy, but also of human activity. Here on the quay, there is a wonderful aroma of bread baking night and day and of succulent meat roasting in the inns. Freshly cut wood and everywhere spices—ginger, curry, thyme, and basil, not to mention the onions and garlic—permeate the air. Sitting here now, there is the aroma of sweet flowers all around. Even the stone buildings smell differently than those in Constantinople. There they are old and reek of years of smoke from ten million fires, lit to warm the chill of a thousand winters. The buildings here smell cleaner, newer. Surely, Venice must be a healthier place to live. The air is fresh here and everyone knows that fresh air is the key to good health."

"We have laws that prohibit noxious fumes from the city. That is why, years ago, we moved the glassworks to Murano. All the industries that spit their smoke and fumes into the air are contained within the Arsenal on the far eastern end of the city, where the prevailing winds blow it away from our dwellings, to the east, and out to sea."

"Finally," Seraglio continued, "I can smell excitement instead of excrement. There was a strange mixture of spices, perfumes, ale, and nervous anticipation that filled the inn last night. Even the lowliest whore in that place had a pleasant fragrance."

"Did you partake of any of our whores?"

"I tried but they seemed to prefer other men. But I am used to that. There was one, though, who was quite young . . ." Seraglio rolled his eyes as he worshipped her memory.

"It is well that you did not try to seduce her. Here in Venice, the court might have forced you to marry her."

"You are not serious, surely?" asked Seraglio incredulously.

"Deathly serious. You did not use foul language last night, did you?"

"My years in the monastery reformed me from any inclination toward profanity."

"That is also well. Swearing is not tolerated in public here in Venice. Blasphemy is severely punished. Priests have been publicly pilloried for uttering a simple profanity."

"You would have done well to warn me of these curious customs, Antonio."

"But, Seraglio, I know a man of culture when I see one. It is obvious that you did not get into any trouble or else you would not be here, now. Tell me, what do your ears tell you about Venice?"

"As you can see, they can tell me quite a lot!" he chuckled, tapping his large ears.

"In Venice, one never escapes the sound of water in motion. The lagoon laps against the quay, the canals gently flow into the lagoon. Gulls and other sea birds make a racket but there are few land birds here compared to Constantinople. There are fewer dogs and I saw horses and wagons only on the quayside. It seems that few people actually *ride* horses here. Venice must be the quietest city on earth. It is . . . ," he groped for the word to describe his impression, "serene. *La Serenissima* is well named." His brow furrowed, indicating that he was deep in thought. He paused and then continued.

"The quiet does something inside you. It makes you feel closer to God. Closer to the way the world should be. I have felt, since I came here yesterday, that I was in a place halfway between heaven and earth—a sort of manmade Garden of Eden. Have you had that feeling too?"

"Every time I return to her, Seraglio."

"It is as though, in Venice, man has married the comfort and excitement of city life with the serenity and ease of country life," observed Seraglio.

"Yes, and we have done it without suffering the vile smells of the farm or the disturbing noise of the city."

Antonio looked at his friend. "What does your tongue tell you?"

"The wine is good—much better than Greek wine. The food abounds with spices that make every piece of meat or fish taste good. Back in Constantinople, too often, one could perceive a spoiled taste. I remember thinking that each time I ate, I wondered if I would be able to finish my meal before I began to deposit it in the privy. But here, you are lavish with salt and that, I have found, makes for the best and safest food. Our fruit is no better than yours, but most of all, I like the taste of your water. Constantinople's wells are very old. There, the water tastes like the Turks have pissed in it, but here, your wellheads teem with fresh, sweet water. How is that possible?"

"Our wells are driven deep into the earth and are not contaminated by animal or human waste, as in other cities. There are few live animals in the city. The salt water of the lagoon continuously washes our liquid streets clean each day with the ebb and flow of the tides. Yet it never mingles with our drinking water."

Seraglio slowly shook his head in amazement.

"What do your fingers tell you?"

"That everything in Venice is well made. The quality of the goods here is the finest I have ever seen." He drank some water from his cup. "The wood of this cup is smooth, the way it should be. No chance of suffering a splinter in the lip. My chair does not wobble on this stone slab. The legs are cut evenly and the floor is level—an architect's assistant notices these things. The coins you gave me were double-struck, their images more pronounced than Byzantine or Turkish coins. Even the cloth of my clothes is tightly woven and dyed brilliantly. Just look at this bright yellow color."

"A man who tries to sell poorly made goods here will find himself without patrons and if he cheats with short weights or adulterates, he risks prison.

"What do your eyes tell you?" continued Antonio.

"I have seen little so far. I have barely left the inn. But from my window perch I could see the sky. Perhaps, because Venice is formed on islands in the middle of the sea, the sky seems higher and wider here than it does on land. The rich blue hues are intense and the clouds are like wisps of silk and ivory. The sun shines brighter here and its rays penetrate the water, turning the lagoon to a milky blue-gray hue. Like an ornate frame that surrounds a fine painting, the sea and sky form a beautiful frame around your man-made masterpiece." Seraglio leaned back in his chair, his hands behind his head.

"Seraglio, a city derives its beauty from more than its physical setting and its grand buildings. More than anything else it is made beautiful by its people. And there are no finer citizens, no greater collection of exotic souls from the ends of the earth, to be found anywhere than here in Venice. We are truly the crossroads of the world, where West meets East."

"True enough, but remember, I am still an architect's assistant. My heart soars at the thought of what man can accomplish with his mind and hands in stone and wood. People have never been an object of my admiration—until I met you, they have only been my tormentors."

Seraglio was right, of course, thought Antonio, feeling a bit somber.

"I was wrong, Your Honor. Now would be a perfect time to see Venice."

Where do I begin? Antonio thought as they walked along the quay. As he turned to look at Seraglio, he could see the Bacino di San Marco, the city's main harbor that stretched from the Quay of the Slavs west to the Molo, the broad landing next to the Doges' Palace. It was midday now and it looked as though an army of ants had climbed out of the lagoon as thousands of workers labored everywhere along the long stone pier.

The gray winter waters were teeming with ships flying magnificent colored banners. Ships from France, Spain, England, and Egypt were intermingled with ones from exotic, faraway ports in Muscovy, Morocco, the Hanseatic League, Portugal, and Lithuania. The harbor was so densely packed this day that, as Antonio looked back toward the Acropolis, the dense rows of wooden hulls topped by a forest of spindled masts and spars looked like the endless reflection of an object in two opposing mirrors.

There, moving between the majestic vessels like flying fish, were the gondolas ferrying ships' passengers and crews to and from shore. Just then, a bright red one caught Antonio's eye; its gondolier was gaily dressed in his striped shirt and black hat. As Antonio watched him adroitly maneuver the rocking boat, he knew *that* was how they must see the city—lazily slipping along the canals in the Venetian way.

As they walked the remaining distance to the Molo, they talked about Antonio's eventful homecoming. Seraglio congratulated him on the birth of his son but when he learned about what had happened to Giorgio, he suggested that they postpone the tour of the city. Antonio would not hear of it.

"I need to think, Seraglio, to draw strength and inspiration from somewhere. A tour of Venice is exactly what I need. It has been so long since I have seen her."

Antonio hired a powerful-looking gondolier who led them to his thirty-six-foot-long emerald-green and black lacquered craft. The empty boat rocked wildly, tied to a striped wooden pole rising defiantly out of the water. Made from hundreds of individual pieces of fine hardwoods, the gondola's shallow draft provided the perfect design for maneuvering through the narrow and shallow canals.

The gondolier helped Seraglio down into the craft, as he nestled comfortably into the wide fur-lined armchair at the back facing forward. Antonio climbed down next to his friend. Satisfied, standing on the end behind them, the gondolier cast off his line.

Slowly at first, the boat began to pump its way forward, propelled by the powerful strokes of the gondolier as he pushed his oar right and then left, moving the boat out into the choppy waters of the Bacino di San Marco. He continually shifted his feet, flexing his supple knees to maintain his precarious balance. He seemed to defy gravity as he danced on the bouncing stern, working his oar with well-learned dexterity.

They moved with delightful slowness past the Istrian stone and brick government buildings and manicured gardens on their right that hid the sprawl of the Piazza San Marco beyond. As the large buildings slipped out of sight behind them, Antonio spoke.

"We will save the Piazza San Marco for last. First, I will tell you about Venice.

"Our empire stretches from the northern Italian plain all the way to Crete. But the jewel in our crown is this city, for which our empire is named. The city of Venice is comprised of one hundred and seventeen islands, crisscrossed by over one hundred and fifty canals. Scores of bridges span these waterways, connecting the six *sestieri,* or official sections of the city. Just up ahead is our most prominent feature, the two-mile-long Grand Canal that winds its way through our city like a liquid serpent."

"How did Venice become so wealthy?" asked Seraglio.

"Trade. Everything here exists to promote trade and business. Our industries produce the finest glass, textiles, ironwork, leather, salt, and ships. A hundred crafts are carefully taught to our young in the *Scuole.* These guildhalls continually refine our methods to constantly improve our workmanship.

"We control the Oriental spice trade to the east. Our own Marco Polo and his uncle were the first Europeans to travel to Cathay and to map the Orient, establishing important trading relationships there. We also control the Alpine trade with Germany to the north. Nearly every country on earth depends on us for essential goods and we are not afraid to charge what the people will pay.

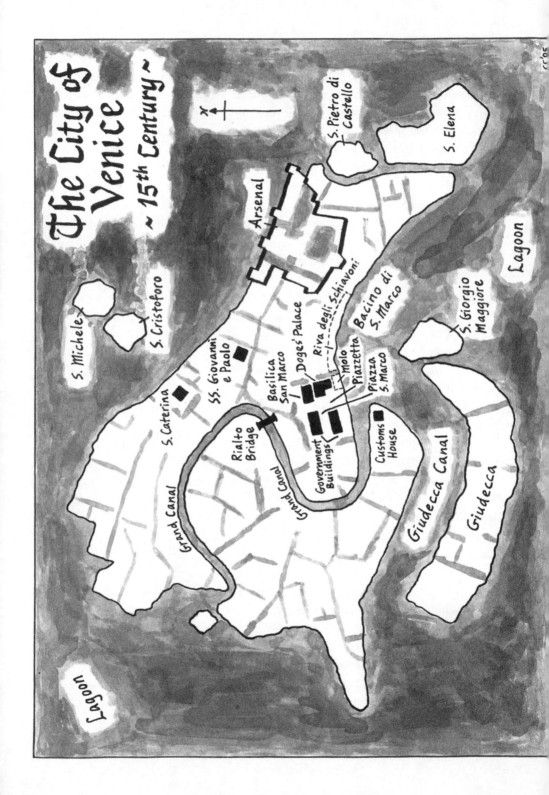

The City of Venice
~ 15th Century ~

S. Michele
S. Cristoforo
Lagoon
Arsenal
S. Pietro di Castello
S. Elena
Lagoon
S. Caterina
SS. Giovanni e Paolo
Basilica San Marco
Doge's Palace
Riva degli Schiavoni
Bacino di S. Marco
Grand Canal
Rialto Bridge
Grand Canal
Government Buildings
Molo
Piazzetta
Piazza S. Marco
Customs House
S. Giorgio Maggiore
Giudecca Canal
Giudecca
Giudecca
Lagoon

"Last year, Venice's exports exceeded ten million ducats—more than any other city in the world. That is because we Venetians have invented many of the business practices in use throughout Europe today. We were the first to have money made from paper, in the form of redeemable government bonds. The Bank of Venice originated the exchange of accounts, allowing traders to transfer ducats between accounts, eliminating the need to barter goods or carry heavy bags of coins to pay for them. We also introduced marine insurance, spreading the risk of inevitable maritime disasters among all of our trading houses." For a fleeting moment, he recalled his troubles.

"In the last century, we have regulated sanitation and drinking water, prices of staples to protect the poor and physicians and apothecaries as part of our system to provide for our citizens' health. We had Europe's first postal service, and the Republic provides pensions to orphans, widows, and retired government workers. We even created a bureau of economic statistics to better understand our economy and to determine how to best improve it."

By this time, they had entered the mouth of the Grand Canal.

"Look to your left, Seraglio."

As he turned, he could see the end of an island.

Seraglio's introduction to La Serenissima was exceeding his expectations, but Antonio was frustrated by his inability to articulate his deepest feelings about Venice.

As Grand Canal began to narrow, they could see rows of the grand palazzi owned by Venice's leading families on both sides, stretching as far as they could see, up ahead.

As the residences of the great patrician families that had produced many doges and procurators of St. Mark's slowly slipped by, Antonio pointed to each one and briefly related its owner's family history—on the right were Corner, Cavalli, Malipiero, Grassi, Moro, Contarini, Mocenigo, and Grimani, with Da Mula, Loredan, two more Contarini, Rezzonico, and Giustiniani on the left.

"There, Seraglio! On the left, is the Ca' Foscari owned by the doge himself."

Seraglio shook his head. "Your wealth is much less concentrated than ours was in Constantinople. It seems many more of your citizens share in the prosperity of your city."

The canal made a sharp turn to the right and snaked in a one hundred-and-eighty-degree arc back to the east.

"There, up ahead, is the Rialto Bridge, the only crossing point over the two-mile length of the canal. At its foot is the Fondaco dei Tedeschi. This is the warehouse of the traders from the powerful German Hanseatic League. From this place, goods come to and from Hamburg, Danzig, Stockholm and Copenhagen, and the other Baltic Sea ports. Also nearby are housed the public officials who oversee trade, navigation, and the supply of food staples into the city."

As they passed underneath the wooden Rialto Bridge, Seraglio could see a beehive of activity on the left in the city's bustling fish market. Scores of boats bobbed in the canal, waiting to unload their day's catch.

"This is the commercial center of the city."

"Venice is so well organized, so well planned," observed Seraglio.

"While Venice was built to accommodate trade from the start, other cities had to be accommodated so that trade could be built. No city is as efficient as Venice at receiving and distributing—and collecting and shipping goods."

Just past the bridge, they curved around to the left again, revealing another expanse of shoreline crammed with more rows of impressive *palazzi*.

"There, on the right is my own Ca' Ziani," said Antonio with no small touch of pride. "Later, I will show it to you. I have a room prepared for you there."

Seraglio could see that Antonio was, indeed, a wealthy man The Ca' Ziani was bigger than the palazzi on either side of it.

"What is that up there on the right?" Seraglio shouted, his breath taken away.

"The Ca' d'Oro," said the gondolier proudly, unable to remain quiet any longer.

"It is the newest and the grandest palazzo in the city," added Antonio.

"It looks as though it is made of . . . gold!"

"That is because it is sheathed in gold. Marino Contarini built it twenty years ago, much to the disdain of the government, which discourages such ostentatious displays of wealth by *nobili*. Since it was built, we even passed a law to limit how much could be spent on a palazzo, but it is not well enforced."

As they silently moved past the Ca' d'Oro, Seraglio marveled at the three-story structure with its painted red-, black-, and white-accented trim surrounding the golden façade facing the canal. Four tall white Istrian marble columns rose from the water to support the alcoved pier. Intricate carved stone Gothic pillars, filigree tracery, and eight balconies completed the edifice. Beautiful private gardens separated the home from the neighboring Ca' Sagredo.

Antonio leaned toward the gondolier. "Turn at the Rio di San Felice."

The man nodded and rowed the gondola into a narrow canal that ran between rows of three-story buildings. No sunlight reached the water there. Seraglio shivered in the cool air and pulled the animal skin up over his chest to keep warm. They passed two canals on their right and then the water opened up into the warm sunlight of the Sacca della Miseracordia. The open lagoon lay before them. Screeching seagulls welcomed them back to the sea as they circled above.

"Put the boat in over there," said Antonio, pointing to a pier on their right.

The gondolier quickly maneuvered the craft to a pier within sight of the church of Santa Caterina. Antonio ordered him to wait for them as they climbed onto the pier. On the way to the church, he told Seraglio that they were going to meet Giorgio and the purpose of the meeting. Seraglio now understood the pain his friend was suffering.

"Your brother has placed you in a difficult position. What are you going to do?"

"I must go to see DeMars without delay and demand proof of his ability to pay on the *Tiger,* if we suffer a loss. If he cannot furnish it, I shall have him arrested."

"What will you do if he is a fraud? Who will insure your ships?"

"When you can furnish profit, you can always find a partner. The question is—at what price? I am afraid that Giorgio has severely damaged our long-standing business relationship with the Candianos. I will try to repair it but it will not be easy. The Candianos gave us low rates. We paid fifteen percent less than anyone else. If we have to insure our vessels with a new partner, it will, no doubt, be at the prevailing price—costing us many more ducats."

A few minutes later Antonio spotted Giorgio leaning against the front of the church, dressed in his black robe. In his hand was the *Tiger*'s insurance contract.

Antonio introduced Seraglio to Giorgio and without further conversation they followed him along the Rio di Santa Caterina. Suddenly, Giorgio stopped and rubbed his head. He looked perplexed. Then, smiling, he pointed and said, "There it is—over there."

He led them into a narrow nondescript building and ascended the dimly lit staircase with Antonio and Seraglio close behind.

At the top of the stairs was a door. Giorgio knocked loudly. No one answered. He knocked a second time. Antonio and Seraglio looked at each other with naked apprehension. They flinched as Giorgio suddenly broke the lock with a violent kick.

The room was empty, save for some scattered papers and two broken wooden chairs in the center. Spoiled food and half-burned trash were piled in the center of the single small fireplace.

Giorgio turned around. His cheeks and forehead were ashen white, his brow covered with perspiration. The barren room spoke for him.

"What are we going to do now?" groaned Giorgio. "He is gone."

"All we can do is trust in the skill of the *Tiger's* captain. Who is it?"

"Our cousin, Andrea Ziani."

"He is a good man. If anyone can bring the *Tiger* and her cargo back safely, he can," replied Antonio. "Now, go home. There is nothing more that you can do today. I need time to think. Seraglio and I will return in a few hours."

Giorgio unconsciously dropped the worthless insurance contract on the dirty floor and obediently left without uttering another word. When he had gone, Seraglio bent down, picked up the document, and unrolled it to examine its contents. As he held it up to the window and read, he suddenly turned to Antonio and asked him a question.

"You and your brother do not speak French?"

"No, Seraglio. Why?"

"Because Monsieur Pierre DeMars' name, translated from French is— 'Pietro, god of war.' It is as though they have reincarnated Pietro Soranzo to torment you."

Antonio closed his eyes as he slowly moved his head from side to side. The magnitude of his hatred for the Soranzos was only matched by his sympathy for his brother. This revelation was the final act of humiliation.

"I did not think it would be wise to mention that to your brother."

Seraglio rolled up the contract and handed it back to Antonio, who carefully placed it inside the folds of his black robe. When they returned to the pier, Antonio climbed down into the waiting gondola with a heavy sigh.

"Take us back to the Molo, past the Arsenal," Antonio ordered the gondolier.

They turned right, along the Fondamenta Nuove. Seraglio could see several islands to his left in the distance out in the open lagoon.

"There is San Cristoforo and San Michele. Farther in the distance is Murano, the site of the glassworks. Beyond is the mainland—*terra firma,*" said Antonio.

To their right, church domes and other public buildings rose above the rooftops, their gold and marble colors contrasting with the red terra-cotta tiles and the pastel painted walls below. As they neared San Michele, they saw rows of stone crypts, standing silently like sentinels, in its large cemetery. Seraglio turned to look at Venice.

"What is that large building on the right?"

"The massive brick structure, with the large dome, is the church of Santi Giovanni e Paolo. It is our pantheon, the burial place of the doges. Recently, the government decreed that all doges' funerals are to be held there to prevent inequality in the grandeur of one versus another. The other large building near it is the city's hospital."

The golden sun was sinking in the west. It was getting cold. The gondolier was tiring as they neared the Arsenal. Above the high brick perimeter wall, Seraglio could see the red rooftops of the long buildings and warehouses. Dozens of ships' masts towered above wooden hulls, in various states of completion, like the skeletons of giant beasts.

"We employ more than twenty thousand workers here. It is the largest manufactory in the world. The main bells in the city peal out the times when its workers begin and end their labors. You might say that as the Arsenal works, Venice works."

Seraglio wrinkled his brow. "I cannot decide, which is more terrifying—this Arsenal and the capacity of you Venetians to make war or the wealth of the palaces on the Grand Canal and your capacity to make money."

"Ah, that is the wonder of Venice, Scraglio. Our ships are designed for speed and carrying capacity—whether they are used for carrying marines or goods. As long as Venice rules the seas, she will prosper and be free. Besides, what is the relationship, really, between war and wealth, Seraglio? War is simply the most efficient way that man has ever devised to acquire or squander wealth. In the end, there has never been a war fought for anything but to take another's wealth or to protect one's own treasure."

He was right, thought Seraglio. Constantinople had fallen to Muhammed II because, more than new adherents to Islam, he desired her great wealth for himself.

They rounded the point of land at the easternmost end of the Arsenal, slipped through the narrow Canale di San Pietro, and made their way back to the harbor.

"Your city is not large, but it *feels* large. There is so much crammed into these islands with their churches, palaces, government buildings, and Arsenal—all protected by the sea. I can see why you have striven for more territory. There is no more room here."

Antonio could see that the gondolier was wilting despite the falling temperature. Antonio ordered him to dock along the Quay of the Slavs, a few hundred yards short of the Molo. As the two friends climbed up and onto the pier, Antonio paid the man, giving him more than he had bargained for.

"Now, Seraglio let us stretch our legs as we walk to the Piazza San Marco. Though you are not permitted to enter the Doges' Palace, I can show you the Basilica and the Campanile of San Marco. You can tell me what you think of our architects."

In a few minutes they reached the Molo. As they faced the Piazzetta, with their backs to the lagoon, Antonio's pride provided the music for his words.

"Seraglio, you have seen much of Venice today, but I have saved the best for last. There," he pointed, "is the Piazza San Marco, built over the years as the vast meeting place for our citizens and our city center."

"We are standing on the Piazzetta that connects the piazza to the Molo."

Antonio pointed skyward. "Crowning these two giant columns, brought back hundreds of years ago from the east, are the winged Lion of St. Mark and on the other, St. Theodore, standing on a dragon with the body of a crocodile and the head of a dog. These are the patron saints of Venice who stand guard over the city, warding off our enemies."

They walked into the piazza, as Seraglio slowly turned in circles and counted the many symbolic winged lions made of stone, found everywhere on the public buildings.

Almost six hundred feet long and three hundred feet wide, the entire surface of the massive Piazza San Marco was covered in a herringbone pattern of brick pavement, with only the western end broken by a small grove of trees, a stonecutter's yard, and a public latrine. In the piazza, which was surrounded by long two-story public buildings on three sides, pigeons and gulls fed in the light and shadows on bits of food left by the previous night's revelers.

"Stand here, my friend, so that you can fully appreciate this place."

Seraglio stood next to Antonio and tried to preserve in his memory the sense of power and grandeur he could feel at that moment.

"There, Seraglio, are the two most magnificent buildings in Venice . . . the Doges' Palace and Chapel, which we call the Basilica of San Marco."

As they walked toward them Antonio put his arm around Seraglio's shoulders.

"The Doges' Palace was completed more than three hundred years ago and has been rebuilt and expanded several times since. This façade was completed just thirty years ago. Inside, the power of Venice is arrayed. Nothing happens in the empire without it first taking shape as a thought within those walls."

Seraglio whistled as Antonio spoke. "It rivals, in size, the palaces of the Byzantine emperors in Constantinople. Though Constantine possessed four, I suspect more has been accomplished in this single one here in Venice."

"That is because the entire government resides in there, Seraglio. While we have our differences within our government, to be sure, as we manage the affairs of the empire, one thing is certain. In times of war, as now with the Turks, the men who guide the ship of state can be relied upon to work together to do what is best for our Republic."

The Doges' Palace, four stories high, was built of Istrian stone and brick. The lower Gothic arcade ran for almost two hundred and fifty feet; eighteen arches supported on colonnades ran the length of the building. Above was a balcony with smaller arches and delicate stone traceries. Up close, as they walked around to the front, Seraglio saw that the walls were decorated with a diamond mosaic pattern of white, brown, and gray brick with six large stone windows, three on each side, flanking a seventh in the middle with a balcony, guarded by the winged Lion of St. Mark. On the left, nearest the basilica, the ornate Porta della Carta, the document door, seemed to be alive as the official notices posted there flapped in the breeze.

"Seraglio, that day back in Constantinople, before we entered the Hagia Sophia, you told me to prepare to meet God. Since He has been driven out of that glorious place by the Turks, I assure you, He will not lament his new home, here in Venice."

They walked past the Doges' Palace and up to the main door. Antonio pointed to the façade. As Seraglio lifted his eyes, he saw an explosion of color and grandeur surrounding the central doorway. Like paint on an artist's palette, the pink, green, blue, gray, yellow, and red variegated marble columns and sculptures guarded five large Byzantine sculpted iron doors. Above, four arches, each more elaborate than the previous, expanded to form a crescent alcove that, in turn, was bordered by two more arches. High above it all, a white balcony ran the entire length of the church.

"Do you recognize those four bronze horses, Seraglio?" asked Antonio.

"I have always wondered what they looked like. It is too bad Doge Dandolo did not take more treasures when he had the chance. There would have been less for the Turks to plunder. If the sultan had gotten his hands on those, he surely would have melted them down and used the bronze to cast more cannon."

Seraglio could see the maze of ornate towers, spires, and winged angels all seeming to salute St. Mark, standing atop his church. The effect was awe-inspiring.

Antonio motioned for Seraglio to follow him inside. As they walked through the door, Seraglio was surprised to see it was so light—as millions of pieces of gilded mosaic tiles reflected and amplified the natural light under the cavernous dome.

"You can see why some call this the Golden Church," whispered Antonio loudly. "The church is two hundred and fifty by two hundred feet and is in the shape of a cross. Ten small domes and one large central dome rise over it."

As they entered the narthex, Seraglio marveled at the mosaics and marble statuary. Antonio stopped him and pointed at a small red marble tablet on the floor.

"On this spot, the Holy Roman Emperor, Frederick Barbarossa, humbled himself before Pope Alexander III in 1177, ending their bitter feud. Doge Sebastiano Ziani, my ancestor, won great glory for Venice for his role in bringing those enemies together."

They walked deep into the interior. Seraglio was astounded at the opulence he saw there. Priceless marbles, porphyry, and most of all, vast expanses of gold-encrusted mosaics filled the place, each lovingly telling a story from the life of Christ.

Suddenly, there in front of him was a large altarpiece behind a dark green marble canopy lifted up on columns of alabaster. He looked at Antonio, who smiled. "Another gift from your city but I can assure you that this one was not stolen.

"It is known as the Pala d'Oro and has been here for almost five hundred years. Look at the other side, my friend."

Seraglio walked around the screen and froze, transfigured. Before him was the most complex and wonderful work of art he had ever seen. Thousands of precious jewels: sparkling diamonds, rich emeralds and rubies and blazing sapphires, regaled in their settings of silver, gold, and enamel. Scores of biblical scenes were portrayed on a surface the size of a large tapestry. Anyone could see that it was unduplicatable, irreplaceable.

"This must be the most valuable piece of art ever created. I wish I could see it better," said Seraglio as he stood on his toes.

"It is not the most prized possession contained within these walls," replied Antonio, as he walked under the canopy. "Here is the tomb of St. Mark the Evangelist, patron saint of Venice and author of the second gospel. His presence here gives Venice her soul, her honor, her reason for being. We are sworn to protect his saintly remains. Every boy learns the battle cry of the Republic—'For St. Mark and Venice!'—before he can say his siblings' names. When he is older, he learns what is written in the book, held in the winged lion's hands. It says, 'I am the great lion himself, and my name is

Mark the Evangelist! Whoever should attempt to defy me shall be banished from my sight!'

"Would you like to see the treasury?"

"No, Antonio," said Seraglio, overwhelmed. "I have seen enough for to-day. Besides, most of the silver and gold probably comes from Constantinople anyway."

"Of that, you can be sure!" said Antonio. His smile turned to a frown as his thoughts plunged back into the problems with his business. The tour had given Antonio a brief diversion but now he could think of nothing else. As they walked through the Piazza San Marco on the way to the Ca' Ziani, Antonio thought about the *Tiger*. She would probably arrive in Marseilles any day now but it would be weeks before he would know if she had safely returned to Venice.

11

Turmoil

Venice depended upon the harmonious cooperation of her *nobili* to effectively manage the affairs of state and build her economic power. Strife between individuals was expected to be resolved quickly or else to be discreetly pursued behind a shroud of respectability. It was considered a serious transgression to resort to violence. Even public disagreements were discouraged. How could the patriciate expect the *cittadini* and *popolani*—the common folk—to respect them and obey their commands if patricians did not respect each other? Antonio and Giorgio could take no action against the Soranzos until they knew what had become of the uninsured *Tiger* and her valuable cargo.

While the days dragged by slowly with no news of the *Tiger,* Antonio attempted to repair the damaged relationship with his erstwhile business partners, the Candianos.

He went to see Vitale Candiano alone to apologize for his brother's ill-advised actions. After exchanging polite greetings, Antonio confronted the problem directly.

"Signor Candiano, I offer no excuses for my brother's actions. If I had been here, instead of in a Turkish prison, I would never have given our business to another insurer."

"I believe you Signor Ziani, but you are too late. As you know, we have the financial capacity to insure only a limited number of ships at one time. After all, we must be capable of making good on any losses that might occur," he said, causing Antonio to cringe. "We have always relied upon the House of Ziani to provide the core of our business, finding others to fill our remaining capacity. When this became doubtful, we moved quickly to find another family to replace yours. Perhaps we can insure a Ziani ship from time to time, but, of course, it would have to be at the normal rate. The special terms agreed fifty years ago by my father and your grandfather are no longer possible."

"Signor Candiano, for whose ships will you now be the principal insurer?"

"Why, the House of Steno, of course. Without their help, we would not have known of your brother's duplicity."

Steno! Antonio fought to maintain his composure.

"Will you be willing to insure the *Eagle*? She sails in a week."

Candiano scratched his beard as he considered Antonio's request.

Finally he said, "I will do it as a favor to you Antonio, for old times. Perhaps you could do one for me in return? My grandson is now old enough to go to sea. Will you sign him on as an officer on the *Eagle*?"

"You ask a small thing in return for your willingness to insure the *Eagle*."

As Antonio stood and thanked the older man, Vitale Candiano replied. "Even though things did not go well for the House of Ziani while you were gone, I am pleased you survived the siege and your imprisonment. You were most fortunate to have had someone looking out for your welfare all those months."

Antonio slowly turned around and looked at him without a trace of emotion.

"And who do you say looked out for me, Signor Candiano?"

"Why . . . St. Mark, our patron saint, of course."

For a brief moment the two men exchanged polite smiles. Then Antonio departed. Even a man like Candiano, who has known me for years, cannot resist applying the knifepoint to my skin about my relationship with the governor of Rumeli Hisar.

In the delicately balanced world of Venetian business, even small changes, if unexpected, could cause unforeseen consequences.

The *Tiger*'s captain had wisely chosen to return to Venice after dark, to give his owners a chance to hear the bad news before it swept through the city. Anchoring far out in the lagoon, three miles from shore, he took a small boat directly to the Ca' Ziani, where he would make his report to Giorgio that very night.

As he opened the door to the study on the second floor, Captain Andrea Ziani was shocked to see that both of his cousins were waiting for him. Antonio jumped to his feet and walked around his large table to embrace him.

"We thought you had been killed, Antonio. Thank God you survived."

"It seems, Andrea, that I survived only to fight another enemy here at home."

Giorgio also rose to his feet. As Andrea Ziani greeted him, he noticed a strange little man with long hair sitting in another chair across the room against the far wall.

"Andrea Ziani, this a good friend of mine. His name is Seraglio. He was imprisoned with me in Constantinople. We shared the same cell for months."

The captain nodded politely and turned to face Giorgio.

"I have bad news, cousin," he said gravely, a frown etched on his face.

"Something went wrong in Marseilles. There was an accident."

"Is the *Tiger* . . . sunk?" stuttered Giorgio as he put out one arm to steady himself against the big table.

"The ship was not badly damaged—it was the cargo. As we sailed around the headland into Marseilles harbor, it was dark and visibility was poor, owing to the infernal fog that plagues that place at this time of the year. I decided to anchor out in the harbor for the night. But the next morning, before I could weigh anchor, a ship collided with us. She struck us on the starboard side, near the stern, and spun us around until the restraining anchor chain yanked us back again like a dog on a leash. The casks of glassware in the hold were thrown one way by the initial impact of the collision and then toppled the other way when the ship reached the limit of the chain. This violent combination played havoc with the cargo. By the time the customs inspectors had finished their work, we found that two-thirds of the glassware was a total loss. All the casks piled more than one high had most of their contents broken despite being packed in sawdust."

"What do you estimate to be the value of the loss, Giorgio?" asked Antonio.

"I make it more than five hundred ducats."

"What ship caused the collision?" asked Antonio.

"By the time we realized what had happened, she was past us and was moving away into the fog and the predawn darkness. She just disappeared!

There was no name on the stern or flag to identify her. She did not have so much as a lantern lit."

Antonio looked at Giorgio. He could see the agony inside of him reflected on his face, as his worst fears had become reality. He looked at Seraglio, who had walked across the room and now stood next to his table.

"What about the return trip? Were you able to sail without a problem?"

"The hull was damaged by a hole far above the waterline. Belowdecks she was a mess. Several of the crew had broken bones and one man, Alvarez, who had been in our employ for twelve years, was crushed to death when a barrel fell on him while he slept."

"Antonio," said Andrea, "due to the loss, we could not purchase the return shipment of wine. The merchant said we had to buy all or nothing and pay in cash. He would not accept our credit. So we sailed back with our hold only one-fifth full with a few things I could buy with my limited funds. When we hit some rough seas in the Strait of Messina I thought we might capsize without the extra ballast the heavy casks of wine would have provided. I do not pray often, but that day I prayed like the pope. Now my crew is unhappy—first there was the collision, and now no prospect of a bonus for the voyage. Some have told me they will quit as soon as they come ashore tomorrow."

"Pay the good ones the bonus they would have earned. Let the others go," said Antonio. "I would rather have them working for one of our competitors."

"As you wish, Antonio."

"What did the authorities in Provence do?"

"They were useless. They said they had no record of a ship leaving port that morning. Antonio, while I have never been able to tell when a woman is lying to me, I can tell when a man is trying to deceive me. They knew more than they were saying."

"What can we do, Antonio?" said Giorgio, weakly.

"Tonight, I am afraid, we can do no more than lick our wounds but tomorrow we shall go to the Molo before Andrea brings the *Tiger* in. We shall listen to the scuttlebutt and see if someone knows too much about what happened in Marseilles. They may lead us to who, in Venice, may be part of this conspiracy besides the Soranzos. Now, let us get some sleep. Tell one of the servants to wake us an hour before sunrise."

Antonio looked at his cousin. "Andrea, I am sorry you were in danger. You have served the family well. I want you to draw your usual pay for the voyage."

"Thank you, Antonio, but I cannot. We must all share in the family's loss. Now, if you will excuse me, I must get back to the *Tiger* to prepare for our arrival tomorrow."

Early the next morning, while Andrea Ziani issued orders to his restless crew to make ready to sail the *Tiger* into the Bacino di San Marco and clear customs, Antonio, Giorgio, and Seraglio mingled amid the throngs who had come to welcome three other ships that had already paid their duty. The harbor was alive as smaller boats of every description serviced the larger vessels. Hundreds of sailors and longshoremen handled cargo along the pier and on the decks, while merchants and investors counted their profits or assembled crews to man other ships that were ready to sail. A long line of sailors ran along the Molo, trying to hire out as crewmen on state-owned ships. Other sailors waited patiently to sign on as crewmen on privately owned vessels.

Along the waterfront, not far from the Doges' Palace, Giorgio spotted Nicolo Steno and one of his captains seated at a small table, enlisting sailors. He had not seen Steno since the night he had vouched for Monsieur DeMars.

Steno was arguing with a crusty sailor while the captain, at his side, exchanged impatient glances with the others in line. The man was angry because Steno had refused to take him on, saying he was too old. Despite his pleas, Steno would not be moved. As the embarrassed sailor retreated, he made an obscene gesture. Steno and the others laughed, caring little that, without work, the man would have no way to feed his family.

Giorgio, his temper rising, decided to confront Steno with his deception.

"Signor Steno, I would like to have a word with you in private."

Steno turned abruptly, annoyed at the interruption. Seeing Giorgio, he quickly stood and stepped away from the table.

"Giorgio, you have been making yourself scarce. Where have you been?"

They walked back to the wall of the Doges' Palace.

"Nicolo, I trusted you. Why did you conspire against me?"

"What are you talking about, old friend? I do not understand?"

"Monsieur DeMars was a fraud. He has disappeared and the insurance I purchased from him is worthless."

"Impossible!" shouted Steno, loud enough to draw attention.

"Why did you tell me he was a legitimate businessman?"

"He was—I mean—I thought he was."

Giorgio grabbed the shorter Steno by the folds of his black robe, pulling him up onto his toes. His eyes burned with anger as they searched Steno's face.

"Vettor Soranzo told you to tell me DeMars was respectable. You knew nothing about him. You lied to me," spit Giorgio through his clenched teeth.

"We have been friends for years. Why would I lie to you? I admit that we have not used him before to insure our vessels, but he had great knowledge of the business. I never dreamed he was not honest. Did something happen to the *Tiger?*" he asked.

"The *Tiger?*" asked Giorgio. "I know nothing of the *Tiger*. She has not returned from Marseilles yet." He tightened his grip and lifted Steno off of the stone pavement, his feet dangling in the air. A small crowd was standing off at a polite distance—just close enough for their straining ears to pick up Giorgio's angry words without appearing to be eavesdropping. Two patricians rarely engaged in such acrimonious conversation.

"But I thought . . ."

"You thought what, Nicolo?" He abruptly dropped him, repeating his question.

"I thought the *Tiger* had sustained a loss. You just said that the insurance you purchased from DeMars was worthless. How would you know it was worthless unless you had tried to make a claim?"

"I know because I went to his office and it was empty. He has vanished—he left in a hurry too. I have looked for him everywhere. He is not in Venice. Yet, he told me that he had sold everything in Marseilles and had come here to stay. He said that his dream was to become the foremost insurer to the major merchant houses and I was to be his first client. Remember, Nicolo?"

Giorgio held him in place with his glaring eyes. Even if Nicolo was not in league with Vettor Soranzo, he was surely guilty of lying to him about DeMars' credentials.

"We are finished, Nicolo—you and me. You have conspired against me and betrayed my trust in you. Get out of my sight."

"Signor Ziani, is that the *Tiger* I see, making her way to the customshouse?"

It was Vettor Soranzo with his toadlike older brother, Cosimo, in tow. Giorgio looked out into the harbor where the *Tiger's* familiar silhouette was moving majestically across the water. He could clearly see evidence of damage on her starboard stern quarter. A gaping hole, six feet across, stared back at him like an ugly black eye. The sight of it made him livid. He turned to face Vettor, who began to speak.

"You must be down here to sign on a new captain? It appears the one you chose nearly lost her. You were lucky. That would have been the first ship lost by the House of Ziani since the *Lion*." Vettor laughed and looked at Cosimo with a self-satisfied sneer that crept through his beard. Giorgio looked at Steno to gauge his reaction. His eyes betrayed a trace of pleasure. Cosimo stared at his brother, amazed at Vettor's audacity.

"Laugh if you like but we know what you have done. There is not a ducat's worth of honor in the Ca' Soranzo."

"A Ziani talks of honor!" hissed Vettor.

The crowd of onlookers was swelling as bystanders on the quayside stopped to listen to the drama unfolding before them. Seraglio spied Giorgio surrounded by other men in black robes. He craned his neck in vain to find Antonio. It was no use. He pushed his way, as best he could, toward the altercation.

Vettor Soranzo pressed home his attack.

"What honor is there in a family led by a man like Antonio Ziani—the only prisoner to return from captivity in Constantinople who gained weight—a man who sold *his* services and *his* honor to the Turks for a bit of food while his comrades starved."

Surprised and confused Giorgio groped for words to fend off Vettor's attack.

"What is your intention, Signor Soranzo?" interrupted Seraglio as he pushed past two onlookers. "Were you imprisoned there too? Did you see what happened?"

"Who are you?" asked Vettor, the tone of his voice more insulting than his words.

"I am called Seraglio. I was with Captain Ziani every minute while he was imprisoned and I can vouch for his honor. It is true that the governor of the prison did place the two of us in a separate cell, but Captain Ziani asked for no special treatment. If you were imprisoned and your captor chose to give you edible food and clean water, would you have refused?"

"Lies!"

"Come on, Vettor," urged the ever-careful Cosimo. "We have work to do."

As they shoved their way out through the crowd, Vettor cast a parting glance at Seraglio that chilled his spine.

Seeing the commotion, Antonio had joined them.

As they walked away, Giorgio and Seraglio told him what had happened.

"We came here this morning to unravel an insurance fraud perpetrated against us," said Antonio, "but, instead, we find ourselves more entangled in our enemies' web of lies and deceit. Now they hatch rumors questioning my loyalty to the Republic, casting doubt on my actions while I was imprisoned waiting for my ransom to be paid."

"But surely, other *nobili* who know you will not believe these lies?"

"Seraglio, that is a chance I cannot take."

ut that incompetent bastard caused Marco's and Pietro's deaths! How could the Republic that I have served with such loyalty for so many years not grant my brothers the justice their souls cry out for?" The veins in Soranzo's neck were bulging, his eyes on fire. He slammed his fist on the table and shouted, "Tell me, Pasquale, how?"

"Giovanni, as I have told you before, it is your word against Ziani's. You have powerful friends and he has powerful friends. The Senate will not be compelled to choose between you. Instead, the doge, his counselors, and the Ten will regard you both as troublemakers at a time when they seek to avoid strife within the ruling families—need I remind you that we are at war? I warn you, Giovanni, if you continue to pursue this . . . this vendetta of yours, it will damage *you* as much as Ziani. Perhaps later you can exact your revenge for what he did but for now, you must stop. If you want to damage Ziani, you must find another way. What good is ruining a man if you also ruin yourself?"

Soranzo respected Malipiero as a powerful patrician who knew the workings of the Republic better than anyone. It was even whispered in the chambers of the Doges' Palace that, someday, he would be elected doge. He had been a close friend of Soranzo's father for many years, but now he was giving him some unwelcome advice.

Soranzo sighed as he reluctantly surrendered to the older, wiser man.

"Very well, Pasquale. You know how much I value your judgment. I will end my campaign to expose Antonio Ziani's incompetence. But I swear, on the souls of my brothers, that one day, I will have my revenge for their deaths."

"Giovanni, I have also heard the whispers that Ziani received favorable treatment while in captivity in return for cooperating with the Turkish governor of the prison. That is old news now. While his reputation has been sullied it has not been seriously damaged. Ziani has too many friends in the government. Let this go too."

"I am pursuing another plan to bring down the House of Ziani, Pasquale. This time, I am not attacking his honor or his loyalty but his purse, instead."

Malipiero smiled at his younger friend. "Take your revenge against him if you must, but be certain his demise cannot be attributed to you. You will be suspected, even if you are not the perpetrator, so be clever as a cardinal."

"You may be assured it will be so. But, Pasquale, is it possible to learn to be that clever without suffering through the Mass each Sunday?"

They both laughed, since neither was a religious man.

"Very well," said Malipiero, "but if I were you I would not pursue charges regarding his disloyalty unless his actions give rise to suspicion about what happened while he was in prison. Perhaps there will be a way to test him and then, if he fails, it can be attributed to this disloyalty—traded in return for favors from his Turkish captors."

Soranzo nodded his agreement. Malipiero was the master of intrigue.

The older man rubbed his beard and sighed, as though struggling with whether or not he wanted to say more. Then he spoke as a teacher to his prized student.

"There is something I want you to do, Giovanni. Make your peace with Ziani publicly. It is easier to attack a trusting enemy than a wary one. Make him think you have reconsidered and absolve him of any guilt. He will quickly forget your earlier accusations against him and concern himself with other things. Your initiative in reconciling your differences with him will be viewed favorably by the doge and his counselors as proof that you are mature and capable of assuming important responsibilities in the future. Then, when the time is right, you can strike decisively. After all, it took two hundred and fifty years for the Turks to take Constantinople, did it not?" He smiled.

Soranzo thanked Malipiero for his help and showed him to the door. As he watched him walk down the street and disappear from sight, he had already begun to devise a way to publicly reconcile with Antonio Ziani.

S oranzo's plan was inspired by his mentor's advice, but it was in his execution of it that he achieved its full potential. A week later, he announced that he would hold a banquet to honor the veterans of the siege of Constantinople on the first anniversary of its fall. He invited all the *nobili* who had survived the siege. To this illustrious group, he added the Ten, the Signoria, and every influential member of the Senate, exalted churchmen, and Doge Foscari. The veterans of the siege all attended out of respect for each other and their dead comrades. Leading members of government and Venetian society attended out of respect for the survivors. Antonio Ziani did not dare to stay home.

Throughout the long evening, everyone watched as the two bitter rivals went to great lengths to avoid each other. Then, when dinner and the lofty speeches replete with platitudes were finished, Soranzo ordered his servants to fill his guests' glasses with his finest Tuscan wine. Then he stood and spoke, filling the room with his powerful voice. The audience, all dressed in their finest robes, stood at attention in rapt silence.

"Let us all toast to St. Mark . . . Venice . . . and the doge!"

For several minutes, the sound of thin Venetian glassware clinking together filled the room, as every man loudly repeated Soranzo's toast to every other man within his reach as they carefully touched the rims of their glasses. As they tasted the rich velvety red wine, Soranzo's voice boomed again.

"And now, signori, I toast to the memory of all Venetians, especially my two brothers, Marco and Pietro, who gave their lives in the siege of Constantinople so that we might prosper and live as free men, here in Venice, tonight."

Shouts of "For St. Mark and Venice" rang out from every table, echoing loudly from the marble floor and walls. Every man repeated the ritual, only this time, with more solemnity and emotion. After Soranzo drank some wine, he carefully set the delicate glass on his table and standing there, with every eye on him, he slowly and dramatically tipped it over, breaking it on the hard wooden tabletop beneath the white linen, staining it blood red. His simple, yet poignant sacrifice complete, he sat down in silence.

The crowd teetered, awaiting the next act in the unfamiliar rite. They had all seen glasses broken at weddings, but nothing like this. Suddenly, Pasquale Malipiero placed his glass on his table and pushed it over in the same way. In less than a minute, five hundred glasses lay broken, the tables and floor below littered with tiny crystalline shards. The wanton destruction of such beautiful instruments of pleasure was shocking yet profound. What did half a thousand expensive glasses matter compared to half a thousand brave Venetians cut down in their prime? Still reeling from the symbolism of the broken vessels and tablecloths stained as with blood, they were amazed when their host again rose to his feet. How could any act—any words, surpass what they had just seen?

But Soranzo had one final surprise planned for the evening. He slowly turned in the direction where Antonio Ziani was sitting, far across the room.

"And now, I propose that every loyal Venetian raise a cheer to the true hero in this room tonight . . . Captain Antonio Ziani!"

The anticipation was shattered as surely as if the room were made of Murano glass. Men sat in shocked silence. Heads swiveled as five hundred pairs of eyes searched among the tables for Antonio Ziani. Rendered speechless by Soranzo's words, Antonio sat at a table in a far corner of the large room, with his back to Soranzo—aghast.

What is happening? he thought to himself, as he could sense the tickle on his neck from curious stares, feeling more confused than embarrassed.

"As many of you know, our two families have contended with each other for many years. But this malice was rooted in events now long past."

His extended arm, palm outstretched, swept dramatically through the air.

"Tonight, I confess publicly that, not long ago, I spoke ill of this brave man but it was grief from suffering the deaths of my two brothers that filled my head with bitter thoughts and compelled my tongue to utter those harsh words against this noble man. Who among you would not have done the same? But now that I have had more time to reflect on those sad events of a year ago, I know that my brothers would vouch for Captain Ziani's bravery and his devotion to our beloved Republic. He was the last Venetian to leave the walls of Constantinople after our heroic defense of the city."

Soranzo walked majestically toward Antonio, who had turned to face Soranzo but had still not fully recovered from the shock. The enthusiastic crowd, now on their feet, parted to let Soranzo through. They began to applaud and shout their approval of the avowed enemies' triumphant reconciliation, but Soranzo held up his hand, signaling for quiet. Then, reaching Antonio, who was also standing, Soranzo embraced him and said loudly for all to hear, "Captain Ziani, I apologize for the cruel words I have spoken in the past, though I do not apologize for the grief that made me speak them."

He lifted a new crystal glass high in the air for all to see as he now addressed the transfixed assemblage of Venice's greatest citizens.

"Everyone, please, let us welcome the newest member of one of the Republic's greatest families. I give you this man's young son, Constantine Ziani, who came into the world on the same day—the twenty-ninth of May—that hundreds of brave Venetians departed from it, dying for the honor of St. Mark and Venice. May he continue the great traditions of his family and reap his just reward for bearing that great patrician name!"

Then, raising the crystal goblet to his lying lips, he drank to his treachery as his guests cheered his enemy's goodness. Captain Giovanni Soranzo's vendetta had become invisible to everyone else but him.

Thirty-year-old Captain Giovanni Soranzo was the talk of Venice that spring. This time, he had won more fame with his charm than with his sword. Like Antonio, he also was revered as one of the true heroes of the Siege of Constantinople.

It had been the hardest thing he had ever done. It made him sick to his stomach just thinking about it, but it had left him free to devise a plan to destroy the unsuspecting Ziani. Pasquale Malipiero had even intimated to him that he had a plan that would once and for all expose Ziani, with unarguable proof, as an incompetent or a traitor.

12

The Plot

As the winter winds ushered in the New Year, Venice prepared for the Turkish onslaught they thought would come with the good weather in the spring. Soon, however, it was apparent that the Republic's wily ambassadors had achieved what had seemed impossible just months before. First, she signed a peace with her rival Milan, ending the thirty-year war that had mutually exhausted their treasuries, bled their people, and exasperated the pope and their neighbors. In the end, for all her exertions, Venice had gained only a single city, Cremona, which she added to her mainland possessions. She also gained a military alliance with her former enemy, and to Milan she soon added another former rival, Florence. Now, with her back protected, Venice was ready to take on the sultan. The Republic's vaunted diplomats had earned their pay once again.

The previous year, the Republic had completed the construction of fifty new war galleys. The Arsenal's incomparable capacity and the efficiency of its dedicated workers ensured that the ships were manned and ready by the spring. However, the drastic reduction in eastern Mediterranean trade placed several Venetian banks in danger of insolvency, while many of the Republic's most influential merchants were struggling to make up losses caused by the war and the depredations of the Turkish navy.

. . .

It had been a year and a half since Antonio Ziani had returned to Venice. One June evening, after working a customary twelve-hour day, as he was sitting on the floor teaching two-year-old Constantine the alphabet, he could not have known that at that very moment, a quarter mile away on the fourth floor of the Doges' Palace, a secret meeting was about to begin. Doge Foscari had called for the gathering at the request of his archrival and self-appointed tormentor, the powerful Pasquale Malipiero, one of the Ten.

I wish to thank Doge Foscari for calling this meeting on such short notice." Pasquale Malipiero looked around the small room at the doge, his six counselors, and the other nine members of the Ten.

"I still do not see the need for this meeting but in the interest of cooperating with you and the others who felt it was necessary to meet, I have agreed to it."

In the old days, I would have told you to go straight to hell, thought the doge.

He would not have dared to refuse our request after all the trouble these past few years, thought his opponents.

"The subjects to discuss are . . ." Foscari looked down at a piece of paper and squinted, his poor eyesight betraying his frail condition. ". . . the dire situation facing several of our banks and trading houses and the Turks' plans for further expansion."

Doge Foscari turned and looked at Guardi, his counselor for finance.

He immediately began to speak. "Three banks have failed in the last month, but four more in danger of closing have been kept solvent by infusions of ducats by the patriciate; several of these were made by men this room."

Everyone dutifully clapped his hands in a polite show of approval.

"Those who contributed their own funds deserve the thanks of the Republic."

"Not so fast, Doge Foscari," interrupted Pisani, one of the Ten and an ally of Malipiero. "Your father-in-law's failed bank, the House of Pruili, has burned its creditors for twenty-four thousand ducats."

Some advocated bringing charges against him. An argument ensued. Pruili barely escaped the humiliation of a public charge or worse, by a tie vote of eight to eight. The doge declined to vote, avoiding the obvious conflict of interest and the trap set by his enemies. Luckily, they could not gain a majority and the sensitive subject was disposed of.

"Now I suggest we discuss how to prevent the Turks from slowly destroying our eastern empire, a city or a province at a time, and with it our very means of dominance in Mediterranean trade."

"What can we do besides oppose their next advance?" asked Guardi, always worried about the cost of things.

"Our massive expenditures since the fall of Constantinople coupled with our considerable losses in goods and property there have rendered all-out war a poor option. Whether we are victorious or defeated in our next fight with the Turks, we will lose—since we cannot afford the cost to fight. Most of the fifty new galleys produced in the Arsenal in the past year had to be paid for with private funds. We cannot continue to rely so heavily on these individual contributions in lieu of levying additional taxes."

"I say, we kill him," said Malipiero, so quietly, it was little more than a whisper.

The room fell into stunned silence, not sure of the words they had just heard.

"I say we kill the sultan," he said again, "and hope that his successor will be easier to deal with. He could be a man of peace like Muhammed's father, Murad II, was."

"You mean, *pray* his successor is a man of peace," chimed in Loredan.

"Could anyone be worse than him? He wants to conquer the world and unfortunately, we happen to possess some of the richest provinces that stand in his way," argued Malipiero.

Now, as men sometimes do when they are bullied and harassed by another, the doge threw in his lot with his enemy to hold him at bay, if only for a while.

"He is right!"

The men in the room were more amazed by the doge's support for the idea than they were when Malipiero had first proposed it.

"The relationship of the cost to the potential benefit is obvious. How much *could* an assassination cost? Surely no more than a single war galley."

The counselor for finance reacted to the doge's words like a ferret slithering down a wet pipe. Guardi's gaunt face seemed to ignite as he stood and raised his hands to draw attention to what he was about to say.

"If this plan works, it will save our treasury and relieve our people from the terrible burdens the war has laid upon them. I say we do it and do it now."

In a moment it was done. There would be no vote; no official record of the plot that could implicate the Republic in an assassination of a head of state.

"Now," said the doge, "who shall be responsible for executing the plan?"

Sixteen men looked at each other as their minds silently considered the question. One, Malipiero, had chosen the name before he had taken his seat an hour before.

"I know just the man who can do it. He was at Constantinople and endured capture and humiliation by the Turks—he should welcome a chance to avenge the deaths of so many of his countrymen and to prevent the deaths of untold others."

"I want no Venetian implicated in the plot, whether it succeeds or fails. Surely the perpetrator will most likely be caught and tortured," said the doge sternly.

"As you wish," bowed Malipiero. "This patriot will not be ordered to actually kill the sultan. Instead, he will only be responsible for employing the actual assassin and directing him. To ensure you are satisfied with his commission, I suggest that he receive it directly from your lips and that no one, save the men in this room, have any knowledge of the plot's existence and even we will have no knowledge of the actual plan itself."

He looked around the room at his colleagues and smiled.

"You seem to have given your plan a great deal of thought," said the doge.

Malipiero nodded confidently.

"What do the rest of you think?"

To a man, each nodded or gave his tacit agreement. Silence was condonement.

"Doge Foscari, we all agree with your desire to maintain complete discretion, shielding the Republic from any complicity in the plot," said Malipiero.

"What is the man's name?" asked Guardi, always the stickler for details. "I must know it so that I can advance him the funds he will require."

Malipiero stood and walked over to a nearby table, reached for a quill, and dipped it into the inkwell. Then he carefully wrote the name of the man who would be ordered by the doge himself to arrange the assassination of Sultan Muhammed II. After carefully blotting the ink and folding the paper, he walked to where Doge Foscari sat and triumphantly thrust it into his waiting hand. The old doge trembled slightly as he unfolded it and read. Satisfied, he held the paper over the burning candle at his side until, consumed by the flame, it shriveled and the black ashes dropped lightly to the floor.

Though the doge often led prayers in public, he was hardly a religious man but earlier he had prayed like a sinner in purgatory, beseeching God to end the torment he was suffering at the hands of his enemies. His initial sense that his supplications had been answered soon turned to uncertainty. He decided that he would pray more carefully in the future. It dawned on him that in the heat of battle he had been outmaneuvered.

I have won, thought Malipiero. If the plot succeeds, I will be acknowledged by the men in that room as the savior of Venice. The dogeship will be mine for the taking. If it fails, Foscari will be finished—most likely deposed.

It was late summer, more than two years since Constantinople had fallen, and still the predicted Turkish threat had not materialized. The sultan, sensing Venice's resolve and aware of her surprising alliance with her former enemies Milan and Florence, had decided to honor the treaty that had been in effect, before the siege. It subjected Venetian merchants to a two-percent duty for goods shipped into or out of Turkish territory. Venice enjoyed the fragile peace while the sultan fully digested Constantinople—but she knew war could erupt at any time on the slightest provocation.

Antonio had finally repaired the damage done during Giorgio's stewardship of the House of Ziani. He had gradually closed the rift with Vitale Candiano, who was now insuring their ships once again, though at higher rates. Candiano's desire to make profit exceeded the disdain he felt for Giorgio. In business, profit can soothe the worst burns.

Though they employed all of their considerable resources, the brothers could find no trace of Pierre DeMars or the mysterious ship that had damaged the *Tiger* that foggy morning in Marseilles. Despite Giorgio's desire to immediately take revenge on everyone involved, Antonio knew they must ensure their vengeance was complete and would not in any way implicate them. That would take time.

Soranzo's banquet had marked an end to open hostilities between the two families. The confrontation on the Molo earlier in the year between Giorgio and Vettor Soranzo was forgotten. There was no more talk of Antonio's captivity and his favored treatment by the Turks. Sometimes he regretted that, at the time, he had not seen how vulnerable his acceptance of Abdullah Ali's hospitality would make him to charges of collaboration with the enemy. He often wondered if he could have refused the governor's hospitality, if he had it to do over again.

Seraglio had become Antonio's inseparable companion, occupying a modest room on the fourth floor of the Ca' Ziani. He valued his friend's honesty and loyalty, trusting him like a member of his own family. Antonio discussed almost everything with him—even things he would not share with his business associates or even Giorgio. He would regularly sharpen his thinking on Seraglio's keen judgment as they talked together each day. He was especially pleased that Giorgio and Seraglio had also become friends.

Isabella and Antonio tried to produce another child, but it was not to be. They were disappointed but were thankful that God had given them Constantine. Isabella doted on him constantly. He was developing a complex personality as his father raised him in a manly way, while Isabella coddled him and often tried to prevent him from engaging in rough play with other boys. Giorgio loved him as his own son. Little Constantine, who worshipped his uncle, followed him around like a puppy.

In contrast, Soranzo seethed under his stoic façade. When the government released most ships and their crews to their owners for commercial use, Soranzo was given command of a squadron of galleys based at Negropont. He chafed every day at the thought of earning a captain's pay while the galleys under his command protected merchant ships belonging to wealthy traders like Antonio Ziani.

Though a man of considerable means, he was frustrated that he was obligated to contribute to Ziani's enrichment by protecting his ships. In Venice, trade made one wealthy and wealth made one powerful. The more Ziani could accumulate, the more difficult it would be for Soranzo to overcome Ziani's power and take his revenge.

Each time that Soranzo sailed from Venice to Greece, on the course he had taken almost three years before, he dropped a silver coin into the sea near the spot where his youngest brother had drowned. Sometimes he swore he could hear Marco's voice crying out to him for revenge from the dark waters below. These infrequent pilgrimages to his brother's watery grave kept the fire of his vendetta alive though he was forced to conceal it whenever he was back in Venice.

Ten year-old Enrico was growing up fast and Giovanni knew that unless he spent more time with him, the boy's need for a man's influence in his life would go wanting. This was something he had tried hard to avoid. Boys who grew up without a father's strong influence became attention-seeking men who created trouble for their families when they could no longer control them.

The official summons took Antonio by surprise. At first he did not believe the messenger, thinking it was some sort of hoax, but after closely inspecting the document he knew that the doge himself had sent for him.

Now, thirty minutes later, he was about to meet with Francesco Foscari for the first time in his life. Like many patricians, he had often seen him at public events and had even spoken to him once or twice. But now, as he paced slowly across the hard stone floor, outside the ornate oak and iron doors to the doge's private apartments, he plumbed the depths of his mind for a reason why Foscari would want to see *him*. Two guards and a member of the Ten, who, by law, observed every person who came and went to prevent unauthorized access to the most powerful man in Venice, stood motionless, but their eyes betrayed their interest. They also seemed to be asking—what does the doge want with this man?

Suddenly, the impressive doors opened and a gaunt man with a pointed brown beard beckoned him to enter.

"I am Signor Guardi, responsible for the Republic's finances. Have you met Doge Foscari before?" he asked as he pointed to the man seated in the center of the room.

Antonio bowed to the counselor and then turned and bowed more deeply, showing greater respect to Foscari, who nodded his approval.

"Of course we have met. Why, I knew Signor Ziani's father, Vincenzo, for fifty years. I even knew his grandfather, the famous merchant Lorenzo Ziani. And who in Venice does not remember the great doge Sebastiano Ziani, who in the twelfth century was responsible for building some of our city's greatest structures?"

Antonio was impressed with Foscari's knowledge of his forebears.

"Sit down, Signor Ziani, sit down," the old man beckoned with a smile.

As he saw him motion to an empty chair next to his, Antonio realized that only the three of them were present in the room. Everyone in Venice knew that the doge was never permitted to receive visitors, even family members, without three members of the Ten present. Where were they? thought Antonio. He had no sooner taken his seat than the doge began, his demeanor now as serious as a gravedigger's.

"Signor Ziani, your country has need of your service. Powerful men in the government who have vouched for your loyalty and your abilities with their very reputations have bestowed upon you a great honor. Do you understand what that means?"

Before Antonio could answer, the doge provided his own.

"It means that you are about to have an opportunity that few Venetians will ever have." As the doge leaned forward and lowered his voice slightly, Guardi stood up and moved away to a large window on the other side of the room, giving them some privacy.

"You can secure your reputation with the Republic's leaders as a man who has done a great thing for Venice. After this, no appointive post would be beyond your reach. Your future as one of the leading members of the patriciate will be assured."

Antonio's head was spinning. What did they want him to do? He had no idea but he knew, already, that he could not refuse the request the doge was about to make.

"Well, what do you say to that?" asked Foscari, his silvery threadbare beard dancing with every word he spoke.

"I am humbled by your confidence in me and pray that I will be capable of living up to your expectations, Doge Foscari," responded Antonio warily.

"By God, Guardi, this man is a born diplomat. If only we had a man like him in Milan thirty years ago . . ." The doge shook his head and continued.

"We are at peace with the sultan but I fear it will not last. Our spies tell us that even now, as he welcomes our new *bailo* in Istanbul, he is preparing to make war on us again. Morea, Negropont, and even Crete are in danger. We must stop this madman, Signor Ziani. No act is too bold for us to consider. Would you not agree?"

Antonio remembered that day in the emperor's palace courtyard when the sultan had cut the heads off of seventeen good men, defenseless men, for the crime of being wealthy and revered by their countrymen. The doge was right. Sultan Muhammed II was murderous and a danger to everyone. No Venetian was safe as long as he reigned.

"Yes, Doge Foscari. I was there in Constantinople. With my own eyes I have witnessed the sultan's treacherous deceit, his barbarity, and his cruelty."

"Well then, let us get down to business."

The words assaulted Antonio's ears—they sounded obscene. They were the same ones spoken by the sultan just before he had ordered the beheading of Contarini, Minotto, and the others. He was struck by the cruel irony.

"The government has decided to prevent the sultan from attempting to destroy Venice, indeed from undertaking any campaign against our lands and our property."

Antonio was startled as he felt a small hand, as delicate as a child's, gently touch him on the shoulder. He turned and looked up. Guardi had returned from his sojourn by the window and was smiling down at him like a candy peddler at a young boy with a handful of silver coins.

"We intend to assassinate the sultan of the Ottoman Empire," said the doge.

Antonio leaned back in his chair and expelled a long breath. The room seemed to revolve around him slightly as he tried to refocus his eyes.

"And you, signore, will have the honor of leading this conspiracy."

The doge's eyes, until now dimmed with age, sparkled as they held Antonio's, carefully searching his face to gauge his reaction.

"Counselor Guardi and I are the only two men in Venice who know the details of this plot. He will now tell you what you must accomplish for Venice and St. Mark."

Guardi moved into full view from behind Antonio's chair and turned. The red of his robe made Antonio think of the blood they were asking him to spill.

"You will leave within the week. It is September and your mission must be completed early in the New Year—by February. We expect the sultan will declare war on us in March just before launching a spring campaign. He will want to secure the element of surprise by giving us as little warning as possible of his intentions. He must be killed before his declaration of war or else his successor would surely be obligated to prosecute the war, in his name, or risk being deposed as a coward. Most important, he must be killed without revealing that Venice is behind his assassination."

Antonio's mind was racing. How would he accomplish such a feat?

"I have been authorized to provide you with two thousand ducats—a fabulous sum for killing one man—even if he is the sultan of the Ottoman Empire," continued Guardi. "The money will be waiting for you in Negropont when you arrive. The governor there will be told you are on a mission to convey a state gift from the doge to the sultan. This will enable you to obtain any transport you require and also avoid suspicion while you are in Istanbul."

"How will you ensure that Venice is not implicated?" asked the doge.

Antonio smiled. It *could* be done. There was a man who could plan such a feat. He was certain of it. If only the man still lived, he thought.

"There is a man, a Jew from Modone—a Venetian citizen. If he still lives, with that man's help, I can do it."

The doge and Guardi exchanged glances, nodding their heads, satisfaction on their faces, as though they had known what Antonio was thinking all along.

"There is one more important instruction, Signor Ziani," continued the doge, as Antonio was still reeling from the details provided by Guardi.

"You must tell no one about your mission, not your family, your friends—not even Domenico Ruzzini, your wife's uncle. If you violate this order, you will be imprisoned and, I promise, the jailer will lose the key. Tell your wife that you must go to Negropont on business. Did you obey my orders to tell no one of our meeting tonight?"

"Just as you ordered, Doge Foscari. I told my wife I was going out on business."

"Good. You must never mention to anyone, ever, that you have met with us today. Now, do you have any questions?"

Antonio had many but only two that he felt he must ask.

"What happens if the plot fails or if I am captured?"

"It will not fail because *you* will ensure that it succeeds. There is no substitute for achieving its aim," replied the doge.

Antonio stared at Foscari with as much defiance as he dared. That answer would not do, even from the doge. Time seemed to stand still as the three men looked intently into each other's faces.

Guardi broke the silence. "If you fail—do not come back to Venice. If you are about to be captured—take poison. The Republic must not be implicated. Do not let the Turks capture you again. This time your jailer will not protect you."

So the rumors of my disloyalty still linger, even here within these walls, thought Antonio. They are testing my loyalty. His mind wandered back to Soranzo's banquet. How could he have thought that such an implacable foe would ever relent?

As Antonio pondered the answer to his question, the doge stood, signaling that the meeting was over. He reached out his frail arm and grasped Antonio's shoulder.

"Young man, it is an honor to serve one's country on such an important mission." He smiled broadly through his thinning beard to amplify his words of encouragement.

"I have one more question," said Antonio.

Foscari sighed impatiently.

"I must take someone with me who speaks Turkish and Greek fluently. There is a man I met in Constantinople and brought back to Venice with me after we were imprisoned together. Do I have your permission to take him with me?"

The two men looked at each other, surprised.

"Who is this man?" asked Guardi.

"He is a Greek named Seraglio—and like no other man I have ever met. He knows Constantinople like the back of his hand and he is fluent in Greek and Turkish."

"Very well, Signor Ziani. But take no one else but him and the Jew you spoke of. Do not tell this man about your mission until you arrive in Modone. Until then you must be as discreet as a confessor."

Antonio stood and bowed. As he walked from the room, he strained his ears in vain to hear anything that they might utter. As he emerged from the Doges' Palace into the dark September night, he shivered as he wondered. Had Foscari decreed the sultan's death sentence . . . or his own? As he walked home, his plan slowly taking shape in his mind, his thoughts turned to a man he had once known—the one man, besides Seraglio, who would be able to help him accomplish his dangerous mission.

13

Istanbul

The meeting in the Doges' Palace four weeks earlier seemed like a distant memory as Antonio stood on the long serpentine stone pier and silently looked up at the old octagonal keep; a sentinel proudly guarding one of the Republic's most important cities. Its domed inner tower rose high above the crenellated walls of the outer tower. A crimson and gold flag with its winged Lion of St. Mark proudly waved above.

Modone, on the southwestern coast of the Peloponnese, was known as the "eyes and ears" of the Republic because of its strategic position astride the trade routes to the Levant and the ancient Byzantine possessions as far away as the Black Sea. Virtually every ship that sailed between East and West stopped there, their crews sharing gossip and intelligence that Venetian agents were sure to hear. It had belonged to Venice since 1204, when she had claimed it as a prize from Byzantium during the Fourth Crusade.

By virtue of its location, every adventurer in the eastern Mediterranean would eventually pass through, staying long enough to entertain a wild plot or to discover a way to make a small fortune—all illegally, of course, but never to be undertaken in Venetian territory. The Republic ruled the city with an iron hand and severely punished crimes of any sort. Antonio had chosen Modone because he knew it was the place where he could find the one man who could help him accomplish his mission.

Now, as Seraglio and Antonio walked in silence to the extreme western end of the stone quay and stopped, for the first time since the voyage began, they were finally alone. Antonio told Seraglio about his mission as his friend listened to every word in silence. When Antonio had finished Seraglio let out a long whistle.

"This will not be easy." Then he broke into a broad grin.

"Is that why you now wear that phial of poison around your neck?"

"Perhaps I should drink it now," said Antonio sardonically. "There is an old friend of my father's here, in Modone. We shall see him tomorrow. He will know what to do. Perhaps, with his help, we will be able to accomplish our mission."

"Antonio, I know people in Istanbul. When the Turks made half of the city slaves they would not have been foolish enough to send these men away. They would have been too useful in helping them to administer the city. They will be able to help us too."

Antonio assumed he would find the man in the same cozy stone apartment that he had called home when Antonio and his late father had last gone there five years before. Then, they had been desperate to find a cure for his father's terrible coughing spells. Josephus ben Levi had been Vincenzo Ziani's principal financier in Modone. A respected leader of the city's Jewish community, he knew all the best physicians. Four of them had examined his father and had all agreed there was nothing that could be done. He would be dead in six months—nine at best. They had been right. Vincenzo Ziani had died, drowning in his own mucous—wheezing and gasping for his last tortured breath. Antonio had eventually found a way to push these thoughts from his mind whenever they surfaced, but now painful images of his poor father wasting away haunted him like guilt.

They walked through the narrow, twisting streets on the way to Josephus' house. Nothing had changed. Soon they rounded a corner and looked down a street, wider than the others. On both sides were shops and storefronts where moneylenders traded their gold and silver for promises. At the end was the ancient synagogue—the only one in the city. It had been deliberately built to look modest on the outside, to avoid attracting thieves or the indignation of the Christian population. Its congregants were the physicians, teachers, and moneylenders of Modone. The first two professions were barred to Christians by a lack of education or by custom, the last by church and civil law.

Just past the old building, Antonio saw the familiar three-story structure.

Josephus' modest apartment was on the second floor. They climbed the narrow stairs to the landing. Antonio held his breath as he knocked on the wooden door.

They could hear bolts and chains rattling from within. Suddenly, the door opened a crack. A young woman's silky voice slid through the opening. They could not understand what she said—she was speaking in Hebrew.

"I am Antonio Ziani and I have come from Venice to see Josephus ben Levi."

"Signor Ziani, please enter," replied the melodious voice in perfect Italian.

A young woman opened the door, revealing a small room with three bare walls but the fourth was decorated with a brilliantly colored fresco depicting, in great detail, King Solomon directing the construction of his great temple in Jerusalem. On the floor was a wool carpet of crimson and gold—a gift from Antonio's father. It bore the colors of the Republic's battle flag but instead of a golden winged lion, a large Star of David adorned the center. Around the star the carpet was faded pink, worn threadbare by steps carefully taken to avoid stepping on the sacred symbol. In the far corner, Josephus ben Levi lay on a small curved bed with his head propped up on a plush silk-covered pillow. He was in his late sixties and so thin, he looked like he weighed no more than a boy. He was a scarecrow of a man and looked in poorer health than the last time Antonio had seen him.

"Antonio Ziani!" said Josephus in a raised, scratchy voice. His smooth, bald head contrasted with his shriveled face. A thin crop of white whiskers cascaded from his bony chin. As he struggled to stand on his frail legs, Antonio helped him to his feet. They embraced for a long time, Antonio patting him gently on the back.

"I never thought I would live long enough to see you again. You honor me with your presence in my humble house."

"Ruth, go and prepare a meal for my guests."

The servant girl nodded and left them, dutifully closing the door behind her.

"Josephus, this is Seraglio. He saved my life in Constantinople two years ago when the Turks were about to kill me. He is my most trusted friend."

Josephus and Seraglio clasped hands.

"I feared you were there. I am thankful that God spared you from the carnage. Now, Antonio, as you can see I am old and sick. Each hour remaining in my life is precious. Tell me why you are here in Modone?"

Antonio cast a glance at Seraglio and then looked into the leathery face of the man his father had trusted more than any other man in all of Greece.

"I am here to ask for your help to complete a mission of vital importance."

"Your demeanor is so grave, Antonio, you act as if you are planning to steal the sultan's treasury." Josephus smiled.

"If only it was just that, Josephus. I have been ordered to take his life."

Josephus slowly sat down on his bed. His sagging eyes betrayed interest as Antonio's words seemed to light a long-dormant fire within him. His tired body stiffened slightly, as some of his old energy and clearness of mind seemed to return.

"Assassinate the sultan? But how?"

"That is for you to tell me, Josephus. My father always valued your ability to solve the most difficult problems. You are the one man I know who could devise a way."

Josephus swallowed painfully. "I could say that I am too old for such an adventure or beg you not to ask me to help you since I have done enough favors for the House of Ziani already." He folded his hands, as if in prayer.

"When you brought your father here, the physicians gave him less than a year to live. Well, now those same physicians have pronounced my death sentence. Five months ago they told me I had less than a year to live. Since then I have been lying on that bed, wasting away with nothing left to live for. The minute before you came to my door, I was waiting to die—there being no longer any purpose for my life."

Josephus reached out to grasp Antonio's hand. Antonio gripped the old man's outstretched sticklike fingers, gently squeezed them, and smiled a toothy grin through his thick beard, baring his teeth to be sure Josephus could see his expression.

"Antonio, I cannot think of a better reason to live than to rid the world of Muhammed II. Though it is a sin in God's eyes to take another man's life, sometimes one finds it is necessary to kill in order to preserve the lives of others more deserving of life. In this situation, I only hope that I am right and that God will forgive me."

Each day they met at dawn and talked until, exhausted, Josephus could talk no more. Finally he agreed to go with them to Istanbul to assassinate the sultan.

A week later, they boarded a ship bound for Negropont. There, they collected two thousand gold ducats from the governor. From there they proceeded on to Istanbul, discreetly booking passage on an Egyptian ship and dressed as Greeks. The weather had turned colder. It was already late October—less than four months left, thought Antonio, as he contemplated his return to the city. He shuddered to think about the carnage he had seen there.

He wondered how it had changed. He hoped the men Seraglio placed such great faith in were still there. They would need all the help they could get.

The new year of 1456 had come. After months of exhaustive planning and preparation, everything was ready. It had all been done in complete secrecy. As in an intricate puzzle, each piece had been carefully set in place. Each participant understood his role perfectly but, like links in a chain, he knew only the one man above and below him. Josephus had proven himself to be a brilliant strategist. His plan insulated Antonio and Seraglio from the act, but provided them with the perfect vantage point to see it done.

Josephus had found that borrowers were always agreeable when obtaining loans. Then they had no aversion to doing business with a Jew. But sometimes his clients were less enthusiastic about paying him back. They would often enlist the help of local authorities to have loans from Jews conveniently declared illegal and therefore not repayable. Having no recourse within the law, Josephus resorted to other means to secure repayment. While never a problem in Modone or anywhere in Venetian territory, where all loans were protected under the law, in cities beyond Venice's control, he would retain the services of an enforcer to help him collect from these men.

Through the years, Josephus had built a network of business associates in every major Greek city, including Istanbul, where, for the last ten years, Michael Gregorius had been his collector. He was as strong as Josephus ben Levi was frail. They complemented each other perfectly. Now Josephus had hired Gregorius, who in turn had hired another man. The two of them would kill the sultan. Josephus had never met the other man. Gregorius had never met Antonio or Seraglio.

In the meantime, Seraglio had obtained useful information about the sultan and his movements from Greeks who had been retained by the Turks in government jobs because of their extensive knowledge of the city and its Greek population, which still numbered fifty thousand. None of these men had met Josephus or Antonio.

While they waited for the fateful day to arrive, Antonio and Seraglio retraced their steps along the streets they had walked together before the fall. They were amazed by the changes wrought by the sultan and how he had altered the human face of the city. There were more Turks than Greeks now. They would stand in front of the Hagia Sophia, now called Ayasofya by the Turks, and watch the worshippers enter. They wanted to go inside, but not being Muslim, they were prohibited from entering on penalty of death.

On the final night, Antonio, Seraglio, and Josephus sat talking softly, sequestered in the small apartment they had taken near the old Blachernae Palace.

"When does your ship sail, Josephus?"

"With the tide tomorrow, about two hours past sunrise. I will be in the Sea of Marmara by the time the sultan is dead."

Josephus narrowed his gaze on Antonio. "Are you sure you want to stay? Seraglio can confirm that the sultan is dead. I believe you are taking an unnecessary risk."

Seraglio decided that he could no longer conceal his true feelings.

"Antonio, you must leave tomorrow morning, before it is too late."

Antonio was fully aware of the risks he would accept by staying, but it was his plan and he intended to see it through to the end.

"No, Seraglio, I have already made my arrangements."

Earlier, unknown to Seraglio or Josephus, Antonio had sent a message to Abdullah Ali, who had recently been named by the sultan as the new governor of Istanbul. Too busy to see him, with 'Id al-Fitr so close at hand, he had agreed to receive him the following day. Antonio thought the meeting would provide him with the perfect alibi. No assassin would willingly put himself into such jeopardy. His sheer audacity would remove him from suspicion in the eyes of the Turks, despite the fact that he was a Venetian. The governor of Istanbul himself would vouch for his innocence.

Seraglio looked at his friend and implored him once more.

"The Turks will react to the death of their sultan like a hive of angry hornets. They will arrest every Italian they find in the city. They will torture indiscriminately to find the assassin. Even I would gladly cry out your name a hundred times to keep my skin from being flayed from my body or a wooden stake driven into my innards."

"Seraglio is right, Antonio," said Josephus unemotionally. "Your nationality is a liability. Can you think only of yourself? Will you be able to remain silent if you are caught and tortured? Would you not betray us to the Turks to save yourself? Do you really believe that the Turks would not round up every Italian in the city and begin questioning them until they get the answers they want?"

Antonio sat silently, their words still ringing in his ears. What could a Venetian do when confronted by the persuasiveness of a Greek, whose ancestors had invented logic, and the steadfastness of a Jew, whose people had invented the art of survival?

After a long silence, he surrendered. "Very well, I will do as you ask, but promise me this. Promise me you will both return to Venice when this business is finished. And that tomorrow, the feast of St. Mark, will be the sultan's last day on this earth."

Seraglio looked at Josephus and smiled. The old man coughed in the damp night air that filled the unheated room and smiled back weakly.

"The plot will succeed," said Seraglio confidently.

"If it does, it will succeed without God's help," said Josephus. "It will succeed because he has looked away."

The smile disappeared from Seraglio's lips as he considered Josephus' prediction.

"I suppose that is the difference between us and the sultan. If he is spared and he kills us instead, he will give the credit to God for our deaths."

"That is why we must succeed," said Antonio. "Now, let us retire. I want to sail with the morning tide so that I am miles away from here when the Turks throw open the gates of hell and they exact their terrible retribution. I will book passage on a different ship than yours, Josephus—It will be too dangerous for us to travel together."

As he embraced Seraglio and Josephus, Antonio felt sadness unlike any he had ever experienced before. It was too much for him. He turned away, inclining his head so they would not see the dampness in his eyes, and walked from the room.

Ramadan was nearly over—and none too soon for the inhabitants of the city. Most of the Turks had carefully observed the mandates of ritualistic fasting and good behavior for the past month, warily eyeing each other to ensure the law was obeyed. The Greeks and other Christians had made themselves scarce when outside of their homes and places of work, not wanting to accidentally violate their conquerors' unfamiliar religious rules.

The new moon would signal an end to the month of self-denial and usher in a great celebration—'Id al-Fitr—the Festival of the Breaking of the Fast. As soon as he had taken the city, the sultan had ordered a new marketplace, the bedestan, built where the old market had been, near the Golden Horn where Antonio had first met Seraglio. The next day, as soon as the midday prayers had ended, the festivities would commence. Beginning there, amid the covered shops with their high-priced wares, the revelers would fan out into every quarter of the city, noisily celebrating their return to normalcy.

Dawn crept silently, like a cat, across the stone floor and up the wall. Seraglio awoke to find Antonio, already up and dressed, sitting in a chair by the window staring down at the empty street below.

"It is dawn. Josephus is going to meet with Michael Gregorius in a few minutes to go over the plan one more time. Is there anything else I can do?"

"No, Seraglio. You and Josephus have done a fine job. I must go in a few minutes."

Seraglio walked silently out of the room to see if Josephus was also stirring. As he opened the door to the room, he could see him sitting on the edge of a stool, saying his morning prayers. Seraglio waited respectfully until he had finished.

"Today is the day, Josephus. Antonio is already up and preparing to leave."

"Yes, all of our work will come to fruition this day if God wills it. Michael will be here soon to go over the plans one more time."

In ten minutes Josephus and Michael were huddled in Josephus' small windowless interior room with its stout wooden door.

"The sultan will receive important subjects and foreign dignitaries at his palace until an hour before the midday prayer. Then, he will be conveyed through the streets in his palanquin to the *bedestan,* where he will greet the people and signal the start of the celebration. After that, he will be taken to his harem where he will, no doubt, expend some of the sexual energy he has been forced to control for the past month." Josephus looked at Michael. "Now tell me again. Where are you and your man going to be?"

"My man will be in the building you found for us near the *bedestan.* The top floor is uninhabited. It is used as a warehouse for storing rugs, just like you said. I must say that your knowledge of the city is remarkable. Who is your source?"

Josephus ignored his question and continued.

"Did your man find the secret room suitable for our purpose?"

"It is perfect. He has been hiding there since early yesterday. When he hears the midday prayer later today, he will post himself at the window and await my signal."

"You are certain he is a good shot?"

"Good enough; he will be armed with a crossbow and the bolts you gave me."

"What is the signal?" asked Josephus methodically between coughs.

"There is a sharp turn where the street from the palace bends right and runs into the *bedestan,* near the seawall. When the slaves carrying the sultan's palanquin enter the turn, they will have to go slowly to avoid tipping the sultan. That is when I will release a black pigeon. When my man sees the bird in the window, he will shoot."

"Good," said Josephus. "Now, how will your man escape?"

"He will immediately return to the secret room and hide there for three days, living on his supply of food and water. There is no way the Turks will find him there. The door seam is impossible to see unless you know where to look for it."

"How much have you paid him so far?"

"A third of his fee. He will only collect the rest if his arrow finds its mark."

"What elements of the plan could go wrong?"

Michael's massive forehead wrinkled as he stroked his bushy beard, his expression like a child's whose teacher had just asked him a difficult question.

"One of the sultan's guards could spot him in the window before he shoots. That is the only time he could be seen. Otherwise, the only other thing that could go wrong is that he could . . . miss. But that will not happen, I assure you," he said confidently. "I know only one man in all of Istanbul who is a better shot than him."

"Then why did you not hire that man?" asked Josephus, surprised.

"Because *you* did." He winked and made like he was firing a crossbow.

"Your man has his poison?"

"Yes, and he will take it too. The Turks will never capture him alive."

"Good. Now tell me, Michael. Where will you be?"

"Where we agreed I would be—several houses farther ahead from where my man will be stationed, so I can get a clear view of the sultan from the front as he nears the *bedestan* before he enters the right turn in the street."

"You know your work?"

"Of course. And I have my poison too. The Turks will never take me alive either."

The muscular Greek towered over Josephus as he approached him closely.

"There is one thing I have been wondering about all these weeks. Tell me, why would a Jew from Modone want to kill the sultan?"

"I have my reasons. That is enough for me—and should be enough for you,"

"Well, I must go to work now. After this day is done, I will meet you in Modone or in hell." As he walked out of the room, Michael laughed at what he had just said—wait until the Jew finds out there really is a hell, he thought.

After his footsteps had faded away down the stone corridor, Seraglio opened the door and entered the room.

"Did everything go as you expected?"

"Yes," replied Josephus, already sounding weary. "I must leave soon."

"Why *are* you helping us?" asked Seraglio, perplexed.

"Because I am old and I am grateful. Antonio's father was good to me—though I was a Jew. That kindness I am now repaying to his son. And as I do, I will help rid the world of a tyrant who would have every man, including me, believe in only his God; something I could never do. If we are successful, I can go to my grave contented. Today, I will complete the last and most important act of my long life."

Seraglio could see the steadfast determination chiseled into the old man's face. The same expression, he imagined, that Moses and Joshua and David must have worn as they had faced their powerful enemies. Seraglio hoped that Jehovah would again look with favor on the strivings of one of his chosen and intercede on his behalf.

The twenty slaves were tiring fast as they trudged under their heavy burden along the uneven cobbled street. Although it was cool, they were dripping with sweat in their heavy black woolen ceremonial robes as they struggled to give the royal palanquin and its occupants a smooth ride—the way the sultan demanded of them. Large enough to carry four adults, its solid wooden construction and gold sheathing made it too heavy. They thanked Allah that the sultan had ordered the heavy canopy removed so that the people could better see their master.

The trek through the labyrinth of stone-paved streets from the old Blachernae Palace had been mostly downhill as they worked their way through the crowds toward the *bedestan,* but now, as the road rose slightly in front of them, their load was becoming unbearable. Though they were carrying but four people, and two were small young women, the weight was immense as the sultan carried a quantity of gold coins with him this day to be dispensed as gifts. Even worse, he was sitting in his new armored seat.

Normally, the five slaves who supported each of the four poles worked as a team, resting one at a time, while the other four actually carried the weight. But this day everyone's strength was required to hold the palanquin aloft. They all knew what would happen if they ever dropped the sultan. Abdul was the one spared by the sultan the last time his livery slaves had dropped him. The sultan had allowed Abdul to live so that he could describe, in detail, the fate of his nineteen executed comrades to the new crew of slaves. His description had been effective—this crew had never failed its sultan.

The long parade moved slowly uphill. The perspiring slaves stole pained glances at each other as they grimaced and panted for air. The cheering crowd up ahead blocked their way, but the Janissaries, who were forbidden by the sultan on this occasion from using the flats of their swords or even their short whips, pushed into them to clear a path.

Just when the slaves thought they could not go on, mercifully, the sultan ordered a rest. With one unified and much-practiced motion the slaves quickly, yet carefully, set the palanquin on the ground and instantly dropped from their feet onto the hard stone pavement, exhausted. As they lay gasping for air, their Janissary overseers moved away to avoid smelling the odor of their sweating bodies.

Their rest was brief but it was long enough. Several took advantage of the unplanned break to relieve themselves. After a ten-minute respite, the order was given to proceed. Refreshed, they took their places, lifted their load, and resumed their labors.

Michael Gregorius could see the sultan clearly now, as he waved to the wild crowd. The Janissaries had cleared the occupants from all the buildings along the parade route to reduce the risk to the sultan. More than five hundred, he estimated, guarded the entrances or formed part of a moving cordon along both sides of the street. As the sultan's palanquin passed along the line of soldiers, the rearmost men would sprint up to the head of the column to maintain the human barrier between the sultan and the people. As the retinue advanced toward him it inched ahead like a giant white and black caterpillar.

Michael looked down at the two iron pots, brimming with steaming broth. No one would suspect that a loaded crossbow was lying on the bottom of one. He knew that at this close range the bolt's wet fletches would not adversely affect its flight enough to make him miss his target. He laughed as he thought of the two pompous Janissaries he had served earlier who had gagged on the foul-tasting liquid. He had even overcharged the bastards for good measure. A few minutes after that, a lone Janissary had approached him and asked him what was in the broth and, after smelling it, had silently moved on. He was a smart one, thought Michael. In the two and a half years since the siege he had never encountered a Janissary who spoke Turkish with such a strange accent.

There was still no sign of his man, Theophanes, in the window. Where was he? Michael stared nervously at the head of the parade as it moved inexorably closer. He estimated five minutes at most and the sultan would be at the turn, just sixty feet from where he stood and approximately one hundred feet from the window where Theophanes was supposed to be stationed. Where in God's name was he? Damn him!

"The crowd is joyous today, Master," shouted Abdullah Ali above the din.

The sultan nodded; it was pointless to try to talk above the roaring masses as the fascias of the stone buildings along the narrow street amplified the noise.

"We are nearing the *bedestan*," shouted the governor again, pointing up ahead. "Just beyond that turn."

Since the fall of Constantinople, Abdullah Ali's star had risen rapidly. He had become one of the sultan's most trusted lieutenants and had recently been made governor of Istanbul, the greatest city in the Ottoman Empire.

"Are you still feeling ill?" the sultan's wife shouted in his ear.

"Yes, but never mind. Do not speak to me," he replied, irritated.

Abdullah Ali grasped his favorite wife's hand and squeezed it tightly. She smiled back at him, happy to have been chosen over his three other wives to accompany him on this important occasion.

Up ahead, Michael could make out the features on the faces of the nearest Janissaries now. He could see the sultan sitting above and behind the governor. Again he looked up at the window and thought he saw someone but it was still empty. Only two minutes now. I should have chosen someone more dependable, he thought. He turned around his long spoon and dipped the hooked handle into the steaming soup and caught the crossbow on the bottom. He lifted it slightly to ensure he could quickly withdraw it when the time was right. He had practiced the maneuver a thousand times. His diligence would pay off today, he thought.

Theophanes slowly pulled open the masonry door as it slid silently on its well-oiled bronze hinges. A roar from outside rang in his ears as he picked up his crossbow and the three arrows and stuck his head out of the door. The corridor was empty. Quickly, he crawled across it and through the open door into the large room that overlooked the street. Piles of cheap rugs and reddish-brown earthen urns lined the walls. More stacks of carpets rose from the floor, forming a mazelike series of passageways, almost as tall as a man. He had stacked some small mats near the window, to just the right height, the day before. Now he crept up behind the pile and peeked over the top.

He could see the buildings on the other side of the street through the open window. All their windows were empty. He draped the black sheet he had brought with him over his head and slowly pushed the pile of mats toward the open window. As he did, the street below slowly came into view. Soon, he could see hundreds of bobbing heads and the tops of the Janissaries' helmets as they stood guard, oblivious to his well-concealed presence.

He looked to his right and spied his quarry. There, seated on the palanquin behind the governor, was Sultan Muhammed II—*Fatih*—Conqueror. He checked his crossbow. The bolt was nestled against the stock straight and ready. He unconsciously patted the weapon. It would not be long now. His mouth was dry as cotton as he looked to his left. There he is! Michael was looking straight at him, but Theophanes could tell by the way he kept looking up and then down that he could not see him. He was virtually invisible to anyone down on the street—just as they had planned it. But one man did see Theophanes in the window. From the other side of the street, the Janissary with the strange accent standing guard in front of an empty building knew where to look for an assassin.

Antonio Ziani had deceived Seraglio and Josephus. He had not sailed with the morning tide. Though he knew that Seraglio was out there somewhere, dutifully waiting to verify that the sultan had been killed, Antonio had decided that he would witness the assassination for himself—despite promising his co-conspirators that he would sail at dawn. As soon as it was over, he planned to leave the scene disguised as a Janissary and then later change into his own clothes and hide out in an inn where he had rented a room.

Tomorrow, he would meet with the governor and ask him for permission to leave the city on the next ship. Since Venice and the Ottoman Empire were technically at peace, and he would not be suspected of complicity in the assassination, he was betting his life that the governor would help him.

Michael could see the Janissaries steadily coming closer, forming their cordon. In thirty seconds they would reach the front of his stand. Each new soldier took his place at the head of the line, facing in the opposite direction of the man next to him—giving the Janissaries a view of the sultan and the crowd. Suddenly, he saw Theophanes move in the window. Everything was ready now.

An earsplitting cheer rang out from the street as soldiers and civilians alike shouted for their sultan. He waved to the crowd as the exhausted slaves carefully began to round the turn, slowly carrying their load toward the *bedestan*. Letting go of the spoon, Michael bent over and picked up a small silk sack and reached inside. With one quick motion, he pulled out the pigeon and threw it skyward as he cheered. The Janissary to his front reached for his sword until he saw the bird that Michael had released to celebrate the end of Ramadan and the sultan's triumphant procession.

When the pigeon suddenly burst in through the window, Theophanes was startled, and dropped his weapon. It cut him slightly as it bounced off his knee and clattered onto the stone floor. He picked it up, replaced the arrow, and held the stock against his cheek. As he looked down the sight, he could see the leading slaves clearly. Ten seconds to go.

As Michael bent down to stir his soup the curious Janissary looked away. He dipped the spoon deep into the cauldron and caught the crossbow's handle. As he pulled it from the steaming liquid, in one fluid motion, he tipped the cauldron toward the street with his free hand. The scalding liquid gushed and splashed onto the legs of the three nearest soldiers, burning them. As they screamed in agony, hopping and falling to the ground, their cries were masked by the roar of thousands of voices. No one noticed Michael Gregorius as he quickly dropped down, inserted the bolt, aimed his weapon, and fired. Invisible, the thirteen-inch-long bolt ripped through the air and found its mark as its razor-sharp Persian steel point crashed dead center into the sultan, pinning his turban to his forehead as his brains exploded through the back of his shattered skull and splattered on his young wife and the slaves and cobblestone street behind him.

Up above in the window, as Theophanes slowly squeezed his trigger, his target suddenly fell backward, moving in the opposite direction from the other three passengers. His arrow zinged through the air and hit the governor in the shoulder—he had missed the sultan! Though he had two more bolts, he panicked, thinking of nothing now but saving his own life. With the crossbow clenched in one fist, he crawled quickly along the floor, like a cockroach, to his hiding place and shut the door behind him. Safely inside, Theophanes unconsciously rubbed his sore knee as he kept his eyes fixed on the door. He strained to hear any sign of intruders over the pounding of his heart.

Meanwhile, pandemonium had erupted on the street below. A few slaves ran away while the rest tried to hold on to their poles but the added weight was too much for them. The golden palanquin toppled onto the street with an earsplitting crash, throwing its human cargo onto the cobblestones. Two officers, not realizing what had happened, began to beat the slaves with their short whips as they cursed them back to their duty.

As the governor slumped to the ground, barely conscious and in great pain, his hysterical wife cradled his head in her arms. Nearby, the sultan lay on his back, a black finger-sized hole in the middle of his forehead. The shaft of the bolt had broken cleanly off when his body had fallen to the ground. A stream of crimson trickled from the wound down the side of his nose, over his mouth, and soaked into his beard. He was unconscious. As his young wife wiped away his blood that had spattered on her olive face, she screamed for someone to help her. The Janissaries nearest to him backed up to shield their master from another attack. Others, farther away, began to viciously swing their swords to cut their way through the crowd that had surged forward to see what had happened. They were already searching the nearest buildings.

Antonio had seen Michael fire the killing shot and quickly drop the crossbow back into the remaining kettle of soup. It had all taken less than five seconds. As the assassin walked away down a side street, he was not alone. Most of the crowd wanted no part of the Janissaries' frenzied search for the assassin—many had chosen the same street to make good their escape. In a minute he had disappeared around a corner in the wild throng.

Antonio walked in the opposite direction, into the *bedestan*. He ducked into an empty booth and quickly discarded his headgear and uniform, revealing a nondescript robe underneath. Then he quickly walked two streets away, to the room he had rented earlier after he had left Seraglio and Josephus that morning.

Word quickly reached the *bedestan* that the sultan had been assassinated. The crowds of would-be celebrants there quickly melted away, their joy turning to despair. The city rang with shouts and screams as the news spread from neighborhood to neighborhood. The sounds of thousands of running feet and cursing men echoed in the streets as people tried to wildly push past one another. Every man ran like he was the assassin, fearing that if he did not, he could be caught and tortured into admitting he was.

After the four Janissaries had climbed to the top of the stairs they fanned out to search the rooms facing the street. One entered the room filled with piles of carpets and went to the window. As he looked out, he could see the sultan lying in the street, surrounded by those who were sworn to protect him. Turning to leave, he noticed a few tiny crimson droplets on the floor, just inside the window. He knelt and touched a drop and slid it between his thumb and his forefinger. It was fresh blood. As he looked around, he saw more drops. Their trail led him into the corridor. His eyes followed the trail up to a wall where it abruptly stopped. He ran his hands, lightly, along the masonry. He could just make out the trace of a seam. He quickly went in search of his comrades.

The Janissaries cried unabashedly as they carried their master's body back to the palace. The man who had given them their greatest victory was dying; the back of his head had exploded like a ripe melon—a gaping mass of red and gray jelly. As the bolt had torn through his skull, splattering his brains out against the armored chair that could not protect him, it had instantly rendered him a living corpse. The range could not have been more than fifty feet. They swore to each other that they would make the Greeks pay.

Theophanes froze. He could hear faint noises outside. His hand reached for the small phial of poison dangling from his neck. Two quick thuds broke the silence. Suddenly, the door exploded as pieces of stone and plaster pelted his face. The Turks fell upon him just before he brought the poison to his lips. As they dragged him to his feet, one held his crossbow and the two unused bolts. They had caught the sultan's assassin!

The door to Josephus' room opened, startling Seraglio. There, in the doorway, silhouetted in the afternoon light, stood a tall, husky bearded man. "Who are you?"

"I am Josephus' paymaster and you have earned yours today."

The man eyed Seraglio suspiciously. Then a broad grin split his face.

"The Janissaries are on a rampage," said Michael proudly.

"Emperor Constantine may now rest in peace," replied Seraglio, head bowed.

Then he reached into his robe, produced a leather sack, and tossed it to Michael.

"Where will you go now?" asked Seraglio.

"It is better that you do not know—but away from this place, I can assure you."

He saluted Seraglio and without uttering another word, he was gone.

After a moment's reflection, Seraglio walked from the inn that had been his home for the past three months and stepped into the street. It would not be safe to remain in the city, but it would be more dangerous to attempt to leave. Now that he had paid the assassins he would go to the tavern where he had first met Antonio, take the room he had rented and wait until some poor bastard who was suspected of being the assassin was caught. Only then would it be safe to leave the city.

My men found a Greek in the upper room of a building directly above the turn where the sultan was shot. They found a crossbow and two bolts exactly like the ones that struck you and the sultan." The officer stood at attention, pleased with his report.

"I want no torture—not yet. I must question him first," ordered the governor. Abdullah Ali rubbed his shoulder where the physician had stitched up his wound. It still burned with pain, despite the elixir he had drunk. As he turned and walked back into his private quarters in the sultan's palace, he wondered what would happen now. The sultan's only son, Mustafa, was barely two years old. Who would rule?

Suddenly, the door opened. He spun around, his hand instinctively reaching for his sword. A Janissary officer had wandered into his room.

"What are you doing here in my quarters? Get out! Leave me at once."

The young officer smiled impudently through his short beard. His un-kempt stringy hair hung down the sides of his face like a barbarian. He brazenly ignored the governor's order. Abdullah Ali flew into a rage.

"Guards!" he shouted.

Two large Janissaries instantly burst through the door.

"What is going on here?" screamed Ali, wildly, as he drew his sword.

"I will take off your head, you insolent beggar!"

"Easy, Abdullah, a man cannot be killed twice in one day."

The governor froze. The voice was familiar. It was the sultan's!

"But . . . I . . . I . . . do not understand."

"I will explain it to you, my friend, for I witnessed the whole scene. You see, today, I was one of the officers beating the slaves who dropped you onto the street."

"But who was that man behind me . . . who was killed?"

"He did look like me. These days it does not pay to be handsome, eh, Abdullah?"

The sultan shook with laughter as he removed the false hair, revealing his shaved head. One of the laughing Janissaries left and quickly returned with a large white turban that he carefully fitted onto the sultan's shining head.

"We must find whoever did this, Abdullah. Do you realize I have been growing that beard since I was a young man? I had to cut it off to make my deception work."

"But how did you know someone was plotting to kill you?" asked the governor.

"Each morning when I rise, I know that it *could be* the day that someone will attempt to kill me. Three days ago, I came into possession of the knowl-edge that enemy agents were at work in the city trying to find out my plans for the festival. I reasoned that if I could present the perfect opportunity for my enemies to assassinate me, they would not be able to resist the chance. I thought it better to have the attempt occur at a time of my own choosing—so I could foil it."

"But why allow your subjects and the rest of the world to think it suc-ceeded?"

"By creating the illusion that the attempt was successful, I knew it would be easier to expose and arrest those who were behind it and demoralize those I cannot catch. I want to crush their spirits. I want my enemies to know that I am invincible."

"Who do you suspect?"

"The Venetians, of course. But I must have proof."

"But, Master, we have already caught the man who did it—he is a Greek."

"I have already finished with him, while the physician was repairing your shoulder. He told me nothing, except the name of the man who hired him. Have you ever heard of a man in the city named Michael Gregorius?"

"No, Master."

"We shall begin with him. But we shall have to climb a ladder, though, to get to the man who ordered my assassination. As Allah is my witness, the old doge will be seated on the top rung. The Venetians have the most to gain by my death."

The sultan stroked his partially shorn beard. He looked almost comical to the governor, who easily controlled any urge to chuckle at the sight.

"Leave us!" commanded the sultan to the guards. "Now my trusted friend, I will tell you what we shall do . . ."

14

The Aftermath

Antonio spent the long night tossing and turning in the squalid little room, staring at the cracks in the darkened ceiling. By the time the sun's rays finally pierced the single greasy windowpane, he had only slept for a few hours. As he dressed, rubbing his aching limbs, he thought about what he would say to governor Abdullah Ali.

The governor shared his residence with the sultan in the old Blachernae Palace. A new palace, under construction on the banks of the Bosphorus, was not yet completed. Antonio was ushered into an antechamber by a gigantic eunuch who eyed him suspiciously as he stood waiting to see his old acquaintance. A few minutes later, footsteps announced the governor's arrival.

"Ah, Captain Ziani, it seems we did not meet next in Venice after all."

"Allow me to offer my regrets on the death of the sultan."

"It is not every day that a great man, such as he, is cruelly taken from his people, Captain Ziani. He possessed a quality most rare in a leader—he made ambitious promises to his people *and* he kept them. They loved him for that. That is why my responsibility to find the sultan's assassin and bring him to justice weighs so heavily on me. Now, what did you want to see me about?"

"I am honored to see you again, my friend, and congratulate you on your appointment as governor of Istanbul," said Antonio.

"As much as I would enjoy one of our thought-provoking discussions, I regret that, today, I do not have time for such pleasantries. Again, what do you want?"

Antonio breathed deeply and began. "I came to Istanbul with the intention of repaying the money you paid for my ransom and to conduct some business. But now, I find, I must again ask for your help. I had planned to sail for Venice tomorrow, but I have heard that no one is permitted to leave the city. Can you arrange a passport for me?"

"That is true. The perpetrator must be caught and executed. As a Venetian you would, of course, be an obvious suspect," said the governor with an ironic smile. "It will be most difficult but perhaps I can arrange something."

"For that, I would be most grateful, Governor. Now, how much did Seraglio's and my ransom cost you?"

"Do not trouble yourself, Captain Ziani. As you can see, I have been made governor of Istanbul. Fortunately, the pay for this job is better than a jailer's."

"Surely, there must be something I can give you to repay your generosity."

"Give me the sultan's assassin," shot back the governor, his fierce eyes penetrating into Antonio's, signaling the serious turn in the conversation.

"That I cannot do. I do not know who the assassin is," said Antonio truthfully.

"Then, just give me your solemn word, sworn to your God, that you had nothing to do with this despicable crime."

Antonio had anticipated his request.

"Abdullah Ali, I swear it."

"Very well, Captain Ziani, come back tomorrow at this time. I will arrange for your passport. You can collect it from Mustapha, my eunuch."

"Thank you, Governor," replied Antonio, his deception achieved.

The next day, Antonio was on a Syrian ship bound for Corfu. From there, he knew he could catch a ship bound for Venice.

As the first strips of flesh were carved from his chest and buttocks, Theophanes had broken, much to the disappointment of his torturers, who had delighted in introducing the sultan's assassin to Turkish justice. Shrieking for mercy, Theophanes had quickly admitted that he had accepted money from Michael Gregorius to kill the sultan, but that his employer had actually fired the deadly missile himself.

Governor Abdullah Ali took charge of the government while the sultan remained in his palace. He immediately ordered a massive hunt for Michael

Gregorius. The enraged Turks searched the city like a swarm of angry hornets whose nest had been torn open. No excess was spared as the Janissaries spread out across the city and its environs, scouring every neighborhood and hamlet as they desperately sought the man responsible for their beloved sultan's death. Michael had eluded a careful search by the guards as he passed through the city gate that first night, squeezed into the false bottom of a specially constructed wagon. But within twelve hours he was found and captured while he slept in his cousin's crude stone hovel, outside the city.

The Turks tortured and killed Michael's cousin and family before his eyes. Later, subjected to the same cruel torture as Theophanes, he had slowly and agonizingly bled to death, but not before revealing that a Jew, who had hired him, had been the plot's mastermind. He courageously died before he could be made to reveal the Jew's name.

The authorities arrested every foreigner who attempted to leave Istanbul for two days after the assassination. Seraglio hid out in his tiny room above the tavern, not venturing outside for any reason. After waiting for three days, he walked brazenly to the harbor and booked passage on an Egyptian ship bound for Alexandria. One look at him convinced the Turks he could not have been a part of the conspiracy.

Seraglio watched the city slowly fade into the hazy purple twilight, as the sinking sun's rays bathed the walls and towering minarets in gold. That night, safely tucked in his hammock, gently swaying with the rolling ship, he finally succumbed to exhaustion, comforted by the thought that he had avenged the fall of his beloved Constantinople.

Antonio was the first to disembark from the ship, eagerly wanting to tell the doge how he had successfully completed his dangerous mission. The voyage had seemed even longer than when he had been repatriated from Rumeli Hisar more than two years before. He walked as fast as he would allow himself toward the Doges' Palace, across the Piazzetta to the Porta della Carta. As he passed through the ornate portal to the seat of Venetian power it all felt more familiar to him than the last time he had been there. He flew up the steps three at a time all the way to the third floor, attracting curious stares from faceless, robed men. At the top he abruptly stopped, almost losing his balance, as two imposing ducal guards barred his way, their hands threateningly resting on the hilts of their swords. He brusquely asked to see the doge, stated his name, and then stood silently as one guard disappeared down hall toward the doge's apartments. Fifteen minutes later, the man returned and beckoned him to follow.

As he entered the room where he had met the doge five months earlier, it felt different from how he remembered it. It was filled with tension. This time, three black-robed men, the members of the Ten assigned to watch the doge day and night, were present. One pointed to a chair. Not a word was spoken in the morguelike chamber while they waited on the doge. Finally Francesco Foscari entered through his private door and took his seat, the whole time his eyes avoiding Antonio's, betraying no clues to the thoughts that lurked behind them.

"Signor Ziani," he said, "I am told you have just returned from Istanbul."

"Yes," replied Antonio, "I have come here directly from my ship."

"Tell us what happened there," he said gravely, almost inaudibly.

"The sultan is dead," Antonio said with a flourish, showing his pride.

Before Antonio could collect his expected congratulatory reward from the doge, Foscari struggled to his feet. Standing transfixed, his face contorted in a look of anguish, he then fell back limply into his plush chair, gasping for his breath. He had the blazing eyes of a caged beast as he extended his arm, pointing a bony finger straight at Antonio.

"Villain!" he screamed, his face a deathlike mask of disaster.

The black-robed men began to shout. Amid the tumult Antonio tried to comprehend what was happening. Then one of the Ten held up his hand for silence.

"Signor Ziani has bungled his mission badly—so badly, that he does not even know what happened, but you, Doge Foscari, and your foolish plan, have caused Venice irreparable damage."

The doge sat silently, head in his hands, defeated.

"But . . . but I still do not understand," stammered Antonio. "He *is* dead, I tell you!"

"He lives!" said the man with certainty—as one who knows an indisputable fact.

Antonio looked at the others' faces but could find no comfort. He thought he would go mad. Finally one of the others spoke.

"Signor Ziani, we have received word from the sultan himself that he is very much alive. The document bore his *tugra*—his official monogram. The man you assassinated was a slave whose sole talent was his uncanny resemblance to his master."

Antonio's heart was pounding, his mouth dry as sand.

"The news could not be worse," the first man continued. "The Turks say they tortured a Greek they caught at the scene who led them to another who, also horribly mistreated, revealed that he was hired by a Jew—a Venetian citizen."

Antonio closed his eyes as he anticipated what he was about to hear next.

"The sultan has informed us that he will climb every rung of the ladder until he finds our doge at the top."

Antonio instinctively shifted his eyes to Doge Foscari, who looked as though he could not hear the conversation as he stared blankly into space.

"Where are your two accomplices, the Jew and your Greek companion? Did they return with you to Venice?" asked the second man.

"We all left separately. The Jew, a man named Josephus ben Levi, left Istanbul for Modone the morning of the assassination attempt. The Greek, Seraglio, should arrive back in Venice in a few days," he replied. "He left the city after I did."

Antonio looked directly at the man.

"It is unlikely that either assassin knew that ben Levi is a Venetian citizen."

"Then how do you explain the sultan's assertion that he is?"

"I do not know," replied Antonio, at a loss for words.

"How do you know that your accomplices actually made it out of the city? What if they did not? What if they too were captured and tortured? Would that not explain the sultan blaming Venice?" the man narrowed his glaring eyes.

"Would the sultan be able to learn from either ben Levi or Seraglio that Venice was behind the plot to assassinate him?"

"Yes, signore. There would be no doubt," Antonio answered, truthfully.

He had failed because the sultan had discovered the plot and had cleverly countered the attempted assassination by employing a double as a decoy. Now the failed plot would provide the sultan with a *casus belli* to break the fragile peace with Venice. They had unleashed the whirlwind.

"You have failed to perform your mission, Signor Ziani," said the first man as he looked severely at the doge.

"You must say nothing of this business to anyone. Do you understand? The people must never know that their government has undertaken such a foolish enterprise. Now, you have been away for many months and should be reunited with your family."

His two colleagues nodded their agreement. As Antonio walked from the room, his head was spinning. Though he had been absolved from sole blame for the disaster, it was the worst day of his life. He wondered if the government would ever entrust an important task to him again. He could not bear to think of a future without the prospect.

. . .

N early perfect," said Soranzo. "The only better outcome would have been if the sultan *had been* assassinated and Ziani had been caught and executed for the crime."

Malipiero narrowed his gaze as he placed his half-empty glass on the table.

"Giovanni, you have been blinded by your desire to exact revenge on that man. Do you not see what has happened? In his weakened state, Doge Foscari will now be even less capable of providing the strong leadership the Republic will require to oppose the sultan, as he will now surely seek revenge on us."

Soranzo leaned back and sighed as he struggled under the weight of his mentor's words. He knew Pasquale was right. His hatred for Ziani was a mere trifle compared to the perilous situation the failed plot had created for Venice.

"Pasquale, surely the solution to the Republic's problem is to remove Foscari."

"True, but remember, in our entire history, no doge has ever been deposed."

Both men sat pensively, finishing their glasses of wine. Finally Malipiero spoke.

"Promise me you will put an end to this business with Ziani, once and for all. His reputation has now been damaged considerably. Surely that is enough for you."

"It is true that Ziani has damaged his family's reputation in ways even his ancestors could not have imagined. But he also caused my brothers' untimely deaths—though I realize that only matters to me."

Soranzo could not disguise his frustration as he stared as defiantly as he dared at his powerful friend.

"But look how he has continued to undermine the Republic. First, he sold his honor to curry favor with the Turks while his comrades rotted in that prison—and what did he suffer for it—a damaged reputation? Now this failed assassination business may drag us into renewed hostilities with the Turks. No, Pasquale, I will not rest until he is made to pay, personally, for all he has done—to me *and* to the Republic."

W hile her leaders toiled to keep Venice in a perpetual state of readiness for all-out war with the Turks, only a few men at the top of the government—the doge, his Signoria, and the Ten knew of the failed assassination plot. The government could not tell the people just how dire the situation really was without publicly admitting Venice's complicity in the plot— something they could never do. A public disclosure would damage Venice's reputation with every other country in the world. As a result, greater demands were placed upon the wealthiest patrician families to finance warship construction, build fortifications in her far-flung eastern Mediterranean possessions, and supply the needs of her land forces. Unpopular war taxes on the general populace were not justifiable so long as the Turks did not openly undertake the attack that the doge and his inner circle knew, one day, would come.

As the months passed the tension grew unbearable. Some of the Ten had lost confidence in Doge Foscari, but a slim majority, led by Domenico Ruzzini, balked at the suggestion by Lorenzo Loredan, supported by Malipiero, that the doge be deposed. That radical step was unthinkable to them, especially since the failed assassination plot against the sultan could not be used as justification with the people. By the time the warm summer sun slowed life in the city to a languid pace, inside the Doges' Palace the chilly relations between the doge and his tormentors had turned frigid. The Ten had even gone so far as to accuse the doge's wayward son, Jacopo, of treason.

Lorenzo Loredan demanded he be hung between the two columns on the Piazzetta in public disgrace but the vote failed in the Great Council. Instead he was sent to Crete where he was imprisoned. In poor health, he died six months later.

Isabella's uncle has told me that from the day Doge Foscari learned of his son's death, he resolved to wash his hands of the men who have dogged him and whom he holds responsible for Jacopo's death—the Ten, led by Loredan and Malipiero. Now he refuses to lead. He no longer attends meetings or fulfills his official duties. It is apparent that he wants to embarrass the Ten by daring them to violate our constitution and depose him. This may be the last straw. I fear he is done for."

Seraglio raised his eyebrows at the prospect of the bloodless coup.

"There has never been a doge who was forced to resign?"

"Never."

They could not have known then how prophetic Antonio's words were. A short time later, after months of wrangling, the Ten, meeting in secret, finally agreed that the doge must go. His greatest foe, Lorenzo Loredan, and Domenico Ruzzini, whose swing vote finally sealed Foscari's fate, made an official visit to the doge and urged him to abdicate. When told of the Ten's decision, the old doge responded forcefully.

"The Ten have no authority to demand my resignation; only a majority of the Great Council may force me to abdicate. If you come with that authority, I will consider it. Otherwise, this conversation is finished."

The Ten were not to be denied. The man was incapable of ruling and had to go. Now it was Loredan who delivered the Ten's harsh ultimatum.

"If you abdicate now, you will receive an annual pension of fifteen hundred ducats, a most generous offer. Otherwise, you will be cast out of the Doges' Palace and all your personal property will be confiscated, leaving you with no means of support."

The threat worked. Tired and broken, the doge finally surrendered. Francesco Foscari became the first doge ever deposed in the history of the Venetian Republic.

Pasquale Malipiero was quickly elected as the new doge. One week later, on All Saints' Day, Francesco Foscari died a broken man. In the first year of Doge Malipiero's reign, thirty-six-year-old Antonio Ziani, as a member of the Great Council, was privy to much that was happening, politically, in the world. However, in the wake of the failed assassination plot, he resigned himself to devoting most of his attention to the House of Ziani and his business interests. He knew there would be no invitations to perform the Republic's business. He would have to pay for his failure by enduring the worst punishment imaginable to a Venetian patrician—he would be ignored by the Republic he loved, as important and exciting duties would be given to others—many less able than he. At least he would have time to develop his plan for the long-overdue revenge against Soranzo, Steno, and the mysterious DeMars for their treachery.

During this difficult period he and Seraglio were inseparable. They met almost every morning for a breakfast of bread, salted fish, and wine. It had become a ritual. On a rare morning that began differently, Antonio would feel incomplete all day. He always looked forward to their time together. Often, they would discuss Constantine's schooling. He was now five years old and full of the mischief most boys display at that age. To supplement the tutelage the boy suffered under the stern teacher Antonio had employed, Seraglio also devoted long hours teaching him in the Greek way—discussing and learning about the world around him.

"In less than a year, Doge Foscari is deposed and then Pasquale Malipiero is elected to replace him. Now there is news that Pope Calixtus III has died in Rome. What changes God wreaks on the world," sighed Antonio.

"Pope Calixtus reigned for almost four years—plenty of time for him to accomplish so little," observed Seraglio with a disrespectful grin.

"Except that, while he always talked publicly of a new crusade against the Turks, instead, that Spaniard devoted most of his energy to building his family's power in Rome. Within a year of becoming pope he brazenly raised three of his nephews to cardinal, though the eldest was just twenty-five. He awarded him the most prestigious post in the papal court—commander of all papal troops even though, as a cardinal, the upstart flaunted his mistress around the streets of Rome. I hope his successor, who is surely aware of his predecessor's transgressions, will restore dignity to the Holy See. Hopefully, we have seen the last of the Borgias!"

Seraglio smiled mischievously and launched into one of his unique assessments.

"Alphonso Borgia's election was a perfect example of Roman Church efficiency. The Italian cardinals could not agree on which among them to make pope, the bribes being nearly equal, so they agreed on a seventy-seven-year-old Spaniard, who was so sickly, they were certain he would die quickly. Their work finished, they left the accursed little chamber they had been locked away in for weeks to get some fresh air and good food. Then, after a few months, thinking by then, he would have died, they thought they would be able to begin their deliberations anew, receiving yet another set of golden inducements to cast their votes, this time, for one of their own—an Italian Pope."

"You speak irreverence this morning, Seraglio," laughed Antonio.

"Fluently," replied Seraglio.

Finally, responding to threats from the west, Muhammed II grew tired of peace. With the eastern reaches of his empire secured from recent Persian incursions, he again turned to the rich West to expand his empire. He was still only twenty-six and filled with zeal to bring Islam to the infidel. Also, he knew his history. His people loved a conqueror and deposed or assassinated sultans who appeared weak or lacked the fiery zeal they expected in their leaders. Having already survived several assassination attempts, he had no intention of turning from his warlike ways. Now the sultan fixed his eyes on Venice's Greek possessions, Serbia, Bosnia, Crete, Rhodes, and even the Italian peninsula itself. The following year, the battle lines would be drawn for the inevitable fight to determine if Europe would be Muslim or Christian.

. . .

As they shared some wine together, Seraglio waited patiently for Antonio to tell him what was on his mind.

"They say Pope Pius II has called for a crusade against the Turks at the congress in Mantua. Nearly every Christian state was represented there," began Antonio.

"What will Venice do? Will she fight?"

"I do not know, Seraglio. We Venetians have not forgotten that we alone, save Genoa, came to the defense of Constantinople while the rest of Christendom sat on their hands and did nothing. I, for one, think we should stay home and tend to our business."

"But our fleet makes us an essential participant in any crusade. Without Venice the west can not succeed against the Turks," observed Seraglio.

Antonio's reply was laced with frustration.

"With our extensive Greek possessions, we have the most to lose if a war against the Turks is lost. The other Italian city-states, which are our rivals in commerce, have more to gain than we do if a crusade is successful. Their share of the spoils would enable them to better compete with us."

"Then Venice should diplomatically agree to join in a crusade if all the other states will wholeheartedly support the war. The congress will degenerate into futile discussions and no action will ensue. Lawyers and diplomats never act; they only talk. Venice will save face and preserve her advantage," replied Seraglio emphatically.

"That is exactly what Doge Malipiero suggested in the Senate yesterday."

Antonio Ziani had used his abilities to expand his family's trading interests. His considerable wealth compensated for his lack of service to the Republic as he slowly rebuilt his reputation among the members of the Great Council.

He was a member of the faction that usually opposed Doge Malipiero, led by Isabella's powerful uncle, Domenico Ruzzini. Antonio suffered in silence as the wily Malipiero played mentor to his rival, Giovanni Soranzo. However, he secretly admired the doge's leadership as he skillfully avoided war with the Turks, while preserving peace with the other Christian states that were constantly rattling their swords to take back the Holy Lands. In this, Antonio differed with Ruzzini and his friends, sometimes voting his conscience and supporting the doge, despite Ruzzini's urgings to the contrary. Antonio did not know that it had been Malipiero who had drawn him into the failed plot to kill the sultan, which had nearly ruined his reputation among the patriciate.

As he sat down behind the heavy oak table, Antonio could barely contain his excitement to share his meticulous plan with Seraglio. He reached for the bottle of wine and without uttering a word filled their glasses. His eyes never strayed from his friend as he began to slowly speak.

"Six years ago, my family suffered considerable financial losses at the hands of the Soranzos and their pawns, the Stenos—all because my brother entered into a fraudulent insurance contract with the elusive Monsieur De-Mars of Marseilles."

Seraglio stopped picking at his fish and smiled sardonically at Antonio.

"Now, I have finally found the means to make them pay for their crime."

"Have you discovered DeMars' whereabouts?"

"Better . . . I have found a way to wring his neck, and Vettor Soranzo's own hands shall do the deed."

Seraglio laughed, breaking the tension. "That, I would like to see," he said as he banged his fist hard on his table.

"I have been searching for almost a year for a man who possesses a unique talent—one that is essential to my plan. Yesterday, I found him."

Seraglio pushed his plate of barely eaten fish aside and leaned forward, his short arms stretched across the table; lines of anticipation were carved deep into the shiny furrows of his olive forehead.

"Who is he?"

"I have found the man who is reputed to be the greatest forger in all of Italy. His name is Signor Fabbro of Milan."

Antonio withdrew a yellowed paper from his robe and carefully unrolled it on the table. Seraglio leaned forward.

"Do you remember this?"

Seraglio craned his neck, struggling to read it upside down in the dim light.

"DeMars' insurance contract," whistled Seraglio, nodding slowly.

"Yes, and how I wished, the day I first saw it, that Giorgio had never signed it!"

Antonio's eyebrows suddenly jumped as he pointed his finger to a place at the bottom of the document.

"But fortunately, Monsieur DeMars also signed it—and, I have learned, he is also the one who wrote it."

Antonio leaned back hard in his chair, causing the tight-fitting joints to creak.

"Signor Fabbro—the Forger. I like a man who is confident in his abilities." Seraglio smiled. "Tell me, Antonio, what is your plan?"

"Signor Fabbro is here, in Venice. He arrived yesterday. He can duplicate Monsieur DeMars' hand so that it is indistinguishable from the original."

"How can you be sure?"

"Because I had the second-best forger in Italy confirm it without Signor Fabbro's knowledge," said Antonio, without stopping to gauge the effect of his words.

Seraglio was becoming more impressed with Antonio's plan as each new detail was revealed. He thought, momentarily, of old Josephus ben Levi. Two months after returning from Istanbul they had heard from his devoted servant that he had died peacefully in his bed. He would have been proud of Antonio at this moment.

"Fabbro will write two letters, both in DeMars' handwriting. The first will be to Vettor Soranzo. It will say that Steno has betrayed Vettor to me. Now I am blackmailing DeMars, threatening to expose him to the State Police, here in Venice, unless he admits to his crime, implicating Vettor as the man who paid him. If he does not, I will have DeMars killed. The second letter, he will write to Nicolo Steno and name Vettor Soranzo as the betrayer. This one will say that I am forcing DeMars to tell the police that Steno was the culprit or else the same fate awaits him at the hands of the Zianis. In each, DeMars' price for silence will be five hundred ducats. He will promise that if he is paid promptly, he will disappear, never to be seen or heard from again."

"Do you think Vettor and Steno will fall for this deception?"

"Yes. Remember this well, Seraglio. A man who knows that he is not trustworthy does not trust other men. Each of them will attempt to solve his problem without consulting the other."

"What do you think they will each do?" asked Seraglio.

"Steno, the weaker of the two—and the richer, will gladly pay DeMars to disappear. Oh yes, I forgot to mention that DeMars will specify in the letters how the money should be paid. Of course, it will be handed to an intermediary, one of my men, who will happen to be in a room in a certain inn in Marseilles."

Seraglio, caught up in the plot's details, interrupted Antonio's predictions.

"And Vettor Soranzo, the more violent of the two, will go to Marseilles and will persuade DeMars to disappear without paying him the five hundred ducats. He might even kill him, just to be sure he disappears for good."

"Exactly," agreed Antonio. "And Vettor will be told to go directly to DeMars, once he arrives at the inn in Marseilles. He will then promptly lead my man to DeMars—where he will confirm that Soranzo has killed De-Mars or else, knowing DeMars' hiding place, my man will deal with him af-ter Soranzo leaves."

"How?"

"He will kill him."

"Old ben Levi could not have devised a better plan," observed Seraglio. "But why kill DeMars? I never thought you were capable of cold-blooded murder."

Antonio sat across the table from his friend, stung by his words.

"I have no doubt it was DeMars who instructed the captain of that phantom ship to ram the unsuspecting *Tiger,* that morning in Marseilles. His treachery killed one of my loyal crewmen—a friend. No, it shall be a life for a life, Seraglio. Years ago, I even put away a special coffin, just for him."

Seraglio nodded silently. He had forgotten about the crewman's death.

"But I have saved the best part of my plan for last."

"Tell me," said Seraglio, a broad grin etched across his face, as Antonio peeled another layer of his plot like the skin off a ripe onion.

"Signor Fabbro has agreed to do his work—*gratis.*"

"I am almost afraid to ask how you arranged that."

"I told him he could blackmail Vettor Soranzo by threatening to turn him in to the local authorities as DeMars' murderer. They will not be happy when they find out that a Venetian has come to their city and killed one of their fine upstanding citizens."

"But how could Signor Fabbro prove that Vettor Soranzo was DeMars' killer?" countered Seraglio, confused.

"It will not be hard for Italy's greatest forger to furnish a letter proving that Signor DeMars was being blackmailed by Vettor Soranzo, a Venetian patrician, and that he murdered DeMars when, after years of payments, he finally refused to be blackmailed any longer.

"Faced with never being able to ever set foot outside Venetian territory again, without risking capture by agents from Provence, Vettor will surely pay."

Finished, Antonio rose to his feet to attend to some business. As he left the room, Seraglio laughed as he thought that with one more peel of the onion, Antonio would have had Fabbro blackmailing the pope and the sul-tan too.

. . .

It took three weeks for the plot to run its course. After receiving his ominous letter, Nicolo Steno unknowingly paid the money he thought DeMars had extorted from him to Antonio's agent, who met him at an inn in Marseilles.

When Vettor Soranzo received his letter, he sent a distant cousin to kill DeMars instead of doing it himself, choosing to remain safely in Venice. Antonio had taken the precaution of pointing out Vettor Soranzo to Signor Fabbro when he had come to Venice to meet with Antonio. With a forger's eye, he had etched Vettor's features deep into his memory. When the Forger noticed that Vettor had sent a surrogate, the Forger wisely informed a policeman friend of the murder plot. The policeman followed the killer to DeMars' house and just as he entered, the policeman overpowered and arrested him. Then the Forger and his accomplice ransomed the would-be killer back to the Soranzo family, though for only three hundred ducats—he was a second cousin.

The man Antonio had sent to Marseilles was then free to deal with Monsieur DeMars. He had followed Vettor's cousin to DeMars' house to find out where he lived. After the policeman had gone and DeMars was alone, he struck. First he took all of DeMars' gold—about four hundred ducats— using a portion to pay the balance due to the Forger. Then, he ensured that DeMars would never leave Marseilles again as he dropped him, whimpering, into the cold waters of the harbor, tightly nailed inside the large cask of broken fine Murano glass that Antonio had taken from the *Lion*.

Three years passed until the day that news swept across Venice like the autumn rains that blow up the Adriatic from the coast of Africa. Muhammed II had finally attacked as the Turks spilled over their borders, like a raging torrent, into the Balkans. The sultan's army had advanced to the gates of Belgrade, taking almost all of Serbia. All summer long, the fate of the city had hung in the balance.

Seraglio burst into the room, wild with excitement.

"The Hungarians have done it! They have defeated the Turks under the walls of Belgrade. János Hunyadi, prince of Hungary, and his knights have handed the sultan his first defeat."

"Our diplomats have succeeded again," replied Antonio. "Our alliance with the Hungarians has been successful beyond our hopes."

"They say that after just two weeks the Turks were in full retreat. Hunyadi and his army surprised and defeated them decisively. The sultan was unable to supply his army because the miserable ancient Roman roads from Istanbul turned into quagmires. They were starving. Now they will be forced to haul their huge siege guns back across the Sava River, which will be swollen with the summer rains."

"This good news may be bad for us," warned Antonio. "Like a powerful wave that breaks upon the shore and then recedes back into the sea, the Turks will retreat to their bases along the Aegean. The sultan, stung by his failure and conscious about his image among his subjects, will now concentrate on easy prizes closer at hand."

Antonio was right. First, the sultan ejected the troublesome Genoese from Pera. He had never forgiven them for taking both sides during the siege of Constantinople nine years before. Then he resolved to take southern Greece and the remaining Aegean Islands he did not already control. Many were Venetian possessions or sought protection from her against the Turks, but Venice pursued a policy of appeasement toward her powerful enemy. She gave up most of them without a fight, except for her heavily defended naval base at Negropont and Morea.

After systematically reducing a few of the defiant islands' defenses with their irresistible guns, the Turks moved south toward ancient Athens. The sultan swept aside the feeble Florentine dukes of Athens who ruled there—as they nobly relinquished their realm without a fight, saving the city's historic treasures from sure destruction. Finally, with most of Greece under the crescent, the sultan turned with relentless energy toward threatening the Peloponnese and the Venetian province of Morea.

Morea had been a Venetian possession since 1204, when she had claimed it as spoils after the sack of Constantinople during the Fourth Crusade. Since the fall of Constantinople to the sultan, only the ancient city of Corinth had tasted the wrath of the Turks when, four years earlier, they had taken the old city from Thomas and Demetrius Palaeologus, the two brothers of the late Byzantine emperor. A short time later, the Turks abandoned Corinth when an uneasy temporary peace was concluded with Venice. The Turks retired to take up their positions north of the four-mile-wide Isthmus of Corinth.

Giovanni Soranzo had been stunned by the unexpected news. Doge Malipiero had suddenly died. He hardly knew his successor, Cristoforo Moro, an old man whose leading qualification to be doge was that he offended no one—making him acceptable to everyone. Now Soranzo would have to oppose his enemy without the strong presence of the most powerful man in Venice. Worse, Venice had lost a strong leader in her fight against the Turks.

Antonio was not happy. Though he had always believed that Malipiero meant him no good, as a Venetian, he knew Malipiero's death placed Venice in danger.

"Pope Pius II has announced his plan to the Christian world to person-ally lead a crusade against the Turks. Doge Moro received it yesterday."

"But before the pope could enlist the help of Venice, without whose ships and gold a crusade would not be possible, his friend and supporter, Doge Malipiero, has suddenly died," replied Seraglio. "What will the Re-public do now?"

"Our people want peace but the pope will exert great pressure. We shall see."

15

The Expedition

Seething to take revenge on Venice for her abortive plot to kill him and sensing the West had no desire to come to her aid, if attacked, the sultan now sought to provoke the Republic. He decided to attack Argos, just south of the Isthmus of Corinth.

As the unsuspecting residents of Argos celebrated Lent—the holiest season of the year—and also the enduring peace they had enjoyed under seventy-five years of Venetian rule since their Byzantine despot had sought the Republic's protection, the Turks struck. The Venetian fortress and its formidable garrison that had provided a comforting sense of power and security as it towered over Argos like their own private Olympus fell in a *coup de main*. By morning, the entire garrison had been mercilessly put to the sword and the leading citizens carried off as hostages.

It did not take long for the news of Argos's fate to make its way to Corinth, twenty miles to the northeast, and quickly on to Venice, where it struck with the force of a lightning bolt. The sultan had made an unprovoked and savage attack upon sovereign Venetian territory, violating the tenuous peace between Venice and the Ottoman Empire. The Republic now had to face the realization that every appeaser eventually must, and the sooner, the better. Aggression must be courageously opposed by resolute force. It had been ten years since Venice had fought the Turks at Constantinople. She could avoid a military confrontation no longer.

Over the ship's starboard side, far off in the distance, they could see the massive bulk of the twin-peaked Acrocorinth—Corinth's ancient acropolis, which towered like Zeus's throne more than eighteen hundred feet above the olive trees, vineyards, and modest whitewashed dwellings that dotted the rocky plain far below. As Antonio squinted into the bright morning sun he could just make out the walls that crowned the impregnable position, enclosing almost sixty acres. It had been a haven and refuge for the Corinthians for nearly four thousand years. Blessed with a source of water—the Peirene Spring—its defenders could hold out as long as their food lasted. Only one narrow and easily defended path led up to the top. Antonio thanked God it was firmly in Venetian hands.

"Is that not the most magnificent promontory you have ever seen?" asked Giorgio as he joined him at the ship's rail.

Antonio shifted his gaze to his brother. He was strong as an ox. Gazing over the rail, he looked every inch a warrior with his hand firmly resting on the pommel of the sword.

Their relationship had changed after Antonio had returned from Constantinople and had seen Giorgio's limitations as a merchant and weaknesses as a man laid bare. Ever since then, both he and Antonio had accepted their altered roles. They recognized that, in the world of commerce, brains counted more than physical strength. But there were still times when they would revert back to simpler days, when Giorgio could feel more like Antonio's equal. In battle, strength still mattered. Knowing what lay ahead, Giorgio looked forward to fighting alongside Antonio for the first time in their lives and to regaining his older brother's confidence.

As Antonio looked at his brother, he thought about how war changed men. His mind drifted for a moment to his bitter rivalry with Giovanni Soranzo. Like Venetian *nobili* had done for centuries, he was glad they could put aside their differences and stand shoulder to shoulder to fight the hated Turk. It was the Venetian way. He did not notice Seraglio joining them on deck.

"So that is the fabled Acrocorinth. I have never laid eyes on it before. It is magnificent. An attacker would die of exhaustion just climbing up there before its defenders' arrows could do their work."

"Captain-General Loredan's ship is signaling for the fleet to turn to starboard."

"Our captain just told me we shall arrive at Corinth's port in a few hours," broke in Seraglio as he joined the brothers.

The three men stood talking side by side on the deck. Seraglio, of course, had much to tell them about Corinth. After ten years, Antonio was not surprised, but Giorgio occasionally shook his head in disbelief as he listened intently to the Greek.

"The Franks built those walls on top of ancient remains. They are over a mile in length. It is the oldest and largest fortress in the Peloponnese"— Seraglio still obstinately referred to Morea by the Greek name. "They say that at one time, more than one thousand cult prostitutes lived up there in the temple of Aphrodite, perfecting their art with the priests and serving all who would make pilgrimage there." Seraglio winked at Giorgio, who laughed at the thought.

"It is little wonder that they built a mile of walls—how else could they keep every man within twenty miles from making a weekly pilgrimage up there?"

Antonio looked at Seraglio, so short he had to stand on his toes just to peer over the side. He could see he was filled with excited anticipation at the thought of returning to Greek soil. Antonio hoped their encounter with the Turks would be more successful this time, but he confessed to himself that he was not so sure. The ominous shoreline seemed too empty—too alluring. A few miles beyond it he knew the Turks would be waiting with their massive guns. Though there would be more Venetians this time, thirty thousand altogether, he still wondered—would it be enough?

After the sultan's unprovoked attack on Argos, Venice had acted decisively—finally ignoring the warnings of the appeasers who had blocked a stronger response ever since the siege of Constantinople. Now, even they agreed, the Turks had to be stopped.

It took two exhausting days for the Venetians to disembark their army. The ancient port of Lechion, a mile from Corinth, was too small to easily accommodate such an armada. The fleet numbered nearly a hundred war galleys and more than two hundred transports and carried thirty thousand men. Their mission was to defend the Isthmus of Corinth against a Turkish invasion. They were also to expel the Turks from Argos, reclaiming it in the name of the Republic. It had taken Venice all summer to outfit the army and conclude diplomatic arrangements with her allies the Hungarians, who had bravely repelled the sultan's attack on Belgrade a year earlier. Now, as

October's chilly winds began to blow, no one was looking forward to a winter campaign.

Antonio and Giorgio went ashore along with the expedition's other officers and civil officials. Just beyond the town they could see the captain-general's impressive tent, in the center of the sprawling camp, towering above the long rows of smaller shelters. The expedition commander, Captain-General Alvise Loredan, a cousin of Lorenzo Loredan, had called a meeting of most of the officers as the troops continued to stream ashore on boats commandeered from the local fishermen by the Venetians. To maintain security, the fleet had departed Venice without informing the officers of the battle plan. After stopping briefly in Zara and Corfu to take on additional men and replenish water and supplies, they had sailed directly to the Gulf of Corinth. Unlike during the voyage ten years before, thought Antonio, this time the weather had been perfect.

Several hundred men milled about, inside and outside the huge tent, drinking wine and ale, staples of every campaign, provided by the captain-general for their refreshment. Though not cold, the air had turned brisk. The ground around the camp had already been churned to dust by thousands of feet. The first rain would turn the camp into a quagmire. There was little wood about to make floorboards, although Captain-General Loredan had brought some for his tent all the way from Venice.

Captain-General Alvise Loredan was the second cousin of Antonio's mentor, Domenico Ruzzini. By virtue of Domenico's influence and Antonio's previous experience in fighting the Turks, Antonio was made an aide-de-camp to the *condottiere* Sigismondo Malatesta of Rimini, the commander of the expedition's land forces. Like Giustiniani at Constantinople, he was a renowned expert at defensive fighting.

As they waited in line to enter the tent a familiar face caught Antonio's eye. He could see Vettor Soranzo's unmistakable profile ahead of him. He quickly looked at Giorgio, who was oblivious to their enemy's presence. Antonio decided not to say anything. Better to concentrate on the upcoming fight with the Turks. War made for strange bedfellows, thought Antonio, as Vettor disappeared inside.

Standing on a two-foot-high wooden platform, the captain-general called the council of war to order. He was tall, lean, muscular, and in perfect health, though his beard was graying with age. Men have always preferred to be led by one more imposing than themselves. He had piercing brown eyes, the kind that could skewer any man who would dare to hold their gaze. Dressed only in black patrician robes, shunning his exquisite armor, he looked more like a man about to speak in the Great Council than the commander of a powerful army. If his reputation and appearance alone were not enough to command attention, he also possessed a deep, sonorous voice. He did not need to demand respect from others—they freely gave it to him.

"I am pleased to report that under the fine seamanship of Vice Captain-General of the Seas Cappello not a single ship has been lost or damaged on the voyage to Corinth." The buzz of the crowd confirmed their leader's praise. It *had* been an uneventful voyage. Antonio shared a sense of power and unity of purpose with his comrades. As the assemblage quieted the commander continued.

"Last April, the Turks illegally seized Argos. They killed more than three hundred of our countrymen when they took Fortress Argo—giving no quarter. At the approach of our fleet, the Turks ransacked it and carried off some of its citizens as hostages. Though Argos will soon be liberated, we have a far greater task that is still to be accomplished."

The captain-general signaled for a large map to be brought up to the platform.

"This is the area we shall defend. We are here, at Lechion," he pointed. "A mile to the south is Corinth and to the southwest is the Acrocorinth. Several miles to the northeast, the Isthmus narrows to where it is pinched on the west by the Gulf of Corinth and on the east by the Saronic Gulf. Now, look closely. Across the isthmus, right here, runs the wall originally constructed by the Byzantines."

"This wall runs the length of the Isthmus, just south of its narrowest point. It is more than four miles long, stands twelve feet high and nine feet wide, and has more than one hundred thirty mutually supporting towers. To its front, on the Saronic Gulf flank, the Turks will have to contend with the remains of Nero's ditch, an unfinished canal he attempted to dig to transverse the Isthmus, saving the one hundred eighty-five miles necessary for a ship to circumvent the Peloponnese. The project was abandoned before it could be completed. Our own government has contemplated completing the work, but funds have never been allocated—other needs taking precedence."

"We will surprise the Turkish pickets posted on the wall and occupy it before the sultan can react. He cannot maintain more than a few thousand men south of it around Argos, living off the land. Unlike us, the Turks do not possess enough transports to supply a large army in the field. Our spies confirm the sultan is in Istanbul and his army is encamped a few miles south of Athens, his supply source. We will create a dam of steel and stone to hold back the Turks from our possessions in Morea.

"There is a powerful fort at each end of the wall that will be well provided with crossbowmen to discourage flanking attacks. The Turks will have to penetrate the wall itself if they want to defeat us. By stationing heavily armored reinforcements at strategic intervals behind the wall who can move rapidly using the paved military road, we will be able to respond quickly to any point the Turks attack."

The audience voiced their approval.

"If we can hold them until winter, the Turks will never be able to sustain their army in the field and will be forced to retire to Athens until spring. Can we hold?"

"For St. Mark and Venice!" cheered the crowd wildly as they sprung to their feet.

"Count Lorentano." The officers sat in silence as a silver-haired man stepped up onto the platform. Dressed in a blue robe with a Cross of St. George dangling from a heavy gold chain, he exuded aristocratic pride and confidence.

"Welcome to our land. My people are eager rise up and fight for their freedom from Turkish oppression. They know only too well what the Turks did to Argos."

This pronouncement of local support further buoyed the Venetians' enthusiasm.

Antonio leaned over and whispered to Giorgio, "Perhaps, *these* Greeks will fight!"

"Now," said the captain-general, "let us see to our men and animals. By tomorrow, we must be in position on the wall to repel any Turkish invasion."

The council of war was over. The officers filed out, in high spirits, and returned to their commands. By the next day, thirty thousand Venetians were arrayed along and behind the wall with the fleet guarding their left flank resting on the Gulf of Corinth. If they could hold for a month, it would be over. The Turks would be forced into winter quarters in Athens, or perhaps, even retreat farther north, all the way back to Istanbul.

The Venetians had been on the wall for eight long days. They awoke each morning cold and stiff, expecting the Turks to attack, but instead the enemy remained in their camps, which stretched like banks of clouds across the Isthmus of Corinth, a half mile to the north, far beyond the range of the Venetians' arrows and wall guns.

At their post in a tower near the center, Giorgio and Seraglio strained to see across the plain. In the morning light, they could just make out the Turkish flags flying from hundreds of white tents, some as large as houses.

To their left, they could see the fleet in the Gulf of Corinth. The ships were packed so thickly, it was difficult to see the blue water. To the right, the Turkish fleet similarly filled the Saronic Gulf. A massive naval battle would have ensued if not for the four miles of land that separated them.

Giorgio looked down the length of the wall extending two miles in each direction.

"Leave it to the Greeks to determine that a straight line is the shortest distance between two points," observed Seraglio. "Think of all the stone and labor they saved when they built this wall perfectly straight."

Suddenly they heard a loud cheer. As they turned around, they could see Captain-General Loredan and the *condottiere* Malatesta, accompanied by Count Lorentano and several others, including Antonio. A large company of cheering soldiers opened a path for them as they rode toward the tower. Giorgio smiled down at Antonio, who saluted back smartly. They had seen each other only twice since the council of war. In a few minutes, the captain-general and his retinue had climbed the tower stairs and were standing with Giorgio and Seraglio, looking out at the Turkish camp in the distance.

"Any sign of enemy activity this morning?" asked Malatesta.

"None," replied Giorgio.

"Why do they not attack us?" asked Loredan. "What are they up to?"

The men stood silently, gazing across the expanse of rock-strewn plain separating the two armies. Each man racked his brain as he searched for the answer.

"Have you seen any sign of their guns?" asked Malatesta. "Some require hundreds of oxen to move them. They would surely be visible even at this distance."

"No sign of their siege guns yet, Captain-General," replied Giorgio.

"Begging your pardon, Your Honor," Seraglio broke in. "Surely there must be some local residents who could provide us some answers to what they are up to."

Antonio quickly spoke. "This is Seraglio, the man who saved my life during the siege of Constantinople ten years ago."

The captain-general seemed not to hear Antonio as he turned to the others.

"What have we learned from your people, Count Lorentano?"

"They are reluctant to give us information. The Turks took hostages from each of the nearest towns. The people are afraid the Turks will kill them if they help us."

"But how would the Turks ever know that they helped us?"

"They think that if winter comes and there is no battle, when the Turks depart, they will release their relatives and friends. If we initiate action, it will be a sure sign to the Turks that they have collaborated with us. So they tell us nothing."

"This is hardly the kind of support we expected and that you guaranteed us, Count Lorentano," exclaimed Malatesta harshly.

Stung by his words, Lorentano replied, "My people will fight if we are attacked, but they will not provoke the Turks."

"I suggest we meet again tomorrow and review the situation," said Malatesta. "Perhaps by then, we shall learn something of the Turks' intentions."

Holding up his hand, the captain-general stopped the conversation. With nothing resolved, the meeting broke up as quickly as it had begun.

Lorentano disappeared into the stairway leading down and out of the tower, as Malatesta waited behind so that he could depart without speaking to him. As he left too, Antonio lingered, his hand fixed on Seraglio's shoulder to hold him in place.

"Captain-General, may I make a suggestion?" inquired Antonio.

The commander, who was still preoccupied with studying the Turkish lines, abruptly turned around. Though weighted down by his awesome responsibility, he looked at Antonio with his clear, icy-gray eyes.

"What are you thinking, Antonio?"

"Seraglio, here, is fluent in Greek. If we ride to the local villages of Isthmia, Cenchreae, Naphlion, and Argos and talk to the people there, perhaps we can find out what the Turks are up to."

Loredan considered the request for a moment.

"I hate these councils of war. They accomplish nothing except to gain agreement to have another. I suppose there may be a chance that Count Lorentano may have missed a piece of information that could prove useful. Go ahead, but come back by the day after tomorrow. I will advise Malatesta that I have dispatched you."

"We shall leave at once," replied Antonio.

Antonio and Seraglio had ridden since morning, finally reaching Argos late in the afternoon. They had learned nothing in the three towns they had already visited. Argos would be their last stop before returning to the front line. Antonio's report to the captain-general, at this point, would not contain one shred of useful information.

After boarding their animals, they looked up at the impressive fortress on the hill above the town, once again flying the red and gold winged Lion of

St. Mark above its battlements. As they walked around the square, they asked everyone they saw for information about the Turks, but they were met with the same wall of silence as in the other towns. One man revealed that the Turks took six of the most important townsmen away when they abandoned Argos after hearing news of the approaching Venetian fleet.

They took a room at an inn, intending to have something to eat and retire. Dejected and exhausted, they flopped into their chairs and ordered lamb and vegetables and a bottle of wine. As they washed the dust from their throats and dug into their food, Antonio noticed a man timidly approaching their table. Antonio could tell by his clothing that he was a simple villager. He motioned for the reluctant man to come and join them.

"My name is Nicholas Kasoulos. I own a fish shop here in Argos."

Antonio poured him a cup of wine as he spoke, still standing.

"I have heard you are looking for information about the Turks."

"Yes," said Seraglio. "What can you tell us? Why is everyone afraid?"

"We are a poor people. Our only pleasure in life is our families and friends. The Turks, knowing this, have taken six hostages from our town. No one would endanger them by providing information that could start a battle. The Turks said that when winter comes and the risk of battle is ended, they would let them go and return to us."

"Do you really think you can trust the Turks to do that?" asked Seraglio.

"What other hope do we have?"

"Did you come here just to tell us that?"

"No, I have come to tell you a story. May I sit down?"

"Of course, sit, sit."

Kasoulos pulled up a stool and emptied the cup of wine Antonio had poured for him. Fortified by this, he began, speaking in a grave but low voice.

"Last April, when the Turks attacked our town, it was during our Lenten observances. That very night, my two young and beautiful daughters disappeared. We never knew what had happened to them. Though their bodies were never found, we thought they had been killed in the fighting."

Antonio looked at Seraglio. He held up his hand for the man to wait as he translated for Antonio. When he had finished, Seraglio nodded to Kasoulos to continue.

"A few weeks later I discovered what had become of my little girls." A tear slid down the man's weathered face and dropped into his empty cup. He began to sob. Seraglio placed his hand on the man's arm and urged him to continue.

"One day a Turkish officer from the fortress came to my shop to buy fish for the other officers. He paid me with this."

He reached into his shirt and held up a tiny silver chain. Suspended at the end, slowly twisting and sparkling in the candlelight, was a silver cross of St. George.

"I gave it to my youngest daughter, Thera, on her twelfth birthday." The man gripped the table with his dirty hands. "I asked the soldier how he, a Muslim, came to possess the cross—a Christian symbol. He laughed and said he found it. I was certain it was Thera's. So I asked him if he was not mistaken and did it not belong to a little girl? He just laughed and said he hoped that little girl was not mine because . . . because of what they did to her . . . what they were *still* doing to her!" He broke down uncontrollably, sobbing in his grief. After a while, he looked up. "I hate the Turks worse than Satan.

"A few months later, during the summer, I was out with one of the local fishermen. We sailed north up close to Nero's old canal. We could see the Turks unloading wagons filled with dirt onto a ship. I think they have tunneled into the earth from the old canal, southward toward the wall you Venetians are defending."

Antonio looked intensely at Seraglio as he quickly translated.

"My family is ruined. I will never see my precious daughters again. But perhaps you can ruin some Turkish families. Make it so they will never see their sons again."

Kasoulos abruptly stood up and without saying another word he turned and walked across the room and out of the inn. Antonio took a silver *soldo* from his purse to pay for their meal. As he placed it on the table, he noticed Kasoulos had left the little silver cross and chain on the table, glimmering in the dim candlelight. He vowed then that he would make them pay for what they had done, as he walked from the inn.

"Seraglio, they have dug a tunnel under the wall to collapse it, creating a breach, or to place troops behind us some night when we have been lulled by their inactivity."

He rubbed his forehead. "But why would the sultan not just smash the wall with his guns? The wall we are defending at Corinth is not nearly as formidable as the walls were at Constantinople. Why resort to such an approach?"

"Perhaps the sultan is not able to bring his artillery with him this time."

"Enough talk," said Antonio as they hurried toward the stable. "If we ride all night, we can be back at the wall by tomorrow morning.

Antonio made his report to Captain-General Loredan as soon as they returned, just after sunrise. He immediately summoned his senior commanders, telling them what they had learned in Argos, but their reaction was not what Antonio had expected.

"The rocky ground here would not be easy to tunnel through. Perhaps they excavated the dirt for some other purpose," observed Lorentano.

"Then why would the Turks go to such great lengths to dispose of it by carting it away on their ships?" asked Loredan.

Receiving no answer, he turned to Antonio and Seraglio. "Did the man have any other information?"

"No, Captain-General," replied Antonio.

"Still no sign of the Turks' siege guns yet?" asked Loredan.

"No," answered Malatesta.

"Where *are* they?" he looked into the empty faces assembled around him.

"It would take considerable time and effort to drag those monsters all the way from Istanbul. Perhaps the sultan thought he could sweep us aside here without going to all that trouble. After all, he could not have anticipated that we would raise such a large army and make our stand here. Without their guns, how can they successfully attack us?"

"If they are not making preparations to smash through the wall with their guns it can only mean one thing. They intend to tunnel under it. How else could they defeat us? We have too many defenders for them to storm the walls in a frontal assault," observed Malatesta. "That would be suicide."

The others nodded their heads in agreement with the *condottiere*.

"Signor Malatesta, if you were them, where would you dig it?"

He scratched his beard in silence, thinking. "It would depend on whether I was going to undermine the wall, blowing a breach in it with black powder, or if I was going to use the tunnel to place troops behind the wall."

He began to pace as he continued to analyze the situation, every eye fixed on him.

"They could never bring enough men through the tunnel in one night to defeat us in a pitched battle the next day. No, their intention is to blow a hole in the wall and attack through the breach. I would bet my reputation on it."

"Where would that breach most likely be made?" pressed the captain-general.

"Where the least number of our troops would be able to plug it, near one of the ends of the wall," said Malatesta.

"And that would likely be the eastern end, where their fleet could support the attack with their arrows and guns, rather than encounter ours on the western end to oppose it in a similar fashion," surmised Loredan.

"The men from Argos saw the Turks removing earth from the eastern end," observed Seraglio.

The captain-general, convinced they had divined the sultan's intentions, gave his order. "Before dawn tomorrow, I want all the support troops we can spare from the western end of the wall moved behind the eastern end—no less than four thousand of them. That is where the Turks will attack."

The next day dawned dreary and drizzling. By late morning the rain had turned into a depressing downpour. As Antonio and Seraglio stood on top of the tower near the eastern flank, the mist obscured the Turkish positions. Antonio wondered how many times, down through the ages, men had cursed the rain for the misery it had added to the mean conditions war imposed upon soldiers. It was the first rain since they had arrived at Lechion. Though it would replenish their foul drinking water, it also soaked them to their skin and made them shiver with cold. At least on the wall, there was no mud. Antonio looked down at the miserable troops below, stumbling through muck up to their shins as they tried to build fires with any sticks they could find. Malatesta, always cautious, had limited the fires on the right flank and had ordered extra ones built on the left to prevent the Turks from realizing that they had transferred most of their reserves.

"Miserable weather," observed Seraglio as he looked up at the teeming heavens, his black hair matted to his forehead. Antonio smiled as he was reminded of the time he threw Seraglio in the water outside of the Acropolis Inn back in Venice. That day, he thought, the weather had been glorious.

Suddenly, Seraglio grabbed Antonio's hand as he strained his eyes at something below, in front of the wall.

"You bastards!" he shouted across the plain at the Turkish camp. "Did you think you could fool us so easily?"

"What is it, Seraglio?"

"I have been looking out there for an hour." He pointed to the sea of mud that stretched from the base of the wall toward the enemy camp.

"I had the feeling that something was not quite right. Look, Antonio, over by that large rock. Do you see it?"

"See what?"

"There, by that rock." He pointed again. "See the deep depression in front of it?"

"I do not understand. What do you see?"

"It is what I *do not* see, Antonio." Seraglio turned and faced him. "Look out there. Every depression in the ground is a puddle of rainwater, except there, in front of that rock. Do you not see it? The water is draining from that hole. There can be only one reason. There is an open space below it."

"The tunnel!" spit Antonio, as though he were cursing.

"The devils are clever, I give them credit. But the Turks did not use a level so the roof of the tunnel has strayed too close to the surface. When we used to dig the sewers in Constantinople, we would pour water above our tunnels to be sure they were dug deep enough. If the water did not pool, leaching through the soil instead, it meant the sewer was too close to the surface and risked collapsing. The sultan should hang the whole incompetent lot of his miners!"

"Seraglio, stay here. See if you can discern any other similar depressions. I will inform Signor Malatesta."

It did not take long for the Venetians to formulate their plan. Malatesta immediately ordered his men to dig their own lateral tunnel that would intercept the Turks' tunnel just before it crossed under the wall. Usually, the most difficult challenge with laterals was to dig them at the right depth. In this situation that would not be a problem because the rock under the soil began at about six to eight feet deep—their lateral could only be dug at one depth—the same as the Turks'.

Digging commenced that morning and would continue day and night until they found the enemy's tunnel. Miners were an integral part of every Venetian army. While they scratched and scraped at the rock-filled earth, specially equipped soldiers stood at the ready in case an unexpected breakthrough resulted in a sudden savage melee. The soldiers assigned to the tunnel were armed with short stabbing swords—long daggers really, and armored gauntlets with spikes on their knuckles. Each man also carried a sack filled with small caltrops—four-pointed spikes in a shape that always resulted in one spike standing straight up while the other three formed a base. Originally used to defend against cavalry, the small caltrops would delay the enemy's pursuit in case the miners had to beat a hasty retreat in the confines of a tunnel.

The rocky ground forced them to dig their lateral tunnel in an irregular zigzag course, avoiding the large rock deposits that sometimes broke through the surface. Progress was slow, but suddenly, late on the second day, they heard faint noises in the ground. Work slowed to a crawl to prevent the Turks from detecting their presence. By the next day, they could hear distinct voices. This meant that less than a foot of earth separated the two tunnels. It was then that Malatesta sent for Seraglio.

"Signor Seraglio, they tell me that you speak Turkish."

"Perfectly."

"Will you go down in the tunnel and interpret what the Turks are saying? We must learn their ultimate aim in tunneling under the wall. Do they plan to collapse a section of the wall with powder or are they up to something else?"

Seraglio was afraid. No man wants to die—he was thirty-nine, not really an old man. But that was not the greatest source of his fear. He was afraid because he felt that the best years of his life lay ahead of him, in Venice. He did not want it to end now, not in a black hole in the Peloponnese, surrounded by strangers, powerful men, fierce men—exactly the same kind who had tormented him for most of his life. But if this were the price of becoming a Venetian, he would go down there—and do his duty.

"I will do it, but since I am risking my life, who is to lead this adventure?"

"The best tunnel man in Italy. *Il Ragno*—the Spider—is built like a block of granite and short, like you. He can stand erect in most tunnels. No one can outrun him under the earth. He is the man you want at your front or your back down there."

Suddenly a guard entered Malatesta's tent and announced that the Spider had arrived. As the man threw back the tent flap, Seraglio's eyes bulged as he saw a younger version of himself—though certainly more handsome. The young man could not have been older than twenty-five. A shock of light brown hair fell over his alert eyes as he stood his ground, his thick forearms folded against his compact barrel chest. He was just six inches taller than Seraglio and outweighed him. He looked like he was capable of plugging a tunnel so tightly with his frame that not a ray of light could pass, let alone an enemy miner. This man is a killer, thought Seraglio.

Malatesta introduced the two diminutive comrades and left them to their work. The Spider was pleased to learn that Seraglio spoke Turkish. As they walked from the commander's tent, he explained their mission. Seraglio's confidence grew as he listened. He quickly determined that the Spider was a master at his deadly craft.

Soon they were looking down into the lateral's foreboding dark opening. Seraglio could see a wooden ladder barely lit by a faint yellow glow. Before he could speak, the Spider was on the ladder, rapidly descending into the hole. Seraglio followed as fast as his unsteady legs could take him. After climbing down about six feet he touched the floor of the tunnel. The smell of damp earth filled his nostrils. The shaft was high enough for Seraglio to stand erect. The Spider stood with his head bent sharply, eyes peering forward under his thin eyebrows. About twenty feet away was a single oil lamp suspended from an arrow driven into the earthen wall. Farther down the tunnel he could see several more lamps before the shaft veered to the left and disappeared around a corner.

"Seraglio, welcome to my subterranean world. If you do exactly as I told you, you will not get me killed—then I will be able to prevent the Turks from killing you."

He stuck out his muscular hand. Seraglio grasped it tightly.

"Signor Spider, I will do exactly as you said. But I have one question."

"What is it?"

"When we encounter the Turks . . . will we really be able to hear them without them knowing we are there?"

"If you only use those ears of yours and keep your mouth shut. If you talk too loudly, I will have to slit your throat."

As Seraglio stared into his eyes, the Spider's grin disappeared. He meant it. The Spider abruptly turned and led the way, head down, as Seraglio followed him, thankful God had made him just the right height for the job. They walked for about three minutes in complete silence, when up ahead of them, they could see a soldier with his short sword drawn, sitting on the floor of the tunnel. He motioned for them to be quiet. They carefully walked the remaining distance to where he sat. Reaching him, Seraglio noticed a bypass had been dug on each side making the tunnel three times wider. As they passed, Seraglio noticed another soldier crouching on the other side. Up ahead, the tunnel abruptly stopped. At the end was another kneeling soldier. He saluted the Spider and pressed himself back against the wall to let them pass.

The Spider reached into a fist-sized leather sack hanging from his belt, carefully withdrew a small bottomless, tapered tin cup, and delicately placed it against the tunnel wall. Then he placed his ear to the cup and motioned for quiet. Seraglio could hear human voices but they were not discernable. The Spider motioned for Seraglio to take a turn listening. Seraglio took the cup in his gnarled fingers, carefully placing his thumb through the handle to secure it. As he leaned his ear against it and pressed it to the wall, like magic, the noises were transformed into words. After a few minutes, he had heard enough. Handing the cup back to the Spider, Seraglio motioned for him to follow.

When they had reached the bypass, about fifty feet from the end of the tunnel, Seraglio stopped to whisper what he had heard.

"They will stop soon and will not begin digging again until morning. They are afraid we will hear them if they tunnel at night. They noticed the water dripping into the tunnel and realize that they are too close to the surface in some places. They intend to patch the roof of the tunnel to avoid discovery, but they are too late, eh Signor Spider?"

"What else did they say? Did they say what their aim is?"

"No. But I think they said someone called *Kapi* would be inspecting their work tomorrow."

"What does *Kapi* mean?"

"*Kapi* means opening . . . a gate," said Seraglio, instantly understanding.

"We must warn Loredan," said Seraglio as he quickly turned.

It was the dead of night by the time the hand-picked attackers assembled around the lateral's access shaft. The steady rain added to the dreary scene as the tired soldiers around them slept, weapons by their sides, with their oil-skins pulled over their heads. The Spider would lead the way, followed by Seraglio. Four short but powerful-looking soldiers comprised their escort; each man was armed with a short sword and spiked-knuckle gauntlets. Seraglio nervously squeezed his fist around the handle of the razor-sharp knife the Spider had given him.

"Remember the plan, now," said the Spider. "We must overpower any guards we find and then locate the powder chamber. If we are pursued, we will throw down caltrops and beat a hasty retreat, drawing our pursuers past the two men hidden in the bypass. Any questions? All right then, follow me."

The party descended the ladder, one by one. Two soldiers carried flickering oil lamps to help light their way. As they neared the end of the tunnel, the Spider extinguished each lamp on the wall as they passed, darkening the tunnel behind them. When they reached the bypass, the sight of one well-armed crouching shadow hidden on each side comforted Seraglio. Soon they reached the end of the tunnel. The Spider extinguished the last lamp as each soldier placed a specially fitted black cloth cover over his lamp, shrouding its glow without extinguishing it. Now, in almost total darkness, the Spider produced his tin cup, placed it against the wall, and listened for a moment. Then, shaking his head and smiling, his white teeth barely visible, he withdrew his dagger and began to quietly scrape away the clay that divided the lateral from the Turks' tunnel.

In a minute, a tiny ray of yellow light burst from the earthen wall. The Spider had broken through. Even though Seraglio had never done this before, his instincts told him this was the critical moment. Would the tunnel be empty—or would the Turks suddenly crash through the thin layer of earth, stabbing them with their razor-sharp blades?

Suddenly, in the faint light, Seraglio could see the Spider drop to his knees and then stretch out on his stomach on the tunnel floor. He was making his entrance hole as low as he could to avoid detection. Using his dagger flat on the floor, he cut across the bottom and began to work his way up, perforating the wall on each side, barely allowing the point of his blade to protrude beyond the wall into the Turks' tunnel. The Spider certainly knew what he was doing, thought Seraglio.

In five minutes, the wall was prepared. It was time. Without a warning, the Spider pushed his face through the thin layer of earth and swiveled his neck, quickly looking left and right down the Turks' tunnel. He pulled back and looked at his comrades and nodded, a leering grin on his face.

Working in unison, like rowers at their oars, they removed all the dirt, cleaning the floor of the Turks' dimly lit tunnel of any debris. Then the Spider motioned for them all to follow him. As they slipped through, one man crawled away to the left in the direction of the Turks' lines. Two others followed the Spider in the opposite direction toward the Venetians' lines. The last remained with Seraglio, guarding the entrance to the lateral as Seraglio gingerly held the two hooded lamps.

The Spider moved swiftly through the tunnel, as though he had six legs, as the two soldiers struggled to keep up on all fours. The Turks had cut their tunnel twice as wide as the Venetians' lateral, but only a little higher. As they neared a turn, cut around a large rock, the Spider heard voices and stopped to allow the two perspiring soldiers to catch up. With his dagger drawn, nearly standing erect, the Spider moved in for the kill.

As he peeked his left eye around the corner, he could see two Turks sitting on the floor illuminated by a single brightly burning lamp on the wall halfway between them and the Venetians. Blinded by the lamp, the Turks would not be able to see their attackers until it was too late. The Spider quietly removed his shoes; the two soldiers followed his example. Then, like a spider in his web, *Il Ragno* struck. With three pumps of his powerful legs he dove through the air, using one of the Turks to cushion his fall to the ground as he skewered him through the side of his neck. Then the Spider turned on the other Turk, as the startled man reached for his sword, but one of the others neatly dispatched him with a vicious slash to the throat. The attack had lasted five seconds—barely a sound was made.

They quickly moved to the end of tunnel and found what they were looking for. Opening up before them was a large chamber the Turks had excavated with great effort. It was large enough to hold more than a hundred barrels of black powder, enough to level twenty or thirty yards of the wall just a few feet above them, but the room was empty—there were no barrels of powder anywhere in sight.

The soldier assigned to reconnoiter in the other direction returned to where Seraglio stood at about the same time as the Spider and the others returned. The breathless soldier spoke in an excited whisper.

"I crawled all the way to a turn where the tunnel went completely dark."

As Seraglio listened to his report, he noticed the Spider and another man were wearing Turks' clothes.

"Where did you get those?"

"We borrowed them from a few Turks we met down there." He pointed.

"They will not miss them," smiled the other man, pulling on his bloody shirt.

The Spider signaled for quiet and for all five men to follow him down the tunnel and into the darkness toward the Turkish lines. As he moved quickly with a deft hand on one wall to guide him, he opened a gap between him and the others as his catlike eyes, accustomed to years of darkness, searched for his next victim. He reached the turn. Far away, a faint yellow glow danced on the wall of the tunnel—it was almost a hundred yards away. It took five minutes before he reached the spot fifty feet from where the light painted the tunnel wall. As Seraglio and the others caught up to him, they could hear voices reverberating on the walls. How many Turks would there be this time?

As they moved to within twenty feet of the light, Seraglio and the others realized the spot was actually the opening to another tunnel, perpendicular to the main shaft.

"Damn," whispered the Spider.

"Alberto," he motioned for the soldier dressed as a Turk. "Explore this side tunnel. The rest of you, follow me."

As he proceeded down the now-darkened main tunnel, once again gliding his hand along one wall, the Spider's foot suddenly touched something hard. He stopped. It was a barrel. The powder! He began to count—ten . . . twenty . . . thirty . . . forty . . . fifty . . . sixty. Now faint light danced on the walls ahead. He stopped and stretched his arm across the tunnel to restrain the others.

"Were there barrels on the other side?" he whispered.

"Yes, I counted sixty," hissed one of the men.

"That makes more than a hundred. In the room up ahead we will find victory or death. Seraglio, you stay here. If we unleash the demons of hell, run as fast as you can and report what we have found." He turned to the three soldiers. "Ready?"

Assuming a prone position, the Spider quickly looked around the corner. Pulling back, instantly, he stood and reported.

"Five. This will not be easy. By my reckoning, we are still far from their lines. If there are no others nearby, we will make quick work of them. For

St. Mark and Venice," he whispered. Then, crossing themselves, the Spider and his three brave men disappeared around the corner. This encounter was not as quiet as the last.

Three Turks were quickly dispatched with well-placed stabs as they realized too late that the Spider and the others were Venetians, but the two farthest away from their assailants had time to reach for their weapons. As one instinctively turned to fight, the other began to crawl away. The fighting Turk skillfully blocked the passage as he slashed the first Venetian soldier with his sword, partially severing his right hand, rendering him defenseless. Before the Spider could climb over his wounded comrade, the Turk had skillfully sliced the wounded soldier across the throat, leaving him to bleed to death. Wild for revenge, the Spider struck before the Turk could cock his sword hand for another stab, and plunged his dagger deep into the man's eye socket.

Without stopping to admire his work, the intrepid Spider set out after the terrified lone Turk, down the tunnel into the dank, dark unknown. As fast as the Spider could run, he feared he might not close the distance fast enough to catch his crawling prey. He made a quick decision and reached into his sack, pulled out a handful of caltrops and threw them with all his might. As they bounced along the floor and walls of the tunnel, the Turk suddenly howled with pain as the spikes penetrated his palms and knees. The tunnel amplified his cries. Knowing the thick leather soles of his shoes would still not protect him from their needle-sharp points, the Spider slid his feet along the floor, sending caltrops flying. Reaching the screaming, writhing Turk, he crashed onto the man's back with his knees making quick work of him, as he knocked off his hat, pulled up his head by the hair, and slit the man's throat. There would not be much time now, he thought. The Turks could hear that one screaming all the way to Athens.

The Spider scrambled back up the tunnel and climbed over the dead Venetian. He continued to where the two soldiers, who had already broken open two barrels, were pouring a line of powder along the floor of the tunnel away from the Turkish lines. As they worked, Seraglio nervously lit their way with the lamps he still held in his hands.

"The Turks will soon come storming up the main tunnel," warned the Spider, no longer whispering. "We must buy some time!"

The two young Venetian soldiers looked at each other.

"This barrel is almost empty," said one. "So is this one," said the other.

"Good men. Remember, fight, then block. Let no Turks pass. Tie yourselves together with your sashes. It will take them longer to untangle you."

The two soldiers disappeared, crawling down the tunnel toward the Turks. The Spider turned to Seraglio and uttered just one word.

"Brave!

"Now it is just you and I—and Alberto. Let us finish this and be gone!"

Seraglio's heart was pounding. As the Spider emptied the last barrel, Seraglio formed a thick stripe of powder behind it with his hands. Suddenly they could hear shouts and cries from the direction the two young soldiers had gone.

"That will do," said the Spider as he grabbed one of the lamps Seraglio had placed on the tunnel floor. He bent down and dumped the burning contents of the lamp onto the powder. It instantly sparked and flamed as it began to burn a path toward more than a hundred powder-filled barrels just fifty feet down the tunnel. As Seraglio stood transfixed watching, thinking of the two brave soldiers who now faced certain death at the hands of the Turks or from the explosion, the Spider yanked him by the arm and screamed at him.

"Run, damn you!"

As they turned to run for their lives, the flame sputtered and died. The Spider was already ten feet ahead of him when Seraglio instinctively stopped. Not thinking of the danger, he ran back toward the powder. Stooping quickly to pick up the second lamp that, luckily, the Spider had not emptied, Seraglio raced to the spot where the powder had gone out and relit it. The crude fuse was now just two-thirds as long. Seraglio ran for his life until he thought his chest would burst.

Up ahead was the entrance to the perpendicular side tunnel that Alberto had disappeared into. As the Spider reached it, he too disappeared. Twenty seconds behind, Seraglio followed him. No sooner had he escaped from the main tunnel than a dazzling flash lit the place brighter than if some giant hand had ripped off the top of the entire subterranean complex. Violent shock waves knocked them to the floor as a sheet of flame singed the clothes on their backs. Seraglio could feel pieces of the ceiling falling onto him as he covered his head. He saw the face of death as he lay there thinking a wordless prayer. He felt closer to God than he had ever felt before.

The first explosion was followed a split second later by another smaller blast that again bathed them in light. Seraglio's aching ears were bleeding from the concussion. His head felt like he had been hit with a mallet. As he rolled over, he could see dust billowing through the main tunnel from right to left away from the direction of the blast.

Seraglio and the Spider struggled to their feet, shaking the dirt and dust from their hair and wiping their faces. Grit stung their eyes. They crawled back into the main tunnel over pieces of earth strewn on the floor. It was then that they saw Alberto, dressed in Turkish clothing, crawling fast toward them in the perpendicular tunnel. They waited anxiously for him, safe in the knowledge that no Turks would be pursuing them in the collapsed main tunnel. On he came through the dust. It was only when he was twenty feet away that they realized it was not Alberto.

"Turks!" shouted the Spider as they both turned and ran for their lives.

The Spider let Seraglio take the lead. As Seraglio ran with all the strength he could muster, he was determined not to let the Turks catch up with his protector because of his slowness of foot. His stubby legs pumping, Seraglio frantically looked for the passageway on his right that led to the Venetians' lateral tunnel. Suddenly, he saw a man's face peering out from the wall. He prayed it belonged to a Venetian—it did.

Seraglio tore into the passageway with the Spider hot on his heels. The silent soldier slid a stiff animal skin coated with earth over the hole, attempting to hide it from the pursuing Turks. Then he crawled after the Spider toward the bypass where the two heavily armed and hidden soldiers waited. The skin crashed to the tunnel floor as the pursuing Turks poured through the hole, like angry ants defending their nest. Seraglio allowed himself a quick look over his shoulder. He thought he could see at least three or four chasing the crawling soldier. Just when he thought he could run no longer, Seraglio finally passed the two soldiers waiting in the bypass followed a few seconds later by the Spider and the desperate crawling soldier.

As the pursuing Turks drew even with the two hidden soldiers, the Venetians struck with the precision of executioners, dropping the two in front with single thrusts of their swords. The two Venetians turned to face the others, but the Turks beat a hasty retreat, not wanting to see what other surprises the Venetians had in store for them.

Seraglio and the Spider slowly climbed the ladder and emerged from the underground hell, breathing in great draughts of glorious fresh air. Seraglio had not realized how dust-filled the tunnel had become after the explosion. He and his comrade were covered with black soot and damp brown earth. It was then that Seraglio realized only the front and sleeves of his shirt had survived the blasts. His back was burned and his hair had been singed.

As Seraglio dropped to the ground, exhausted, Antonio's face suddenly appeared above him like a sublime vision.

"What a massive explosion! The whole Turkish camp is in disarray. Now they will be forced to try to take the wall using scaling ladders," said Antonio. "Well done, my friend."

"What I did was nothing compared to those brave young soldiers who sacrificed their lives so that I might live."

"Seraglio, tonight your courage might have saved thousands—only time will tell."

The Venetians' valiant attack robbed the Turks of the element of surprise. The tunnel that had taken months to dig was completely destroyed along with more than a hundred barrels of black powder. Seraglio had entered the subterranean world of tunnel fighting and lived to tell about it. The Spider had done it before. Seraglio made a solemn vow that he would never do it again.

16

Corinth

The morning broke dull and dreary. The incessant rain had tapered off slightly, leaving the sun an eerie pale disk peering through the dark clouds. Venetian officers shouted at their soggy troops, rousing them from their beds of sticky mud. Thousands of coughing, sniffling soldiers stretched their aching arms and legs as they struggled to pull off their dripping clothes. Standing naked, shivering in the raw morning air, they twisted them to wring out as much water as they could before putting them on again.

The early risers were eating their stale unleavened bread, dipping it in puddles to soften its rock-hard texture. Any man unfortunate enough to break a rotten tooth would suffer days of excruciating pain and could slowly starve if he was unable to eat. Some were munching on fresh olives and salty cheese made from sheep's milk, gathered from local farmers. Others were eating a few scraps of dried meat or fish. There were few fires since all the available scrub wood within a mile of the wall had been burned days ago.

The soldiers who slept along the length of the wall were not as filthy, but like those below, they were also soaked to the skin. While Seraglio lay curled up against a crenellated stone block, dead to the world, collecting his hard-earned sleep, Antonio, who had spent the night there, and Giorgio began to awaken the men. They knew that dawn would bring danger. The Turks were just a third of a mile away. Even in the mud, with a determined attack they could reach the wall in less than half an hour after forming up.

"Seraglio proved his mettle last night," said Giorgio.

"Yes. When he awakens, he will probably fill his pants when he realizes how close he came to being killed."

They laughed for the first time in days. The cold wet weather had made everyone short-tempered and sick of the whole miserable affair. There were signs that the Venetians' legendary discipline had begun to break down. Men were fighting over trifles. Just the day before, one soldier had to be flogged for stealing another man's oilskin.

As the sun began to burn through the drizzling sky, the tired and worn Venetian army took up its positions, as it had each day for the previous two weeks. When the order was passed down to the companies of irritable troops along the wall, and to those in reserve behind it, to put on their armor, even the newest volunteer sensed that things were about to change. Every man had heard the explosion the night before.

As the army unfurled their battle standards, dotting the wall with crimson and gold, the air rang out with the clanking sounds of men pulling on their heavy armor. Each soldier, depending on his station, fastened a bascinet, barbute, or salade onto his head. Some were topped with bright colored plumes. Crossbowmen inspected their bolts while common soldiers wiped the rain and mud from their rusting steel weapons. The few men with wall guns, a relatively new addition to the Venetian army, sighted down the ornate handmade barrels and checked their powder and fuses to be sure they were dry.

Uppermost, in each man's thoughts, was his desire to acquit himself honorably in the eyes of his comrades. True, he was fighting for the Republic, but his greatest fear was that, in a moment of weakness, his courage would fail and he would suffer the eternal reproach of his company of comrades, those men he knew best.

Soon, the men's attention turned from their own state of readiness to the Turks, far in the distance across the narrow Isthmus. Antonio looked down at the ground in front of him and imagined thousands of Janissaries carrying scaling ladders, trying to climb the wall to get at the Venetian defenders. At Constantinople, there had been too much wall and too few defenders. With a quick calculation he figured that the density of defenders on this wall was more than three and a half times greater than it had been then.

"Antonio, what are you thinking?" interrupted Giorgio.

"This time, we will hold them—not like at Constantinople."

"God help us if we cannot." Giorgio turned and pointed at the hilly open expanse of the countryside behind them.

"We will have too far to go to reach the safety of our ships and we cannot outrun their cavalry. We must hold," he said as he turned back to face Antonio.

"I wish I could stay here to fight alongside you, but I must go see what orders Signor Malatesta has for me to do today."

"Do not worry about me. No Turks will reach the top of the wall where my men stand." He patted the pommel of his sword for effect.

No sooner had Antonio disappeared into the stairwell when the sound of a thousand shouting men, quickly joined by ten thousand more, made him stop. He quickly retraced his steps and emerged into the soft daylight that illuminated the brilliant crimson, gold, and steely silver of the Venetian lines as rows of soldiers contrasted starkly against the gray sky. He looked toward the Turkish positions, now visible for the first time in days. They were collapsing their tents and forming ranks.

"They are breaking camp!" shouted one man.

The loud cheer that echoed from atop the wall heartened the men behind it, on the ground, as they clamored to find out what lay beyond their sight.

"We have done it!" shouted another. "They are going home for the winter."

Suddenly, as if a signal had been given, the cheering stopped. The Venetians fell silent. The only sound was the faint blaring of trumpets from the Turkish camp.

"Look! There are the guns," shouted one young soldier, pointing out what every other man could see for himself. "They were concealed in those big tents all along!"

"Look at the size of them! They will smash this flimsy wall to pieces."

Antonio strained his eyes as he tried to count the enemy's guns. He gave up at twenty. One had the longest barrel he had ever seen. The sultan had indeed brought his vaunted artillery with him after all. How could they have thought that he would not?

"There will be hell to pay now," said Giorgio quietly. "What can we possibly do in the face of such firepower?" His eyes searched Antonio's for an answer.

Antonio said nothing. There *was* no answer. Once the wall was smashed, only flesh and bone would stand between the Turks and all of Morea. Outnumbered and out-gunned, the Venetians did not stand a chance. They could only hope that the Turks would impetuously attack prematurely, before their guns had time to finish their deadly work. At Constantinople, the Turks had an incentive to attack prematurely—to plunder one of the richest cities on earth, but here, behind the wall, were just some farms and small towns. Antonio knew they would wait patiently until the Venetians were forced to abandon their once proud wall after their guns had reduced it to rubble.

The sun finally began to warm the land. Its rays poured through the billowing clouds bathing the landscape in a strange light, brighter than one would expect for a late autumn day. All along the four-mile wall men stood silently, eyes fixed on the huge cannon, each certain that one of the ominous black barrels across the plain was pointed directly at him. Many crouched or ducked as they moved, unconsciously surrendering to their fears. The officers, feeling no safer than their charges, were obliged by their rank to walk as though taking a Sunday morning stroll in the Piazza San Marco. This angered the troops who knew they could not leave their positions until their officers, convinced it was foolhardy to remain there, ordered them to move back out of range of the guns.

Twenty-two thousand Venetians—every man posted on the wall—watched as the Turkish gunners methodically set themselves to work. They were loading each gun with black powder and a stone or iron ball. The only sound along the wall was the beating of human hearts, pounding in the breasts of desperate men, too afraid to talk, too proud to complain. It was a scene frozen in time.

Giorgio Ziani reached out his long arms and wrapped them around the shoulders of the two nearest soldiers.

"Well, men," he said loudly, for everyone nearby to hear, "do you think we are in range of those guns?"

The two men turned and looked at him, confusion in their eyes.

"Is it possible that we are beyond their range?" asked the younger one, hopefully.

"I am afraid not," countered the grizzled old veteran. "They probably emplaced those guns months ago, after firing a few shots to be sure they had the range. They have done this before, you know," he growled in disgust. He looked at Giorgio with eyes that begged for the truth. "What do you think, Signor Ziani?"

Giorgio knew he had to bolster his men's courage—somehow.

"Easy now, men. Those guns are so massive; they can each only fire a few rounds a day. The chance of a shot hitting you is so small it is not worth worrying about."

The men were not convinced. Altogether, Giorgio counted more than thirty guns grouped into six batteries. Two looked as though they were going to concentrate their fire directly on the tower he and his men were defending.

Giorgio shook it off as an illusion and grimly began to explain to his men
what he wanted them to do.

Suddenly, a chorus of trumpets rang out again from across the plain between the two armies. Tens of thousands of Turks now responded to the call
to arms. Within minutes, the sultan's army was assembled into perfectly
formed ranks. Endless rows of red, orange, mustard, and green uniforms
topped by hundreds of pennants and flags fluttered in the sea breeze like a
fiery rainbow. Out in front, squadrons of elite *sipahis* wildly raced back and
forth on their Arabian warhorses, pennants snapping in the wind, exhorting
the infantry to prepare for battle.

The *bashi-bazouks,* the sultan's fierce territorial troops, who were paid
only in booty, were arrayed on each flank. Every man was armed with a
sword or mace and a spear. They would be in foul temper since the only loot
they would find would be on the bodies of dead Venetians, there being no
city for them to sack. From the Venetian lines the sultan's army looked like
a patchwork of undulating fields of ripened crops. The center of the Turkish front line was comprised of a motley array of lightly armed provincial
troops levied from every corner of the sprawling Ottoman Empire. Behind
them stood the elite Janissary infantry and behind them in a second line
stood the Janissary archers. In the rear were more than twenty thousand cavalry, ready to burst through the first breach in the wall to slaughter the retreating defenders.

It would not be long now, thought Giorgio. He took a few steps back
and gazed over the inner side of the wall at the reserve troops, now lined up
in their ranks. The sense of awesome power he had felt a few days before
had vanished. Now, the Venetian line looked thin and vulnerable. Like most
of his comrades, he felt helpless, though he could not show it. All the Venetians could do was resolutely wait for the Turks to attack.

In a tower a half mile to the west, the two Venetian commanders stood
alone in the stairway. Guards were posted at the top and bottom to give
them privacy while they discussed the perilous situation facing the army.

"How long do you think it will take for the Turks to breach the wall
with their guns?" asked Captain-General Loredan.

Malatesta shook his head. "I do not know for sure . . . no more than a
day, perhaps. This wall is not capable of withstanding their artillery. It is too
old. The mortar is brittle. In some places, the stones were cut so skillfully, no
mortar was used at all."

Then, without emotion, he looked at Loredan and spoke his greatest
fear.

"Those three monsters in the middle are the largest guns I have ever seen. A well-placed shot from any of them could destroy five or six feet of wall. It is not a question of whether they will level our defenses but merely whether it will be today or tomorrow."

"I think we should move our troops off the wall and resume our positions after the bombardment, just before the Turkish infantry attacks."

"I would advise against that," counseled Malatesta. "That would create uncertainty among the troops. They will not understand why it makes sense to stand in a place that was too dangerous for them only minutes before. In my experience, once a position is abandoned, it is very difficult to reoccupy."

"But if we do not move the men off of the wall, they will be slaughtered where they stand," observed Loredan, showing a rare trace of emotion. "Our only chance then would be to hope that the Turks do not have enough projectiles or powder to use their guns long enough to breach the walls."

"There is another strategy we might employ," said Malatesta, coldly. "Our first aim must be to preserve our army, intact, to oppose the Turks. If we cannot fight them here at Corinth, we must withdraw until we can meet them somewhere else on more favorable terms, when they cannot use their artillery to the same effect."

Loredan looked at Malatesta, beginning to understand. "You mean, embark the entire army back on board the fleet?"

"Yes, Captain-General. That is exactly what I mean."

"But that would take a day at least," said Loredan incredulously. "You just said that we could hold the wall for no more than a day—with our entire army!"

"It is already late morning and the days are not so long now as in the summer. The Turks will not want to attempt a frontal assault against such a strong position with the wall intact. Even with those guns they cannot reduce it until nightfall—given their slow rate of fire. If we leave a small but active covering force, say one in ten men, to demonstrate boldly on the wall during the bombardment, the assault will not come until tomorrow. By then, the rest of the army will be safely on board our ships."

The *condottiere* stood confidently, hands on his hips, and awaited the captain-general's reaction to his plan. He is right, thought Loredan. I must sacrifice a portion of the army to save the rest to fight another day. Our position here is hopeless.

"Very well, Signor Malatesta, all the men in and adjacent to every fifth tower, about four thousand in all, will remain on the wall. The rest shall begin their retreat immediately. The Turks will not be able to observe their movement as long as the men are told to march alongside the wall. Once

darkness falls, we shall march away from the cover of the wall, back to Lechion where we will embark, unseen by the Turks. I will send word to
Captain-General of the Seas Cappello to gradually move the fleet into position, careful to conceal our intentions from the Turks until dark."

"I will advise the commanders of the troops who must remain on the
wall."

"No, Signor Malatesta. As commander, it is my duty to undertake such a
distasteful task. I want you to inform the commanders who must lead the
retreat."

"As you wish, Captain-General." Malatesta bowed. He admired Loredan
for his insistence on delivering such difficult news personally to those who
would stay behind.

The two gray-haired commanders emerged from inside the tower and
separated. After dispatching an *aide-de-camp* to advise Cappello of the plan,
Captain-General Loredan found Antonio and ordered him to accompany
him. As they rode toward the eastern end of the wall, Antonio was relieved
when Loredan told him the plan.

The big gun roared flames fifty feet long as it threw its projectile across
the third of a mile between the opposing lines. The massive stone flew
over the wall and tore a deep furrow in the soggy ground a hundred yards
behind a company of Venetians standing in reserve, behind a tower near the
center of the wall. By the time the other guns had fired their first shots, all
but two had missed. One landed just short of the wall and bounced against
it, cracking a block of stone but doing no real damage. The other bounded
across a section of wall near the east end of the line. As the hot iron ball
ripped across the top, it killed four men instantly, tearing their bodies to
pieces, turning their bones and armor into deadly missiles that wounded
three more. The Venetian army, trained for close quarters combat, could
only fight back with their silent resolve to resist their instinct to run away.
The Turks reloaded and began firing their guns at will, each one throwing
between one and four shots every hour, depending upon its size.

At the eastern end of the wall, with their horses' hooves nervously
stomping at the water of the Saronic Gulf, Captain-General Loredan gave
Antonio his orders.

"I will inform the commander of the bastion here that he and his men
must cover the retreat of the army, remaining here until morning, when they
will be free to make their way back to Lechion. We will leave sufficient craft
to ferry them out to the fleet. The rise in the ground over there will obscure

our movement behind the wall from the Turkish fleet out in the gulf." He pointed to the ridge along the coast next to the bastion.

"Ride west along the wall until you reach the tenth tower, where you shall deliver the same order. Then proceed to every tenth tower and give the order to the commander there, until you reach the western end of the wall. I will follow and inform the rest of those who will comprise the rear guard, starting with the fifth tower. That way, we will be able to more quickly inform those who are to remain on the wall."

"As you wish," saluted Antonio, as he turned his horse and rode off.

When he informed each officer whose troops would stay on the wall, he delivered a hard message. He told them to do everything they could to convince the Turks that the entire army was still on the wall and to remain in place until morning. Only then could they make a run for it. Every officer knew that if the wall was breached and the Turkish cavalry got through, they would be caught in the open and butchered.

After an hour, Antonio reached Giorgio's tower. It was the sixtieth. He would have to stay. Antonio felt sick as he dismounted. The troops on the ground, behind the wall, had already begun to march away to the west, keeping close to the wall to avoid detection. To the east, thousands were streaming down and out of their towers or already marching along the wall. Those remaining were spreading out to fill in the departed troops' positions. As Antonio walked up the stairs, he summoned all of his strength.

"Antonio! What is happening? How can we be retreating before the fight even begins?"

Antonio placed his arm around his brother's shoulder and steered him back inside the tower, away from his men, where they could talk alone.

"The news is bad. The army is going to retreat and embark tonight, after dark."

"But why?"

"Captain-General Loredan and Signor Malatesta have determined that the Turks' guns will smash the wall and we will be unable to resist the assault that will follow."

Giorgio was silent, listening intently, his mind racing.

"You and your men must remain as part of the rear guard, doing everything you can to convince the Turks that the entire army is still here and that we intend to stand."

Their eyes locked. Finally, Giorgio spoke.

"This is a damned tough thing to chew. The men will not like it."

"They must do this for the Republic. They must help to save the army."

"When we do it, it will not be for the Republic—not this time, Antonio." He glared bitterly. "We will do it for one another. Each man's devotion to his comrades will not permit him to be the weak link that destroys the chain. Stand we must and stand we shall." His familiar smile returned. "And then . . . just before sunrise, we will all run like rabbits—but not until then, I promise."

Antonio embraced his brother. They squeezed each other hard. Pulling away, Giorgio uttered the words Antonio had dreaded hearing.

"If I do not make it back, tell Constantine his uncle died like a Venetian."

"Make it back, Giorgio. Somehow, some way . . . you must make it back."

There was no more to say as his brother turned to go.

"I will send Seraglio down," he called back. "He cannot help us here."

Soon, Antonio heard footsteps. The familiar face was wrinkled with questions.

"Giorgio says you want to see me. What is happening? Why are we staying?"

Antonio's eyes held his friend's in their sad but firm gaze.

"Giorgio and his men must form part of a rear guard to cover the army's retreat."

So they are to be sacrificed like those two brave young soldiers in the tunnel were the night before, thought Seraglio. He looked sympathetically at his friend. His suffering weighed on him like a great stone.

"I want you to leave with the others," said Antonio.

Though Antonio's words told him he would not have to share Giorgio's fate, Seraglio felt a sickness in the pit of his stomach. He had to turn away.

The Venetians executed the difficult retreat with precision. As each company of men abandoned the wall, though shivering with cold, they left their capes or robes with those who remained behind, who used them to create the illusion that the entire army stood defiantly on the wall. The Venetians even raised every battle flag, including the captain-general's personal standard, prominently along the wall.

The skeleton force of four thousand men braved the Turkish fire all afternoon. Their only advantage was that their reduced numbers made it harder for the Turks to inflict many casualties, but by the time the sun set over the Isthmus of Corinth, the walls had been reduced to rubble in a dozen places.

Normally the defenders would have used the night to repair the breaches but the rear guard made no attempt. Instead, the forlorn men stood watch, praying that their commander was right—that the Turks would wait for daylight to attack. Even the weakest probe would reveal that the bulk of the Venetian army had gone.

Meanwhile as soon as darkness fell, Captain-General of the Seas Cappello moved his fleet to Lechion, three miles away. The new moon provided just enough light to guide the hundreds of small boats ferrying the troops safely to the transports. Throwing vast stores of food into the sea and slaughtering the animals to deny them to the Turks, the Venetians required only one night to embark twenty-six thousand men.

Just before dawn lifted night's curtain, signaling that the final act in the defense of Corinth had begun, the band of actors left on the stage discarded their armor, filed out of their towers, and ran for their lives. The Turks, believing they would easily breach the ruined walls the next day, had not probed the Venetian positions during the night.

A long the Turkish lines, across the plain, the new day revealed to them that something had changed. Though the Venetians still occupied the wall, there was no activity. Wisps of smoke wafted above their positions from a few places, but the men on the wall seemed as though they were still sleeping. Most of the Venetian fleet had also moved from their position guarding the western flank of the line to Lechion.

The sultan turned to Abdullah Ali.

"It appears that the Venetians have gone. Send a squadron of *sipahis* under the wall to draw fire. If there is none, it will confirm my suspicion."

"Master, if they have gone, there are far too many soldiers for them to make a stand on the Acrocorinth. I believe they will, instead, embark onto their transports. That will take time. We can catch them with one foot on their ships and the other on land."

"We must breach the wall, at once, to enable our cavalry to pursue them," said the sultan. "Direct all of the guns to fire at that section of wall between those two towers and reduce it to rubble." He pointed. "Then take the cavalry and ride them down, destroy them. I want no prisoners."

"As you command, Master," bowed the governor of Istanbul as he departed.

G iorgio had decided to keep on his armor and bascinet, but after running a few hundred yards, he was falling behind his men. As he looked at the mass of the Acrocorinth up ahead, he discarded one piece of armor after another as he ran. He briefly looked back toward the wall. The commander of the bastion on the eastern end of the line had decided it was too far to Lechion, preferring to defend his fortress rather than be cut down on the plain or in the hills behind the center by a wave of pursuing Turkish cavalry. Ranged across the low hills up ahead Giorgio could see a dozen small companies of men streaming away to the southwest and the safety of Lechion.

On the small stone pier at Lechion, Antonio and Seraglio struggled to see any sign of the rear guard nearing Lechion, but there were none in sight.

Footsore and exhausted, Giorgio and his thirty men struggled over the rocky ground, broken by small ravines and hills, to make their way to the west of the Acrocorinth. Somewhere beyond that point was Lechion. Judging by the sun, it was two or three in the afternoon. Only a few more hours of daylight remained. Despite the cold, they were dripping with perspiration.

They stopped to rest for a few minutes. Some men used the respite to relieve themselves. Just as he ordered his soldiers to resume their trek, a soldier shouted and pointed to a low ridge a half mile to their rear. A lone rider, a white turban on his head, his lance pointed in the air, sat motionless on his horse and then disappeared.

"The *sipahis* have breached the wall!" shouted another soldier.

"Easy now, Lechion cannot be far off. We must bear down, men. If we do not run, we will never make it." Giorgio broke into a steady trot. The others followed. For fifteen minutes they ran, lungs bursting and feet bruised and sore from the countless rocks that dotted the hilly plain. As they climbed to the top of another small rise, a panorama opened before their eyes.

To their left, the Acrocorinth towered above, too far to reach and an impossible climb in their winded condition. At its foot, to the right, were the ruins of the ancient city of Corinth. A mile beyond, farther to their right, they could see the tiny white buildings of Lechion. Just over the rooftops, was a familiar sight—the Venetian battle fleet. It seemed to Giorgio that he could almost reach out and touch it.

Giorgio waved his men onward. There were still about twenty-five in the company behind him struggling up the hill. Farther back, five stragglers, weaker men who had all but given up, were barely visible against the undulating landscape. Ten minutes passed. Two more steps, he puffed, and I will reach the top of this wretched hill . . . the cold sea breeze blew his long hair and beard as he surveyed their situation.

He could clearly make out individual Venetian ships now riding at their anchors in the Gulf of Corinth. Lechion was less than half a mile away. A few of the heartiest soldiers now crawled up alongside of him, gasping for breath, steam billowing from their mouths, the biting air sticking their dripping nostrils together. A few hundred yards to his right, Giorgio could see a company of about fifty men moving quickly through a grove of olive trees, between his position and Lechion, several hundred yards behind the wall.

"Turks!" shouted a voice from below. Giorgio spun around. A half mile behind them hundreds of horsemen, their white robes flowing behind, were pouring over the crest of long ridge, like a frothy wave, and riding toward them.

"Follow me!" shouted Giorgio, as he decided to make a dash for the port.

Suddenly, another cloud of cavalry rose up out of the earth and galloped toward the olive grove. The fugitives amid the gnarled trees began to shout and disperse in every direction, desperately searching in vain for a place to hide. The *sipahis* shouldered their lances and crashed through the rows of small trees, skewering the lightly armed Venetians. In five minutes the ground was littered with their slaughtered corpses.

Now, exposed and in the open, their direct escape route to the sea cut off, Giorgio and his men had only one choice. They veered left and ran for a small hillock in front of a mass of jagged rocks and scrub brush. There, they might have a chance to defend themselves against the Turkish cavalry.

They ran with the fear that the threat of imminent death brings to all creatures. As the Turks converged on them from two directions, he could hear screams as the *Sipahis'* lances found the backs of his stragglers.

Waiting until the last moment, hoping against hope, Antonio and Seraglio had finally taken one of the last boats out to the fleet. On the deck, a quarter mile offshore, they stood helplessly as they watched the Turks butcher the men in the olive grove. Suddenly Seraglio pointed to another group running toward a hillock where they could just make out some more soldiers amid the rocks.

"A fitting place for brave men to die," observed Seraglio stoically. "For two thousand years that place has seen its share of death and destruction. Everyone from Alexander and his father, Philip of Macedon, to the Romans, the Goths, the Slavs, and the Franks has sacked Corinth. And then, the depredations of man being insufficient, even God has seen fit, in his infinite wisdom, to ravage the place with earthquakes."

"The only thing I know about Corinth, Seraglio, is that it is the final resting place of Xenophon, the famous Greek general."

"It is going to be for those poor devils too."

Every man on board the Venetian ships watched helplessly as their countrymen prepared to make their last stand in the shadow of the ruins of

Corinth. Taking up positions near the marble stones, the Venetians prepared their defense.

Vettor Soranzo and his men cheered as they saw their comrades running to join them. They had occupied the same position fifteen minutes before. Posted closer to the western end of the wall, he and his men were nearer to Lechion than most of the rear guard. They would have made it to the port before the *sipahis* had blocked their way, thought Vettor, if only he had not wasted so much time, lost, leading them down a deep ravine. By the time they had finally found a usable path through it, it was too late.

Now they were isolated, cut off from Lechion and the fleet and too far away to reach the refuge of the Acrocorinth. He knew his men were too exhausted to escape over the jagged rocks, covered with entangling scrub brush to their rear. He looked to his left and envied his cousin, Giovanni, somewhere out there, safe on board his war galley.

Loud shouts jerked Vettor back to reality. The *sipahis* from the olive grove had spotted the new company of Venetians, running toward him. Vettor had seen what the Turks had done to the poor devils in the orchard. So had these twenty fugitives, who were racing as fast as their tired legs would carry them. Suddenly, his jaw dropped. There, right in front, was Giorgio Ziani. He had never imagined he would be glad to see him.

Vettor's men cheered as Giorgio's men streamed up the hillock and dropped to the ground, exhausted from their dash. They could see the *sipahis* reigning in their mounts, as they waited for more horsemen in the distance to join them. Their commander knew he had trapped his quarry. There was no reason to hurry now.

They faced each other for the first time since that day on the Molo. Vettor's cheeks and forehead were cut and bleeding. His neck had an ugly bruise. He had thrown away his armor and now looked like a common soldier with no trappings of rank—no trace of military bearing. His ashen face betrayed that he was possessed by a cold, paralyzing fear. Giorgio knew, at once, that he would have to take command.

"How many men are with you?"

"About fifty," answered Vettor. "There must be hundreds of *sipahis* out there."

"At least," observed Giorgio icily. "There were more than a hundred chasing us. They will come thundering over that high ground, there, soon enough."

"What are we going to do?" implored Vettor, as though hoping for some magical solution to their mortal danger.

"What is back there?" asked Giorgio abruptly, pointing to the rocky broken ground to their rear.

"Nothing but jagged piles of rocks and thick underbrush. Even if we made it through, there would still be a quarter mile of open ground for us to cover to reach the sea. With all that Turkish cavalry out there, we would never make it in time."

Giorgio thought fast. He was right. Their men were already exhausted. By the time they cut through it, the cavalry would be between them and the sea. They would have to make their stand among the rocks where the *sipahis* would have to dismount to attack them. If death was inevitable, he preferred to sell his life dearly and kill some Turks rather than be slaughtered in the open like those poor bastards in the orchard.

"Form your men on the left and center. We will take the right. Our rear should be safe. Are you certain no horsemen can get in there?"

"Yes."

Vettor felt a strange sense relief, relinquishing command to him. Now as he thought not of the men he led—Giorgio would see to them—he thought only of himself. What was he doing here in this dung heap of a country, defending people he cared nothing about? Why should he sacrifice his life for them?

He could see the Turks milling about in the distance, their numbers swelling by the minute. A retinue, accompanied by trumpet blasts, appeared on the right as it crested the ridgeline. Its commander was obviously someone of great importance.

Vettor looked at his men. Let them look to Giorgio for leadership now. He allowed himself a furtive glance at the broken terrain behind them. He looked back at Giorgio, barking orders to his men. A smile curled his lips as he rubbed his aching neck and walked slowly and purposefully toward the far left end of his line.

Giorgio expertly posted each man. Most were scared, some were resigned—all were obedient. They knew their only chance was to do what the big patrician said. Vettor's men were rejuvenated by his martial bearing and decisive tone, so different from Vettor's bumbling that had prevented them from reaching Lechion and safety as they had hacked their way through the tangled thickets in the ravine.

His preparations completed, he crouched down and rested. All they could do now was await the Turks' onslaught. They had been in the rocks for a half hour. Surely the Turks would want to finish them off before sunset—now less than an hour away.

Abdullah Ali was in personal command of the *sipahis'* pursuit of the Venetians. A few minutes after reaching the ridge, a quarter mile from the ruins of ancient Corinth, he had made his plan. He would deploy his cavalry to fight as infantry. They would dismount and use their bows to kill as many Venetians as they could from long range. Only then would they move in to finish them off. They would attack from three sides. He sent a squadron of forty of his mounted bodyguards around behind the Venetians' position to cut down any who might try to escape through the rocky ground to their rear.

The dismounted *sipahis* drew their bows as they worked their way around the Venetians, placing them in a deadly cross fire. In minutes, more than half the defenders were down, shot by arrows. The Turks gave no quarter, the Venetians asked for none.

As the Turks pressed home their attack, Vettor Soranzo had sidled steadily to his left, shouting hollow words of encouragement that made little impact on his bitter men, who blamed him for their impending doom. With his eyes on the Turkish bowmen, he reached the two men on the far left of the line as arrows began to rain on them.

"You two, come with me," he snapped.

The two soldiers looked at each other in amazement.

"He wants us to scout for a way out through that rough ground to our rear." He jerked his thumb in the direction of the undefended ground.

"Follow me."

The two men obediently rose and followed him, unnoticed by their comrades, who were now fully occupied with the arrows that were flying at them from three directions. In a few seconds they had climbed over some rocks and disappeared into the thick brush.

"You two go on ahead. Find a trail if you can, but head for the fleet—over there. I will be along in a minute."

As the brush closed behind the two men, Vettor peered from the safety of his hiding place at the carnage below. Men were dropping dead or writhing in excruciating pain. He could see Giorgio waving his arms, still leading the resistance, trying to gather his few unwounded men together for a final stand. Suddenly, as he stood, he spun and dropped to the ground. His decision to slip away confirmed by what he had just seen, Vettor turned and ran to catch up with the two soldiers.

The arrow had ripped into Giorgio's chest with such force, it knocked him hard to the ground. Breathless, he rolled onto his side and looked in the direction of the fleet. Somewhere out there was Antonio and beyond . . . far beyond, was Venice. He lay there oozing life as he fought to remain conscious.

The screams of his dying men rang in his ears as each life was mercilessly ended.

Suddenly, towering over him was a tall *sipahi,* his sword raised threateningly. He motioned quickly with his left hand for Giorgio to hand over his purse. Fleeting thoughts of surviving as a hostage, ransomed like Antonio, danced in his confused mind. He obediently pulled up his shirt, revealing his leather purse. The Turk knelt down to loot him as he lay there in too much pain to resist. Then the Turk stood and emptied the contents into his hand—a few ducats and some silver. He smiled, satisfied with his find. Then he slowly raised his sword high above his head.

In the end, just before the razor-sharp blade sliced through his neck, Giorgio Ziani closed his eyes. But not before they caught sight of the smiling face that belonged to the golden winged Lion of St. Mark emblazoned on the crimson flag that was draped, like a trophy, around the *sipahi's* powerful shoulders.

From his position high on the ridge, Abdullah Ali could see the man's head bobbing above the scrub brush as he ran for his life away from the fight. To his right, his *sipahis* had already disappeared behind the rough ground to intercept him. He congratulated himself on his decision to block the Venetians' retreat.

The three fugitives crouched at the edge of the brush and looked out at the shoreline and the waiting Venetian fleet. Their spirits soared. With only a quarter mile to go, in five minutes they would be on the beach. Vettor cautiously raised his head in the fading light and scanned the open ground. The coast was clear.

"Now!" he shouted. The two men burst from the brush and began to run, neither looking back. Just as Vettor was about to jump from the brush, he heard the blare of a trumpet—Turks! He dropped low and began to crawl back, deep into the underbrush. He could hear shouts and the thunder of horses' hooves. Soon all was quiet. He was alone.

Only a few hundred of the rear guard, mostly from the western end of the wall, made it to Lechion and the safety of the fleet. Captain-General of the Seas Cappello waited all the next morning for more survivors to appear. Then, as the sun burned through the morning mist, revealing thousands of Turkish soldiers along the shoreline, salvaging whatever they could along the beach, he moved his ships away into deeper waters. He knew that even though the Turkish fleet was at least four day's sail away in the Saronic Gulf, the Turks could turn a few of the larger boats he had left on the beach into fire ships.

That afternoon, Captain-General Loredan ordered the Venetian fleet to sail for home. The defense of Corinth had gained the Republic nothing and cost more than three thousand of her bravest men and a mountain of supplies. Now, with Morea as good as lost, Venice retained only Crete, Corfu, and her island fortress of Negropont—all that remained of her former Greek possessions.

17

The Dilemma

It had been a week since Giovanni Soranzo had peered far over his ship's rail, seething with anger, as he had watched the demoralized Venetian army retreat from Corinth and shuttle back out to the fleet in the hastily assembled armada of small boats. He had no way to know whether his cousin, Vettor, had survived. Had he been a part of the rear guard? Turning to his adopted son, Enrico, he had cursed the decision to abandon the wall, leaving Morea to the mercy of the Turks without a fight.

Just nineteen years old, Enrico Soranzo had tasted war for the first time, even if it was from a distance. He had heard the booming of the Turks' guns and had seen the *sipahis* slaughter the men in the ruins, so far away that it had been nothing more than an interesting tableau—without pain or death. Frustrated by having to remain aboard the ship all those days, out of the action, he wrestled with his fears and his desire to prove his manhood. Enrico was the image of his dead father. Now, this morning, anchored in the harbor at Corfu, he looked forward to leaving the accursed ship for the first time in months. He thanked God that Captain-General Loredan had decided to disembark a strong garrison to reinforce the strategic island fortress before sailing for Venice.

Giovanni and Enrico walked along the pier, crowded with officers anxiously exchanging rumors, sprinkled with facts, about the Battle of Corinth. Giovanni quickly scanned each man's face, desperately searching for Vettor.

"Captain Soranzo!" shouted a familiar voice.

Soranzo spun around. It was Captain-General of the Seas Cappello.

"Allow me to congratulate you."

Soranzo had no idea what he was talking about.

"A miraculous escape. Never seen anything like it. What courage."

Vettor. He is alive!

"Captain-General Loredan just told me of your cousin's exploits. Remarkable."

"Where is he? I have not seen him in weeks. I feared he was dead."

"He is there, in the center of that crowd, with the captain-general," he pointed.

Soranzo could see a large group of officers. In the midst of the noisy gathering was Loredan and standing next to him was Vettor, a broad grin on his face. Soranzo broke into a run. By the time he pushed his way through the crowd of amazed admirers, Vettor was recounting the story of his desperate fight and amazing escape.

"Giovanni! Enrico!" he shouted like a conquering hero, as he spied his cousin.

They embraced briefly and then Vettor plunged back into his dramatic account.

". . . Then I could only watch while the Turks butchered my men as they tried, in vain, to hold their indefensible position. I cannot for my life understand why Giorgio Ziani foolishly ordered us to make our stand in that place. I tried to tell him that we could escape through the rough ground to our rear but he would not hear of it. It was as though he was determined to die—right there, near the ruins. That was fine for him and the poor souls under *his* command but he had no right to order *my* men to accept the same fate."

Vettor cast a quick glance at Loredan, who smiled with approval while veiling his embarrassment at Vettor's words. He was making strong accusations against the Zianis. Loredan did not want to be stuck in between the feuding families.

As he listened, Giovanni could hardly believe what he was hearing. Another Ziani mistake but fortunately, this time, it had not proved fatal to Vettor.

"Just as we were about to fight off a company of dismounted *sipahis,* Ziani finally ordered me to take two men and search for a way out of our death trap, but by then it was too late. As we scrambled up the embankment behind the ruins, we could see our position overrun. The Turks massacred them all. There was nothing we could do except save our own lives. We managed to escape from the killing ground by running through the dense brush until we reached a place a few hundred yards from the beach. I am certain our entire force could have escaped that way had Ziani listened to me earlier.

"We concealed ourselves there until dark but unfortunately, in the end; I was the only one strong enough to swim out to the fleet—the others, too exhausted to go on, drowned. They just slipped under the surface of the water. I was too weak to save them. Only with God's help was I able to make it back to the fleet."

"I think you must have been the last man to make it back to the fleet," observed the captain-general. "When we return to Venice, I shall see to it personally that you receive an award for your bravery."

Giovanni allowed a modest smile as he shared in his cousin's celebrity that reflected so gloriously on the family. And now, Giorgio Ziani was dead—and he had died ignominiously. He knew only too well how his death would devastate Antonio Ziani. As Giovanni joined Vettor in accepting congratulations from dozens of his fellow officers he could not see the profound sense of emptiness that crushed his adopted son. Giovanni did not understand how desperately Enrico needed to be a part of the family's success—to prove himself worthy. Instead, this day, Vettor's victory was Enrico's defeat. Feeling like an outsider, he slowly walked away.

Within minutes, after the crowd dispersed, Vettor's story spread like wildfire along the length of the pier, evolving and embellished. A thousand men swore they had heard it with their own ears as they retold tales of Vettor Soranzo's Homeric exploits and Giorgio Ziani's ignoble death that had caused so many to needlessly perish with him.

Antonio and Seraglio had gone ashore to try to find someone who could tell them of Giorgio's fate. It had not taken them long to hear Giorgio's name punctuating an animated conversation between two young officers. The young man did not spare Antonio's feelings as he told him about his brother's death and Vettor Soranzo's miraculous escape. He did not know that he was speaking to Giorgio Ziani's brother.

"Liar!" screamed Antonio, wild-eyed, as he violently pushed the unsuspecting man to the ground. He walked to the edge of the pier, followed by Seraglio.

"It is not possible," moaned Antonio to the sea.

He was shattered. It would be said that his only brother had met an ignoble death, in vain—one that had caused many other brave men to die.

Every nerve, every muscle, every sense in his body told him it could not be—not Giorgio. He could accept that he was dead. After all, he had been part of the forlorn rear guard. But could he be responsible for the death of almost a hundred men? Impossible.

"Antonio, there must be some other explanation. If Vettor Soranzo was the only survivor, there is no other witness to corroborate his version of what happened. In order to escape, perhaps he ran away before Giorgio and the others were overwhelmed."

Antonio slowly turned to face Seraglio. He seemed to lean against the majestic battle fleet arrayed behind him. His patrician bearing returned as he regained his composure. There were no tears in his eyes, only the stoic stare of a man inured to pain and suffering, who refuses to surrender to the unfairness of life. The terrible news that had filled him with compassion and remorse, anger and frustration, had now turned into a firm resolve to carry on.

"I refuse to believe that Giorgio caused those men to die in vain."

Seraglio placed his stubby arm around Antonio's waist.

"We should be getting back to our ship. The tide is in now."

Antonio looked at Seraglio, his eyes heavy with pain.

"How will I tell Constantine? When will I ever be free from the Soranzos?"

A fair wind billowed the sails of the Venetian battle fleet as it sailed into the Bacino di San Marco, but it was not a traditional homecoming. The Molo was not packed with the usual teeming crowds of adoring citizenry. There was little for anyone to cheer about. Captain-General Loredan had sent a fast messenger ship on ahead while the fleet had put in at Corfu, alerting the city to the army's disastrous retreat from Corinth. Though the dejected city mourned her three thousand dead, a week later when their names were posted on the Porta della Carta, the greatest source of her sadness was that the Turks had again prevailed. They had ruthlessly cut another valuable appendage from the body of the Republic's *terra firma* empire. Morea, a Venetian possession for more than two hundred and fifty years, was all but lost.

Antonio climbed from the small boat, followed closely by Seraglio. The short walk home would barely provide enough time to decide how to tell his family about Giorgio. He had put off thinking about it on the voyage home but now, as he racked his brain, he could not find the words. He knew that any words, no matter how carefully chosen, would seem pathetically inadequate. He thanked God that Giorgio had no wife or children. Telling them of his death would have been too much to bear.

As he crossed the Piazza San Marco, his mind wandering in self-defense, he admired the grandeur of the buildings and felt comforted by the familiar surroundings. He thought about Isabella and Constantine. After his long absence, he could not wait to embrace them. But how could he tell his ten-year-old son that Giorgio was dead? He knew the boy had always held a special place in his heart for his dashing uncle.

Finally home, Antonio kissed Isabella as he wiped away her tears of joy. But as he bent down to embrace his son, his heart broke again. Straightening up, he grasped Constantine's shoulders and inclined his head.

"I have bad news. Your uncle Giorgio is dead."

Isabella tried to throw her arm around her son, but he gently pushed it away.

"But how, Father?" he asked as he fought back tears.

For an instant Antonio struggled with terrible images of Giorgio fighting for his life, surrounded by bloodthirsty Turks. He pushed them from his mind.

"He was part of a rear guard. He sacrificed his life so that the bulk of the army could withdraw from a hopeless position." He knew he could not stop there. Constantine's friends would know the official version, as told by Vettor Soranzo.

Constantine struggled with the thought of his beloved uncle laying down his life even for such a noble cause.

Antonio placed his curled finger under his son's chin and lifted his face. His eyes told the boy that what he was about to say was important.

"Some will say that he did the wrong thing—that he needlessly sacrificed the lives of his men—that he was not brave. Constantine, it is not true. Do not believe it. Someday, I will explain to you why some men will say such things about the man we all loved. Until then, just know that what they say is wrong. When other boys tease you, do not fight with them. Pity them because they do not know the truth."

He looked at Seraglio and then took a step back, facing his son and wife.

"Someday, Giorgio's soul will rest in peace. Until that day, we must all be strong and love his memory even as others, in their ignorance, speak ill of him."

Constantine took the news like a man. Within a few weeks the boy's bitterness had turned to admiration—Giorgio's memory would live forever within the stone and plaster walls of the Ca' Ziani. As Antonio and his family had buried the memory of their beloved Giorgio, so Venice buried her dead as well. Though news from the East was relatively quiet as the Turks digested their Grecian meal—converting Morea into a province of the Ottoman Empire, the West was finally moved to action.

T he pope's death has enabled the Milanese to create a problem for us," observed Antonio as he picked up a delicate glass and filled it with dry Tuscan wine.

"They have seized Genoa?"

"Yes, they have taken cruel advantage of her long-declining fortunes. She was once a proud city-state, but Genoa has been mortally weakened by the loss of her eastern Mediterranean colonies to the Turks. Her loss of Pera was the final nail in her coffin."

"But while they have taken Genoa, you Venetians have captured the pontificate itself. Pietro Barbo, cardinal of San Marco, has been elected as the new pope!"

Antonio shook his head. "And a poor choice he is. Unsuited for doge or even a senator of the Republic, we will now send him to Rome to talk to God. He is so vain, I hear that he originally proposed to take the name Pope Formosus . . ."

"He wants to call himself Pope Good Looking?" Seraglio laughed heartily as he translated the Latin.

"But now his better judgment has apparently prevailed so he has decided to take the name of Paul II instead," continued Antonio, chuckling too.

"Why him, of all the men in Venice?"

"It is not in our interest to have a powerful pope—even if he is a Venetian."

"But surely, Venice must gain some advantage from a Venetian pope?" asked Seraglio quizzically, not understanding Antonio's concerns.

"Like so many popes before him, he will prove ineffective at raising the ire of Christendom against the Turks. He will assault them with words and grant indulgences to all who say they will fight, but his election will actually work against the Republic."

"Is that because, as a Venetian pope, he will naturally be expected to procure the wholehearted support of Venice for a crusade against the Turks?" asked Seraglio. "And while your so-called allies in Florence and Milan content themselves with holding Venice's cloak as she is locked in her death struggle with the Turks, they will seek to increase their power at home on the peninsula at her expense?"

"That is precisely our fear, Seraglio," smiled Antonio. "Are you quite certain you were not in the employ of the emperor's foreign minister rather than his chief architect?"

"No, I am quite certain. Although there was talk that my mother knew the foreign minister—frequently! She concluded many alliances, though she still suffered frequent invasions." He smiled.

Five years passed as Venice deftly resisted her mortal enemy while she held on to her treacherous allies on the Italian peninsula. The Turks continued to nibble at her remaining Greek islands in the East, taking small bites that they knew Venice would not muster the will and force to oppose. She doggedly played for time in her attempt to delay having to choose between two unappealing options.

To preserve her possessions, she could engage in an all-out fight to the death with the Turks risking her oriental trade, the very lifeblood of the Republic. But this would make her vulnerable to the treachery of her city-state neighbors and erstwhile allies Milan and Florence, who would be content to watch Venice spill her blood and gold in the defense of Christianity.

Or, she could make her peace with the Turks, perhaps only temporarily staving off the inevitable loss of her remaining eastern Mediterranean possessions, as Genoa had suffered. But this course would bring down on her the wrath of the Christian world.

Venice resorted to diplomacy, statecraft, and bribery to placate her allies while she avoided openly antagonizing the sultan. She continued her alliance with the Hungarians to resist western expansion by the Turks, as she offered huge bribes to the shah of Persia to make trouble for the sultan in the East. Her other allies saw her exertions and seeing an opportunity, finally began to waver as they sought new concessions from her.

Why do the other Italian city-states detest you Venetians so?" asked Seraglio.

"Remember the day we first met? You told me the other boys beat you because you were different. Well, I suppose in this case the other city-states are all essentially the same and *we* are different. They fight over ducal succession, having no free elections of their dukes; the popes constantly meddle in their affairs; and they live in fear that a larger state will invade and reduce them to a mere conquered province. We have free elections, consider the pope a formidable nuisance; and we are assured by our geography and our navy that we will not be successfully invaded by anyone—not even the Turks."

Seraglio looked thoughtfully at his mentor and then spoke carefully.

"But, Antonio, things change. Will your elections always be free? Will the popes always remain impotent in affecting Venice's fate? Can you always count on the large nations, like France and Spain, to be disinterested in your charms forever? And might not these rival city-states you speak of join and attempt to make Venice be like them?"

"You make good points, Seraglio, but remember, we are free to choose our own destiny. If times demand action, we are free to adjust our strategy and avoid disaster."

"But as long as Venice depends on others for trade, raw materials, and food, you are not free. Byzantium believed she could hold back the march of time but she could not. Now where is she? I will tell you. She is a conquered province with a sultan as her master—a footstool of the Ottomans."

Seraglio was right, of course, thought Antonio. In the history of the world no empire had survived forever—not Greece, not Rome, not the Franks. How could Venice think she could be any different?

The sultan had finally decided that the time had come to end the Venetian presence in Greece. He had utterly defeated them at Constantinople and Corinth but they had continued to resist him. Now he would strike them a mortal blow, once and for all. He would take the one possession, within his power to seize, that was most prized by *La Serenissima*—Negropont, her largest naval base in the eastern Mediterranean and the key to the island of Euboea with all its wealth. It was the prize of the Aegean. With no place to base their fleet, the rest of their possessions would be indefensible.

Venice's spies and diplomats reported that hostilities were expected to begin in the spring. While Venice resolutely prepared for her supreme test of strength with the sultan, knowing the rest of Europe would sit idly by, watching her fight, like a champion of old, holding her cloak, and publicly cheering her on to victory as they privately attempted to loot her purse.

The cavernous Great Council chamber was alive with excitement. More than fourteen hundred uniformly black-robed men—every patrician over the age of twenty-five—had assembled to discuss how Venice would deal with the Sultan's threat.

Antonio Ziani found an empty seat on a bench along the wall between the towering many-paned windows. Many who had come after him were standing along the far end of the room, opposite from where Doge Moro and his six councilors sat, five steps above the crowd on a dais. These venerable old men, dressed in scarlet, flanked the doge, who was in his gold-embroidered and ermine-collared robe, horned *corno* on his head. As a sign of respect, no one else was permitted to wear any headdress except the doge.

Antonio smiled as he thought about the men who filled the room. To an onlooker, they all looked almost identical, dressed in the same simple black robes, some a bit older or younger, some taller or shorter. But in their hearts and heads ran as many different thoughts and emotions as there were fish in the sea. The subject of the day's debate was so important to the survival of the Republic, every opinion would, no doubt, be heard.

Though he did not know the name of every man around him, there were few faces that Antonio did not recognize. Centuries of intermarriage among the *nobili* had made more than two hundred of them his distant relatives. As he studied the crowd he could feel it begin to settle. The black-robed figures sank into their places. The room quickly hushed as the diminutive doge rose to his feet. The air was dense with the smell of desperation. This would be a night to remember.

Doge Cristoforo Moro was old. Despised by some for dragging the Republic into the abortive crusade, undertaken five years before at Ancona, they blamed him for the resumption of hostilities by the Turks. Short and crooked with a deformed back, he cut an unimpressive image as he prepared to call the meeting to order. His high-pitched voice cut the silence like the whining of a dog. As he slowly read from a piece of paper, more than a thousand black-sheathed torsos leaned in his direction to catch every word.

"Our purpose today is to agree on how we should respond to a grave threat to our interests. Information has come to us that the sultan Muhammed II has begun to concentrate his much-enlarged fleet in the Dardanelles. We have also learned that he will march south from Istanbul at the head of his army—more than eighty thousand strong. His intention is to take Negropont and all of Euboea. I do not need to remind this body that such a loss would be a disaster for us of the first magnitude. He must be stopped."

"But how?" shouted an unseen voice from among the legion of black robes. Others joined in the chorus. Soon arguments erupted. The six in scarlet stood, signaling for quiet. The tempest subsided. The doge continued.

"We are here today to decide how." He paused a long time and then continued, "I wish to outline the decisions we must make today. First, we must authorize an additional war tax to finance whatever action we will take. Second, the Arsenal, which has recently been expanded, will produce more than twenty-five new galleys in the next month. They must be paid for. Third, we must choose a new captain-general of the seas to command the fleet. Finally, Governor Erizzo, aware of the Turks' movements, has requested more troops. We must respond to his request."

The doge deferred to his councilor for financial matters, who detailed the recommended tax of two hundred thousand ducats. It passed by a vote of nearly ten to one—those voting against it arguing the need for an even larger tax. Since the burden would be borne almost entirely by the men voting in the room, the expense of the new galleys was easily authorized. Now would come the most difficult part.

"Who is fit to have the rank of captain-general of the seas?" the doge put the question to the vast assemblage. Only a man with proven experience and years of selfless service to the Republic would be able to secure the support of the Great Council.

"Who will the candidates be?" asked the doge impatiently, as he searched the room for someone to respond to his request. But no one rose to place his own name or another's before the council. The coveted position of honor, normally hotly contested, was lying unclaimed on the floor of the Great Council chamber, so great was the fear of the sultan's military power. Word had reached Venice of his recently enlarged fleet. Finally, one man rose to speak, pulling every head in the room in his direction.

"I wish to place the name of Nicolo Canal in nomination."

Many were aghast. Though a famous physician and senator and well respected for serving the Republic for more than thirty years, he had little military experience. He had only served as a *sopracomito,* the supervised commander of a small galley, typically the first responsibility a young patrician was awarded on turning twenty-five.

Those around them encouraged other more qualified men, but none would allow his name to be placed in nomination. Every man qualified to lead the fleet also knew his future career would depend on his performance in the upcoming campaign against the Turks. The prospects of success were so dim, not one of them was willing to accept the risks of command to oppose Canal, who was also willing to personally pay for the cost of a new galley, a requirement for becoming captain-general of the seas.

"Surely, there must be others who would command the fleet," begged the doge.

Silence. Minds percolated as men sat motionless in their chairs to avoid drawing attention. This rare display of reticence demonstrated to all the terrible effect the wrath of the sultan had on the council. Almost every man in the room would fight, but only one was willing to take on the awesome responsibility of leadership.

"Very well," sighed the doge. "There being no other names, we shall vote." He paused one last time as though his silent plea for another candidate would be answered.

"Who is in favor of Nicolo Canal?"

Giovanni Soranzo was horrified, as were most of those around him who were also naval men. They began to raise their voices to oppose the quick vote, but more than a thousand hands shot into the air and Canal was chosen by an overwhelming, if not deserved, vote.

Before the arms had dropped, their owners were already contemplating the effect of what had just happened—so fast, yet so final and so far-reaching in its meaning. A virtual novice had been placed in command of the greatest fleet in the Mediterranean because he was the only man there who was willing to lead in such dire circumstances. The best candidates had sat silently, too protective of their reputations to volunteer for such a difficult commission. Ignorance gives rise to false courage, thought Soranzo.

"The final item to consider is an authorization to send five thousand troops with the battle fleet to reinforce Negropont," said the doge, quickly, as though he could minimize the impact of what had just happened by changing the subject.

No one present really believed that these reinforcements would arrive before the Turks had blocked their entry into the city. Governor Erizzo and his garrison would have to hold out in their well-fortified position until the fleet could come and drive off the Turkish army after defeating the Turkish fleet. The measure was approved anyway.

As the meeting ended, most of what needed to be done had been accomplished, but as the patricians emerged from the chamber, engaged in animated conversations, Nicolo Canal's name was on every man's lips. What experience did he have? Would he rely on the advice of his lieutenants? Could he do it? Compared to the highly esteemed commander at Corinth, Alvise Loredan, they were different as night was to day.

The *podestà*, governor of Euboea, was fifty-three, vigorous, and smart. Tempered by years of unselfish service to the Republic, like a fine steel rapier, Paolo Erizzo combined the unique qualities of the flexibility to deal easily and effectively with colonials and the rigidity to enforce Venetian law without exception or mercy. He looked more like a Roman senator than a Venetian patrician, with his short-cropped auburn hair and neatly trimmed beard. He issued his commands in a deep voice, with each word spoken in a rolling rhythmic flurry, like the notes from a fine musical instrument. They were invariably obeyed. Venice could not have had a better man to govern the one-hundred-and-twenty-mile-long island with its critical naval base and port of Negropont. His sheer competence commanded the attention and respect of others.

Since he had received word of the sultan's intentions two months earlier, he had worked like a demon—whipping his garrison into fighting trim and taking every precaution possible to hold Negropont for the Republic. His forage parties had scoured the countryside around the city for miles, going as far as Eretria, farther east along the coast, to gather enough supplies to sustain them during the impending siege and to deny them to the enemy. The city's population had doubled as thousands from the surrounding villages sought protection inside its formidable walls.

As the flaming sun dipped behind the distant Boeotian hills to the west, Paolo Erizzo stood atop the walls of the citadel of Negropont and pondered his predicament. A score of tasks, still to be completed, filled his mind as he tried to concentrate on the strategic situation. Just over those hills near Thebes, thirteen miles to the west, were the advance scouts of the sultan's horde.

Across the island, there were no major ports on Euboea's Aegean Sea coast, comprised of endless miles of sheer cliffs and dangerous shoals. Negropont was situated halfway up the western coast. At that place, the long channel between the Euboea and the mainland, called the Euripos, normally between five and ten miles wide, narrowed to less than two hundred feet. A wooden bridge had spanned the narrows there since the fifth century B.C. The first *bailo* had arrived in Negropont just eleven years after Venice took possession of the island from the Byzantines after the sack of Constantinople during Fourth Crusade. His first act had been to improve the bridge with an arched stone center section—now weathered by more than two centuries of wind and rain.

As Erizzo looked down at the smooth waters of the Euripos, he could see them rush by as the tide came in. Seven times a day, in each direction, it swept the funnel-like channel creating a flow so powerful that it made crossing without the bridge impossible, though if a man timed his crossing just right, he could wade across in chest-deep water. A local legend told that Aristotle, who died there, had thrown himself into the Euripos and drowned, so frustrated was he with his inability to explain the mystery of the tides there.

In 1390, Venice took direct control of the city, installing a *podestà* who ruled over the rest of the island that remained under the control of feudal overlords. Recognizing the city's vulnerability to attack, the government ordered a strong diamond-shaped citadel built and later surrounded the city with high walls punctuated by strategically placed towers. Recently a small turreted castle, really an elaborate tower, had been built on a small outcropping of rock near the midpoint of the bridge. It stood guard over the bridge like a giant sentry, its stone walls astride either side of the arched stone roadway that ran through the castle's gate.

Negropont's value as a naval base was unquestioned. It provided unsurpassed shelter to the fleet from storms and plenty of fresh water from a nearby lake. The city was also the Republic's collection point for large quantities of grain, wine, oil, wax, silk, cotton, and livestock produced on the island—next to Crete, it was the largest in Greece. Trade with Euboea was so lucrative, powerful Venetian families routinely attempted to gain control of parcels of land through marriage. Just three months before, Erizzo had signed the deed granting the Zorzi family title to large holdings there. He laughed ironically at the thought that poor Zorzi, who had only recently come to inspect his new possessions, might not have them for long. He wondered how many ducats he had paid. Unlike Zorzi, who had just arrived, Erizzo was due to be recalled soon. He would be sorry to leave Euboea, but after nine years, he missed Venice, only making the six-week voyage back there four times since he had been made governor. His seventeen-year-old son, Michele, had spent half his life on the island. His young daughter had been born there. He regretted that they did not know Venice and even after returning, he feared they would be looked upon as not really being Venetian but instead, *terra firma* colonials.

"Father, Mother sent me to find you. It is time for the evening meal."

"Tell your mother I will be along shortly."

"Can we hold off the Turks until help arrives?" asked Michele as he lingered.

"We must, my son. We have no other choice."

"I want to be posted in the castle, there." He pointed to the highest turret in the little castle guarding the bridge across the Euripos.

Erizzo looked impatiently at his son. "I raised you to be brave, like a Venetian, not stupid, like a Greek *villane*."

Michele recoiled at the rebuke, surprised by his father's reaction.

"Michele, the men who will defend that place will be corpses. The Turks will slaughter them to a man. Do you not understand? The only safe place will be in the citadel. That is where you and your mother and sister will be."

"But I want to fight like the others. I will not be coddled and ridiculed."

Erizzo exploded. Before he could gain control of his emotions, he slapped his son's face hard. "Listen to me! You will do as I say. This is not going to be some phony war fought with sticks on the bridges of Venice during carnival time. This will be brutal and bloody. Limbs will be hacked off and many will die horrible painful deaths."

He placed his arm around Michele, still smarting from the unexpected blow.

"I admire your courage, my son . . . and I admire your spirit. But I see death where you see glory.

"Now, go and tell your mother I will be there soon."

In ten minutes, the governor had worked out where he would post the six thousand men who would defend the city. Tomorrow, he would order the defenses manned at half strength, allowing the others to rest. The Turks might try a sudden attack before the bulk of their army arrived but it was not likely. He knew the sultan preferred to employ overwhelming force—especially after he used his vaunted artillery.

C aptain-General of the Seas Nicolo Canal stood on the prow of his flag-ship and surveyed his fleet, arrayed astern in four long columns. The captain of each ship was careful to maintain contact with the ship ahead of his, but remain far enough away to avoid a collision. Behind him were fifty-two powerful galleys, many of the newest design, fresh from construction at the Arsenal, along with eighteen smaller ships. They would rendezvous with a dozen others at Candia, in Crete, including seven that had sailed from Negropont to avoid the Turkish fleet. They would bring important news about the state of the city and possibly the strength of their enemy.

As he scanned the horizon to the west, shielding his eyes from the afternoon sun, he could see the impressive fleet plowing along in the moderate seas, battle flags waving proudly from every mast. Though he felt an immense sense of power, he also had the weight of the world on his shoulders. He had allowed himself to be swept up by his pride and ambition, held in check for so many years. He had been unable to contain it in the heady emotion of the Great Council meeting. When he had walked into the chamber, he had no ambitions for the office he now held. What was I thinking? he asked himself.

Three ships back in the line led by Canal's galley, Soranzo withdrew a golden ducat from his pocket and solemnly walked to the rail. As he looked down into the sea, he could see the dolphins running with the ship, darting forward and dropping back along the side. If only Marco could have swum like them, he thought.

As he dropped the coin from his hand and watched it make a tiny splash and disappear, he thought about his adopted son, Enrico. He had recently turned twenty-five, the age when, as a patrician, he could take his seat in the Great Council. Giovanni had waited until then to tell him the real story about what had happened to his father so long ago at Constantinople. Until that day, since he was a boy, Giovanni had carefully shielded Enrico from the truth. It had been Vettor who had seen to it that his younger cousin was properly infused with the genetic hatred of the Zianis that was passed on by every Soranzo since his grandfather. But Giovanni had forbidden anyone to tell Enrico the truth about Constantinople. He had reserved that duty for himself.

Giovanni had chosen the time and place carefully. It was night before they were to sail with the fleet to relieve Negropont. He and Enrico had gone to inspect his galley. Finding things in good order, he had stopped Enrico by the bow as they were inspecting the anchor chain. Giovanni could still recall every word.

"There is something I must tell you," he had said gravely.

Enrico had the face of a lamb being led to the slaughter, so trusting and unaware.

"Your father's and Uncle Marco's deaths could have been prevented."

Enrico's peaceful expression was swept aside as confusion and uncertainty filled his mind. As he tried to find words to speak, Giovanni continued unabated.

"My brother, Marco, was drowned because his commanding officer did not look to his well-being. He was allowed to go up on deck in a fierce storm and was washed overboard."

"But, why did you not tell me that his drowning could have been prevented?"

Giovanni fought to maintain his composure as he explained.

"My ship, which followed his, passed over the very place where he slipped beneath the waves." He struggled to speak the words as he ignored the question.

"Then, later, at Constantinople, that same officer led your father to the walls with four hundred other marines. Less than fifty returned alive. Your father was not among them. What I must tell you now is that this officer *did* survive. Further, while he was imprisoned he received favored treatment by the Turks. He was not starved like the rest. All that points to one conclusion. That man is not fit to command men in battle."

"Who is this man?" demanded Enrico, as he grasped Giovanni's arm.

"It is Antonio Ziani. The brother of the man who almost cost Vettor his life."

"Ziani! The merchant who makes his living with his ships? Ships that you have protected all these years?"

"The same."

"Why are you telling me this now?"

"Because you are now old enough to know the truth. Now that you have taken your seat in the Great Council, you would have found out anyway. There are many there who know the story. After the siege there was an inquiry but, in the end, the government took no action. They said there was insufficient evidence, but I know better."

Enrico released his grip and turned toward the city.

"All my life, I have wondered why God took my father and put you in his place. I have tried to love you like my real father, but ever since Corinth, I have felt that you would have preferred it if Vettor were your son instead of me."

Enrico looked at Giovanni with defiance in his eyes.

"I will make Ziani pay for what he has done."

"Enrico. That is not what I intended by telling you this. I wanted you to know you can never trust the man. I wanted to share my burden with you because it has become too heavy for me to bear alone. You see, your father asked to be removed from serving under Ziani and I admonished him for it. His concern was vindicated by his death. I was wrong. I should never have permitted him to serve under the man whose incompetence had already led to Marco's death."

Giovanni hung his head as memories and self-recriminations washed over him.

"Father—and I call you that name, knowing all you have done for me and my mother—you hold the wrong man responsible. Ziani was on the walls—not you. You *have* told me this for a reason. I am young and strong. I swear I will find a way to even things with him. But do not worry, I will be careful."

Since that day, Enrico had burned for revenge, even more than Soranzo did himself. Every day, on board the ship, Enrico talked of almost nothing else. Giovanni wondered if Enrico's path would cross with Ziani's at Negropont. His strong fingers gripped the rail as he thought of the day that Ziani had told him that Marco had drowned. How strange fate was. Now they were returning to Negropont, the site of all those bitter memories.

. . .

Antonio had left Seraglio back in Venice, much to his friend's disappointment. The Turks could not tunnel under the solid rock the citadel was built upon. Constantine had also begged to come but Antonio had forbidden it. By leaving Seraglio at home he was better able justify his decision to leave his son behind.

As he looked at the pastel-colored twilight sky he could see the dim moon rising. Soon they would reach Crete where they would take on food and water before the final run to Negropont. He remembered the last time he had been there. Then, it had seemed like the worst day of his life. Now at forty-eight, he thought, he should be enjoying a life of peace and tranquility, but instead he was going to war again. When would it ever end? He yawned as he rubbed his thinning hair and scratched his beard. Despite his best efforts lice had invaded it. He decided that it was time to see to his men.

18

Negropont

The sultan sat astride his horse, high up on a hill overlooking the Euripos, surrounded by his retinue. He could easily make out the walled city and two harbors, one on each side of the bridge that blocked the strait. The week before, his main fleet had entered the strait from the south while another contingent had swept down from the north, hoping to catch the small Venetian fleet between them, but they were too late.

The Turkish fleet had disembarked several thousand men to clear the countryside of the enemy, denying them access to any more provisions. This would be the first knot in the noose the sultan intended to tighten around the city. It was already mid-June and getting hot. The army, which had marched all the way from Istanbul, was exhausted. He would give them a rest while his guns battered the walls.

Erizzo could see the Turks on the hills above the Euripos laboring to emplace their heavy artillery. He wondered why they were not using the curve of the strait there to triangulate their fire on the city walls, placing them in a long line, instead. He expected they would begin by taking the small castle in the strait so they could post archers in it. This would compel his men on the walls to keep their heads down while Turkish sappers built a pontoon bridge to transfer the sultan's main army across the tidal straits. The stone bridge would be too dangerous to use being so close to the city walls. Any troops using it to cross the strait would be subjected to a withering fire from the Venetians.

When Erizzo had asked for volunteers to defend the outpost, he had been overwhelmed by the response. More than a thousand men had asked to be placed there, but he had only detailed a hundred. It was so small, any more would have just been in each other's way. All that mattered was that they make the Turks devote time and blood to take the place—giving the Venetian fleet more time to come to the city's aid.

An explosion shattered the quiet. Erizzo could see the puff of white smoke drifting with the wind, from the ridge opposite the city. The ball splashed harmlessly into the Euripos in a fifty-foot-high geyser of water. As the rest of the Turkish artillery opened fire, soon more splashes sent waves rolling in interlocking circles all along the channel. Suddenly an iron ball crashed against some stone at the top of the little tower with an ear-splitting crack, showering fragments into the water. One defender, killed instantly, fell from the turret; his limp body splashed headfirst into the water and quickly floated away.

The bombardment continued for an hour and then suddenly stopped. As clouds of white smoke drifted lazily between the two armies, a cheer shattered the quiet. Waves of shouting Turks, in their customary pointed helmets and chain-mail–covered white shirts, ran down the ridge on the other side of the strait and plunged into the water. Others, carrying ladders, stormed across the bridge. They ran toward the castle as hundreds of archers began showering the Venetians with flights of arrows at close range. They proved their accuracy when some lightly armored defenders fell from the unprotected turrets.

Erizzo and his garrison could only watch. He had ordered his crossbowmen to hold their fire, saving their bolts for the defense of the city proper. The order had angered many of the men on the city walls, since he had given it only after the volunteers had already taken their positions in the castle—too late to reconsider their brave decisions.

The Turks' feet rattled on the bridge's wooden ramps until they turned to high-pitched clicks when they reached the stone bridge. The first Turks to reach the base of the little castle were immediately killed by a hail of rocks dropped on them by the defenders. The rest of the attackers immediately threw down their ladders and hastily retreated. This temporary victory heartened the defenders, but the Turks came on again and within minutes the castle was surrounded. The Turks were attempting to scale the walls on all four sides. But the defenders knew their business. Most wore suits of armor and were almost impervious to the arrows shot by the Turks from two hundred feet away, except for the occasional lucky shot that pierced a vulnerable spot where the armor joined. Those defenders who were more lightly armored took refuge inside the castle.

Each time a band of Turks placed their ladder against the wall, the Venetians would wait until they had almost reached the top before calmly pushing it over on the attackers. Soaking wet but mostly unhurt, unless struck by a falling comrade, the Turks would pick up their ladder and try again. So far, the affair had been relatively bloodless.

"The Venetians are not supporting those defenders in the castle with flanking fire from the city walls. There must be a shortage of crossbow bolts. Our troops make too good a target for them to hold their fire."

The sultan turned quickly to Suleyman Bey. "Call off the attack!"

Soon trumpets sounded and the soaking wet attackers began to retreat out of the Euripos and back up the ridge. A tumultuous roar from the city walls joined the cheering from the little castle's defenders. One man defiantly waved the crimson and gold Lion of St. Mark from the turret, mocking the Turkish attackers, daring them to come on again.

Soon the Euripos was empty except for the bodies of those killed, which quickly floated back into view with the onrushing tide from the south. As both sides watched the strange spectacle, a lone soldier suddenly emerged from the castle, running for the city gate, his armor clanking as he awkwardly struggled to maintain his balance.

Within minutes, he was standing before Governor Erizzo.

"Castellan Duodo requests permission to retire under cover of darkness."

"What?"

"He commands me to tell you that if, in the next attack, you cannot support us with fire from the city walls, we are doomed."

The man was perspiring profusely even though he had taken off his barbute, with its T-shaped slits for his eyes and nose.

"We already have suffered eighteen wounded and seven dead. The castellan believes that the Turkish archers' fire is too accurate at this close range and with the turrets being unprotected, our men are too vulnerable."

The man was right, thought Erizzo. They were too brave to deserve to die alone out there without any help from their more numerous comrades.

"Very well, tell Castellan Duodo he may give up the castle at sunrise."

"Do you think that is wise?" asked Zorzi, the rich landowner, who had been listening to the conversation. "The more time we can buy, the more likely the fleet dispatched from Venice will arrive in time to rescue us."

"I will not order brave men to throw their lives away and we cannot afford to support them with our crossbows. We must conserve our arrows for the main attack. The only way the Turks can take this city is if they breach these walls with their guns. That will take days. Sacrificing these men would have no effect on that. If the Turks were in a hurry to smash the city walls with their guns, they would have already begun."

Erizzo turned away from Zorzi to find that the messenger, not wanting to give the *podestà* time to change his mind, had already left him to return to the castle.

Back on the heights across the strait the sultan was exuberant. He turned to his retinue, and issued an unexpected order to cease the attack.

"Mark my words, the Venetians will abandon the castle tonight."

"Shall we intercept them when they try to retreat back through the city gate?"

"No!" shouted the sultan, his eyes ablaze. "I want those survivors allowed back inside the city, encouraging the rest to value their individual safety over their duty to be brave. Never miss an opportunity to encourage cowardice in your enemy. War is a curious thing and not always what it seems. Those who value their lives the most often lose them first." The sultan smiled. "In his attempt to save a few miserable lives, the Venetian commander has endangered every life in the city."

"What are your orders for tomorrow, Master?"

"Use all twenty-one guns to immediately begin reducing the walls and move the bridging materials into place."

The sultan turned to his admiral who had responded to his earlier summons.

"The Venetians will surely send their fleet and attempt to lift our siege. I want you to engage it when it tries to enter the straits from the south. I have already given orders to the flotilla in the northern straits to sail around Euboea and join you. No Venetian ships are to reach as far north as the bridge, understood?"

"Yes, Master," replied the man dutifully.

"I trust you will be more useful than Admiral Baltoghlu was at Constantinople."

Though it was seventeen years before, the man had heard about the punishment meted out to the unfortunate admiral that day. He would not fail his master.

"While you are awaiting the Venetian fleet, I want you to ferry half of my *bashi-bazouks* across the strait, a half mile south of the city, to complete our blockade of the place. I want no one to leave or enter the city." Then he turned to his commanders and said, "If you catch any defenders trying to escape, bring them to me for interrogation."

The next day dawned rainy and cooler—a welcome relief for the sultan's parched troops and a depressing sight for the Venetians. While the Turkish infantry lounged, regaining their strength after the long march, their gunners began to pound away at the city walls. They concentrated every gun on a single stretch of wall along the strait, hammering it remorselessly. As the behemoths shattered the morning's stillness, firing their two-foot-diameter balls, thousands of slaves carried heavy boats, planking, and chains to the reverse side of the hill above the Euripos, out of sight of the defenders. The materials would be used to construct a pontoon bridge across the strait.

The next day, Erizzo and the other city leaders watched from the highest tower in the northwestern corner of the wall as the Turks began building their bridge under cover of their guns. They blasted the stout walls, cracking and loosening sections of stone, preventing the Venetians from firing at the sappers as they labored in chest-deep water. After working for an hour, they would wade back to the far side as the swift current made it impossible for them to continue, while the chains held the partially finished bridge fast. An hour later they would return and begin their work again with renewed vigor.

In six days, the diligent Turks had completed their bridge. Now, with almost twenty thousand Turks surrounding Negropont's walls on the north, east, and south, and the guns slowly wrecking the west wall facing the strait, the defenders grimly prepared for the ferocious assaults they knew would soon come.

By the time Captain-General of the Seas Canal led his fleet of seventy-one ships around the northern headland of Euboea, the Turks had besieged Negropont for two weeks, launching four major assaults against the city. Reports from local fishermen provided the Venetians with a grim picture. The sultan's mighty artillery had reduced a portion of the city's western wall to rubble. Each assault had been repulsed but the defenders were weakening. Without reinforcement, their defense would soon collapse.

Later that evening, becalmed about thirty miles north of the city, Canal took advantage of the lack of wind to send word to his captains to join him for a council of war. Soon every ship's captain was gathered on Canal's flagship.

"For the entire voyage we have encountered only one Turkish *fusta*. Her captain revealed to us, under extreme duress, that the Turkish fleet is anchored in the Euripos, *south* of the bridge, with the obvious intention of intercepting us. Though it has taken us longer, we have sailed north around Euboea to attack the Turks from the direction they do not expect and cannot oppose us."

"Forgive me, Captain-General Canal, but the extra six days' sail, required by your plan to attack from the north, may cause us to be too late to relieve the city."

"Perhaps, Captain Mocenigo, but I have been charged first and foremost with preserving the fleet; only then am I to accomplish my second aim, which is to relieve Negropont and prevent it falling into the hands of the sultan."

In the flickering torchlight Captain-General of the Seas Canal, dignified and confident, stood his ground. It was his decision and he had made it. No one was sure just how strong the Turkish fleet would be. They all knew the reports from Istanbul that said the Turks had closed the gap between their naval strength and the Republic's.

"Captain-General, what is your plan of engagement?" asked a veteran captain.

"The Turks have built a pontoon bridge across the Euripos a few hundred yards north of the stone-arched bridge. I intend to sail to within sight of it and intimidate them into lifting the siege. They will be afraid we will destroy the bridge, leaving a portion of their army stranded under the city walls, unsupplied. Their fleet, south of the stone-arched bridge, will be unable to come to the army's assistance since they cannot sail past it, even if they destroy the wooden section, the water being too shallow near the banks."

"What if the Turks are not intimidated? Can we destroy their pontoon bridge?"

"How can we do that?" asked Canal. "The strait is so narrow there, the sultan's guns would smash to bits, at nearly point-blank range, any ships that sailed near to the bridge. Besides, even if some ships smashed through the pontoon bridge, they might not be able to back away to safety before they are driven by the wind and currents up against the immovable stone bridge. They would be doomed, unable to advance or retreat."

"But we cannot just sit idly by, within sight of the city and not attempt to help them!" said Soranzo, impatiently, bordering on insubordination.

"Captain Soranzo, I understand your frustration, but this will be a war of many battles, not just this one. I will not endanger our *only* battle fleet to save *one* of many cities. That I would do only to save Venice herself."

As the captains began to argue amongst themselves, Canal signaled for silence.

"I have been a senator for many years and I have always appreciated that doing the will of the majority is usually the best course of action." He held out his hands in a majestic gesture, as if embracing his captains.

"I am willing to allow my authority to be overruled by a majority. Who among you believes that we must attack and destroy the bridge, regardless of the danger?"

Canal's unorthodox method of command made the captains uncomfortable. They were used to following orders.

"I vote to attack the bridge—now!" said Mocenigo, the most respected captain in the entire Venetian fleet.

"So do I!" said Soranzo in a loud voice.

The landslide had begun. When the votes were counted, the seventy-one captains had voted almost six to one in favor of smashing the pontoon bridge and immediately coming to the aid of the beleaguered city.

"Very well. I will yield to my captains but tell me this . . . will you all be so eager to raise your hands when the doge asks who was in favor of this plan—if it fails?"

The surprised captains looked nervously at one another. Canal had shared his decision with them, but he had also shared the responsibility for its consequences.

"I will confer with several of the senior captains to determine our actual battle plan. Tomorrow we shall sail down the Euripos and the next day we shall attack."

"Captain-General," said Mocenigo. "Our attack must be supported by the garrison if we are to be successful. They must sortie out of the city and attack the Turks under the western wall while we attack them from the shore. Surrounded, we will easily put them to the sword before those deployed along the other walls will have time to come to their aid. With thousands dead and no supplies, we can destroy the rest of the Turks stranded on Euboea while the bulk of the sultan's army can only watch across the Euripos, with our fleet blocking their passage. As long as we can withdraw our ships out of range quickly, the sultan's guns, with their slow rate of fire, cannot destroy more than one or two."

"Who will undertake the perilous mission to get into the city and tell the governor of our intentions and what he must do?" Canal scanned the blank faces in the dim light. There was no response. He pressed his commanders.

"Captain Mocenigo is right, of course. The killing must be done with lightning speed. We must surround a portion of the Turkish army—while we avoid being surrounded ourselves."

Antonio had listened to the debate in silence. He knew that this was something he could do. Someone had to alert the city. Ever since his failed attempt to kill the sultan, he had yearned for another chance to serve the Republic. Besides, he thought, Seraglio had taught him to speak Turkish well enough to talk his way through their lines. What he did not know was whether or not he could get into the city without being mistaken for a Turk.

The prolonged silence was deafening. All these brave men and not a single one to volunteer, thought Canal. Perhaps my original plan will be adopted after all.

Slowly but deliberately, Antonio boldly stepped forward.

"I will go."

The deck was quiet as a morgue. The only sounds were of the gentle waves lapping against the side of the ship and the buzzing of the insects. The hot air was still. Even the flames of the big torches lighting the deck seemed frozen.

"Captain Ziani. How would you accomplish such a dangerous mission?" asked the captain-general.

"I speak Turkish and Greek well enough. That should enable me to get through the enemy's lines. But I will have to convince the garrison to open the gate."

Captain Mocenigo interrupted.

"I will take you down the Euripos tonight. By doubling the oarsmen and rowing in shifts, we should arrive before daylight. I will deposit you a mile north of the city."

"Very well," said the captain-general. "Captain Ziani will enter the city and inform Governor Erizzo of our plan. If anyone has any other ideas, let him speak now."

The crowd stood like stones, relieved that Antonio had volunteered.

"You have the appreciation of the Republic, Captain Ziani. Go with St. Mark and remember. After midnight tomorrow we will make our approach and attack at dawn."

Canal pronounced the council of war finished. As Antonio turned to leave, he reached out his hand. Antonio grasped it as a thought came to him.

"Captain-General, what if the fleet remains becalmed?"

"Then Erizzo must not attack until we arrive."

"But how will he know what day that will be? Surely he cannot keep his forces in a constant state of readiness to attack for more than a few hours."

"Pray for wind, Captain Ziani. If we cannot attack the day after tomorrow, we will attack at dawn the next day. I am afraid if we cannot attack by then, it may be too late and your bravery will have earned you nothing but a place inside a doomed city."

With that sobering thought Antonio turned away to look for Captain Mocenigo.

Antonio and his four handpicked men climbed over the side of the galley and into the small boat. All were fluent in Turkish and Greek. As they quietly rowed toward shore they strained their senses to pick up any sign of danger. If any were caught they would be tortured and killed. Worse, Antonio knew he would undoubtedly reveal the plans locked in his mind, ruining the bold attack and possibly causing the slaughter of his countrymen. He unconsciously wiped some of the grease from his face that he had used to darken his complexion. He felt the stubble where his long beard had been hastily shaved. He had sacrificed years of growth to resemble a common Turkish soldier.

In a few minutes they reached the shore. Antonio could see the black hulk of the galley turning against the tide to return to the fleet. It was hot. He pitied the sweating men straining at their oars in the stifling heat below deck.

"Captain Ziani," whispered Alessandro, "There is a road over there on the other side of those trees." He pointed in the distance.

Faintly visible in the dark, Antonio could see a break in the trees. The five men picked their way over the rocky ground and disappeared into the woods. As they reached the edge of the trees they looked left and right—the road was empty.

Walking in the woods, along the side of the road, they headed south toward the city. In the distance, they could see lamplights, high above the trees, along the battlements. Though the lights might reveal targets to Turkish archers, Antonio thought, they would prevent sentries from accidentally falling off the walls.

A sudden noise broke the stillness . . . a voice . . . speaking Turkish. They quickly stepped back deeper into the trees that lined the road. Soon they were close enough to see a large wagon hitched to two asses. One man was trying to lift one animal's leg while the other was cursing at the beast. The animal would not budge.

Alessandro signaled to use the garrote instead of the blade. It would not do to have blood splattered all over the clothes. It was child's play. The Turks' bodies slumped to the ground without making a sound as Antonio and the other two quickly joined them.

"Stefano, see what is in the wagon. Gabriele, go and see if there are any more Turks up ahead."

While Alessandro dressed in one dead Turk's clothes, Leone presented the other man's to Antonio.

"He was about your size. They should fit."

They were civilian clothes, not military uniforms. The dead men were teamsters. Better still, thought Antonio. It was unlikely that they belonged to a particular military unit. They could go anywhere without appearing to be in the wrong place. He dressed quickly, shoving his sharp dagger into a pocket inside the short robe. Finally, placing the dead man's round cap on his head, he became one of his enemies. The wagon was loaded with lengths of wood and nails, the kind used for making scaling ladders. Antonio rode with Alessandro while the three others concealed themselves back in the trees by the side of the road. After some coaxing, Alessandro convinced the two asses to get back to work.

Though the sun had not yet appeared, its first rays were bending over the hills to the east. In the dim light, up ahead, they could see a ghostlike group of Turks blocking the road. As they approached, their menacing faces became visible.

"What have you got there?" called one as he stepped in front of the animals.

A few more inquisitive sentries stepped toward them from both sides.

"Nails and wood to make scaling ladders."

"Are you sure you have no food in there? Let us have a look."

"It looks like a commissary wagon to me," said one small man who suddenly appeared by the side of the wagon. "Search it for food. I am starving!"

As the hungry Turks pulled back the cover and began to rummage through the back of the wagon, Antonio spoke to their leader in a raised but respectful voice.

"The sultan has commandeered the food wagons to bring up the ladders tonight. We will bring the food tomorrow," said Antonio with all the authority he could muster.

The men grumbled their disapproval, finding nothing that could be eaten.

"How far up ahead is the front line?"

"About three hundred yards up ahead the road bends to the right. There you will find our lines. Be sure to stop, though. That road leads over the moat to one of the city gates. Do not go much farther than that or else the Venetians will probably shoot you from the walls. You would make fine targets in those white robes. Go with Allah."

"Go with Allah!"

Antonio drew a sharp breath and flicked the reins. The animals responded and the wagon lurched forward.

"Just a minute," shouted the small man.

Antonio jerked the reins and stopped. His mouth felt like sawdust.

"You do not look Turkish to me. Where are you from?"

Antonio thought a quick prayer. "My mother was Genoese, taken by a Janissary officer. I am Turkish only on the inside."

"Can you speak Italian?"

"Of course! *Arrivederci, signore.*"

"Perhaps if you stray too close, they will not shoot you after all." He laughed.

Antonio snapped the reins once again. When they were safely beyond earshot of the Turks, Alessandro spoke.

"How do you say 'balls' in Turkish?"

Antonio looked at his companion and grinned.

"I have been thinking, Captain, how are we going to get into the city without being killed by our own men or worse, attracting the attention of the Turks who will torture us and then kill us? We do not even know the password."

Antonio smiled.

"When we get to the bend in the road, we shall make a run for the gate."

"But you have not answered my question. How will the garrison know we are Venetians and not part of some Turkish ruse?"

"Have you ever been hungry, Alessandro? Tonight, the password to enter Negropont will be 'meat,'" said Antonio, " 'fresh meat.'"

The young man looked quizzically at him. Then Antonio pointed to the two donkeys. Instantly understanding, Alessandro broke into a toothy smile and then laughed. A few minutes later, they spotted the bend in the road up ahead in the dim light. Just past it, Alessandro began whipping the two asses hard. The frightened animals broke into a run, quickly pulling the rumbling wagon past a few tired sentries, toward the city. Now clear of the Turkish lines, Antonio and Alessandro took turns driving while they tore off their clothes. Dressed only in their courage and the dark stubble where their beards had once grown, they burst out of the woods about two hundred yards from the city walls.

The old wagon made such a screeching racket surely every Turk within a quarter mile must have heard them. The two wild-eyed asses vainly tried to escape the sting of Alessandro's relentless whip, braying for mercy. As they neared the moat, the sentries on the wall above began to shout and point. Antonio stood, exposing himself, as he screamed every patrician name he could think of. The spectacle of a shouting unarmed, naked man was so bizarre, the sentries lowered their deadly crossbows until they could identify the mad attackers, knowing they posed no real threat to the city.

Rolling up to the moat, in front of the gate. Antonio shouted, "A wagonload of food for the brave defenders of Negropont!"

The sound of arrows whizzing by and spitting at the ground signaled that the Turks had been aroused. Two arrows made zipping thuds as they struck the underside of the drawbridge. Antonio and Alessandro instinctively ducked their heads.

"They are alone. Lower the bridge, quickly," commanded a voice from far above.

Alessandro stood up and pulled on the reins with all his might as the asses veered to avoid the water-filled ditch. The terrified beasts strained against their harnesses as the wagon skidded sideways and bounced to a stop twenty feet from the edge. Antonio and Alessandro jumped from their seats and scrambled for cover underneath the wagon.

They could see the Turks, ghostlike in their white robes, moving along the tree line as arrows crashed into the side of the wagon and bounced off the stone walls. Antonio hoped the defenders did not think it was a Turkish trick. Suddenly, the giant bridge made a loud grinding noise as it began to drop down on its thick chains. They jumped up into the seat. As they instinctively ducked their heads from the rain of arrows, they rolled across and through the gate—uncertain if they would be welcomed or killed.

Their brazen trick had worked! Antonio quickly convinced the captain of the guard that he had a personal message from the captain-general of the seas for Governor Erizzo. Four haggard soldiers escorted Antonio and Alessandro, dressed in clothes the guards had given them, through a maze of stairs and passageways up to the citadel. When they arrived, three men held their swords on them while one went to rouse the governor. A short time later Paolo Erizzo emerged, wearing a nightshirt and rubbing his eyes. The sun was just breaking over the tree-lined hills along the horizon to the east.

Antonio was shocked at his appearance. He had seen him several times before. His hair and beard had turned gray and he looked emaciated. He was obviously sick.

"Who are you?" he coughed, as one of the soldiers reached out to support him.

Bent over with chest spasms, he cursed as he spit a clot of blood that spattered onto the stone pavement.

"Damned cough." He protested as he straightened up with difficulty, visibly embarrassed by his weakened state. Many of Negropont's defenders were sick.

"Do you not recognize me?" asked Antonio as he spit into his hands and began to rub the grease from his face with the hem of his robe. "I am Antonio Ziani." He smiled.

"Ziani! What are you doing here?" The governor managed his first grin in days.

"Captain-General of the Seas Canal sent me. I have a message for your ears only."

Erizzo gave Antonio's escort a quick tilt of the head. "Leave us."

Antonio relayed Canal's plan to the governor, who listened intently.

"So, we are to attack the day after tomorrow? It will not be a moment too soon. The Turks have almost destroyed a section of the city's western wall along the Euripos. I fear that in two or three more days we will no longer be able to repair it during the night."

"How many men can you spare to make the attack?" asked Antonio.

"About fifteen hundred, no more. The walls are extensive and we estimate twenty-five thousand Turks ring the city. That will leave about a thousand to prevent the Turks from scaling the walls. More than six hundred of my men are down with sickness. The city reeks of excrement. I have a touch of dysentery myself and my damned gums will not stop oozing blood." He spit for effect. "It hurts even to eat," he lamented.

"Rumors of your mission will already be sweeping the city. I want you both to remain in my quarters until tonight. Tell no one of the plan until then. We must prevent the Turks' spies from divining our intentions. Surprise is essential." The governor motioned for them to follow. "You look like you could use some sleep."

The stifling summer heat made the day unbearable. Even shielded from the merciless sun, Antonio and Alessandro melted in the windowless room. They were careful to drink only a little wine that the governor provided, avoiding the tainted water. Finally, after what seemed like an eternity, the door opened and Erizzo entered.

"I have told my subordinates to meet me here in fifteen minutes. I want you to tell them the plan. Then I will make the necessary arrangements for them to execute it."

"As you wish, Governor Erizzo," replied Antonio.

The six officers received Antonio's words the same way thirsty men gratefully drink down cool water. Antonio's news had restored their sagging faith in the Republic. Negropont would not be abandoned to its fate. They were not forgotten.

When he had finished, they all thanked Antonio for risking his life for them. Now Governor Erizzo outlined his battle plan.

"You will mass your men along the western wall, between the breach and the main gate. I want fifteen hundred posted there. When the first galley is sighted from the tall tower, we will give the signal. I want five hundred men to attack out of the main gate at the bridge. The other thousand will burst out through the breach using a passage we will deliberately leave unrepaired. Speed will be essential. We must kill the Turks quickly and savagely. We will have no more than fifteen minutes before the rest of them will be aroused and over the moat. I do not have to tell you what will happen if we are caught outside the walls by the bulk of their forces ringing the city."

One man turned to Antonio, a strange look on his face. "Captain Ziani, are you certain that the fleet will attack at dawn?"

"Yes."

The man turned to Erizzo and continued, "Governor, my men are near the limit of human endurance. I know them. This attack must succeed or I fear we are lost."

"It will succeed!" replied the governor emphatically. "The alternative is too horrible to imagine."

The day had been interminably long but now time seemed to stand still. Antonio tried to sleep but in the stifling heat, his active mind could not rest. After finally dozing off for barely an hour, Alessandro shook him awake. Erizzo had provided him with a full suit of armor. Alessandro helped him to put it on. It was well made and fit him almost perfectly. When Alessandro finally placed the heavy steel "pigfaced" bascinet over his head, evenly distributing its eight pounds onto his shoulders, Antonio was relieved to find it was lined with leather. Alessandro told him that it was the governor's personal armor.

Sheathed in German steel from head to foot, with his head protected by the bascinet, Antonio resembled a giant silver bird. The helmet's seven-inch-long conical protuberance narrowed to a sharp point shielding his nose and mouth. Protected by forty pounds of armor, he was only vulnerable to a sword or dagger inserted into a seam or a heavy blow to the head. As long as he remained on his feet he would be a formidable foe.

Antonio and Alessandro, who wore a breastplate and salade, the helmet worn by common soldiers, stepped out into the darkness. In an hour, the attack would begin. Antonio removed his heavy helmet and breathed in fresh air. It was stifling with the bascinet on and in the darkness he was afraid he might accidentally fall off the wall. They soon found the governor standing with his commanders, making last-minute arrangements.

All over the city, troops were on the move, the noise of their activity dampened by the high walls. Except for a few sentries, the Turkish army would still be asleep. Antonio could see hundreds of soldiers streaming to their assigned positions like metallic ants. Each man wore his individual protection—the best armor or chain mail he could afford—and brandished his weapon of choice. Only the *balestrieri,* the dreaded Cretan crossbowmen, wore no armor—it interfered with their rapid and accurate firing.

Antonio and Alessandro fell in with a file of men as they made their way to the western wall where they would join in the attack through the breach. The men were resolute. Some were scared, but most were grimly happy for a chance to savagely punish the Turks for the misery they had been forced to endure in the siege.

Within a half hour, everything was ready. Though it was dark, the fading light from the quarter moon glistened off the steel helmets and axe blades. Up on the wall above him, Antonio could see the crossbowmen arrayed along the battlements to support the attack with their devastating fire. Around him, men whispered nervously. A few joked, denying the gravity of the situation, while others prayed.

Dressed in his splendid armor, easily worth more than thirty years of a common soldier's pay, he had no trouble pushing his way to a spot in the front near the breach. Silhouetted against the sky, he could just make out the dark mass of the long ridge and the Turkish positions just across the Euripos. He looked to his right, over the top of the rubble, in the direction the fleet would come from, but it was too dark to see. Except for a few insects, everything was quiet. There was no sign of activity from the unsuspecting Turks, who were camped a hundred yards to their front on the near bank of the Euripos.

He momentarily thought about home. He was glad he had forbidden Constantine to accompany him, but he missed Seraglio. After so many years of close friendship, he felt incomplete without him at his side. What would his friend think at this moment?

"Look!" whispered Alessandro, pointing to the right. Barely visible, a dark gray mass loomed above the trees—a sail! Two more! The fleet was running down the Euripos, heading for the Turks' pontoon bridge.

The first rays of light were stealing the night. Antonio could feel primitive excitement welling up inside of him, like some ancient warrior on the hunt. Just as he had predicted to the governor, Canal had kept his promise. As the men high up on the wall, with their better vantage point, spotted the leading ships of the fleet, their hushed chatter cascaded down to the infantry massed for the attack.

Suddenly, trumpets began to sound from the Turkish camp across the Euripos. They had also spotted the Venetian fleet, but it was too late. Four big galleys were now visible three hundred yards north of the pontoon bridge, bearing down on the flimsy structure. Nothing could save it now.

"Ready, men!" Governor Erizzo's voice rang out. "Wait until I give the order."

The sound of a thousand zinging swords, drawn from their scabbards, harmonized with the clanking staccato of heavy battle axes and steel visors drawn down over determined faces. The symphony of war echoed through the city.

"When the lead ship crosses beyond that big tree over there, we will attack," said the governor. "We have them now, the bastards!"

The anticipation he felt overcame his natural fear. Antonio thought of nothing except the mad dash he was preparing to make toward the Turks who, by now, would be cowering along the bank of the unfordable Euripos. They would slaughter them to the last man, he thought. The lead ship was only a hundred yards from the bridge now.

Antonio saw the lead ship suddenly drop her sails, then the next.

Someone shouted from above, as the lead ship passed the big tree.

"For St. Mark and Venice," shouted the governor. A thousand voices raised a cheer in response, amplified by the tall stone walls into one vast extended roar.

Antonio and the others in the lead pushed through the opening in the rubble and spilled out into the early morning light with a shout. As he struggled to run in his armor, fighting his sabatons with their damnable points and twice as long as his feet, he froze . . .

The ships were turning—all of them. What are they doing? Cried crestfallen men.

"The cowards!"

"Miserable bastards!"

"They are running!"

Antonio could not believe his eyes. Powered only by their oars, with sails furled, the fleet was turning around. Stunned, Antonio looked behind him. He could see the broken wall, packed in front with hundreds of men, who a moment before had been invincible. Now they were frozen, silent, confused.

A retreating soldier bumped him hard. He stumbled and staggered trying to keep his balance. Alessandro steadied him, preventing his fall. There were no soldiers in front of them now. They turned and followed the last retreating men through the breach in the rubble. Back inside the city wall, the governor suddenly appeared.

"Ziani! What has happened?" he screamed.

"I do not know, Governor. I do not know . . ." his voice trailed off.

Surrounded by a few of the men Antonio recognized from the council of war the previous night, Erizzo looked like a corpse—pale and haggard, he was utterly defeated.

"He has betrayed us," shouted one officer. "My men found Turkish uniforms in the wagon he drove up to the gate. No one could have made it through their lines unless they let him through. He is a spy, I tell you!"

Antonio could not believe his ears. Things were moving too fast. He had not yet absorbed what he had just seen. Now he was being accused of treason!

"No!" screamed Erizzo. "There must be some other explanation."

"Explain that," another officer pointed to the unrepaired breach. "There is no time to repair it now. It is daylight. When the Turks see it, they will attack with everything they have for sure."

"Get a rope. Hang the traitor!"

The word tore into Antonio's ears, defiling them. Alessandro, shaken, grasped Antonio's arm, his young face twisted with terror.

"I am no traitor . . ." Antonio's voice was drowned out by the shouts of the men around him. Suddenly, unseen hands were tearing the armor from his body. His sword clattered on the stone pavement. He was defenseless. Alessandro struggled with one of Antonio's assailants, but another struck him with his mace, knocking him to the ground, lifeless. Someone wrapped a coarse rope around Antonio's neck, tightening the noose around his throat—struggle as he might, he could not resist.

"Stop it! I command it!" screamed Erizzo, trying to regain control. "We are Venetians, not animals. He is as loyal as you are—or you—or you." He pointed to each of the men nearest Antonio. "Let him go! If you want to hang someone . . . hang me. I am the one who ordered the attack. I am the one who ordered the breach left unrepaired."

They reluctantly released Antonio, who immediately bent down to attend to his fallen comrade. Though unconscious, Alessandro was breathing. He would be all right. His salade had saved him from the heavy blow to his head. Antonio stood and faced his accusers.

"I swear I do not know why Captain-General Canal broke off the attack."

"They were only a hundred yards from smashing the bridge like sticks— seconds from victory. We could have slaughtered them. Now they will kill us, if we do not first die of dysentery or starvation. We are doomed," said the leader of his accusers.

Eyes darted, brains worked feverishly but not a word was said. Finally, Erizzo broke the silence.

"Captain Ziani, I fear this terrible betrayal has destroyed the city's morale. We will not last another day in this state. You must get word to Canal. Tell him that if he does not act immediately, we are lost and it will be forever written that his cowardice sealed the fate of Negropont, handing it to the Turks on a silver platter."

"But how can I escape through the Turks' lines now? It is daylight."

The governor wrinkled his pale brow as he pondered the problem. Suddenly a voice spoke up. It was his son, Michele.

"Father, each morning we dump the dead into the Euripos from the bridge. The Turks allow it and do not touch the bodies for fear they will catch a disease. If a man pretends he is dead, he could float like a corpse, pushed along to the north by the morning tide. Perhaps he could elude the Turks and reach the fleet in time."

Erizzo looked at his son with a father's pride.

"It just might work, Captain Ziani," he said.

"You can stuff your clothes with animal bladders filled with air so you do not sink. Just be sure to lie on your back so you can breathe. You will look so bloated the Turks will not dare go near you. Why worry about a possible escaped defender when there is a chance of catching the plague?"

Antonio looked at the boy and smiled. "It might work!"

The crowd around them had dispersed as the officers furiously drove their men to attempt to repair the breach.

"Take him with you . . . please, Captain Ziani," entreated the governor. It was not an order. It was a plea.

"I will not leave you and Mother," said the boy emphatically.

"I am your father and you will do as I say. If you will not obey your father, as a soldier, obey your governor. Go with Captain Ziani and tell the captain-general of the seas how his treachery has ripped the very heart from the city."

Antonio could see the pain in his eyes. He placed his arm around the boy's shoulders. "I need someone to go with me and Alessandro is in no condition to go." He pointed to his comrade, unconscious on the pavement, blood running from his nostrils.

"Very well," replied Michele. "We must go now or it will be too late." He threw his arms around his trembling father and kissed his forehead. In a moment he and Antonio were dodging masses of dejected soldiers, running toward the main gate. As they disappeared among the milling crowds of soldiers, Erizzo broke down and sobbed. It was not every day that a governor lost his city and his son.

Lined up along the wall, inside the gate, were two carts filled with the corpses of those who had died since the previous day. A third cart had been emptied of its grisly occupants who were now lying on the ground in a pile next to it.

In fifteen minutes, all was ready. With inflated bladders stuffed into their clothes, Antonio and Michele lay on the bottom of the cart while soldiers carefully piled the dead back on top of them. Antonio struggled to breathe through his mouth as the crushing weight was eclipsed by the stench that made him vomit, adding to his misery. The hot night had ripened the bodies far worse than Antonio had imagined possible. He and Michele were too sick to talk as they waited for the gate to open.

Wasting no time, the burial detail quickly pushed their carts out onto the bridge. In a minute it was done. Antonio felt a momentary sense of relief as he slid across the wooden bed and fell through the air. When he hit the water, one knee crashed into a bloated stomach, pushing the corpse under the water, as Antonio fell on top of it. The bladders kept him afloat as he placed the curved spine of an ostrich plume into the corner of his mouth. As he rolled over onto his stomach, the hollow feather enabled him to breathe without difficulty. Stiff and motionless, he allowed the swift current to carry him north along with the other bodies. The Turks watched them pass, only interested in killing the living.

The ruse worked. After a half hour Antonio allowed himself a turn of his head toward the western shore. He could see a few Turks but they took no notice of the lifeless bodies. He turned to the east. There was no sign of Michele. He prayed the boy had also eluded the Turks. He told himself it was still not safe to move.

Suddenly one of the bladders, gradually emptied of air, caused him to roll over onto his back. As he fought the urge to wipe the saltwater from his stinging eyes, he could see the blue sky above him. Birds flew overhead, unconcerned. He could not stand it any longer. Wiping his eyes, he looked around. Not a Turk was in sight. Fifty feet to his right, he could see Michele floating on his back—they had both made it!

He began to kick his feet under the water like a frog, without making a splash. There, a mile up ahead, he could see the horizon filled with ships— the Venetian fleet was still there, riding on their anchor chains, sails furled, in the middle of the Euripos.

In less than an hour, Antonio and Michele were safely on board a galley. After putting on dry clothes, they commandeered a rowboat and made their way to the captain-general's flagship. He and Michele could see it in the distance, with its distinctive flag and red and white striped canopy that marked it as Canal's own.

As they climbed aboard, Antonio prepared to deliver Governor Erizzo's desperate plea for help, but he was surprised to see a group of officers under the canopy arguing violently. He quickly determined that they had been called to a council of war that had not yet officially begun. When they saw Antonio, they stared at him as though he were a ghost, ceasing their heated debate.

"Captain Ziani! At least you were not able to get into the city. I can only imagine the damage that would have been done if you had delivered the order to attack," said Captain Mocenigo as he walked toward Antonio and Michele, arms outstretched.

Antonio scanned the anxious faces. Canal was not among them. As he was about to speak, he noticed that there, not twenty feet away, was Giovanni Soranzo.

"Captain Mocenigo, allow me to introduce Governor Erizzo's son, Michele. He and I have just come from the city. It is a disaster. His father has ordered me to tell the captain-general that the city will surely fall unless the attack is made before tomorrow. The events of this morning have destroyed the garrison's will to fight on."

Mocenigo was stunned and embarrassed. He had spoken too soon. He and the others hung their heads in shame and anger.

"I *must* speak to Captain-General Canal," repeated Antonio with authority.

"I am afraid that will be impossible, Captain Ziani. *Signor* Canal is no longer captain-general of the seas. He is under arrest."

"What happened?" asked Antonio, shocked.

Giovanni Soranzo strode out of the pack of officers and took his place next to Mocenigo. He looked into Antonio's eyes and measured him carefully.

"You have brought the governor's plea at an awkward time, Captain Ziani. You see, we were just discussing what we should do. This morning's despicable act of cowardice by the Signor Canal is the worst I have ever seen by a Venetian naval officer and unimaginable by so high-ranking a commander as the captain-general of the seas."

"Captain Ziani," interrupted another captain, "these men have illegally removed the captain-general from his rightful place of command. Some of us object to this, this . . . unheard of mutiny, an act so treacherous that in the annals of our Republic, there is not one example of it ever happening before."

"In the annals of our glorious naval history, there has never been an act of cowardice so profound as Canal's. He will pay for it with his head!" shouted Mocenigo.

"What do you say, Captain Ziani? Should Canal be restored or put in chains?" asked Soranzo, noncommittally.

"I cannot answer unless you first tell me why. Why was there no attack?"

Mocenigo held up his hand, stopping several others from answering Antonio's question. His nostrils flared with anger. His voice trembled with emotion.

"Our esteemed captain-general of the seas lost his nerve."

He spun around and faced those in the crowd who had been defending Canal.

"Is there one of you who believes differently?"

No one dared to defend Canal's decision to call off the attack. Mocenigo was right. They were agreed, but the argument was about what to do with Canal.

"Hang him from a yardarm."

The men turned to see who dared speak such bold words. It was Michele.

"This morning, I saw the officers of the garrison try to hang Captain Ziani as a traitor for delivering up the city to the Turks. We had left the breach unrepaired to better attack the Turks in support of your fleet. They had the right idea but the wrong traitor."

"This boy has the heart of a lion," said Mocenigo. "What about you, Captain?"

Antonio had heard enough. "Remove him from command, put him in chains, and deliver him to Venetian justice but for God's sake, attack!"

Mocenigo turned to his fellow officers. "Nicolo Canal shall remain chained below. As senior captain, I am assuming command immediately."

"And what about the fleet? The city?"

"Captain Ziani, this morning we have lost the element of surprise. An attack is out of the question now. There is nothing more we can do against eighty thousand Turks with those guns—no matter how brave we are. We sail for Venice with the tide."

Antonio and Michele stared at each other in disbelief as tears streamed down Michele's face. As Antonio held the boy's head against his chest, he could see Soranzo steal a glance at him. For the first time since that day in Negropont, all those years ago, when they had exchanged bitter words the day after his brother Marco had drowned, his enemy's eyes were not glazed with hatred. Caught, Soranzo quickly looked away.

. . .

With herculean efforts the forlorn defenders were able to partially block the passageway they had left in the rubble on the western wall. When the Turks attacked, they were beaten back but at a high cost. Unable to use their wall effectively, the Venetians bravely sacrificed themselves to keep the Turks out, but outnumbered nearly twenty to one, they knew they were doomed. By the time the sun rose the next day, while the fleet stood by in the Euripos, within sight of the city, the Turks made their final attack.

As though they knew it was their last day, the exhausted and bloodied defenders simply gave up. The city prepared to die like a majestic elephant, mortally wounded and set upon by a pride of hungry lions. By noon, the last bastion of resistance was the tall tower on the north wall. There, Paolo Erizzo and a handful of heavily armored men, pledged to one another to fight to the death, resisted attack after attack. The Turks were hacked to death, one after another, as it proved impossible for them to climb the narrow stairs to the top. Eventually a wall of their dead blocked the passage hopelessly.

It had been a different scene in the streets below. There, the savage fighting turned into a bloody massacre. The defenders had fought behind barricades, street by street. Women and children even threw boiling water and roofing tiles from high above, but the Turks prevailed. The angry Turks regarded all as combatants. There was little to plunder. Every male over the age of eight was slain and their severed heads were piled in a gory pyramid in the main piazza. They killed the women and children too, All that night, screams echoed across the Euripos as frenzied groups of Turks searched in the cellars and attics for survivors to drag out and slaughter. Negropont was hell on earth as more than five thousand souls were consumed in its fires.

Upon hearing that a handful of defenders still held out in one tower, the sultan resolved to end the impasse. Seeing there was no way out for the defenders and no way in for the attackers, he sent a message to the valiant remnant of the Venetian garrison.

The Turkish officer threw the rock up for the fifth time. Finally, one man caught it. As the governor unwrapped the paper around it, he could imagine its contents.

"What does it say?"

"The sultan has offered us terms. If we surrender, we can keep our heads."

Erizzo looked up at the eleven men. There was no fight left in most of them. We are spent, he thought.

"We have no choice. We must accept. If we fight on, we shall surely die. We have no reason to hang our heads. We have already done the impossible."

He folded the paper and placed it on the small table.

"We shall vote."

Three of the room's occupants were common soldiers. They looked at each other nervously. Erizzo, seeing their confusion, addressed them.

"Today you have distinguished yourselves with your bravery. Today, you are no less Venetians than we are. You, too, shall vote."

"Who wants to surrender?"

Eight raised their hands. One old soldier struggled to his feet, his hand horribly mutilated and wrapped in a bloodstained dirty cloth.

"I was one of the few who escaped from Constantinople seventeen years ago. I do not trust the Turks. They will kill us. I say we take a few of the bastards with us."

"You may be right, but the majority has spoken," said the governor.

"Throw down your weapons and let them in."

After tying their hands tied behind their backs the Turks marched them down to the main piazza. Amid the stench of bodies splayed in every imaginable position too grotesque to look at and past the pile made from the heads of the brave defenders, they were led before the sultan.

"Every inhabitant in this city has been slain as a warning that it is futile to resist me." The sultan stood with his arms folded, the image of his epithet—the Conqueror.

"Which of you is in command?"

"I am—my name is Governor Paolo Erizzo."

"And I am he who has the power of life and death, given to me by Allah," replied the sultan as he narrowed his menacing gaze on the prisoners. Then with a simple flick of his hand a troop of Janissaries drew their swords and stepped up to the prisoners, one behind each, except for the governor. The sultan motioned for one man to withdraw. He obediently stepped away from behind one of the common soldiers.

One almost imperceptible nod of the sultan's head and the terrible deed was done. Nine heads bounced on the square's hard stone pavement. As the bound torsos toppled in all directions, spewing blood in great gushes, the two survivors wretched as they fought back the bile that rose in their throats.

"I beg you to spare my head . . . and his." The governor gestured toward his young countryman.

"Do you claim special treatment simply because *you* were the commander of this pathetic garrison?"

"No, I claim my right to receive the terms upon which we agreed to lay down our arms, saving many Turkish lives . . . terms you offered as a man of honor."

The sultan looked at his retinue of officers who had witnessed the massacre.

"You are right. A ruler must not only be feared but he also must be a man of his word. Thank you, Governor Erizzo, for reminding me of my duty."

He turned to the young soldier who was on his knees, still quivering, unable to take his eyes from the corpses lying next to him.

"You shall bear witness to the doge and his Great Council back in Venice that the sultan of the Ottoman Empire always keeps his word."

"I forbid you to cut off governor Erizzo's head," he loudly proclaimed to his men. "Get two tables, place them close together, lay this man who would teach me about honor on them and saw him in half at the waist. I forbid anyone to curtail his misery."

The sultan's eyes bored into the stunned governor.

"It seems you have made a poor bargain."

It was a disaster of greater magnitude to Venice than the fall of Constantinople had been. Negropont, their largest and most prosperous colony in the eastern Mediterranean, was lost.

Nicolo Canal was formally arrested for his cowardice in the face of the enemy by a committee of ranking captains and brought back to Venice in chains. Found guilty of all six charges, he was fined, removed from his office, and banished for life to the small mainland village of Portogruaro. His surprisingly light sentence was mitigated by the fact that he was not a military man, but rather a political appointee. His friend the pope had also appealed on his behalf to the Pregadi for clemency.

The Turks now seemed unstoppable. Venice was gripped with fear. Some merchants faced ruin. As the Republic fought for her very life, the other Italian city-states watched with mixed emotions. They, too, feared the Turks whom they would, one day, have to fight themselves, but they were relieved that, for now, Venice would stand between them and the sultan—suffering in their place. Now the sultan would digest another Venetian meal as he prepared for his next attack. The fight seemed hopeless to most Venetians, but they resolutely fought on, hoping for a change of fortune.

. . .

More than a year had passed. The dreary gray November sky swept a steady rain up the Adriatic like a vast shroud. It beat against the windows obscuring the vista of the Grand Canal. As Antonio and Seraglio sat drinking wine, talking, they contemplated the news. While Venice lived, her two most powerful citizens had died just days apart.

"In the end, neither man was successful at stemming the Turkish tide," said Antonio morosely. He swallowed the remainder of his wine in a single gulp, absentmindedly placing the fine glass on the table with almost enough force to break it.

Doge Moro was dead after nine years of leading an unsuccessful fight against a more powerful Turkish foe. Under his leadership, the Republic had seen her fortunes in the eastern Mediterranean suffer disastrously, culminating in the loss of Negropont.

The other Venetian to die was Pope Paul II. No more successful than the doge, he left a legacy of verbal support for a crusade without rallying the force to make it a reality. These two men had been unable to inspire the rest of the Christian West to come to Venice's aid. She had bravely and resolutely fought on alone.

"So now Nicolo Tron has succeeded Doge Moro. Do you know, Seraglio, that he made his fortune as a merchant in the eastern Mediterranean but at the price of losing his son, who was killed defending Negropont." Antonio grimaced slightly as he poured another glass, already feeling the effects of the strong wine.

"I have seen him. He has a ridiculously long beard. It is almost laughable."

"He refuses to cut it as a tribute to his dead son," replied Antonio.

"What a strange way of dealing with such a loss. It seems all he gains by that tribute is a few hundred more troublesome lice. He should have avenged his son's death on a few hundred troublesome Turks instead," observed Seraglio coldly.

"He has ordered drastic measures to rebuild our treasury to secure enough money to finance a continuation of the war against the Turks—to the death if necessary."

"Your unselfish patriotism has enabled you Venetians to fight on against your larger foe past the time when any other state would have asked the sultan for terms. In your strength may lie the source of your weakness."

"Perhaps, but our brave stand at Negropont has finally spurred some of the other Christian states into action. The new pope, Sixtus IV, has pledged to join with Naples to fight alongside us," said Antonio.

Tired of retreat and buoyed by these promises of support, in the spring, the government decided to carry the fight to the Turks, using their greatest weapon—the Venetian battle fleet. Like a sword drawn and then slipped back into its scabbard without spilling the enemy's blood, at Negropont the fleet had been unused—not defeated. Since the fall of Constantinople, each time hostilities had broken out between them, Venice had waited for the Turks to attack, and each time the sultan had attacked on land. Now she would bring the fight to the Turks, on the sea—where Venice's superior ships and naval tradition would give them the same kind of advantage that the Turks had enjoyed on land with their powerful artillery at Constantinople, Corinth, and Negropont.

19

Smyrna

Antonio stood on the *Republic*'s deck gazing straight ahead, over the bow rail, at the *Rialto*. She was three hundred yards dead ahead, cutting through the four-foot swells like a sleek blade, her stern churning the sea into a creamy white wake. For years she had been the pride of the House of Ziani until nine months ago, when Arsenal workers had completed the larger and faster *Republic*—one of the first to be built of the new 1471 galley design. Powered by one hundred and twenty rowers and a massive mainsail, she was one of Venice's most powerful warships and the first ever to mount two large cannon on her bow. He had paid for her—every ducat.

Antonio smiled as he rubbed his hand on one of the smooth bronze gun barrels. Then he turned and slowly ran his eyes up the length of her broad cloud-white mainsail. It rolled and snapped in long, loud billowing waves, as it vainly struggled to break free from the towering mast. Above it, the crimson and gold Venetian battle flag flew defiantly from the mast, identifying the *Republic* as a Venetian war galley. Though she belonged to the House of Ziani in peacetime, she belonged to the Republic in wartime.

Swaying with the rolling deck, salt-laced air filled his nostrils and lungs, as the sharp sea breeze gently whipped his face through his silver-streaked beard. I belong here, he thought, as he stood with his feet planted on the deck. I feel so alive, so free, so . . . invincible. A Venetian could never feel like this with his feet on the ground—only on a wooden deck.

After arriving in the Aegean, recently appointed Captain-General Pietro Mocenigo had split his fleet into three divisions, assigning to each responsibility for attacking and sacking a vital Turkish port. The *Republic* and the *Rialto* were sailing with the captain-general's division headed for Smyrna, the largest and most important target. They were in for a tough fight. Antonio was glad he had made the decision to leave Constantine behind in Venice but he had never seen his son so angry.

The day before the fleet sailed from Venice, Antonio, Constantine, and Seraglio had run into the Soranzos on the *Molo*. They all had stood there, frozen in time, minds racing. Antonio had been the first to break the awkward silence.

"Vettor, I hear you are going to fight with the marines on board your cousin's ship. You will, no doubt, add to your heroic exploits at Corinth."

"We have nothing to say to you, Signor Ziani," said Giovanni icily. Antonio had silently stepped aside, unblocking their way as they passed.

"Running away from a Ziani again?" called Constantine.

Incensed, Vettor turned around and faced them.

"What did you say?"

Constantine's piercing glare seemed to be searching Vettor's innermost thoughts. Vettor had to look away, as Soranzo came back and joined him.

"Admit it, Vettor, you ran while Giorgio and the rest died honorably."

He had spoken the words calmly. Vettor was almost seduced by their softness, despite their devastating meaning. The look on the Zianis' faces told him that they knew that events were not as he had reported them.

Convicted, he lashed out at them.

"No, Signor Ziani. When he ordered me to find a way out, I was surprised to see him running behind me. I never told anyone . . . but he was one of the two men who swam with me, trying to make it out to the fleet. It turned out he was wounded, just badly enough to sap his strength. Soon he was swimming far behind me."

Antonio said nothing, but Seraglio had to restrain Constantine as he reached for his sword. Antonio knew that Giorgio was fearless. He never would have run. He had faced death before, against the Milanese, when he had defended his outpost in a small town near Cremona, although outnumbered four to one, until he was finally relieved.

"I heard his pitiful calls for help. The night was calm, not like that stormy night on the way to Constantinople when Marco was lost."

Vettor had sneered the words to inflict maximum punishment on his enemies.

"No, Signor Ziani, he begged me to come back and help him, but I kept on swimming. After a while, his whimpering ceased, so you see, he was not brave. He did not die a fine death in battle. Instead, he drowned, begging for me to save him."

Antonio slowly shook his head and said, "I have heard enough." Then he turned and walked away. Vettor was a liar and a coward, he thought. Constantine obeyed his father but soon began to argue with Antonio about the altercation. He had wanted to go back and find Vettor and demand satisfaction. His rashness confirmed a feeling Antonio had had for some time. He decided that it would be too dangerous for Constantine to accompany him on the *Republic*. He was not ready for battle. When Antonio told him of his decision, the youth tried unsuccessfully to change his father's mind but his decision was final. Constantine would stay behind in Venice with Seraglio. Only his mother was happy.

I s that the *Republic* over there?" asked Vettor as he pointed to starboard.
"Her silhouette is unmistakable at this distance," replied Giovanni.

Vettor turned. "So we will fight with the brave Antonio Ziani at Smyrna."

"Yes, and I will never forgive him for the deaths of my brothers. But I have to admit, what he did at Negropont took great courage."

Vettor turned and looked at his cousin, surprised at his unexpected charity.

"No man is completely bad, Vettor."

"Well, I will not rest until Antonio Ziani is in his grave and unable to cause the death of another member of my family. Look at how I barely escaped certain death at Corinth when Giorgio Ziani's foolish decision almost cost me my life."

Giovanni looked at him with a strange expression, like a man who has grown too tired to feel emotion anymore. He has grown soft, thought Vettor.

He recalled that day at Corinth. In the sanctuary of his mind he saw himself running away as Giorgio and the others stood and died. He remembered the ill-gotten fame he had won with his lies. Now, much would be expected of him in the coming battle. Could he live up to the lie that was the brave Vettor Soranzo?

. . .

It was midday; they were about thirty miles northwest of Smyrna off the western coast of Turkey. The only land visible was the faint outline of the island of Chios, to the south. Antonio was standing with one of his most trusted captains. Leonardo Bravullo had commanded Ziani ships in peacetime and war for fifteen years. Standing with one hand on the rail, hat cocked jauntily to the side, he was the picture of a Venetian galley captain—a *patron*—sure of his skills and intensely proud of his country's glorious naval tradition. For centuries, men like him had been the principal reason that Venice had dominated every other navy in the Mediterranean. How can we lose with men like this? thought Antonio.

"How would you attack Smyrna if you were Captain-General Mocenigo?" Bravullo asked the young lieutenant.

"I would have the fleet approach from the west. Then just before sunrise I would row hard—and attack without using my sails. That way, I could quickly close on the enemy while the western darkness concealed our approach until we were on them."

"A good plan—but it would fail," said the captain, flatly. "Here is why. First, the Turks will have a picket ship anchored miles from their main fleet, in the mouth of the bay, to warn them of an approaching attack. Even in the moonlight, the picket would see us before we were five miles from the city. Worse, by approaching in the darkness our ships would risk colliding with each other. But the greatest weakness of your plan is that it would exhaust our rowers. After ten miles, the oarsmen will be too fatigued to row at battle speed, and hardly fit for combat afterwards."

"Captain-General Mocenigo will hug the coast, along here, as we approach Smyrna from the northwest," added Antonio. "Then, at first light, their picket ship will spot us as we appear from behind this headland—much closer than we would be if we attacked from the west. We will employ full battle sails at first and only begin rowing minutes before we engage them. The winds should be from the northwest—favoring us. By the time the main Turkish fleet realizes their danger they will be unable to maneuver their ships into a good defensive formation, the wind being against them."

Bravullo put his arm around the young man's shoulder and squeezed him hard. "You were right about the time of attack. It *will* be at first light." There will be a bloody fight tomorrow worse than any you might have seen on land. Many will be killed. Promise me that you will not be among them.

A sea battle moves quickly and so unpredictably. Only one thing is certain. After years of defeat at the hands of the Turks, tomorrow we will avenge our defeats and make them pay for their depredations."

The young man nodded as he began to realize, for the first time since the fleet left Venice, that tomorrow, he could be dead.

Antonio stared at the ceiling as the big ship slowly pitched and rolled. The Aegean's shallow depth, whipped up by the strong winds, made for large swells that pushed the hundred-twenty-foot galley over to thirty-five degrees. The sickening smell of the "ship's bowels"—a vile combination of putrid water, vomit, and sweat—wafted under the cabin door. He had never been prone to seasickness but thoughts of the impending battle made his stomach sour. He tried in vain to sleep.

The Venetians had twenty-two galleys. Except for the *Republic* and Mocenigo's flagship, twenty were similar in their design. About a hundred oarsmen powered each vessel seated on long rows of benches below the main deck, grouped in threes. Most states used slaves to row their galleys. Whether captured in battle or criminals, all were intent on escape. If the battle was lost and the ship sunk, the slaves would all go down with it, chained together. If the ship were burned they would be consumed in the fire. If the battle was won, the slaves would go on rowing until the next battle—or they died of disease or the lash. Only the strongest men lasted more than five years. It was a grim prospect for them as they rowed their lives away, devoid of hope.

But Venice was different. Most of her warships were privately owned and financed. They employed free men as rowers. In time of war these intensely proud men—rowed to win, not to avoid the sting of the lash. Instead of shackles on their ankles, swords and axes lay at their feet ready to be picked up when they joined in the battle. This greatly increased the number of armed men on each Venetian war galley compared to their enemy—a key to Venice's naval superiority.

Still awake, Antonio decided to go up on deck. As his eyes tried to penetrate the shroud of darkness, a jagged bolt of lightning suddenly split the black sky, eerily illuminating the fleet for a few seconds before it vanished in a loud rumble of distant thunder. It reminded him of a flashing sword. He thought about what his instructor had taught him. "Always fight with the sun at your back," he would say. "That way, your foes will be blinded by its rays." He thought about his sword, two and a half feet long and made of fine Bavarian steel. It was razor sharp and deadly. As he stood there alone, his active mind refused to be still.

Like every man, he feared the unseen enemy—the crossbowman—most of all. He wondered how many the Turks would have. Everyone knew that an arrow wound was the most painful of all as it ripped deep into a man's flesh and sinew. Thank God, he had not allowed Constantine to come with him. As he returned to his cabin, exhausted, but with his mind still racing, Antonio resigned himself to a long, sleepless night.

Thirty men were required to sail the *Republic,* but she had a complement of forty-five aboard. This enabled her crew to sustain up to one-third casualties and still operate her with no loss in effectiveness. Most of her sailors were Venetians. Some were Slavs. A few were outcasts from England, Spain, Portugal, and other maritime nations. Always the melting pot, Venice attracted mariners from every corner of the world.

The weapons they used in combat were terrifying. Any serious wound usually caused a loss of limb or death due to infection, gangrene, or tetanus. The sword was the primary weapon. Long, short, heavy, light, curved, straight, all were used to stab or slash the victim. The marines preferred shorter swords to prevent entangling them in the ever-present ropes and canvas that were found on deck. Their swords were also light since their adversaries wore only chain mail or thin armor. Marines shunned wearing heavy armor, fearing if they fell overboard they would drown. Long-shafted spears, axes, and maces were also used. Every man carried a razor-sharp dagger.

Antonio could sense commotion on deck. He could feel the heaving motion of the ship. She was under full sail. He laboriously pulled his chain mail over his leather battle shirt and then grabbed his armet and sword as he hurried from the cabin. It was time to form his marines up on deck.

As he threw open the hatch door and emerged from the dim stairway, a dazzling array of color assaulted in his eyes. The white canvas mainsail stretched and strained in the strong breeze. Crimson pennants proudly fluttered and crackled at the top of each mast. All around the deck he could see sailors putting on their light leather armor that contrasted with the dull metallic chain mail worn by the marines over their yellow leather jerkins and red pants. Their helmets were of various shapes according to each soldier's preference. On the fighting castle, Captain Bravullo and his two officers wore full mail and plumed armets, the captain's long white plume dancing freely in the breeze.

Antonio quickly walked up to join them.

"We were spotted thirty minutes ago by that Turk over there." Bravullo pointed to a smoldering vessel about half a mile away. "The Turks are burning their own mainsail, consigning themselves to certain death, as our two galleys close in on them, in order to warn the rest of the Turkish fleet of our approach. They will easily see the smoke. What courage! This is the resolve of our enemies. To defeat them, ours must be greater."

The two Venetian galleys were rapidly bearing down on the Turkish vessel as the flaming wreckage of her mainsail fell across the deck and tumbled into the sea. As the wounded ship began to heel out of control to starboard, they could just make out flights of arrows crossing between the three ships, looking like swarms of insects. They could hear the distant roar of the clamoring combatants as they prepared for their fight to the death. There would be no prisoners taken by either side today.

"For St. Mark and Venice!" shouted the *Republic*'s crew, encouraging their countrymen. The two galleys were within a hundred yards of the smaller Turkish ship, now drifting out of control perpendicular to them. Her blazing sail rained fire on the crew below, setting the deck aflame. They could see the shattering impact of the galleys' prows as they crashed into the Turk almost simultaneously—tearing jagged holes in her hull. The collision was so violent; it snapped the mainmast in two, sending it crashing onto the deck, crushing the men beneath. The Turk rocked sideways, her port side almost rolling over into the sea. The few Turks who were still alive taunted the Venetians, daring them to come aboard, but their bravado was answered with sheets of arrows. The Venetians had no intention of boarding. They were going to kill the Turks with their crossbows. The enemy's mainsail destroyed and his ship locked to his executioners' by their ramming spikes, there would be no retreat for the brave Turkish captain and his gallant crew.

The *Republic* surged on toward the Turkish fleet, one of twenty ships abreast. Suddenly they heard a screeching, scraping sound of wood tearing at wood. One galley was driving the burning Turk ahead with her wind-taut sail and oars, while the other vessel, with her sail now furled, was rowing in reverse, trying to free herself. The doomed Turk's deck was now a blazing inferno. The Venetian battle fleet was running to the southeast with the morning wind. The flaming ball of the rising sun was visible over the hills just off their port quarter. Antonio held his left hand up to his eyes to block the sun's rays as he tried to make out the city on the hills beyond, but it was no use.

A mile ahead lay the Turkish fleet—about fifty *fustae* and other small vessels and six large ships. Two bore the unmistakable silhouettes of captured Venetian galleys. Like a caravan hastily breaking camp, the Turkish fleet was scrambling to get into battle formation.

From their perch, on the fighting castle, they watched the battle quickly develop. Captain-General Mocenigo, in his powerful flagship, was in the lead, about a ship's length ahead of the other galleys. The *Republic* was on the right of the Venetian battle line with only three ships on her starboard side.

"Captain-General Mocenigo is attacking dead ahead with two-thirds of our ships," said Bravullo. "Captain Soranzo is leading his four ships around the enemy's right to attack from the north. Captain Memmo will lead our division of four ships around the Turks' left to hit them from the south. The wind will be with us until we turn north, when we will use our oars. Their only escape will be to the north, against the wind, up the channel to the sea. Captain Soranzo will have the honor to take most of the prizes today."

They were less than half a mile from the Turkish fleet when Bravullo abruptly ordered the helmsman to steer the ship to starboard.

"We will go straight for that big galley on the far right," called Bravullo.

The deck pitched as the ship rolled hard to port. They grabbed the rail, fighting to keep their balance. Far to the left, Soranzo's galleys turned to port making an opposite maneuver. They were going to surround the Turks and pin them against the shoreline.

The Turks prepared for the Venetian onslaught, sunlight flashing off their weapons and helmets. Cheers boiled up from the Venetian ships nearest to the *Republic*. Soon several thousand voices from the other Venetian galleys were added to the wild chorus. Antonio looked aft at the two galleys that had destroyed the Turkish picket ship—now far behind. He hoped they would not be missed.

As he turned to look ahead, he could see several flashes along the city walls, followed by distant reports as he watched the balls fall harmlessly short, throwing up plumes of water near Soranzo's ships. The *Republic* began to right herself and then, rolling over, leaned to starboard. The Turkish galley's slaves were frantically straining at their oars as the ship turned around to line up her bow directly toward the oncoming *Republic*.

"He is a good sailor, that one!" cried Bravullo. "There will be no ramming him." They were about three hundred yards away. It would take little more than a few minutes to reach the enemy ship. "Crossbowmen ready!" shouted Antonio. The archers' commander spit orders to his men, crowded into the bow of the ship alongside the gunners.

"Let them fire first! I want to see their faces before we fire." Bravullo knew that the first cannon shots fired would be the most accurate since they had been carefully loaded earlier that morning with two iron balls each and just the right amount of black powder and wadding. Once the battle was joined, as the gunners furiously reloaded, they would be lucky if the guns did not explode—an all too common occurrence.

The Turkish ships began to discharge their arrows with great whooshing sounds. Death swarmed overhead as the arrows flew in bunches through the air toward the Venetians. Four found their marks, their victims dropping to the deck writhing in agony, as the rest clattered and thudded harmlessly against wood and rope or tore holes in the sails. After waiting for what seemed like an eternity, Antonio shouted the order.

The Venetian crossbowman let loose their bolts as the gunners touched their flaming torches to their cannon. The guns roared and Turks dropped as though cut down by some terrible invisible scythe. The two balls crashed through the rail, scattering parts of men and wood across the deck. The shower of bolts skewered the Turks, dropping nearly twenty men and nail-ing one to the mainmast like a grotesque medallion.

Antonio could see the enemy now, a sea of brown faces, white turbans, steel-plated helmets, and flashing blades, as the range closed to less than fifty yards. A moment later he shouted to hold on as his marines heaved their grappling hooks over the side.

Men frantically grabbed on to the ropes and rails as the stout lines groaned and pulled taught, suddenly halting the ship's forward motion and throwing them all onto the deck. As Antonio scrambled back onto his feet, he could see that they were tethered fast to the Turkish galley by a score of ropes, their large hooks biting deep into the Turkish ship's rail. Men were shouting unintelligible insults as they pulled the two ships together. The Turks, knowing it was futile to try to cut so many ropes, taunted the Vene-tians as they strained at their work.

Antonio climbed to the top of the rail and leapt across, sword in hand. Marines in front blocked his access to the enemy. He looked up and saw Turks with crossbows up in the rigging frantically reloading. He hoped they would not choose him as their next target. They could not miss at this range. He felt naked despite his expensive chain mail. The man in front of him abruptly stepped back and then forward, straddling a fallen comrade. Now, Antonio had only one marine between him and the Turks. The clanging of steel on steel was deafening, painful to hear as it rang inside his metal armet.

Men were shouting and cursing as they hacked away at each other. The wounded screamed piteously as they rolled in grotesque motions on the deck. Blood splattered on his chain mail, face, and arms. He tried to jab his sword point at a Turk through a space between two marines, but he could not reach him. Suddenly, ten feet to his right, a marine crumpled backward onto the deck with a long spear shaft protruding from his stomach, his astonished eyes looking out of place above his contorted mouth and cheeks.

While the Turk desperately struggled to pull his spear from the corpse, Antonio leapt forward and swung his sword at his exposed shoulder. The sword bounced off as, in his haste, he hit the man with the extreme end of his blade. But it was enough to drive him to his knees in pain. Antonio was on him now and swung again, hard. This time, he slammed the blade deep into the man's neck. The Turk died as he fell. Antonio had killed his first man in almost twenty years.

There was no time to reflect on the deed as he felt something jerk him off-balance. A spear had pierced his sleeve below his chain mail; its deadly point was caught in the folds of his shirt. The Turk tore wildly as he tried to withdraw it for another jab. Antonio grabbed the shaft with his left hand and pulled it toward him with all his might. His assailant, trying to hold on to his weapon, was yanked forward, off-balance. Antonio swung his blade at the man's hands, the only target he could reach. In an explosion of blood and flesh, the man dropped the shaft and three of his fingers. With a quick backhanded swing, he slashed him squarely in the chest. Then he pulled his sword back in one fluid motion and thrust it into the man's belly as he fell.

The Turks slowly began to back up. They were losing. Antonio could see a Venetian mainsail behind the wall of turbans and helmets as it silhouetted more Venetian attackers climbing aboard the enemy ship. It was the *Rialto*! The Turks were surrounded.

Right next to him, another Venetian marine was locked in a duel. Antonio attacked. The Turk had no chance. As he turned to face him, the marine drove his sword into the man's exposed side. The marine looked at him for an instant and nodded. Then he spun back around to choose his next victim. Distracted, Antonio did not see the Turk. As the heavy mace crashed into his steel bascinet, his knees buckled and he blacked out.

The *Rialto*'s sixty marines slammed into the rear of the hapless Turks who were engaged with Antonio's men, butchering them without mercy. One of them saved Antonio's life by killing the Turk as he was about to deliver the fatal blow. Two others dragged him along the deck and lifted him across to the *Republic,* where they left him, sitting groggily, legs outstretched, with his back against the mainmast.

Four finely dressed Turks were spared and quickly tied together on the deck. The few other survivors were stripped and thrown over the side to drown. Land was about two miles away, too far for the exhausted Turks to swim. Several Venetians quickly went below to inspect the slaves. Five Venetians were immediately freed to the cheers of their victorious countrymen. The rest were introduced to their new masters.

As Antonio regained his senses, he realized that the young lieutenant was sitting faithfully by his side, a worried frown on his face. Antonio could see Bravullo turn to look at him. His face was flushed red. He did not look like he had just helped to retake a captured Venetian war galley—the ultimate prize. He walked quickly down from the fighting castle to the mainmast where Antonio sat.

"The battle is not going as we had hoped. The Turks had a surprise for us. They moved the buoys marking a shoal and then anchored just behind it. Seven of our ships in the center division have run aground. They will be stuck there for hours until the incoming tide frees them. As soon as we can ungrapple, I intend to proceed to the center where the battle still rages. Can you lead your marines?"

Antonio nodded. The Turks had used a trick similar to the one the Venetians had employed for centuries in their shallow lagoon surrounding Venice. Whenever they were threatened by sea, they would move the pilings that marked the deeper passages to the city, making it impossible for invaders to navigate without running aground.

His head was pounding with pain, he felt faint but after a few more minutes rest, he could fight. The captain pulled a skin from his shirt and handed it to him.

"Drink this, it will help."

Bravullo and the lieutenant helped Antonio to his feet. Over the port side they could see more than twenty ships, with their red, gold, and white banners glistening in the morning sun, among the maze of white sails. It was impossible to tell how the battle was going. Several ships were on fire. They could see sailors choosing the sea over the flame as they jumped to near-certain death, preferring to drown. The Venetians' galleys were now disarrayed in four groups. Five, with the captain-general, were under attack by six times as many Turkish ships—four of them galleys. One of Captain Soranzo's ships was giving chase to six or seven small *fustae* away to the north. Two others were closing with a Turkish galley. The fourth one was coming to the aid of the captain-general's beleaguered ships. The seven Venetian galleys grounded on the shoals were reduced to cheering on their comrades—shouting all the louder since it was now their only weapon. This made Captain Memmo's division the only support available to come to the aid of the captain-general's outnumbered ships, save the lone galley from Soranzo's division.

Giovanni Soranzo stood on his fighting castle and shouted to his helmsman to steer for the Turkish galley alongside the captain-general's flagship.

"I hope we will not be too late," he shouted to Vettor at his side. "By the time the galleys ran aground on the shoal, it was too late for him to break off his attack. He was committed. Now there will be hell to pay. We will be lucky if we get him out of this."

Vettor considered his cousin's words. Again, he momentarily recalled his narrow escape at Corinth. His quick wits had saved him then, perhaps they would again this time.

As the distance closed, Antonio could see the battle clearly. Mocenigo's ship was under attack by two Turkish galleys grappled to either side of it and at least a dozen *fustae*. The other four Venetian galleys in the center division were engaged with the two remaining Turkish galleys and more than thirty smaller craft. Their crews were fighting for their lives, unable to come to the aid of their beleaguered commander.

He felt a sinking feeling in his stomach. For the first time, he realized that they might be defeated. He looked astern toward one of the Venetian galleys that had subdued the Turkish picket ship to open the battle. She was rowing hard to come up, but was still at least twenty or thirty minutes from the fight. The other Venetian galley was farther in the rear, her captain trying to extricate his ship from the burning Turkish wreck.

As the *Republic* bore down on the melee in the center, they could feel the rocking motion as the oarsmen rowed hard. The big ship surged and then glided at four-second intervals as they maintained their backbreaking pace. Their weapons at their feet, the exhausted oarsmen would join the fray as soon as the big ships grappled. They preferred hacking at their enemies' arms and heads to the monotonous, exhausting work of rowing.

Antonio looked over the side as the ship bore down on one of the Turkish galleys, grappled to the captain-general's ship. He could not allow himself to think about the dishonor they would suffer if the captain-general were killed, or worse, taken prisoner and skewered alive on a wooden stake. The distance was only two hundred yards now. His crossbowmen were preparing to fire at the smaller enemy ships. The enemy galley was too close to the captain-general's ship to risk firing a volley at her.

He gave the order to fire. Thirty arrows whooshed through the air. Turks dropped onto the deck. Two fell over the rail into the sea. The Venetians had announced their arrival. The merchant of death had come.

The Turkish galley was nearly perpendicular to them. Through the deck beneath his feet, Antonio could hear the drummer mindlessly beating his relentless rowing cadence. Now, just beyond the Turkish galley to his front, Antonio could clearly see the captain-general and his bodyguards on the flagship's fighting castle, repelling groups of wild attackers who were trying to climb up the two stairways and cut them to pieces. A lone Venetian crossbowman, high up in the crow's nest, was hastily firing his last bolts before the Turks, climbing the rigging, could kill him. Far below, alongside the enemy galley, doomed men swam for their lives, their heads bobbing in the waves, scrambling to avoid the impending collision. Antonio noticed that the wind had picked up, whipping white foam spray into the air. The two ships were only twenty seconds apart now.

"Faster! Faster!" screamed Bravullo.

With one last mighty heave of the oars, the big ship surged forward and crashed into the Turkish galley with a terrible splintering sound. The *Republic*'s bow rose up, dropping her deck down at the stern. Though every man had braced himself for the collision, its tremendous force knocked all but a few to the deck—tumbling uphill, falling hard onto their hands and knees. Temporarily dazed, they tried to recover their senses as they struggled to regain their feet and board the Turkish ship.

The destruction to the Turkish galley was tremendous. She had been lifted up almost out of the sea by the *Republic*'s ramming spike. The collision was so violent it was transmitted to Mocenigo's adjacent ship. Just a moment before, Venetians and Turks had been on their feet, locked in mortal combat. Now, sprawled on the deck, they wrestled one another, stabbing and slashing at limbs and torsos as Antonio and his marines prepared to swarm onto the enemy galley. Waiting to meet them were an equal number of Turks who were clambering up the sides of the Turkish galley from their smaller craft, intent on crossing it to attack Mocenigo's ship.

Antonio's head ached and his legs were unsteady. He resigned himself to giving commands—to engage in combat now would be suicide. As he looked to his left, he could see Bravullo leading his sailors over the rail at the far end of the Turkish ship. Across the enemy galley, under her mainsail, he could see Soranzo's galley closing in. He was going to ram the Turkish ship grappled to the other side of Mocenigo's. Antonio looked in the direction of the captain-general's fighting castle, but the Turk's mainsail blocked his view.

As he prepared to jump over to the Turkish galley, his eyes searched for Bravullo. Suddenly he saw the captain's familiar white plume above the swirling mass of helmets, raised arms, and flashing weapons. He was engaged in the thick of the melee. Antonio instinctively looked up and saw a Turkish bowman take aim. Bravullo dropped to his knees as the arrow penetrated deep into his exposed neck just beyond the protection of his chain mail. As he put one hand down on the deck to steady himself, Antonio could see a blade flash above him in the sunlight. He shouted a useless warning. The white plume flew through the air as the captain's severed head fell to the deck, his body falling forward like a sack of grain.

Antonio stared in disbelief. Waves of anger wrenched his insides. His dizziness left him. He reached for his sword but it was not there. He searched for a weapon—any weapon that he could use. He spied a length of rope running through a thick oak pulley and, seizing it, he mounted the rail and jumped across the four feet of water to the enemy's deck, consumed with his desire to avenge his fallen captain.

He swung the pulley over his head, slamming it into the side of a Turk's helmet, knocking him off-balance. A marine ran him through the gut with his sword. Antonio began to club his way through the beleaguered enemy, leading his men to the opposite side of the Turkish ship. The long rope enabled him to swing the pulley above the heads of his own men and down on his opponents'. It proved to be a simple, yet effective weapon. Once a Turk was stunned with a blow from the heavy wooden block, he was at the mercy of the Venetian swordsmen and axemen.

"Quick," someone yelled, "or the captain-general will be taken."

The Turks had fought their way to the top of one stairway. Though heavily outnumbered, Mocenigo's personal bodyguards were fighting like lions, blocking the Turks' way. Antonio and the men from the *Republic* pushed and slashed their way through the Turks until they were near the far side of the enemy ship. Antonio's company of seventy-five Venetians prepared to rush the unsuspecting Turks, more than two hundred strong, who were bunched in a wild mob on the deck, around the bottom of the stairways and on up the stairs as they tried to expand their foothold on the fighting castle.

The appearance of the fresh Venetians seemed to demoralize the Turks. Unable to advance up the stairs quickly and fearing their new assailants, they began to compress against the fighting castle of the captain-general's ship to make their final stand. The captain-general's defenders, their spirits renewed by the sight of Antonio's force, began to drive the Turks, who opposed them, over the railing, down the stairs, and onto the deck below. The tide was turning in favor of the Venetians.

Suddenly, Antonio's ears were filled with the sound of screaming men. As he turned quickly to his right, his heart sank. Waves of fresh Turks were streaming up and over the sides of the captain-general's galley, from the other side, unopposed. Below, in the water, a half dozen abandoned *fustae* bobbed alongside the larger craft as the last of their occupants climbed up ropes and onto the deck. As these reinforcements charged down the empty deck toward the melee on the fighting castle, some turned to prevent Antonio and his men from crossing between the two ships. The Turks nearest to the captain-general, encouraged, redoubled their efforts to capture him. In all, there were now almost three hundred of them in the fight, their numbers still swelling, packed onto the deck—a little more than a hundred feet long.

Giovanni Soranzo crashed his ship into the Turkish galley's hull, driving it sideways, until it was pressed hard against Captain-General Mocenigo's galley. As his crossbowmen unleashed a devastating volley into the Turks crowded along the divide between the two ships, his marines began to leap across onto the enemy's deck. The first boarders were slaughtered but their brave sacrifice gained their comrades a foothold that they quickly expanded. Drawing his sword, he swore to himself that he would personally kill twenty Turks to avenge Pietro's death at Constantinople. As his marines fought for their lives, he screamed for his rowers to come up from below deck. Up they came, armed with their swords and axes, to reinforce his outnumbered marines.

As he shouted to Vettor to come with him, they jumped over the gap between the ships and began pushing their way to the front as the red- and yellow-clad Venetians expanded like a raging fire on the deck of the Turkish ship.

At the sight of Mocenigo and his men fighting for their lives, Soranzo's men went wild. The exhausted Turks soon began to give way. Slashing their way through them, the Venetians soon reached the far side of the enemy galley. Not a single Turk was left alive on the ship. As Soranzo reformed his men along the rail, they could see Mocenigo clearly, shielded by his small force of handpicked marines and backed into a corner of his fighting castle, heavily outnumbered by the enemy.

The Turks continued to stream onto Mocenigo's ship from the bow, emptying more *fustae*. Soranzo knew the enemy's only chance for victory was to capture the Venetian commander. Instantly seeing what must be done, he grabbed Vettor's shoulder and pointed. Vettor nodded his understanding and began to shout. Soon, he had assembled a company of forty marines. Almost half were bleeding from wounds received only minutes before. They moved along the deck, toward the captain-general, looking for a weak spot as the Turks warily eyed them, preparing to repel the attackers. Vettor shouted for them to begin vaulting over the side and onto the captain-general's ship. Soon, though outnumbered, they began to press the mob surrounding Mocenigo.

Antonio and his men caught their breaths on the deck of Turkish ship they had taken only minutes before. He spotted a bloodstained sword and picked it up. He had twenty marines who were still able to fight. As they stood at the rail, the Turks who opposed them suddenly began to back away. He could see Mocenigo and his men under his tattered red- and white-striped awning, marking the galley as belonging to the captain-general of the seas. Again, Antonio shouted exhortations to his marines to rescue their commander. As they climbed over the side of the ship they could see a new force of Venetian marines and sailors to their front, pouring over the other side. Antonio stood on the rail and prepared to jump across to join in the fight.

For a fleeting moment, he caught a glimpse of the commander of the other Venetian ship, fighting like a lion, well protected in his bascinet and chain mail. Like two powerful jaws, the companies of Venetians closed in on the Turks caught between them. After overpowering and killing most of them, the Venetians intermingled in the center of the captain-general's galley. The Turks who had survived retreated to join their main force still trying to get to the captain-general.

Now, finally on board the Mocenigo's ship, Soranzo grimly launched his attack to rescue his commander. Suddenly he saw a group of Turks leap across to the galley lashed to the other side of the captain-general's ship. They were killing some wounded Venetians strewn on the deck. Wild with rage, Soranzo turned away from his men and climbed up onto the rail, intent on saving as many as he could, but as he landed on the deck with a heavy thud, he felt an arrow pierce his leather boot, penetrating deep into the top of his foot. He fell, dropping his sword and writhing in pain. One of the Turks looked directly at him. Soranzo spied a battle-axe and lunged for it.

Out of the corner of his eye, Antonio spied a Venetian, in heavy chain mail and a shiny steel bascinet, bravely but awkwardly trying to get to his feet and ward off his assailant. He looked wounded and could not withstand the big Turk's deadly onslaught. Antonio flipped down the visor on his armet and jumped across the water onto the deck. But the patrician was already down. There was no fight left in him. Blood was streaming from his foot. The laughing Turk, his back to Antonio, ripped off the Venetian's bascinet, exposing his head as he prepared to slit his throat.

Suddenly, he spun around, ignoring his defeated opponent to face the new threat. His long mustache fluttered as he swiveled his head, sizing up one opponent, then the other. The Venetian with the axe was fought out. The Turk moved to his left, to face Antonio squarely. As he did, Antonio stole a quick glance at the vanquished man through the slits in his armet just before the Turk went for him. He reacted instinctively, as he dodged to his right, eluding the zinging blade by inches. He could not believe his eyes. The wounded Venetian was Giovanni Soranzo.

He parried another quick thrust. His right hand stung from the force of steel on steel. Another quick stab by the Turk almost caught him unprepared. Antonio slashed at him but he was fast for such a big man. He noticed that his opponent wore a helmet and chain mail. He was an officer. The man laughed, as though to say, "Who are you?" As Antonio poked his sword at the Turk, measuring him, he grinned and spit on the deck.

They fought for a minute—it seemed like ten. Finally, the Turk's size began to tell. Antonio made a desperate thrust, but his front foot slipped on the blood-soaked deck, causing him to lose his balance. The Turk saw his chance. Whipping his sword straight over his head with all his might, he hammered the motionless blade Antonio held over his head for protection, breaking it in half and smashing it against his armet. But the Turk was overextended. As he placed a hand on the deck to keep from falling, Antonio threw the useless hilt at him, but it bounced harmlessly off of his chain mail. His eyes frantically searched for something to use as a weapon as the leering Turk slowly stood up. Suddenly a short-handled axe tumbled, like magic, by his feet.

Antonio shot a glance at Soranzo and then quickly picked up the weapon as the Turk moved in for the kill. Taking another big overhead swing, he was not fast enough to strike Antonio as he rolled to his left to avoid the blow. His sword point stuck momentarily into the wooden deck. Antonio quickly rose to his knees and smashed the rigid sword with his axe blade, breaking it in two. The Turk looked up at him in disbelief, both hands still gripping the hilt.

Antonio mercilessly swung his axe at the man's bent kneecap. As the heavy blade sliced through muscle and bone with a cracking sound, the Turk screamed in pain, dropping the useless handle of his once proud weapon. With another well-placed blow, it was finished. The Turk lay dead, the top of his head split open like a ripe melon. With his head spinning and his hands trembling, Antonio turned toward Soranzo.

"Are you badly hurt?"

"You saved my life," said Soranzo, visibly shaken and in pain.

"And you saved mine."

"Ziani!" said Soranzo, through his pain-clenched teeth. Though Antonio's face was concealed by his armet his voice was unmistakable.

Antonio saluted him and turned away to rejoin the fight. As Soranzo tried to rise with great difficulty, he watched his savior leap over the side, back to the deck of the captain-general's ship, and disappear into the melee.

Antonio led the Venetians in their final resolute attempt to rescue Captain-General Mocenigo. Wildly hacking and clubbing through the equally determined Turks, they pressed toward the stern of the captain-general's ship. Altogether, about a hundred Venetians were trying to cut their way to their commander, who, with his eight remaining bodyguards, was still surrounded by almost a hundred desperate Turks.

Antonio shouted encouragement to his men. They knew the terrible shame that they would have to bear if Mocenigo were killed. To a man they instinctively surged toward the fighting castle, savagely dispatching the more lightly armed Turks, killing two for every Venetian that fell. Antonio could see Mocenigo fighting superbly alongside his men, his chain mail drenched in blood. By the way he was swinging his sword, Antonio knew it was not Venetian blood but, instead, Turkish that had stained it.

Sensing their inevitable fate, the Turks redoubled their resolve. Two more bodyguards collapsed on the fighting castle. Mocenigo's situation was desperate.

As Vettor drove his blade through another Turk and tore it from the dead man's stomach, he looked around for his next victim. To his right, he could see marines pushing their way to the foot of the far stairway leading to the fighting castle, about fifteen feet from where Captain-General Mocenigo and his valiant protectors were making their last stand. A band of outnumbered Turks was trying to bar their way.

"Save the captain-general!" screamed Antonio again with all of his strength. His voice resonated over the heads of his men as he waded back into the fight.

To his front, Antonio's men finally reached the foot of the stairs. They were slashing at the legs of the single Turk who had not yet been killed or had climbed to the top of the stairs. The marines quickly dragged his mutilated body down and began to ascend. The first man up received a vicious kick in the face, knocking him senseless. The Venetians now tasted what the Turks had endured earlier as they had tried to climb up to the fighting castle when Mocenigo and his men had opposed them. A valiant Venetian sailor suddenly swung into view, hanging on a rope, and dropped onto the heads of some Turks defending the top of the stairs. The sudden disruption provided Antonio's marines with the opportunity to quickly force their way up the stairs as the Turks hacked the brave fellow to death. Reaching the top, they began to cut their way to the captain-general, who was now defended by just three marines.

As Antonio prepared to climb the stairs, suddenly, he caught sight of a Venetian officer staggering backward toward the rail, the broken shaft of a Turkish arrow protruding from his neck, just above his chain mail. He was struggling to remove his armet. Antonio spun to his right and tried to grab hold of him, but he was not quick enough. As the reeling man's hips collided with the rail, he flipped over it, disappearing into the water below. Antonio grabbed the rail and peered over the side. Below, he could see the man floating on his back—it was Vettor Soranzo.

As Vettor kicked his feet, he tore wildly at his chain mail, shredding his fingertips on a dozen jagged, broken links. The searing pain of his wound and the jarring impact of his fall had left him gasping for a breath. He tried to fill his burning lungs with air as he kicked his feet, but he could not remove his chain mail. He fought his urge to panic. If I do not find something to hold on to, to keep me afloat, I will drown. He looked up at the head peering over the side of the ship ten feet above him. A familiar face peered from under the visor of the red-plumed armet—Giorgio Ziani—impossible, he thought. He rubbed the stinging salt water from his eyes, but the face was gone.

As Antonio turned to rejoin the battle, he could see that the weight of Vettor's chain mail would pull him under. Ironic, he thought, as he picked out another Turk. He wore it to protect him from the enemy and now it will be his undoing.

Vettor struggled as he frantically looked around for a piece of debris to keep him afloat. His body was lifted by a wave. He spied a piece of the captain-general's red- and white-striped awning floating about ten yards from the stern of the ship.

If I can make it, it might support my weight long enough for me to remove this accursed chain mail, he thought. He swam one-handed with his last measure of strength—his wounded left arm was useless. Just as he was about to surrender to his fatigue and pain, a wave suddenly pushed him the last few feet toward it. With only a foot to go he stretched out his good arm and extended his fingers. They scraped at the soggy canvas cloth. He felt something hard—a wooden strip that had held the awning aloft was sewn inside it. Taking hold of it with both hands, he screamed in pain as he pushed down hard and felt the wood frame push back against him. He rolled onto the awning and heaved a great sigh as he tried to regain his strength. After a few minutes' struggle, he pulled the heavy confining chain mail over his head and threw it into the sea.

He did not see the two men in the water behind him. Vettor was not the only swimmer who had spied the life-saving piece of debris. Suddenly, a ripping pain tore through the back of his thigh as the Turkish sailor thrust his dagger up through the canvas. Unarmed and exhausted from his ordeal, Vettor spun around and tried to defend himself against the sudden attack. He screamed as he kicked wildly at the Turk, but then another sailor grabbed him from behind, holding him down while the first man stabbed him, this time higher up, once, twice, three times more—over and over.

Vettor Soranzo had almost made it. His blood seeped and oozed from a dozen wounds. His mind began to cloud over as the searing pain faded. Giorgio Ziani's face haunted him as he rolled off the red- and white-striped awning, the symbol of Venice's most powerful naval officer, and slipped beneath the waves.

Back on the fighting castle, the Venetians had finally encircled the thirty Turks who remained on their feet. They called on them to lay down their arms and said that they would give them quarter. A few chose the sea over the Venetians' offer. The rest dropped their weapons. Captain-General Mocenigo and his two surviving marines were mobbed by some of the jubilant Venetians who had saved them. The rest quickly pushed their Turkish prisoners into a corner of the fighting castle and stripped them, leaving them squatting against the rail like plucked chickens.

The fight on the captain-general's ship was over, ending the naval Battle of Smyrna. The Venetians were victorious. Their superior ships, seamanship, and armor had matched the Turks' superior numbers, but their resolve had been the difference. They had captured four of the six enemy galleys, sinking another. Only one escaped. Not a single Venetian galley was lost. It was a glorious day for the Republic, but they had been within a minute of losing their commander. Captain-General of the Seas Mocenigo assembled the Venetians near his shattered fighting castle and thanked them for their bravery.

"This day we have won a great victory. Though one razed city will not compensate for our loss of the Peloponnese or Negropont, today we have seriously wounded the sultan's pride. But more important, we have demonstrated the superiority of our navy over his. After today, he will think twice about attempting to attack Venice because now he knows he must defeat us first!"

The deck rocked with cheers and shouts. The navy *was* invincible.

Amid wild congratulations, Mocenigo dismissed his men.

"Captain Soranzo," called the captain-general, as Soranzo was about to leave to return to his own galley.

"If not for your quick thinking, coming to my rescue, I would have been lost today. For that, I am grateful, indeed. When I return to Venice I intend to recommend that you be my made my vice-captain."

"I did my duty, no more than any other man would have done," replied Soranzo.

Mocenigo held up his hand.

"Please accept my regrets for the death of your cousin, Vettor."

Mocenigo's well-intentioned words served as a bitter reminder to him.

Soranzo painfully limped along the bloodstained deck, strewn with the dead. Suddenly, he spotted Antonio Ziani, standing alone, with his back to him, by the ship's rail. Leaning beside him, Soranzo placed his hand on the dark wood, near to Antonio's. They stood together, neither man speaking, inches apart, as they stared down at the bloated bodies and debris floating in the water.

Finally, Antonio turned to face the man he had hated for so long and who, he knew, despised him. Today, they had buried their hatred to fight side by side, together, for the Republic—like men of honor.

"I loved Vettor like a brother," said Soranzo, filled with remorse.

Antonio recalled the day when he had delivered heartbreaking news to this same man—reigniting the bitter feud that had divided their families for generations.

"I saw him at the end," said Antonio quietly. "I tried to save him, but before I could reach him, he was gone—fallen over the rail with a Turk's arrow in his neck."

Soranzo's face and beard were spattered with blood, an angry purple bruise visible beneath his blood-caked whiskers. Antonio searched his eyes for a reaction.

Soranzo looked back at him, but there was no hatred, no anger—just a blank stare, his eyes like a shark's—cold and lifeless. Then slowly, his eyelids fluttered and blinked. For an instant, they betrayed a trace of misty emotion before they dissolved into serene resignation. Soranzo placed his hand gently on Antonio's shoulder.

"I know. I saw it. I could not have asked for anything more."

He grasped his hand and squeezed it.

"Antonio, today, you could not save Vettor's life. But you saved mine."

Antonio could feel the tension vanish.

"A Venetian I did not know was in danger, so I came to his aid. I could not let him die if it was in my power to prevent it. By the time I saw that it was you, I was committed. We were both going to live or die together. But I confess that I do not know if I would have tried to save you, had I first known it was you."

Soranzo looked hard into his eyes, anger and gratitude battling within.

"You also saved my life," continued Antonio. "My sword was broken. The Turk had me. When your axe appeared at my feet, it was like a miracle you hear about but do not believe."

"But if I had not thrown you that axe, we both would be dead. Imagine, for twenty years we have caused each other untold misery. Yet today, we stood side by side, like brothers-in-arms, fighting the Turks."

"We had no choice, Giovanni. How can we Venetians survive if we hate each other with greater passion than the mortal enemy who has sworn to his god to destroy us? We must put our differences aside and stand together if we are to defeat him."

Soranzo slowly shook his head as he took a step back from the rail.

"I do not know what the future will bring—but for this day, just this one day, let there be peace between us."

"You speak noble words," sighed Antonio, "but tomorrow, when the danger is past and this battle is a just a memory, what will you say then?"

Soranzo abruptly turned to face him. "Hatred is a hard thing for a man to give up when, for so many years, it has been his reason for living, capturing his very soul and determining his words and his actions."

Antonio could feel the moment slipping away as he replied.

"A man consumed by hatred is not living—he is dying—day by miserable day."

Soranzo's expression hardened. "Do you really think what we did today can end this vendetta that has consumed three generations of your family and mine?"

"If it doesn't, Captain Soranzo, I fear it never will."

Historical Note

That summer in 1472 the Venetians achieved an audacious victory— painfully reminding the sultan that despite his victories at Corinth and Negropont, Venetian galleys still ruled the seas.

After devoting a few hours to binding up their wounds and disentangling their precious dead from the enemy's in order to give them a proper burial, the Venetians went ashore to claim their prize. The city's inhabitants, who had not fled when they saw that the battle in the harbor was lost, quickly capitulated.

There was no massacre and no rape. Instead, the Venetians methodically swept through Smyrna with cold precision, completely ransacking the city, carrying off everything of value, and setting it ablaze. As the plunder-laden sailors and marines rowed back out to their fleet in the debris-filled harbor, they rejoiced that they had also freed more than five hundred Christians from the terrors of Turkish slavery. In their place they would sell five hundred unfortunate Turks, many among the most important in the city, into slavery at Otranto on the way back to Venice.

As the orange flames surging up from the conflagration that had been Smyrna licked the dark gray twilight sky, the Venetians celebrated on board their ships, refighting the day's battle with tales of danger and glory, as they drank to their victory and their rescued leader—Captain-General Mocenigo.

The next day, the Venetians sailed with the morning tide, wary that the lone Turkish galley that had escaped the day before would soon alert the sultan's main battle fleet. After joining the two other divisions that had attacked Halicarnassus and Anatalya with equal success, the combined fleet sailed for home, where they were hailed by the city for their much-needed victories.

But the people knew their time of wild celebration would be brief. Soon yellow dust kicked up by a relentless Turkish army would appear over a hill outside some Venetian city or a ship's lookout would shout his warning as he pointed to a hundred Turkish ships, flying their familiar crescented battle ensign, visible over the gray horizon. It would only be a matter of time before the sultan would seek vengeance for the Venetians' depredations of his cities. The war would continue until one side, or the other, its blood and treasure exhausted, would finally lose its will to fight on. But that is another story for another day.

Author's Note

I have always been an avid reader—fiction, nonfiction, thrillers, histories, biographies, and classics, but as I have grown older, my interest in books has far exceeded the leisure time I can devote to them. It takes a visit to a bookstore or a library to remind me just how much a good book can entertain, teach, and inspire. There are so many interesting books on the shelves, but who has the time to read them all? It seems that today many spend their leisure time like money—calculating their return on the investment. Where was the book I was always looking for that could make me gladly take the time to read it? For years I contemplated the long, arduous task of writing it myself as I searched for a subject, I felt, deserving of the effort. My quest ended after a visit to Venice in 1999 led me to read several histories of the Venetian Republic. Now, there was a story to inspire and entertain! But where was the novel that drew upon this glorious history? And so, I put my shoulder to the task and now, four years later, *The Lion of St. Mark,* the first volume of *The Venetians,* is a reality—the original manuscript completed just two weeks after that infamous day—September 11, 2001.

I believe that a novelist's job is akin to the gourmet chef's. Just as food provides sustenance for the body, so books provide nourishment for the mind. Today, a diner knows he must eat, but he wants more than just a full belly. He wants to *experience* eating—great taste, pleasing aroma, unique presentation, efficient service, and good nutrition to be better off for the experience. One look at a bestseller list reveals that today's fiction reader wants nothing less—a great story, appealing characters, alluring settings, expanded knowledge, and he wants to be better off for spending his precious time with the author and his creation.

I have tried to write the kind of book I search for when I feel the pangs of literary hunger. *The Count of Monte Cristo, The Godfather, Killer Angels,* and the *Matarese Circle* all handsomely rewarded the time I invested in them—drawing me into the story, feeling and thinking with the characters as I learned about each world they lived in. Just as these works of fiction have inspired me to go on and read the histories of these times, so my visit to Venice inspired me to write a story about her history and her people.

But historical fiction must read like a novel as it stays true to the facts—no simple task. This is not alternate history—the main events are as they happened. And as you have seen, the truth *is* stranger than fiction. Many characters are real, Sultan Muhammed II, Doge Francesco Foscari, and Governor Paolo Erizzo, to name just a few. The rest are invented. I hope the reader will not be able to tell the difference. A few surviving shreds of dialog are real, but most of it, as the events occurred half a millennium ago, is contrived, though faithful, I trust, to the speaker's feelings and intent.

As with any great exertion, I could not have written this book alone. As Althea Gibson once said, "No matter what accomplishments you make, somebody helped you." When I was a small child, my Aunt Nellie, a consummate storyteller, introduced me to the power that rare gift holds to spellbind. My parents, Elmer and Barbara, instilled in me a love of reading and bought me any books I wanted—an indulgence to children I highly recommend. My wife, Cathie, and my children, Sara and Tom, read many drafts of the manuscript and never once uttered a word of discouragement—only help and hope.

My agent, Bob Solinger, believed in this book from the start and inspired one of my favorite characters, the irrepressible Seraglio. For all that and more, I am grateful. Peter Wolverton, my editor, taught me the most important thing for a fiction writer—make the story fit your characters instead of writing the characters to fit your story. I hope the reader will agree that the revisions suggested by him improved the overall effort.

Finally, I want to say how grateful I am to be born an American. I think we take our country for granted. Where else could a middle-aged business executive begin a simultaneous career and receive so much encouragement from so many people—even his employer?

I trust readers will enjoy the Venetians and their story and you will be pleased with the time you have spent in their world. I hope the experience will inspire you to visit Venice and drink in her rich history—for there is nothing like it on this earth. And as for expanding your knowledge . . .

I also hope this book will inspire you to think more deeply about our world today where, despite the passage of more than five hundred years, sadly little has changed as the clash of cultures is renewed—fueled today by the same forces and passions as then. Take heart and learn from the Venetians who so bravely defended their republic. Watch them fight on alone against their powerful and terrifying adversary as they strive to preserve freedom and their way of life. Before there was Churchill and the resolute British of 1940, there were the Venetians. Now, as we fight to preserve our own culture, our values, and our very freedom, can we afford to do less than they?